BONE DUNGEON

Elemental Dungeon (Book 1)

JONATHAN SMIDT

Thanks for checking out *Bone Dungeon*.

If you'd like to try out stories from the other fantastic Portal Books authors, sign up to our mailing list to access all current and future FREE books!

You'll be sent over 40,000 words of LitRPG novelettes, including *Rising Tide* by Oliver Mayes and *Survivors* by Alex Knight. Click through below and subscribe, and we'll get the eBooks straight to you:

https://portal-books.com/sign-up

Happy reading!

Best wishes,

The Portal Books Team

www.portal-books.com

I would first like to thank my wife for putting up with my long hours typing away on Bone Dungeon. I also want to thank the team at Portal Books for helping bring a dream of mine to life, as well as putting up with our multi-hour long Skype sessions because I like to go off topic, bwahaha.

Chapter One

"For your sins against the church—"

Sins? In what perverse world did rushing to help someone screaming in distress count as a sin? Sheesh.

"—we hereby assign your punishment. Death!"

Death? That seemed a bit...drastic. Then again, Ryan had attacked a high inquisitor. But the man had ordered those innocent people to be beaten! There was no way the church would condone this type of action by its followers. Oh, wait – this *was* the church.

"Will you repent in your last moments, heathen?"

The man at Ryan's side, clad in all white, was practically oozing distaste for him, though he had done nothing wrong. Ryan opened his mouth to speak, to protest, but his cries were muffled behind the gag they had placed on him.

Well, that's just not fair.

"Even now, you refuse to repent. And so, as the hand of the Goddess of Justice, I set forth your sentence, and act upon it."

The priest's hand moved, and the blade of the guillotine came crashing down.

Damn.

Ryan's head left his body, and he watched in awe as the whole world turned upside down. Part of him had been hoping to at least ruin the high priest's robe with his blood, but no such luck.

Of all the branches of the church to arrive in his small town, why did it have to be the Zealots of the Light? The only sin Ryan had committed was trying to be a good man, certainly a better one than the corrupt followers of the Goddess. His eyes focused on the bright golden sun above for a moment, before his mind drifted off and his world went black.

"I am sorry, child, for the unjust end to your life," a woman's voice whispered in his mind.

Ryan opened his eyes, startled by the emptiness around him. Was he dead? He was pretty sure you died when your head was cut off.

"The least I can do, to atone for the sins of my followers, is grant you another life."

Ryan glanced around, but there was no one. His body, completely intact, was simply floating in nothingness.

"Stay pure to your heart, young man, and I hope you continue to walk the path of righteousness."

The world started to turn dark. Whatever was going on, Ryan was confused. As a heaviness filled his mind, all he could think of was how unlucky this whole ordeal had been. He wondered if he was hallucinating. But deep in his heart, he knew he really was dead.

"Wake up!" A voice, loud and shrill, pulled him from darkness.

How long had he been asleep?

"Heellloooo," the voice continued, louder this time.

Ryan opened his eyes as visions – memories – flashed through his mind and disappeared.

Who am I?

An image of a man in white, a movement, a giant blade.

Ugh, the church. Wait, what's a church?

"Anyone in there?" The speaker, a small, floating thing, stared at him.

She – Ryan was pretty sure it was a she – appeared to be a

young woman, judging from her simple white dress and long golden hair. However, she definitely wasn't human. Feathery wings sprouted from her back, and she glowed with a faint golden light. Ryan tried to respond but realized he couldn't.

With a quick glance, he realized a lot of things. First, he had no mouth. Second, he was certain he didn't have any eyes, yet he could somehow see in 360 degrees around him. Third, his body was a glowing white sphere.

Had he always been a glowing white sphere? The more he inspected himself, he realized he was made of some sort of glowing stone.

"Oh, you are awake." The tiny woman flapped her wings in excitement. The motion sent her flying into the ceiling above Ryan. If he had a mouth, he would have laughed.

He took in his surroundings: a small, confined space, with stone and dirt all around. Was he underground? Had he always lived down there?

The woman in front of him lowered herself to his eye level – so to speak – and smiled. "What's your name?"

Ryan?

The name came to the surface of his mind, and he clung to it. That's right, he was definitely a Ryan! But he still had no way to speak.

The woman stared at him in silence. After a long while, she shook her head, laughing. "Oh, that's right. I have to complete our bond first." Her body started to glow brighter, and she leaned forward, wrapping her arms around him. Their two lights blended, and she gently kissed the top of his stone.

In that instant, Ryan felt a flash of energy rush through him, the light emanating from him filling the room. At the same time, he felt a strange stream of thoughts — a consciousness — in his mind. Reaching out internally, he saw the woman shudder as he engaged it.

"Hello?" he thought to her

She beamed. "Hello!" Her voice was filled with excitement.

"Who are you?" Ryan was thoroughly confused about what exactly was going on. One moment he was in darkness, and now this.

"Oh, of course you don't know. Sorry, I'm just as new to all of this as you are." She fluttered around him, suddenly nervous. "My name is Erin."

"Ryan." He projected his name through their bond.

They sat there for a moment, Erin's face growing steadily redder. The continued silence started to feel awkward, and it didn't seem like Erin was going to be the one to break it.

"So, Erin, what exactly are you? And more importantly, what am I?" For some reason, he had no idea. *Strange.*

"Well, I am a celestial fairy." She spread her wings wide, beaming with pride. "And you, Ryan, are a dungeon."

Chapter Two

A dungeon? What does that mean?

For a fleeting moment, Ryan's mind screamed that this was wrong, but then the thought vanished.

"Technically, you are a dungeon core." Erin pulled his attention back to her. "You are a soul, trapped inside of a magical gem."

My soul is trapped?

"What was I before?"

Erin waved her hand across his 'face'. "Not important."

He thought it was important.

"What *is* important," she said, "is that we get to work."

"Don't you think we're moving a bit fast?" Ryan's mind was spinning, and Erin wasn't doing a good job at explaining anything.

"Fast? Fast?!" she wailed. "Do you have any idea how long I've been stuck in this cramped dirty hole??"

He didn't. In fact, he really didn't have any sense of time in their hole.

"Uhm, considering I just 'woke' up, and have no recollection of anything before then, I'm going to say no."

The fairy crossed her arms and wings across her chest, annoyed.

"No need to be sarcastic," she sighed. "For your information, the Goddess of Justice sent me down here over a month ago."

"Goddess of Justice?"

"Yes, the deity that rules over righteousness and justice in the world. The best goddess there is!"

The memory of a voice tickled across Ryan's mind before it too was eaten by the darkness. He was getting tired of these memories being stolen away.

"She sent me down here," Erin continued, "telling me a new dungeon was about to be born."

"Me?"

"Yes. Though I didn't realize you would be asleep for a month."

"Well, you could have tried to wake me up."

"What do you think I've been doing? Ugh, try to keep up." Well, now she was just being mean.

"I'm sorry, Erin, I really am." He sent a small feeling of comfort through their bond, which reminded him: "Say, what is this 'bond' between us? What did you do?"

She flew off the ground, humming softly. It was apparent she had a lot of unspent energy. "Dungeon cores require a fairy to link with them in order to grow. The dungeon core serves as the heart of the dungeon and is responsible for creating everything within it. As a fairy, my task is to guide you, to ensure you grow at an appropriate pace, and live a long and prosperous life."

"Seems tedious. What do you get out of it?" Ryan couldn't believe she would willingly just help him for no reason. The world didn't work that way. *Strange. Where is this bias coming from?*

"Through our bond, I can share in your power. The stronger you get, the more powerful I become as well. Once I've bonded to you, I can no longer draw mana from the world on my own, so I need you to help me survive."

"What's mana?"

Erin huffed again at his question. They really weren't getting very far.

"Do I have to explain every little thing to you right this instant?"

"Well, isn't that your job?"

She opened her mouth, but stopped, thinking for a second. "I mean, you're not wrong."

She flew over and sat back atop his head. He could tell now he was indeed in some sort of gem, with his inner light making it appear to glow white.

"How about we work out your powers as I explain some things?"

"Sounds good."

If Erin needed Ryan to provide this 'mana' to survive, he should probably get some. He couldn't help but shudder at the thought of being alone in this hole.

Oh, poor Erin.

"Mana is the very energy that runs the world. Everything contains some form of mana. You could say it is the lifeblood of existence."

Makes perfect sense... not.

"Ambient mana exists lightly in the air," explained Erin, "and you will use mana in every aspect of your life as a dungeon core."

"All right, so magical energy, floating around, that I can use. Easy enough."

Erin sent an annoyed jolt through their bond at the interruption, then continued.

"As a dungeon core, you can use your mana to spread your influence into anything you touch. By doing this, a dungeon core is able to slowly build and carve out a desirable shape, or body, for the dungeon. As you grow stronger, the amount of mana you can use, along with how quickly it returns, will increase."

She flew over to the wall, just outside the range of his white light.

"I want you to focus on the energy within you and spread it forward to this wall."

Ryan closed his 'eyes', focusing within. She was right, he could feel a strange power that seemed to stir within. Gently, he reached out to it, and it eagerly jumped towards him, like a pet happy its owner had returned. It filled him with an almost intoxicating warmth.

"Good, now extend that energy towards—"

Ryan was only half listening to her as he focused on the spot she had indicated. He urged the energy towards her, letting it go, and it leapt from him. Erin's scream a second later brought him back to his senses.

"Ryan!" The wall Erin had been hovering beside was now a crater, the rubble and surrounding rock glowing slightly.

"Did I do it?" He could 'feel' that area now and could see everything around it as if he was in it.

"Well… you did. But you can't just unleash random bursts of mana!"

Oops.

"You have to gently reach out with it, otherwise you risk blowing everything up around you, including me."

Her left wing did seem to be smoking just a bit, and perhaps missing a feather or two.

"Right. Whoops. Well, now that we have that out of the way, what's next?" He found this whole mana use thing very exciting, yet oddly draining.

"Well, now we slowly spread your influence. It's going to take a lot of mana to get to the first level of true dungeonhood."

Chapter Three

It took Ryan a whole day to spread his influence into a three-foot sphere around himself. Erin mentioned the measurement to him, noting his core was equal to the size of a human fist. He had no reference for that, so he ignored it.

"So, what do we do from here?"

He floated in the chamber, the latent mana in his body keeping him suspended, while Erin flew around, enjoying the new space. The entire room glowed with a pure white energy, and Ryan could feel more mana slowly filling him.

Erin had explained to him that currently his mana capacity was low, meaning he would have to take multiple breaks as he worked. As such, it took him the whole day to create his small space. At least the larger he got, the more mana he would be able to absorb, and the larger the area he would be able to work on before needing to take a break to recharge.

"Well, this is a good start." Erin landed atop him – a favorite spot of hers, it seemed. "But we're going to need to get a lot bigger."

"You mean *I'm* going to." She really hadn't done anything, other than complain about how slow Ryan was. He may have 'accidentally' blasted through a piece of rock near her when she had started to annoy him. That stopped her complaining.

"Don't be like that, Ryan, I'm helping too." She sent a hurt feeling through the bond.

"Nagging isn't helping." He sent her a chuckle as he felt her anger rise. "But I think I am ready for the next step towards dungeonhood." He was more comfortable with his mana and had definitely become faster at shaping the earth around him. He'd also noted that as he expanded, he seemed to absorb the broken dirt and rock, instantly gaining an understanding of the material. He needed to ask Erin about that.

"Are you listening?"

Oops. He had zoned her out. What had she been saying? *Quick, divert.*

"You have such pretty wings." He watched her face as she blushed and stuttered, her face turning red for a moment.

"Tha– thank you." Erin flapped them a couple of times, watching as the fine white feathers ruffled, then cleared her throat. "As I was saying, this is only the first step in your path towards being a proper dungeon."

She waved her hand, and six strange symbols appeared in front of Ryan, each glowing a different color.

"These are the different affinities you can have as a dungeon." 'Affinity.' That was a new word. "Across the land, there are usually seven different types of dungeons. Each dungeon specializes in a specific type of energy, or specialized mana."

There were different types of mana? Was that why Erin had originally glowed gold when she met him? Was that her type of mana? Also, she said there were seven, but Ryan only saw six symbols.

"Which means?"

"The mana specialization of a dungeon determines what type of mobs it will be able to create."

"Mobs?"

"Eh, adventurer slang for the types of creatures a dungeon has."

"Why do I need these mobs?" She really hadn't explained much of being a dungeon to him. All he knew was to use his mana to grow his influence, so he could gain more mana.

"You are so clueless." She sighed in exasperation.

"Only because my 'helper' doesn't tell me these things. I can't just absorb all your thoughts—" Erin's face grew startled, and Ryan paused. "Can I?"

"No! No, that's… that's not a good thing. Sorry, I'll do better." She seemed panicked; he could feel terror streaming through their bond. *Guess I shouldn't mention absorbing her again.*

"Anyway, as I stated earlier, a dungeon's goal is to grow stronger. One measure of strength is the amount of mana a dungeon can control, which is why growing your influence is important. The larger you are as a dungeon, the more usable mana you have, and the quicker it refreshes. Mana exists naturally in the world, and as a dungeon, you draw it in constantly from any area that you have influence over."

That made sense and explained why he was now pulling in much more mana than when he had barely had any influence on his surroundings.

"The main way for a dungeon to become stronger, though, is by defeating adventurers and gaining experience."

"So, I use my mobs to beat them, and they just hand over this 'experience' when they lose? What exactly is an adventurer?" Erin's face grew grim for a moment.

"Well, they don't just 'hand' anything over. When an adventurer dies in your dungeon, you absorb them, and you gain experience based on how strong they were. Experience is the other way in which a dungeon grows in strength. You know what, Ryan? We will cover experience a little later."

Death. Ryan remembered a giant blade, a quick slice. He didn't want to kill anyone.

"All right. But Erin, is there a way to grow without killing? I don't like that idea." Erin's face brightened, though her eyes were still sad. She wrapped him in a hug.

"I know. As a celestial being, I am generally against it as well. You can slowly gain experience by spreading out your influence and absorbing new materials around you, but it takes a much longer time to gain experience that way, and the Goddess told me she wants you to grow fast. Besides, adventurers know the risk, and take it willingly."

He couldn't fathom why people would willingly go towards death. Maybe Erin would explain it later.

"But we are a bit off topic," she was saying. "So, long explanation short, as a dungeon, you will make mobs, which will fight adventurers who come into your dungeon. Killing adventurers equals more experience for you, which makes us stronger."

"Simple enough. So, I have to choose one of these affinities in order to begin making mobs?" He felt Erin's pride at his question through their bond. *I got something right. Go me.*

"Yes. Each affinity affects the basic types of mobs you can begin creating. By knowing what type of mobs you will make, you will be able to begin forming the first level of your dungeon. Then we can start trying to attract adventurers."

Adventurers equaled power. Ryan was all for the path to power, especially as it seemed to make Erin happy. The killing part was still unfortunate, though.

"So, what are my options?" he asked.

She pointed to the red symbol first, which was shaped like a flame. "Fire affinity starts with small lizard-like mobs, eventually allowing you to create lesser dragons."

An image of a giant, fire breathing lizard filled his mind from their bond.

"Those seem cool."

Erin nodded before pointing towards the next symbol: a blue teardrop. "Water isn't really an option for us, as we aren't near the water, and adventurers usually complain about exploring those anyway."

All right. So far, it's looking like fire.

"No water, okay. Next."

"Wind," she pointed at a nearly invisible silvery symbol that appeared to be a few squiggly horizontal lines, "gives way to various air-based wisps and elementals, as well as winged beasts. Usually, a wind dungeon is high up in the mountains, which we are not."

So, still dragons.

"Not an option. Okay."

"Earth affinity dungeons begin with low-level animals, but quickly expand to great beasts." Images of massive clawed and furred creatures filled Ryan's mind as Erin pointed towards the next symbol. "Earth dungeons typically also have golems within."

A humanoid pile of moving rocks seemed intimidating at first, but he felt it would get old fast. Ryan was definitely still liking that dragon option.

"Boring."

"Celestial, or light magic as some call it—" She pointed towards the golden symbol, a perfect golden sun, "—begins with gentler, magical creatures, which eventually evolve into divine." She sent an image of a beautiful unicorn, as well as a large, glowing version of herself: an 'angel,' she called it. "However, celestial dungeons usually grow rather slowly. Like I said, celestial creatures are averse to killing."

Well, that won't help me get stronger, so that's out. "Doesn't seem like a good path to power. No offense."

"None taken."

"And the next one?"

"The last one is darkness. It is the power to raise the undead. Dungeons aligned with darkness raise skeletons and zombies, and can bring forth anything that has died in their dungeon as their own monster. In that sense, a dark dungeon could have creatures from the other affinities as well, but in the undead form."

That seemed intriguing, but Erin didn't seem keen.

"Hmm. Going to have to say dragons are the coolest." Ryan glanced at the six symbols and recalled Erin's earlier comment. *Shouldn't there be a seventh?* Maybe she had misspoken.

Erin let out a sigh, as if she had been holding her breath. "Thank the Goddess. The church hates dark dungeons."

The church, you say? Ryan saw a brief vision of a man in white, and a feeling of disdain filled him. Ryan was pretty sure he didn't like the church.

"So," Erin was saying, "just stretch out your mana to the symbol for fire, and that will bind your dungeon to that affinity. After that, we can really get started." Erin pointed towards the fire symbol.

Ryan grinned to himself, moving his mana ever so slowly out

towards the fire symbol. *I really don't like the church*. The thought pushed into his head. *And if the church doesn't like the darkness…*

Something within him snapped, and suddenly his mana shot towards the dark symbol: an impossibly black human skull. The moment his mana touched it, the darkness wrapped around Ryan's light and rushed into him. It left a black imprint on his stone, the same shape as the skull symbol.

"Ryan, WHAT HAVE YOU DONE?"

Chapter Four

"Erin. Erin. ERIN!"

His cries were ignored. The fairy's emotions were a mixture of rage and sorrow. *What have I done?*

"Look, Erin, I'm sorry."

"You're vile. How could you? Only evil souls choose darkness or chaos."

Chaos? *So there* are *seven.* Ryan made a mental note to ask Erin about that one later on, when she wasn't extremely mad at him.

"Look, Erin. I'm not evil, I promise." He tried to convey his sincerity through the bond. "Something came over me. I couldn't control myself. Pull the other elements back up, and I'll switch back to fire. Having fire-breathing lizards seems so cool."

Tears fell from her eyes as she shook her head. "It can't be undone."

What? "But—"

"Once you pick your affinity, there is no going back. You're stuck with a dark affinity." She said it with disgust. Was darkness really that bad?

"Oh." Why had he acted so impulsively? What strange force had come over him to make him chose the dark energy? What had the church ever done to him?

"It doesn't matter." Erin was fighting hard to get her emotions back in order. "I've let the Goddess down."

She broke down again.

Poor girl.

"Erin, you haven't let anyone down. You've been a great help. It's not your fault you got stuck with a stupid dungeon core."

She looked up, a small smile starting to form. "The dumbest."

"Yup, that's me, dumbest dungeon there ever was."

She laughed; it was light and musical. Ryan could feel himself smiling.

"Now, then, how about you help this dumb dungeon try to work past his mistake?"

She flew back onto him, wiping her eyes as she landed. "Well, thanks to you, we are stuck with darkness."

"Nothing we can do?"

"Nope."

"Well, then, I guess it's time for the next step in becoming a dungeon. You mentioned something about mobs?"

She sighed but pulled out two crystalline triangles. They grew until they were each just a tad smaller than Ryan and floated in front of him. They appeared to be inversions of each other.

"Your affinity helps us decide what type of mobs you are able to create. Those," she pointed towards the triangles, "show us your current level, as well as the amount of experience you have towards the next level."

She flew to the first triangle. "This is the level gauge." She pointed at the triangle's wide base. "The bottom is the Bronze tier and consists of eleven levels. Next is Silver, with nine levels. Then it's Gold with seven, Platinum with five, Diamond with three, and at the top, is God tier."

"Hey, awesome. I'm made of diamond. Am I a one, two, or three?"

"You're made out of idiot." She laughed again. "All dungeon cores are made of diamond. Besides, what your stone is made of doesn't determine your level, silly." She pointed to the bottom left-hand corner of the triangle, where a single, much smaller triangle, glowed black. "This is your level. You are currently a

Bronze Eleven darkness dungeon." Oh, so he was at the very bottom. *Ouch.*

"And this shows you are about halfway towards the experience requirement for your next level." She pointed at the other main triangle – the inverted one – which had the narrow bottom portion partially filled with a black glow. "This triangle is split into six levels." Ryan could see six different lines cutting across it, each creating a larger section. "For Bronze, you need to fill the bottom portion to level one. For Silver, you'll have to fill the second. To reach Gold, it's—"

"—the third level, Platinum the fourth, and so on?" Looking at that, it meant each level would grow increasingly more difficult to progress past. *Ugh. Being a dungeon is going to be hard.*

"You caught on to that quickly." Erin waved her hand, and the two triangles sank to the ground. "If you absorb these, you will be able to call them forth whenever you choose, to check your stats." She didn't have to tell Ryan twice. He instantly absorbed them both. Unlike the previous objects he had absorbed, though, these weren't broken down, and a rush of knowledge didn't fill him regarding them. *Darn, they seem interesting.* He wondered how they worked.

"Now, call your level triangle back out," suggested Erin.

He looked at her, wondering how he would do that. "How?"

"Just… think of it?" Erin didn't seem to know either. *Awesome.*

"Fine." He imagined the triangle he had just absorbed, and on cue, it appeared shimmering before him. "I did it!"

"At least you can do some things right." She seemed to still be a tad upset about the darkness thing.

Oops.

"So, the mobs you can summon depend on multiple factors. First, your affinity. Second, your level."

"And mobs get stronger as I do?" He was liking this whole 'interrupt Erin with thoughts of his own' game. She had seemed happy with his guesses earlier.

"Not quite." Drat, he was wrong. "Mobs are assigned a point value. Based on your level, you have a certain amount of points available with which to create mobs."

Ugh. Does this mean I have to do math?

"At Bronze Eleven, you are allotted fifty points." She pointed to the bottom leftmost triangle, and a white '50' appeared over the darkness. *That's helpful.* "As you increase in levels, you will be allotted more points."

This all seemed simple enough.

"So, I can create fifty points' worth of mobs right now?"

Erin shook her head. "They would have nowhere to go."

Ah, right. They were still in a single sphere-shaped room.

"So, we have to expand first?" *Ugh.* Expanding took forever. Ryan wanted to see what else he could do.

"Correct. Before you summon any mobs, you need to create the first level of your dungeon."

"Just one level?" He tried not to sound disappointed. He wanted to be big.

"Yes. Your allotted points apply across all your floors, so I don't think expanding out to more than one floor would be wise at this time." Oh, valid point. He wasn't sure how much different mobs cost yet, but he had a feeling fifty points wouldn't go very far.

"Try to make three rooms for now. A boss room right before this area, and then two other rooms. That seems to be the basic setup for most low-level dungeons." Erin flew atop him again, patting his head. He sent a pained groan through their bond.

"The sooner you get this done, the sooner you get to summon your first mobs," she told him, sending a wave of distaste through their bond. Yup, she hadn't forgiven him at all.

He silently set to work spreading his influence out. Perhaps if he worked hard enough, Erin wouldn't hold onto her obvious grudge. Besides, darkness couldn't be that bad.

???

The deep reverberation of bells woke him from his slumber. His eyes opened slowly, and as he sat up, he scanned the room. The skeletons that surrounded him as he slept stood silent and unmoving.

He paid them no heed as he stood, calling on the surrounding gloom to cover him. He emerged from the room riding a wave of darkness, heading to the heart of his castle

The walls he passed were adorned with ancient paintings, relics from times long forgotten. He recalled 'acquiring' the castle from his master and smirked to himself as he remembered that sniveling fool. He hadn't even been worth bringing back as a minion.

He passed patrolling zombies and skeletons on his way – his loyal servants, all humans too weak to stand before him in life. At least they were useful in death. He grinned again as his eyes passed over his pets. Every undead face reminded him of a battle, of death. He did so enjoy killing. Perhaps that was why he had so readily accepted his calling and embraced his dark powers.

His thoughts paused as he reached his goal: a massive underground chamber, with a single pedestal resting in the center of the room. Atop the pedestal sat a crystal, the only one of its kind in existence.

It was able to determine when a dungeon of darkness affinity had awakened. And clearly, it had detected something, for the crystal was glowing with a dark light. Beside it, an acolyte, the only other living being in his castle, was clanging the bells. As he entered, the acolyte faltered, and stepped away from the bells, bowing in his direction.

"Contact your master," he growled to the acolyte. "There is a new darkness dungeon."

Chapter Five

Ryan began by focusing his mana outward, spreading himself through the dirt and stone. He instantly absorbed anything and everything he touched, clearing out a space. Erin had given him a brief description of how the boss room and other two rooms should look, and he wanted to make her proud.

While he worked, Erin curled up on top of him, and was soon asleep. Apparently, she thought the basic labor behind dungeon building was uninteresting. Ah, well. That just meant he would be able to surprise her when she woke up.

He set to work, pushing out and creating a space large enough to be called his boss room. He still wasn't sure what a boss was, but Erin would likely tell him when he finished. As such, he pushed his influence out until he had created a vast — well, vast compared to his small three-foot area — room. It had to be close to four – no, five – times the size of his own chamber, with square walls and a domed top. He liked the aesthetics of that curved ceiling, though the room itself was otherwise rather nondescript. He would have to ask Erin about ways to touch it up. If people were going to be in the room, he wanted to give them something worth looking at.

Focus!

He shook his head and created an arching doorway leading out of the room. As he worked, Ryan casually called forth his experience triangle, watching the bottom portion hungrily. The plus side of this expansion was he might just be able to get another level out of it! Erin had told him a dungeon would gain a small amount of experience as it spread its influence to new areas and created larger rooms.

He created a winding pathway out of his boss room, slowly angling it up. Ryan wasn't sure how far underground they were, but he figured he had enough space to add a little depth and elevation to his first floor. As he carved away, he also noticed strange variations in what he was absorbing. By the time he had carved out his second room – this one a large, cavern-like expanse – he had found a few neat things.

First, several different metals had made themselves 'known' to him via his absorption of them. He found iron and copper, though Erin hadn't woken from her sleep for him to ask her about them. He had also found a small strain of gold, but again, he wasn't certain if that was valuable. The only reason the metals stood out was because they were different from the normal rocks and dirt he had been eating away.

The other things he had stumbled upon were the skeletal remains of a variety of creatures. Ryan wasn't sure if it was his affinity for dark mana, but as he absorbed the remains, he instantly gained an understanding not only of bone, but also of the creatures the bones had belonged to. Frustratingly, though, some of the skeletons were incomplete. As he pushed forward with the excavation and his final room, he found himself hoping for more bones to complete his collection.

"Finished that boss room yet?" Erin stretched as she rose from her nap. How long had she been asleep? He really had no idea of time down here.

It *was* taking a while, mainly because he needed to take breaks from his work to give his mana time to refill. On the plus side, as he grew larger, his mana began refilling faster, increasing the rate at which he could work. A busy dungeon was a happy dungeon, it seemed.

Once he reached his final room, he had been able to make changes without feeling much of a drain, but the boss room had taken him at least a day, if not two, to create. If he had to guess, he figured he may have been dungeon building for a week now? And Erin had slept the entire time. *Lazy fairy.*

"You could say that." He was only half paying attention to her, having found a human skeleton as he was finishing up his final room. *Spiffy.* That made four different skeletons in his collection. In the silence, while Erin took a nap, he may have become a bit obsessed with completing his sets, to the point of creating a few offshoot tunnels here and there as he searched near the remains he did find.

"Well, let me take a look." Erin stretched her feathery wings and took flight, heading through the small opening he had made between his room and the boss room, per her instructions.

Erin told him he couldn't completely cut it off from the dungeon, but that his room should be hard to find. As such, he made a tunnel from his chamber that snaked up and a down a few times, before connecting through a small hole at the top corner of his boss room. He felt it was sneaky.

"Ugh, you couldn't have made that easier on me?" Her voice was filled with irritation as it came through their bond.

Well, you can't please everyone.

Ryan finished his final touches on the first room: a sprawling expanse like the second, seeming almost natural, not dungeon made. He wanted to talk with Erin about a few things before adding to it.

"I like this ceiling. This room feels eerie," said Erin.

Dark stone illuminated only by a faint white glow – it *was* eerie. Especially since the room was too large for the light to chase away the darkness. But hey, Ryan didn't have any way to add extra light. The only reason there was a slight glow was because it permeated everything Ryan had influenced. Erin had told him the glow represented objects that had been worked on by a dungeon's mana.

"Well, eerie can be good, right? We are a darkness dungeon." He sent his humor through the bond. Maybe she had forgiven him.

"Oh, how could I ever forget?" She huffed as she flew on to the next room. Erin zipped around the large space, inspecting the walls, muttering to herself here and there.

"Ryan?" She was inspecting one of his offshoot tunnels. *Oops.* "What is this?"

"Um, I was looking for something." He could tell this was about to go south.

"Oh, like metals?"

"Yes, totally those." *Phew, that was close.*

She poked around in the offshoot tunnel, looking at the soil, checking the portions he had absorbed away. He watched her through the walls and realized something just as she noticed it. He had absorbed the skull he had found there but forgotten to absorb the rock around it. The effect: a piece of stone with the perfect imprint of a human skull.

Crap.

"What have you been doing?" she screeched.

Yup, she was mad. So very, very mad.

"Come on. Throw me a bone!" *Ha.* Probably a poor time for that joke. "I didn't do anything with it, I just absorbed it. I needed it for my collection."

"YOUR WHAT?"

Oh, note to self: anything dark-related is a touchy subject.

"My bone collection." He was quickly filling in all the other offshoot tunnels he had made. She didn't need to know about those. It was easy enough; he found he could create anything he had absorbed with a simple thought and a minuscule mana drain.

"I'm going to act like I didn't hear that for now, and finish inspecting the dungeon." Her tone, and her feelings, told him this was not over.

Chapter Six

"So, what did you think?" Erin had finished looking over Ryan's hard work, and was now sitting atop him, albeit silently. She hadn't spoken to him since his mention of his bone collection.

"It's a good start."

Oh, that's promising.

"But it is pretty basic."

Ouch.

"Well, you didn't really give me much to go on," he grumbled.

Great plan, shift the blame back to the angry one. I really need to think about things before I say them.

Erin growled and hit him. Obviously, being a diamond, he didn't feel it, but he got the message. She was mad. *Really* mad.

"Sorry, I tend to speak without thinking sometimes." He sent his remorse through the bond.

"You 'tend,'" she stressed the word, "to do a lot without thinking."

Fair point. His mind was currently sneaking around the walls, seeing if he had missed any bones. Ryan found he could send his consciousness to multiple places at once, allowing him to multitask.

Oh look, another bone.

"Ryan."

Oh no.

"Ryan, you're searching for more bones, aren't you?"

His emotions must have traveled through the bond while he was speaking with her. She'd felt his sudden excitement and figured him out.

"Um, will you be mad if I say yes?" he asked.

Ryan still hadn't quite gotten used to being bonded with her. She seemed able to make guesses about what he was thinking based on what emotions she could sense him experiencing. It was rather unnerving.

Her anger came across the bond, and he prepared himself for another fit from her. However, the emotions slowly faded to sorrow.

"What am I supposed to do with you?"

"I'm really sorry, Erin." He sent waves of his own sorrow through the bond. Ryan hated to hurt people, and he really had started to care for the fairy. "I'm just trying to become a dungeon you can be proud of."

"I know, I know. I'm just a little biased. You chose practically the worst dungeon type you could. The only one worse would have been chaos."

"You know, I don't remember that being an option." He really was curious about this chaos affinity now. "Did you hide it from me?"

Erin quickly shook her head. "That's not it. I would never purposefully hide anything from you."

Ryan wasn't sure if that was true, but he was listening.

"Chaos is the direct opposite of celestial. Because you are paired with me, and I am a celestial fairy, chaos wasn't an option. In the same way, a dungeon with a chaos fairy cannot choose celestial. "

"If it makes you feel better, I wouldn't have chosen chaos."

Ryan didn't know what Chaos was, since Erin hadn't explained much on it, but something in his core told him he would have stayed away from it. He wasn't evil.

"You know what, how about we get to building some mobs?"

Erin's mention of mobs drew his full attention. She certainly knew how his mind worked.

"Awesome. What do I have to do?"

"As I mentioned before, darkness dungeons utilize skeletons and zombies as their basic monster types."

He remembered that, hence his bone collection.

"All right, so how do I make them?" His mind was already swarming with ideas.

"Normally, darkness dungeons begin with making mobs from bones they have found through expansion."

Ryan beamed. "Well, I have found a lot of bones so far."

"Then try to reanimate one of those sets."

Reanimate? "How?"

"Well, send your mana into the set of bones you've found, and it should naturally begin to bring the creature back to life." She seemed to hate giving him these instructions.

"Can't do that."

"Why not?"

Now who's the slow one?

"Because I absorbed every set I found." How else would he have a bone collection?

"Oh." She paused. Ryan was curious what she was thinking about; her emotions were all over the place. "Hey, Ryan, I think I just solved our problem."

"What problem, and does it get us to this whole 'making mobs' thing? I really want to make some." He had been waiting a long time for this.

"I think I found out how I can accept you as a darkness dungeon."

Oh, that was definitely more important than mob summoning.

"I'm listening."

"So, part of the reason why darkness dungeons are destroyed by the church is because of how dangerous and evil they are."

"Well, I can guess raising things from the dead is usually frowned upon."

Erin nodded in agreement, continuing, "That's part of it, Ryan. The other issue is how strong they can become in a short amount of time."

"How?" *Isn't getting strong fast a good thing?*

"Remember I mentioned you are limited to how many mobs you can have based on your level?"

"Yup! At Bronze Eleven I have fifty points. But I'm sooooo close to leveling."

"Right, well, when a dungeon reanimates a skeleton or a fresh corpse that it has found and didn't create, they don't count against that value."

Oh, that's interesting.

"And those mobs can leave the dungeon." She let that hang in the air, like it was a big deal. Ryan had no idea why, and his confusion must have gone through their bond.

"Normally, dungeon mobs can't leave the dungeon," Erin explained.

Well, then.

"So, having mobs that don't cost anything and can leave the dungeon to roam the land presents a danger?" he said. "That makes sense."

Ryan guessed masses of undead meandering about killing innocent people would cause quite a stir. Hell, he could almost sympathize with the church for fearing dungeons like that. Almost.

"But I'm not going to do that." He felt Erin's mood rise, though she looked at him with a confused face.

"What do you mean?"

"I don't want to raise people from the dead, and I don't want to be destroyed before we get strong." Ryan wasn't evil, and the thought of bringing people back from the dead left a bad taste in his mouth.

"I knew you weren't evil. This is why I think my solution will work for us." Erin was glowing a little brighter, and her mood was infectious.

"You still haven't told me this solution," he reminded her. He was glad they could get this to work, glad she seemed in a good mood, but he was still confused what her solution was.

"Well, as long as you promise to never raise the dead or create mobs from fallen adventurers—"

"I promise."

"—we can make our mobs completely from scratch using our own dungeon bones."

She waved her hands in the air at the last part, a smile across her face. If Ryan had to guess, she had just come up with that name.

"Works for me. So, can we get to mob summoning now?"

Chapter Seven

Erin's mood changed completely the moment she realized Ryan wasn't planning on using the bodies he had found as his mobs. In fact, now she seemed almost as excited about mob summoning as he was.

"So, first I'm going to explain the basic mobs you can make as a Bronze-level dungeon." She had his full attention. "There are two main mob types: skeleton and zombie."

As she spoke, she flashed images of both to him.

"But, as a Bronze dungeon, there are four types you can summon, as each main type has two sub-types: beast and human."

Now we're getting somewhere.

"Beasts are broken down based upon their sizes. As you get stronger, you will be able to create larger beast-type skeletons and zombies."

Ryan shuffled through his knowledge on what types of beasts he had absorbed. He had found complete skeletons for rats and squirrels, an incomplete deer, and an incomplete wolf. He had also found a single human skeleton, but it was missing an arm for some reason.

"At Bronze level, your human-based skeletons and zombies are limited to basic versions, but when you level up, you will be able to make them tougher, and even give them armor and weapons to use."

"So, can I make fifty human skeletons?" *Each mob counts as a point, right?*

"No, different mobs have different point values."

Ugh, so much to learn.

Erin held up her fingers, and started ticking away at them, as if trying to remember the information herself.

"Small beast skeletons are worth one point, small beast zombies are worth five points." *Oh, that's easy enough to remember.* "Normal human skeletons are five as well, and human zombies are ten."

"Are their values based on their strength?"

"More or less. A single human skeleton is stronger than a small beast skeleton, but five small beasts *might* be able to take on a human skeleton. Variety in dungeons is key. It will take you a while to figure out the combinations that will enhance your dungeon. Most high-ranking dungeons even modify each and every floor to hold different mob types and adapt them to highlight the strengths of those mobs."

"Why do zombie beasts cost five times as much as skeletal beasts, while human zombies cost only twice as much as human skeletons?"

Erin stared at him for a moment, mouth agape. After a second, she shook her head.

"These are just the starting costs. At Silver, your medium skeletal beasts and zombie beasts only differ by five mob points, or twice as much."

"Then why such a large difference now?" He really wanted to know.

"No one really knows why mobs cost what they do, Ryan. However—" She paused, her face growing dark. "There is a belief that the God of Death wanted to tempt dungeons into summoning more human mobs than beast mobs early on."

Ryan shivered at this. Just what type of being was the God of Death?

"Well, that was dark." *Ha.* "So, what do you recommend we make?" he asked Erin. He was at a total loss, not to mention nervous about taking the first step to becoming a powerful dungeon.

"What do your collections look like?"

"Well, I have full sets of rat and squirrel bones. My deer and wolf sets are almost complete as well, and my human is missing all the bones of his right arm." He wondered if something had dragged away that arm after the human died.

"Hmm. The wolf and deer are both medium beasts, so you won't be able to use those yet." *Darn.* "Rats and squirrels could be interesting, and a human missing an arm."

Erin fell silent, thinking.

"This dungeon building is hard," Ryan whispered, trying to imagine the best possible combination. Fifty points suddenly didn't seem like much for his three rooms.

"So, I think we should use a human skeleton for your boss," Erin finally said. "And if we mix up skeletal squirrels and zombie rats for the other rooms, we can at least give adventurers a bit of a scare, and maybe kill one or two to help you get a little stronger."

Ryan started doing some basic math. A human skeleton for his boss would cost him five points, leaving him with forty-five points spread across two rooms. Should he try to even them out? Or should he make the mobs harder as adventurers came deeper?

"Just a single skeleton in my boss room? Isn't a five-point mob pretty low for a boss? The other rooms are going to have forty-five points divided between the two. Seems a bit off." Shouldn't his boss room be his strongest?

"Oh, bosses are different. They cost five times the basic cost of the mob you use. Your single skeleton is going to cost you twenty-five points and will be unique."

"What?" That would leave him with twenty-five points for the other two rooms. That hardly seemed adequate.

Erin ignored his outcry and continued. "So, Ryan, how about you put five skeletal squirrels in the first room? And two zombie rats with ten points of skeletal squirrels and rats mixed in for the second room?"

The numbers added up, though Ryan still couldn't get past

the massive cost of his boss skeleton. Why was it so high? *Oh, well. First things first: skeletal squirrels.*

"Well?" Erin broke the silence that had filled the room.

"How do I make a mob?"

"Oh!" Erin started laughing, and while Ryan loved the sound of her laugh, this time he was annoyed. She was laughing at him, and it hurt.

"I'm serious."

"I–" More laughter. "I'm sorry, I forgot to tell you." She had tears falling down her face. "As a dungeon, not only do you learn everything about the things you absorb, but you can then create them at will."

He would have smacked his own face if he had one. He had been creating dirt to fill holes and manipulate his dungeon, but he hadn't realized he could do it with other things, too. He turned his focus back to Erin as she continued.

"Think of your squirrel skeleton, and push mana into the image, willing the bones into existence." He started to concentrate. "In the first room!"

Whoops. He had been about to try and summon the skeletal squirrel in the room with them.

Ryan focused his attention, looking over the skeletal remains he had absorbed, and pushed his mana into imagining a skeletal squirrel in his first room. He felt the dark mana respond, and suddenly a pile of bones appeared out of the ground in his first room. Ryan repeated the process four more times.

"Now what?" The bones weren't moving; they were just piled up.

"Now, push your mana into them, imagine them as alive. Your darkness affinity will do the rest."

"Easy enough."

He did as she said, and suddenly, a dark mist swirled around the bones. Then, the bones began to clatter, and suddenly Ryan had five very animated skeletal squirrels scampering around. *Neat.*

"Those little guys will follow orders you give them and will instinctually attack anything that enters the dungeon."

They clattered around, the sound of bones on stones echoing throughout the room. It was a rather creepy sound.

"Next, your zombie rats." Right, he wasn't done. "By absorbing the rat's bones, you understand the creature as a whole, correct?"

"Yes." He knew everything about rats.

"Good, so imagine a decayed rat, and summon that body."

"How decayed? Does it matter?" He was curious whether the amount of decay would affect its strength.

"Your dark energy won't let you make a living creature, and part of a zombie's strength is its potential to spread diseases. So perhaps give it enough decay that the flesh has begun to rot, but not enough that it's falling apart."

Oh yeah, really clear instructions. Thanks, Erin.

Ryan focused on the task, imagining it as Erin said. In his mind, he could see the rat, fur falling off, flesh exposed and beginning to decay. He knew that would enable it to carry disease and make it dangerous to whoever it attacked. As before, he pushed his mana into the image, and when the rat's body appeared, Ryan sent his dark mana into it.

With a squeak, his zombie came to life, its decayed eyes glancing around the darkness cautiously as it seemed to sniff the air. Ryan quickly created the second rat and then spread a mix of five squirrel and five rat skeletons to the room. He was left with twenty-five points, just like they had planned.

Next up: his boss mob.

Chapter Eight

"So, the first thing you need to do is summon your human skeleton."

Before Erin finished speaking, Ryan already had his skeleton formed and walking around. It was getting much easier to call forth his mobs now that he had some practice.

They both watched the monster amble about, and Ryan couldn't help but feel annoyed that it was missing an arm. Where were those blasted bones?

"All right. Now you have your skeleton, you can begin to make him your boss mob."

Oh, more instructions. Time to listen.

"What do I do?"

"Well, if you'll look, you have twenty points left on your triangle." Ryan quickly called forth his level triangle, confirming the number was down to twenty. "Yup, at least we can both do math."

Erin ignored his comment and continued. "Now, focus on the mob and push your mana into him, willing his point value to increase."

He did so slowly, and dark tendrils crept up the skeleton, the monster looking down blankly at them. For a long moment, nothing else happened.

"Need a hand?" Erin started giggling.

Is now really the time for puns? Ryan pushed his attention back towards his mob, watching his triangle at the same time. The dark tendrils began to snake across the entire skeleton, and suddenly Ryan's triangle dropped to nineteen. Then eighteen, more darkness; seventeen, it started to swirl through the air. Sixteen, it was filling the gaps around the bones.

This is taking too long. Ryan slammed all his mana into the mob.

The tendrils turned into a wave, and suddenly the skeleton was covered in a dark blob that completely hid its appearance. At the same time, Ryan saw the remaining numbers of his point total tick rapidly down until they hit zero.

"Is it finished?" His mana stopped flowing, but the cocoon of dark energy remained.

"I'm not sure. Let me go check." Erin flew from the room, and Ryan watched the fairy go. Hopefully she would be okay.

A moment later, she appeared in the boss room, her golden light a stark contrast to the black mana that permeated from where his skeleton had stood. Cautiously, she flew up to it, inspecting it.

"Well, to be honest, Ryan, I don't know what to do from here." She continued inspecting it. "You're my first dungeon. I've only been instructed as to what you should do, not what happens afterwar–"

She screamed and flew towards the ceiling as the dark energy started to crack.

"Oh, something's happening." Ryan ignored her panic, excitement filling him. His boss mob was hatching.

The dark energy continued to crack, and Ryan was able to make out a slight white glow coming from inside. All of his skeletons – everything he touched with his influence, in fact – held that slight glow. More and more cracks splintered across the cocoon, until finally, it shattered.

"What is that?" Erin's voice was filled with a strange mixture of excitement and disgust as she stared at Ryan's creation.

The skeleton had grown close to eight feet in height. His bones had thickened, and dark tendrils wrapped lazily around his body. The bones along his left arm had also developed sharp, blade-like edges, which Ryan imagined would make decent weapons. What was really unique, though, was the skeleton's right arm.

Where before there had been an annoying lack of bones, now there floated a random assortment of them, pulled from throughout the skeleton's body and suspended by dark mana. It looked disturbing to say the least, but Ryan wasn't quite sure what they were for.

"Well, if I had to guess, I would say that's our boss mob." Ryan could barely hold in his excitement. His mind was racing as he wondered how his other mobs would react to the boss mob's transformation.

"You don't say." Erin's voice was filled with sarcasm as she flew above the skeleton, watching it warily.

"So, what now?" Ryan had definitely noticed his attention span decreasing since his awakening as a dungeon. He wanted to constantly be doing something, and now that his task of creating a dungeon filled with mobs was complete, he was already looking for something new and exciting to do.

"Well, now you've completed the basics of your dungeon, I would say it's time we created an entrance for adventurers."

Oh, yup, that sounds like the next new and exciting thing to do.

"Okay, one entrance, coming right up." He turned his focus to his first room and, before Erin could protest, extended the full might of his influence towards the end of the room. The walls glowed a bright white as he focused on what he was doing.

In his mind, he saw a straight tunnel leading from the room at a slight incline until it reached the surface. His mana responded, and a beam of energy and influence ripped through dirt and rock. His dungeon shook from the violence of the blast, but Ryan didn't care. He felt his influence hit the surface, blasting rock, soil, grass and trees aside as his dungeon created its opening.

"Ryan." Judging from her tone, Ryan guessed he had ignored her as he worked on his opening.

"Ye-es?" He was only half listening as he devoured everything that touched his influence. He learned what oak trees were, and grass, and a strange set of various other plants he would investigate later. What he was really focused on was the fact that his influence wouldn't spread past his new opening.

Even still, he found if he focused on his entrance, he could 'see' everything around him. Vast trees loomed, casting shadows even as sunlight filtered through their leaves. The force of his excavation had blasted a clearing of about ten feet around the entrance, though it was clean of debris thanks to Ryan's quick absorption.

"You're supposed to do that slowly. Now you've gone and just created a giant hole in the ground, haven't you?" Erin was in lecture mode.

"Well, not quite." Something had caught his attention. "Say, Erin…"

There was movement outside of his dungeon. Figures – humans – standing and dusting themselves off.

"What?" The fairy was annoyed at him, which he was used to by now. But her emotions suddenly leveled out as she registered his tone.

"What is it, Ryan?" She was worried because he was worried.

"I think we're about to get our first adventurers."

The group of four had regrouped and were eyeing his opening. If he had to guess, he had blasted them away. There was violent motioning, an argument of sorts, and then the largest man in the group, clad in a mass of armor, started walking towards his entrance. As the man drew closer, he pulled out a large silver sword, and motioned for the others to follow.

"Already?" Erin was resting on top of Ryan, looking down into his dungeon core, which allowed her to see everything he could.

"Oh, they don't look happy." She looked down at him accusingly. "What did you do?"

"I, uh, I think I blew them up."

Chapter Nine

A few moments earlier

"How much longer are we going to just sit around?"

Blake was sitting with the others around a campfire, staring lazily into it. He had been excited when the Adventurers' Guild had been alerted to a new dungeon awakening. A new dungeon meant an opportunity for him to finally get started as an adventurer.

He had been even more excited when his father, a Platinum-level paladin, had announced Blake could come along as they went to check out the dungeon. His father never allowed him to accompany him on missions, as they were far too dangerous for him. Blake was, after all, a brand-new adventurer, while his father, at Platinum level, was one of the strongest.

Whenever a dungeon awoke, the Adventurers' Guild would send out an expeditionary group to determine whether the dungeon would prove a good training ground. The group usually consisted of three high-level members, to ensure no accidents occurred. The foursome Blake was a part of consisted of his paladin father, a Gold-level cleric from the church, and a newly appointed Gold-level mage from the Mages' Guild.

The team had assembled and departed the day the guild was alerted to the dungeon's presence, and had arrived about a week later. That had been nearly a month ago, though, and there still wasn't a sign of the blasted dungeon.

"Patience, Blake." His father's voice was strong, yet kind. "It usually takes up to a month before a dungeon is ready to create an opening."

"Say, Sean, why did you even bring the boy?" The cleric glanced up from his book, looking between father and son.

Blake's father, Sean, looked every bit the high-level adventurer he was. He was clad in heavily enchanted plate armor, said to have been blessed by the Goddess of Justice herself. His divine sword was even crafted from a rare celestial ore, known as orichalcum, that could only be found within the Goddess's personal dungeon. Blake, on the other hand, had just reached the first level of adventurer, Bronze Eleven, and his gear betrayed that fact. He was armed with a simple iron sword and light leather armor. Being Bronze meant Blake wasn't even strong enough to choose a class to specialize in, so he was just a generic fighter.

"Yeah, why'd you bring the noob?" The mage looked with disgust at Blake. Noob was a derogatory term used to describe brand new adventurers.

"First," Sean's voice was deep and powerful, and it almost seemed like the earth around them was rumbling with his growl, "insult my son again, mage, and you will regret it."

The ground rumbled again, and the mage's eyes grew wide. Was Blake's father causing that rumbling? He did have the mana reserves required to affect the very earth around him, after all.

"Second…" More rumbling as Sean looked at the cleric. Blake's father seemed unconcerned with the rumbling, so Blake decided it must be his father flaunting his power. The mage had done nothing but complain the entire trip, after all. It was likely Sean had finally had enough. "I brought him because if we deem this dungeon safe enough, I want my son to train here."

The cleric sighed and nodded, turning back to his book. Blake could tell the cleric was just as done with the mage as his father was.

"Third—" The rumbling intensified, and before Sean could

finish, the ground immediately behind him exploded. As the earth tore open with a tremendous roar, Blake saw the air around the group shimmer with a golden light. The divine shield, created by his father, kept the debris from smashing into the group, though the force of the eruption still sent the four of them tumbling into the woods.

"What the hell?" The mage cursed as he stood, brushing himself off.

Blake slowly rose to his feet as well, inspecting his body. The speed at which his father responded to the eruption told of the skill a Platinum-level paladin had, and Blake couldn't help feeling a little proud of his father.

Someday, Blake wanted to be a paladin surpassing even his father's level, but he still had a long way to go. He groaned as he stood, having slammed into a tree from the blast.

"I would say our wait is over." Sean was already back in the clearing, looking at the ominous hole that had suddenly erupted into existence.

It looked like a gaping mouth, leading down into a sinister void. Blake couldn't help but shiver. What power did a dungeon have, to rip the ground apart like that? What awaited him in that dungeon? He took a moment to calm his nerves, reminding himself he was with his father. Sean was one of the top adventurers in the land; it was highly unlikely anything within that dungeon would be able to even scratch him. Blake had nothing to fear.

"Leave the noob out here and let's get going." The mage was still grumbling as he neared Sean.

"How about I sacrifice you to the dungeon? I'm sure it wouldn't mind a low Gold mage as its first meal. Might even help it level up a bit." Sean's voice blasted over the mage as Blake and the cleric approached the two.

"Sean, let us get this over with, and then you can teach the mage a lesson. He needs to be alive to provide his report to the guild." The cleric's voice was calm and soothing, and Sean seemed to let his anger fade by a small degree.

"Fine. Let's get this over with." He started towards the

dungeon entrance, drawing his sword as he did. "Stay close, Blake."

They began their descent into the dungeon. Blake was shaking, and he wasn't sure if it was from fear or excitement.

The time for his first dungeon dive had finally arrived.

Chapter Ten

Sean led the group through the first tunnel, unworried about potential attacks. It was nearly impossible for a Platinum-level adventurer to take damage in a brand-new dungeon.

"What type of dungeon do you think it is?" Blake whispered to the cleric as they walked, examining the walls, noting how they seemed to glow with a faint white light.

"We won't know till we come across some mobs." The cleric's own body was glowing with golden light. "I would love to see a celestial dungeon, other than the Goddess's, at least once in my lifetime."

The mage snorted.

"No one likes those. Adventurers can't get around the idea of killing off fluffy animals and unicorns."

His hand burst into flame.

"I'm hoping it is a fire dungeon. Rumor is, you can occasionally capture a baby dragon from one of those and train it as a pet."

Oh, a pet dragon would be cool, thought Blake.

"As long as it isn't chaos or dark, it'll do," Sean called back to the group.

Blake shivered at the thought. Chaos dungeons summoned demons and were to be destroyed on discovery. Dark dungeons were nearly as bad, using dead bodies as monsters.

"Place your bets now." Sean's voice had taken on a lighter tone as they neared the first room. Blake knew his dad, just like all adventurers, loved the excitement of exploring a brand-new dungeon.

The group called out their choices, and Blake decided to bet on an earth dungeon. Given his lack of gear, he figured he could at least take on the small beasts that normally existed in new earth dungeons.

They stepped into the first room, a large rocky cavern. The faintly glowing walls didn't offer much in the way of light, and shadows seemed to dance across them. Blake wondered if his guess had been correct. A strange clicking sound began to echo across the room, as though something hard was scurrying across the rocks.

"Be on your guard." Sean took a step forward, and suddenly a white streak leapt from the ground towards him.

His sword flashed with inhuman speed, and the creature attacking him simply fell apart. White bones clattered to the ground.

"Darkness," the cleric hissed, clutching at his holy symbol. His golden light brightened, and Blake was able to make out a few other skeletal creatures scurrying across the floor towards them. They almost looked like—

"Squirrels?" he asked out loud as the next one leapt at his father, and again the creature was struck down.

As they walked past the piles of bones, Blake confirmed they did appear to be squirrels, though their tails seemed a lot more sinister as bones, rather than as cute and fluffy and covered in fur.

"Aye, a darkness dungeon can create mobs using any creature it finds." The cleric was inspecting one of the small piles as they moved by, his face deep in thought.

"Guess this dungeon is going to be a bust." The mage laughed as he sent a fireball into the group of three skeletal squirrels that remained.

The blast sent them flying into pieces, turning the white bones black as it charred them. The mage brought another fire-ball to life on his hand.

"Hopefully there's a zombie for me to roast before we destroy this dungeon." The flickering flames made his face look terrifying.

"We haven't decided if this dungeon will be destroyed yet," the paladin called back as he neared another tunnel, likely leading to the next room. "Looks like this room only had five skeletal squirrels."

He looked around.

"No sign of loot yet. Definitely a new dungeon." Sean walked through the tunnel, leaving the others to chase after him.

The next tunnel headed slightly deeper underground, a gentle yet noticeable descent. Blake was still shaking with excitement, but his mood had dropped. He had been hoping this dungeon would serve as the starting point for his career as an adventurer, but if the mage was right, it was going to be destroyed when they reached the end.

"Blake, take point." His father's voice pulled him from his thoughts, and he jogged forward, drawing his sword.

"Yes, sir." He rushed past his dad, but in his hurry, and due to the dim lighting in the tunnel, failed to see the uneven ground at his feet. He suddenly found himself flying forward, sword leaping from his hand. The weapon clattered to a halt just inside the next room.

"The noob is going to get himself killed." The mage was laughing hysterically behind him.

"Go get your sword, Blake." Sean's voice had a touch of anger, and Blake knew he had embarrassed his father.

He stood and went after his blade, this time paying attention to the ground. All Blake wanted to do was make his father proud.

Blake entered the next room, smiling as he neared his sword. He would prove himself to his dad. He leaned down, but as he grabbed his blade, he noticed a strange motion in the darkness near him. A sharp pain erupted from his ankle. His cry of agony turned to one of horror as he saw a decaying rat clamped tightly to his leg.

"Zombie!" He swung his sword down, the blade slicing the rotting creature in half.

To Blake's horror, the front half continued to claw at his ankle, the mouth still biting down. He kicked his leg wildly, eyes scanning the room for more enemies as his father and the others rushed in after him.

"Oh, that bites." The mage laughed at his own joke, and moments later the zombie on Blake's ankle was blasted by a fireball from the mage, causing it to erupt in flames before it fell away and died.

Chaos broke out around them as a mass of skeletal creatures attacked. For the next few moments, the group swiftly dispatched the creatures, sending bones dancing all around the room. Another zombie rat tried to attack Blake while the others were killing the skeletal beasts, but this time Blake was ready. He thrust his sword through the creature's skull, and it died instantly.

Blake looked around, noticing the movement from the others had slowed down, and he realized in the time it took him to kill one mob, the others had slain… ten?

"You all right?" his father asked gruffly as he looked around the room, scanning for any other enemies.

"Yeah, though that first one managed to get a good bite on me." He looked down at his wound. It could have been the poor lighting, but it seemed the blood oozing from it had a strange, dark color.

"That's going to turn nasty if we don't heal it." The cleric walked up and knelt by his ankle, placing a hand on his wound.

Golden light surged around his ankle, sending warmth into Blake, and suddenly, the wound closed.

"Zombies are resilient, but their biggest threat comes from the diseases their attacks spread into the blood. Left unattended, even a high-level adventurer would succumb."

Blake nodded at the cleric, thankful for his help.

"I'm guessing, since this is a new dungeon, the next room will have the boss." Sean walked towards the tunnel at the end of the room. "Be careful in this next fight, Blake. Even brand-new dungeon boss mobs are dangerous. Judging from how you did in here, it'll be too much for you to handle."

Blake could practically feel his father's disappointment. His first dungeon dive was a failure.

Chapter Eleven

"Are all adventurers this strong?" Ryan asked as they watched the group decimate his second room. He had been excited when his rat bit the youngest one; Ryan had even sent his second zombie after him. The others, though, seemed way too powerful for him.

"No, I think this group is just checking your dungeon out. Adventurers usually send a scouting party to determine the type of dungeon, and whether it should be destroyed." Erin's eyes were glancing around at the group. "If they decide not to destroy you, we will likely be seeing more adventurers like the young one soon."

"That's good, because they really aren't helping my self-esteem right now." He watched as the man in the white robes healed the young one.

"They've been making quick work of your mobs." Erin paused as the group began moving again.

"Oh, at least we get to see how my boss does." Ryan still had no idea how his boss actually worked. He was curious what the bones floating in darkness were for.

"Mm-hmm." Erin pressed herself closer to him as they watched the group enter the room.

The man in the armor – a paladin, Erin had called him literally glowed with golden light. He was definitely the strongest of the group, and mana radiated from him in waves.

"Here it goes." Ryan sent his excitement through the bond, as the group hesitated upon entering the dark room.

The skeleton turned towards the group, towering over even the paladin. The bones in the dark mana of its missing arm elongated, sharpened into points, and then, without warning, shot toward the group.

"What the—" Ryan laughed at the mage's startled cry, but his humor faded as the bones smashed against a shimmering barrier in front of the paladin. He was projecting some sort of mana shield that prevented any attempts to damage him.

How annoying.

The bones, instead of falling to the ground, were pulled back towards the skeleton and re-attached to it by the dark mana tendrils. *That's actually pretty cool.*

"Keep Blake safe," the paladin called to the others as he walked slowly towards the skeleton. From the way the cleric and mage moved in front of the younger adventurer, Ryan could only guess that was Blake.

"This paladin really is overpowered," Ryan said.

His skeleton slashed at the paladin, and the man raised his silver sword to block the strike. When bone and blade met, a flash of golden light filled the room. The bones shattered.

"Yeah, that's Sean." Erin's voice had taken on a dreamy tone. "He's a Platinum-level paladin to the Goddess. He's like a minor celebrity among us celestials."

Great. She had a little crush on the guy decimating his boss.

"Well, your boyfriend is about to kill our last mob," Ryan replied, annoyed.

Sheesh, talk about having your priorities wrong. Didn't she care that their boss was being so easily defeated? Ryan winced as Sean brought his sword down on the skeleton, white light arcing through its form. The bones collapsed, and as they hit the ground, Ryan knew his boss was dead.

"Aannd that just happened." He sighed.

He had been so excited about his first encounter with adventurers. Needless to say, he was very disappointed in himself.

"Shhh. Sean's talking." Erin had her ear pressed against Ryan's core, and he brought his attention back to the group.

"So, that boss would actually prove a decent fight for new adventurers," Sean said as he sheathed his sword.

"Aye. Formidable, with both a ranged attack and good melee potential." The cleric leaned down, investigating the large glowing bones.

"This dungeon is crap. No traps, no loot, lame mobs," argued the mage.

That mage was just being hurtful. *Wait. Traps? Loot?*

"He makes a good point. Why didn't you have any traps?" Erin questioned.

"If I knew what traps were, I would have them."

Sheesh. He was new at this; couldn't she cut him some slack?

Sean was speaking again. "Yes, sadly, I think we may have to destroy this dungeon." Sean looked at the group. His words sent a sinking feeling through Ryan.

"Darkness dungeons are a danger in and of themselves. Even more so with the rumors of a necromancer to the south," Sean said. "The last time a necromancer and a darkness dungeon came together, the church barely managed to defeat them. Without any loot, I don't think we can justify keeping this dungeon alive."

Ryan did not like the sound of that. Was this it for his short dungeon-hood?

The mage nodded at Sean as he spoke, while Blake looked downcast. The cleric was still looking at the boss mob's bones. *Why?*

"Say, Sean," the cleric said to the paladin. "Did you notice all of the mobs seem to have been created by the dungeon?"

His words made the paladin pause.

"Hmmm." Sean stared down at the still-glowing bones. Ryan had been just about to absorb his boss so he could learn the pattern to recreate him.

"That is interesting. Even brand-new darkness dungeons are usually filled with undead mobs raised by the dungeon, not created by them." Sean's face was thoughtful, but then he shook his head. "However, even if this dungeon hasn't raised the dead just yet, that doesn't redeem it enough to let it survive. The risk just isn't worth the reward, especially with the lack of loot."

"What's this loot he keeps talking about?" Ryan could feel Erin jump as she pressed her palm to her face.

"Loot is what mobs are supposed to drop. It can range from common items – in your case, a bone or two – to armor, weapons, and precious metals."

Oh.

He had plenty of precious metals.

"Loot is what makes a dungeon worth fighting. It's the reward that makes the risk to life worth it." She shook her head. "But we didn't drop any loot for them the entire time."

Sean closed his eyes and raised his hand, turning towards where Ryan was hidden. A golden light began to form in his hand.

"So, should we drop some loot now?" Ryan was panicking. Sean was certainly about to destroy them.

"Drop everything." Erin was panicking as well.

Ryan focused inward, thinking of anything he may have absorbed that the adventurers might want. He dropped chunks of copper, iron, and gold. He summoned one of the plants he'd absorbed. Hell, he even absorbed his boss so he could drop one of the bladed arm bones.

The paladin opened his eyes, looking at the pile of loot growing, and for a second the light wavered. In his panic, Ryan summoned one last item, hoping it would stop the paladin. That was all he could do — he was out of mana.

A single, glowing feather drifted down between the adventurers. It drained a surprising amount of his mana to do so.

"What is that?" Erin's voice echoed in his mind as the adventurers all asked the same question.

"One of your feathers. I absorbed it accidentally when I scorched you on our first day." Ryan watched as Sean lowered his hand, the light fading. Ryan was saved.

"Oh. Oh, no," Erin barely whispered, a sense of dread coming across the bond.

"What?"

Why wasn't she happy? Sean was no longer trying to kill

them. Instead, he was holding the feather in his hand as the cleric stared at it.

"A celestial feather?" The cleric's voice filled with awe. The way he looked at it, Ryan suddenly didn't feel so good about dropping that as loot.

"I never thought I would see one," the cleric said. "This must be a sign from the Goddess. She wants this dungeon to be saved. How else would a brand-new dungeon, much less a darkness dungeon, have such a treasure?"

The cleric reached out towards it tenderly, reverently. Before his fingers could brush it, though, the room was suddenly bathed in flames.

"Hand it over, or the boy dies."

Chapter Twelve

"Uh, what's going on?" Ryan couldn't help asking as he watched the scene unfolding before him in awe.

The mage had grabbed Blake and was holding an arm around the young man's neck, a fireball in his hand. Both Sean and the cleric stood still, looking from the feather to the mage.

"Let my son go," the paladin growled, but the moment he moved, the flames grew brighter.

"You may be Platinum, but we both know my flames can incinerate your son before you can kill me." The flames cast eerie shadows across the mage's face.

"Celestial feathers are one of the rarest items in the world. Only angels and celestial fairies have them," Erin said to me.

Oops. Probably shouldn't have dropped it.

"They can heal any wound, and even save someone from the brink of death," she went on. "But they can only be used once."

So, Ryan had given them something extremely powerful and now they were fighting about it. He couldn't help but feel sorry for Blake.

"Anything we can do to help?" He scanned the room, noting the fear on Blake's face, and Sean's obvious internal conflict.

"Their mana will keep you from spawning new mobs in that room," Erin said. "Have you absorbed all of the mobs in the rest of the dungeon?"

"Yup, already did that."

"Okay, so if you look at your level triangle, what is your mob count at?" She was watching the scene before them. The mage's eyes were crazed, and his hands were shaking, bringing the flames closer to Blake, making the young man sweat.

Ryan summoned his triangle and frowned. He had absorbed all of his mobs; why was he only at twenty-seven?

"Hey Erin, how come I am only back up to twenty-seven points?" he asked. "All my mobs are dead."

"Ah, that's another mechanic of dungeons. It seems whatever strange powers govern dungeons decided it would be unfair for you to just instantly keep spawning wave after wave of mobs on adventurers."

Ryan couldn't help but imagine fifty skeletal squirrels running at adventurers repeatedly. That would get a bit old.

"As such, you are refunded a small amount of your points the moment you reabsorb your mobs, and then the rest of the points are returned after a set amount of time, depending on the type, and cost, of the mob slain."

"All right, so, in the essence of time," Ryan groaned, "I'm going to say I understand that. What shall we do with the twenty-seven – oh, now twenty-eight – points?"

He really wanted to help Blake now. The poor guy was obviously new to all of this. Plus, that mage had said some hurtful things about Ryan.

Erin spoke again. "Well, you can't summon mobs in the room with the adventurers. Their mana will prevent you from interfering in there. However, you can summon mobs in the second room."

Ryan could guess where this was going.

"Boss mob?" He could summon one; he had enough points. And with its ranged attack…

"Boss mob." Erin smiled a mischievous smile.

Ryan summoned his monstrosity, forming it instantly now that he had the pattern for it. Erin had said the mob would follow his orders, so now he was going to try it out.

He pushed his consciousness into it, ordering the boss mob to quietly approach the group from behind, and to attack the mage when he was in range. In his commands, Ryan stressed the point that Blake was not to be hurt. He figured Sean wouldn't forgive him if Blake died, and Ryan was afraid of the paladin.

"I hope this works." The fairy was trembling, and the scene in the boss room didn't look promising.

Sean, torn, handed the feather to the cleric.

"Give this to him and get my son." The paladin spoke, and the cleric carried the feather to the mage.

The crazed mage took the feather but held on to Blake.

"I'll release him once I get out of here. Otherwise, I know you'll just kill me the moment I let him go." His flames grew brighter, making Blake cry out in pain.

However, even as Sean prepared to move, he froze, his eyes fixed on the darkness behind the mage. The cleric too was frozen, staring into the darkness. For some reason, the darkness was staring back.

"Ha," Ryan whispered.

The boss mob, now visible in the tunnel thanks to the mage's flames, launched his attack. Bone spikes suddenly protruded from the mage's body, and his flames died instantly. The boss mob pulled the mage's body, frozen with shock, towards himself. As the mage got closer, Ryan's boss mob slashed into him with the bladed bones of his other hand. At the same time, Sean darted forward, skewering the mage through the stomach.

The helpless man let out a single, agonized scream before he died.

The moment he passed, multiple things happened. First, a rush Ryan could only guess was from experience gain filled Ryan. Second, the mana that had been keeping him from absorbing anything near the mage vanished. As a result, Ryan quickly reabsorbed his boss mob, the mage, and of course the celestial feather. He figured he should take that particular item away before any other strange things happened.

"Did the dungeon just save Blake?" Sean held his son, looking at the cleric.

"I think… I think it did." The cleric shook his head, looking from Sean to Blake. Ryan could see his disappointment that the feather was gone. "I can't believe I'm saying this, but I think we have found a darkness dungeon we can allow to exist."

His words brought a smile to Blake's face, and Sean nodded in agreement, letting go of his son.

"I think we have. Might as well make our reports so we can start getting some of these new adventurers training." He patted Blake on the back, smiling.

The cleric smiled and nodded as well. He pulled out a crystal. "I wonder what other surprises this dungeon has. A darkness dungeon blessed by the Goddess," the cleric muttered under his breath. The crystal in his hand glowed, and suddenly the trio were gone.

Chapter Thirteen

"So, what should we do first?" Ryan and Erin sat in the core room, which was filled with almost visible levels of excitement.

After the adventurers had departed, Ryan had been able to check his triangles. The mage had provided him with enough experience to gain four levels. It had taken Erin nearly ten minutes to calm him down to the point of coherence.

Now, Ryan was a Bronze Seven dungeon, and he was eyeing the seventy mob points on his triangle hungrily. Much better than his paltry fifty earlier.

"Well, those adventurers did mention some issues with your setup." Her words caused Ryan to wince.

"But that guy was Platinum." Sean had been way too over-powered. It wasn't fair.

"That doesn't mean you can't improve yourself," Erin scolded him, though her eyes took on a dreamy look at the mention of Sean.

"You just have a crush on him." Ryan sulked as he thought back to the adventurers. That mage had mentioned Ryan was lacking in traps.

"I do not."

Ha! She was blushing. For some reason, though, her reaction only made him smile for a moment before he felt something else. *Jealousy? Why am I jealous?*

"Uh-huh. Whatever you say, Rin." He paused, seeing if the nickname would stick.

She glanced at him and smiled lightly. *Yes.* Her smile made him shine a little brighter.

"How about we get to work, Ryan?" she said. "Any ideas on what you want to fix first? We probably have a few weeks before more adventurers start arriving."

"Well, that mage did mention I didn't have any traps. How about those?"

"Oh, that mage just continues to come in handy." They both laughed. His attitude may have been crap, but the mage had been the most useful of all the adventurers from Ryan's point of view. Free levels. Free advice. Free complete skeleton.

"Yeah, he really did give us a hand. And an arm, and—"

Erin groaned, cutting him off. "I get it, you have a full human skeleton now," she said. "First things first: traps."

"Tell me," Ryan said, rubbing his hands together – metaphorically speaking, of course.

"Traps are, well, traps."

"Oh gee, that really helps."

"Traps are something a dungeon can put in place to try and hinder or kill adventurers," Erin said. "Some dungeons use traps like pitfalls, others use trick passages, falling objects. There are really countless ways to trap your dungeon."

"Okay. Does it matter which type we use?"

"Well, usually dungeons try to make traps that synergize with their mobs, and the type of dungeon they are. Fire dungeons usually use lava in pitfall traps to burn adventurers alive. Earth dungeons have been known to chase down adventurers with boulders on steep slopes, to crush them."

Ryan visualized an adventurer running through a dungeon, trying to escape as a giant boulder rolled after him. The idea made him smile.

"All right. What type of traps do darkness dungeons usually have?" he asked.

"Honestly?"

"No, I want you to lie to m—"

She slapped him lightly and went on.

"The darkness dungeons I've heard of usually had massive pits where they would trap adventurers and kill them. Then they would bring the zombies back to life, and just keep filling the pits with zombies, until they had enough to release throughout the dungeon."

"Oh, let's not do that."

"Agreed," Erin muttered.

"I can still do some pits, though. Maybe make some narrower areas for the adventurers to pass, which will allow my mobs a better chance to attack? If the adventurers fall, they go into a pit, and we send in the mobs to finish them quickly?"

"As long as you only absorb them and do not resurrect them."

"I promise."

Sheesh, didn't she think he was a dungeon of his word?

"Well, stop floating around and get to work, then," Erin ordered.

She curled up, obviously prepared to take a nap while he worked. Ryan didn't mind, though; it would give him space to modify more than just traps.

He started with his first room, remembering how easily the adventurers had walked through, killing his mobs. Ryan knew he was going to put more mobs into that room but decided to modify it a bit more to give them a better chance.

He created narrow tunnels all around the walls and under the floor, much like he had for Erin from his room, so his mobs could move about undetected. Then he hollowed out a few portions of the room, leaving just a thin layer of stone on top. If anyone stepped onto one of those areas, their leg would break through and become trapped. Not enough to kill anyone outright, but Ryan could imagine it would at least sprain or break something and give his mobs a chance at a kill.

Next, the tunnel leading into his second room was just too simple. Instead of an easy walk, Ryan decided to add in a twist. He widened the hallway, but then cut away most of the floor on either side. This created a narrow, winding walkway, with a ten-foot drop on either side. The adventurers would have to walk single file, or risk falling into one of the pits. He littered the pits with random broken bones. Nothing he was going to reanimate, but he figured it would scare the adventurers as they walked past it.

His second room was where he was hoping to do some damage. He knew the zombie rats could create wounds that would potentially hinder adventurers against his boss, and he wanted to capitalize on that. Ryan started growing rock formations out of the ground, obscuring visibility in the room, so that his mobs could hide more easily.

He littered this room with tunnels for his mobs as well. Never again would anyone waltz through as easily as those other adventurers had. He made the tunnel leading from his second room to his boss room the same as the first tunnel, wanting to keep the adventurers on edge as they neared his final room.

Once he finished, Ryan gave all his work a once-over. His dungeon was still dark, the lightly glowing walls providing poor visibility. There were decent traps layered throughout, and he thought he had done a good job for his first attempt at trapping. Erin was still asleep, though, so Ryan decided to add a little more to his dungeon while she slept.

First, he sifted through the plants he had absorbed when he created his opening. He found a few that he felt looked nice and urged them to grow in his second room. Now the room had a nice mixture of dark stone and simple flowering plants and mushrooms. Not only did they add a little color to the room, but they would help muffle the approach of his mobs.

Next, he decided his boss room needed a door. He didn't want adventurers being able to see his boss from the hallway, and besides, leaving the boss visible would open him up for attacks outside of his range, which hardly seemed fair.

However, just as Ryan made the decision to start, he immediately stopped. *How do I make a door?* A stone slab was useless, and hanging the cloth from the mage's robe wouldn't really do much. Plus, he hated the way a hanging cloth over an entryway looked.

He did summon some of that cloth into his room, though. It added a nice splash of color, and he was sure Erin would like it. He smiled as he decorated the arched entryway into his boss room with glowing skulls, deciding he would revisit it when Erin was awake.

Finally, Ryan decided his main entrance needed a little work. Right now, it was just a gaping hole in the ground. He had his pride as a dungeon to uphold, so he got to work. He slowly pushed his influence into the ground around his opening and started pushing the stone up. Ryan grinned as he formed the stone; since his dungeon had a theme, he might as well embrace it. Checking his work over, he smiled to himself, and decided it was time to wake his fairy.

Chapter Fourteen

"I LOVE THIS."

Erin sat on the ground, running her fingers along the fine material the mage's robes had been made of.

Ryan forced a smile. He was glad she was happy, but he was also a bit annoyed. He had put all this work into modifying his dungeon, and yet she cared more about the cloth in the room.

"So, about my new dungeon," he said.

She flapped her wings as she reluctantly lifted off the ground.

"Fiiine, I'll go look."

She flew through the tunnels connecting his room to the boss room, and Ryan made a mental note to make that a smoother flight for her.

"Boss room looks the same," she said.

Judging from her short comment and tone, Ryan figured his mental note was a good one. All the twists and turns seemed to put her in a foul mood. Happy fairy, happy life, or something like that.

"I didn't think we needed to change much in there—"

"No traps? Nothing?"

"Nope, just the boss. He seems able to handle himself against a weaker group." Sean had said as much, after all.

"Okay, well, hopefully the next—" She paused as she left the room, noticing the glowing skulls on the arch. "All right, Ryan, that is a nice touch."

Erin shuddered as she glanced at it one more time.

"That gives off a creepy vibe," she said.

"I want to make the adventurers a little wary of entering my boss room."

He knew he limited his raw power by refusing to use the dead as his mobs, so Ryan had decided he could mess with adventurers' minds a little. *Nothing wrong with mind games.*

"Well, that definitely works." She flew lazily across the winding path, noting the narrow walkway and the bone-filled pits on either side. "Your dungeon definitely feels more dangerous now."

Erin stopped as she reached his second room, now filled with rock formations and plants.

"This is amazing," she laughed.

She zipped around, going to different flowers, smelling them with a smile on her face. Each of the plants she flew to, and even the mushrooms, all had the same faint white glow that everything Ryan created in the dungeon had. It gave the room a mystical feeling.

"What do all of these do?" she asked.

"Well, I just put them in to make the room look better, and because I figure my mobs would be better hidden. But—" He flipped through his knowledge on everything he'd put in there. "Some of the mushrooms are edible, and others are poisonous, so that's fun."

He glanced at the plants. Most of them were just nice to look at, but the winding three-leafed ivy he had intertwined throughout the room had a property that made him chuckle.

"The three-leafed ivy you see is called poison ivy," he said. "It will cause a painful rash on humans, if what I've learned from absorbing it is correct."

He could imagine that would inconvenience at least a few adventurers as they walked through the room, though he wasn't certain how quickly it would take effect.

"All right, well, nice job on this room." She flew towards the next room, noting he had mimicked the tunnel design from the boss room to the second room. "A bit unimaginative."

Ouch. That was rude.

He looked at his path, feeling a little less proud about his work. She was right; he shouldn't have both tunnels exactly the same. "Well, I am new to this."

Erin crossed her arms, disappointment clear on her face.

"I know, and you were doing so well with the first tunnel and your second room," she said. "I was expecting another surprise, is all."

"Well, I have hidden traps all through the first room," Ryan countered. "I hollowed out small holes and left just a thin layer of rock over them. When someone steps on them, they should get stuck."

Erin nodded at that, examining the rest of the room as he spoke.

"I also put smaller tunnels all throughout the dungeon, letting my mobs have a chance to attack without getting blasted apart like earlier," added Ryan.

"I like it," Erin said.

That made him smile. He was so caught up with her praise that he almost let Erin start flying back without checking out his entrance.

"Wait." He stopped her. "You should go look at the entrance." He was proudest of his work there, and he wanted her to see it.

"Oh, I didn't think you'd done anything there!" she said, clapping her hands with glee. She flew off, her excitement evident through the bond. As she neared the light, she slowed.

"Just go towards the light," Ryan said.

He mentally nudged her forward, realizing she hadn't been outside since her Goddess had sent her to him. Her form seemed to glow even brighter as the sunlight touched her, and Ryan couldn't help but admire how beautiful her wings were in the light. He felt a pang of guilt that she was stuck in a darkness dungeon.

"WHAT IS THIS?"

Her voice ripped him from his feelings of guilt as she

screamed excitedly through the bond. He watched as she zipped through the air, up and down, looking over his entrance.

It had been hard, but he had formed the stone around his entrance to emulate a massive wolf skull. A bit tacky, perhaps, but he felt it gave the dungeon a much more fitting feel. He was a darkness dungeon, after all. Just because he couldn't make a wolf skeleton yet didn't mean the adventurers knew that. Plus, he had a hunch that human skulls as entrances had likely been overdone already. And who would be scared of a rat or squirrel skull?

"Do you like it?" he asked as Erin finished inspecting it, her eyes sparkling with the pride he could feel through their bond.

"I do. This is amazing. You are really becoming a proper dungeon." She admired the skeletal maw before her. "Now, how about we build some more mobs and set up a loot system before the adventurers arrive?"

She flew back inside, chuckling to herself.

"They are going to be in for such a surprise."

Chapter Fifteen

"How should we mix up the mobs?"

Ryan and Erin were looking at his level triangle. Nearly half of the bottom layer of his triangle was filled with dark energy, and a white '70' shone brightly.

"I was going to let you decide."

Erin was sitting on him again, though she had wrapped part of the silky cloth around herself. Ryan wasn't sure how to feel about her statement. He was happy she trusted him enough to do this, but he was still uncertain. That last group had knocked his ego down quite a bit.

"I don't know."

He knew his doubt was flooding through their bond, and he hated that fact. Ryan just wanted to do his best, but what if it wasn't good enough?

"I believe in you." She smiled, patting him. "Besides, you can always change things up again later on. You're a dungeon. You live to grow and change."

Oh, she had a good point. He could easily absorb anything in his dungeon, and just create mobs elsewhere if he didn't like how they were performing. That thought took a bit of the stress off of him and gave him energy.

"All right," he said.

He closed his 'eyes' as he shifted through his catalog of

bones. The only thing Ryan had gained was a completed human skeleton, so he figured he would stick to the same mob types he had already used.

"First, I think we should use the same boss," he mused.

Erin nodded, and he summoned his massive skeleton in his boss room. The eight-foot monstrosity rose with a clatter, dark power swirling around him, bones floating where his missing arm was. Ryan now knew those bones were a potent weapon. He could already imagine the panicked reactions of adventurers when they encountered him.

"Ryan?" Erin pulled him from his thoughts.

"Yes, Rin?" Calling her that made her blush a little, so Ryan had decided to keep at it.

"What are you going to name your boss?"

Huh? Name him?

"Does he need a name?"

"Well, generally, all the mobs in a dungeon have different names." She had failed to mention that before. "And adventurers can identify the names of the mobs. Some can even observe basic information on mobs. Their weaknesses, their strengths, etcetera."

Oh, that sounded like an interesting ability. *I wonder if I can do the same to adventurers?*

"So, I have to name everything?"

"That would probably be for the best," Erin said.

"Ugh. You know, you keep forgetting to mention these things."

Ryan immediately regretted saying that as he felt the hurt from Erin flow through their bond. The poor fairy's eyes were practically shimmering, tears threatening to spill over.

"I— I— I—"

Oh, no.

Her voice cracked, and tears started to fall. Ryan silently cursed himself as his mind raced. How could he make her happy? Maybe he should apologize?

"Rin. Don't cry." His voice was soft, and he sent a soothing feeling through the bond. "I'm not mad at you. I was just...

there is so much to being a dungeon. It gets overwhelming at times."

He could feel her calming, but her tears were still falling, and she wasn't looking at his core. Trying to hide her face was pointless, though, since he could see everything within the dungeon.

"But... but..." She could hardly speak past her sobs. "I'm supposed to be here to help you, and I keep failing."

Welp, that unleashed even more tears.

"You're a great help, Erin. I wouldn't have gotten this far without you. Now, how about you turn that frown upside down —" *Ugh, what a tacky line.* "—and let's get to naming some mobs. I'll let you name the boss."

She steeled herself, trying to smile. "You aren't mad?"

"Nope. I could never be mad at you," Ryan said, wishing he had a mouth with which he could flash her a smile.

"Oh, okay." She paused and wrapped him in a hug. "I'll try to do my best for you, Ryan."

"I know."

He glowed a little more brightly from her touch, and he felt pleased with himself as he went back to summoning mobs. He couldn't help but feel a little guilty though, too. Ryan had just passed naming the boss mob onto Erin because he had no idea what he should name that thing. *Maybe I'll just let her name everything for me.*

Ryan pushed the thought from his mind, doing some quick math in his head as he summoned his normal mobs in his first two rooms. Five skeletal squirrels in the first room. Two zombie rats, five skeletal squirrels, and five skeletal rats in the second. He glanced at his level triangle, smiling at the remaining twenty points while absentmindedly trying to come up with different options for his two rooms. He knew he wanted some more mobs in his first room, but how many?

"Ryan?"

He turned his attention back to Erin. "Yes?"

"I've thought of a name."

This should be interesting. He pushed the numbers out of his head and gave her his full attention. "And what awesome name have you come up with!"

"The Handyman."

If Ryan had eyes, he would be staring at her blankly.

That is terrible.

"I'm just kidding," she laughed. "I was really thinking we could name him 'One-Armed BS."

"What's the BS for?" he asked.

Erin giggled at his question. Had he walked into another trap?

"Bone Slinger." *Oh, that sounds nice*.

"Can we just call him the Bone Slinger?" he asked.

"Well, usually bosses have an actual name with a descriptor."

"Okay, so we need a name for him, and then we just add on Bone Slinger?" Ryan asked.

"Yup. Thoughts?"

How had he gotten roped into helping with the naming? Hadn't he pushed this task off onto her? Tricksy fairy.

"Umm… Steve the Bone Slinger?"

That sounded so corny. Why had he chosen the name Steve? *I hate this*.

"Works for me," Erin laughed.

Well, all right. Guess my first terrifying boss is now going to be named Steve.

"How do we name him?" he asked.

"Focus on your mob, and then mentally assign the name to him."

Ryan turned his attention on Steve and did as Erin instructed. After a moment, white letters shimmered above the skeleton's head, forming his name in bold: **Steve the Bone Slinger**. Immediately after they formed they faded away.

"Hurray! We've named your first mob," Erin cheered, punching the air.

Erin was a lot happier about this than Ryan was. He promised himself his next boss was going to have a much cooler name.

"Hey, Rin, can you name the other mobs while I finish off adding them to the rooms?" He needed to get back to crunching numbers, and he wasn't too enthused about naming more mobs.

"Sure thing, hun."

Hun? Did she just call me hun?

She started humming, and Ryan decided to just go back to his task.

He decided to add five more skeletal squirrels to his first room. Ryan didn't want to overwhelm adventurers on the very first room, and figured zombies wouldn't be as helpful, since the adventurers could just leave the dungeon to heal if they got bit so early on.

That left him with fifteen more points for his second room. He quickly summoned a zombie rat, which scurried off into the foliage on the floor. Ryan paused before deciding on his next set of mobs, in part because all this summoning was exhausting.

He could add more skeletal beasts, or even a few more zombies now. After a few moments of thinking, he added five more of each skeletal beast, watching his mob points sink to zero on his level triangle. His mana pool was also significantly drained.

"All done," he said. He was beaming through their bond, and he could feel similar feelings coming from Erin.

"Me too," she replied. "I've got the names for all the mobs down. Now we just have to assign loot, and we will be ready for round two."

"Right," he said, trying to keep the wariness from his voice. "Let's hear these names and get going, then."

They couldn't be as bad as "Steve." Could they?

Chapter Sixteen

"Are you serious?"

Ryan couldn't believe what Erin had just suggested – keeping the names literal. So skeletal rat, skeletal squirrel, and zombie rat. He was going to be the laughing stock of all dungeons.

"Yup, I think those names are the best."

"Nothing creative? No unique, fun mob names?" Ryan asked.

Skrat, Skuirrel, and Ratbie were names he had come up with on the fly. How had she not come up with any names during the time he was building mobs?

"I couldn't think of any. I'm sorry."

Oh, now she was giving him the sad eyes. She knew he was a sucker for the sad eyes.

"Tell you what, Rin, how about I give them some names I thought of, and we'll name the rest of the mobs together, once we get stronger?"

She smiled at him, nearly smirking. He had fallen into her trap, and they both knew it.

"Deal!"

"I swear I got stuck with the most manipulative—"

"What was that?"

"Nothing, hun."

She blushed as he called her hun. Ha, add that as a win for Ryan. Quickly, he assigned names to his mobs, noting how the names showed up in grey, and weren't bolded like Steve's name. Interesting.

"All right, now that's done—"

Erin was giggling.

"What?" Ryan snapped.

"You do realize your skeletal squirrels are just called squirrels now, but spelled differently," Erin said.

Everyone's a critic.

"I thought it was witty," Ryan said.

"Whatever you say. It's your dungeon."

"At least I came up with actual unique mob names."

She shot him a glare before breaking out into a light laugh.

"Yup, Steve and the Skrat pack," she said. "Behold, Steve and his fearsome skuirrels. That's skuirrel with a 'K,' not a 'Q.'"

"Are you done?" He could feel his indignation starting to rise.

"I suppose. For now." She flew off of him so she could look at him properly. "Besides, next up is everyone's favorite part. Loot."

Yay! Loot.

"So, you going to throw me a bone and help me figure out some loot?" he asked. *Ah, bone puns.* He needed to make a list of useable puns, though; he felt like he had used that one before.

"Please don't try to bring your puns back from the dead." Erin winked.

Oh good, now Erin was playing the pun game. He wondered if he could get her to play more later. But first, he needed to focus.

"Maybe we should get back to the loot."

"Probably for the best." She nodded and closed her eyes, thinking. "So, the whole point of loot is to try and give adventurers a reason to come into your dungeon. Loot and experience are the two reasons why adventurers risk their lives in dungeons."

"Experience? Like what I got from killing the mage? Do adventurers and dungeons level up the same way?"

"It is very similar – as a dungeon, you level up through experience, which you gain from killing adventurers, and in small part from spreading your influence," Erin explained. "Adventurers gain experience by killing mobs in dungeons. The amount of experience gained by both dungeons and adventurers is dependent on the level of the slain foe. For instance, your skrats and skuirrels will give the smallest amount of experience in your dungeon, while Steve will give the most. Just like you, once adventurers have gained enough experience, they can rank up!"

"Hmm, I suppose that makes sense," Ryan grumbled. "So the higher their level, the stronger they are, and that's based on the experience points they have accumulated. Do they have level triangles?"

"They do, though not physical ones like yours. Those are dungeon specific and can only be provided by a fairy. The other sentient races have different ways of viewing theirs."

"Do you have one?" he asked.

Erin opened her mouth as if to reply before closing it again and shaking her head.

"I'm linked to you now. Fairies turn their triangles into physical materials in order to pass them on to their dungeon. Once we've done that, we lose our individual levels as we share everything with the dungeon we are bound to."

So, the triangles she had given him were originally hers? Ryan's emotions shifted swiftly at the knowledge. Was it admiration? Gratitude? A tinge of sorrow? He tried to push them aside and get back on topic.

"So, back to loot," he began. Erin shook her head, as if clearing away a bad feeling, before smiling at him.

"Loot," she went on. "First, you need to select loot appropriate for the mobs being killed and the level of your dungeon."

"So, easier mobs drop less valuable loot?" he asked.

"Exactly."

"How do I know the value of my loot?" Obviously, he didn't want to drop any of Erin's feathers again.

"Ah, well, luckily for you, most items – with the exception of coins – have a rarity assigned to them."

"Rarity?"

"Yes. Loot is classified by common, uncommon, rare, ultra-rare, and legendary."

"How do I know which is which?"

"By the color of their name."

Wait, what?

"What do you mean?" he asked.

Erin drifted down to the ground, sitting on the cloth. "Summon one of my feathers in here."

He did as he was told, and the white feather slowly floated between them. She grabbed it and held it up towards him.

"Now, focus on it like you did with your mobs, and its name will appear," she ordered.

Ryan did as she said, and after a moment, golden letters appeared: 'Celestial Feather.'

"Now, reabsorb this, and try to pull up the name of the cloth you summoned in here for me."

The feather disappeared from her hand, and Ryan focused instead on the cloth. He hadn't summoned the entire robe in here, just the material, so he was curious as to what it would be called. After a moment, green words appeared above the cloth: 'Fine Silk Cloth.'

"Oh, I see what you mean."

"Common items are white, uncommon are green, rare are blue, ultra-rare are red, and legendary are golden." So, he had dropped a legendary item for Sean and the others. *Oops.*

"Since you are a low-level dungeon, your basic mobs should only drop common and maybe uncommon items. You can have your boss drop uncommon items, and maybe the occasional rare item." She flew back on top of him, sitting in her favorite spot. "Of course, you can also drop coins of varying value. Did the mage have any?"

"Yeah, he did. Some copper, some silver, and a single gold coin."

"Hmm, all right. Well, you should have your easiest mobs drop copper coins, and your ratbies can drop silver occasionally. As for Steve, if he isn't dropping an item, you can have him drop a single gold coin."

"Why can't we just drop high-level loot for everyone?" Other than the feather, none of the objects seemed to take much mana to recreate. And wouldn't it encourage people to come if he dropped rarer items? He could make gold coins pretty easily. Why not just fill the dungeon with those?

"First, because it is bad dungeon etiquette to just give out high-level items and gear." Erin fixed Ryan with a stern look. "Second, if you start dropping too-rare items, you will be overwhelmed with high-level adventures like Sean who will just waltz in, kill your mobs, and leave."

That didn't sound pleasant.

"And third…" She paused.

There's a third?

"Because I said so."

Not much of a third.

"Do you understand?"

"Clearly," Ryan managed to say, struggling not to laugh at how serious she was acting. "Now, how do we set up the loot? Do I just summon loot for them when they kill my mobs?"

He imagined randomly dropping coins around the room when his mobs died. It seemed amusing, but he was sure it would get old quickly.

"Most dungeons just assign loot to the mob type. When the mob dies, one of those types of loot will randomly appear."

Oh, it's like magic. Wait, it is magic.

"Just focus on the mob in your head, and mentally assign your different loot types to it," said Erin. "Then, when it dies, a piece of loot will randomly be selected, with rarer levels of loot having a rarer chance to be selected and dropped. It's a part of the magic system that exists for dungeons."

Ryan wasn't going to question the workings of ancient magic, so he decided to just take this at face value and go with it.

"Okie dokie, time to assign some loot."

He closed his eyes, focusing on all the items he had received so far, then turning his attention to his skuirrels. They were the first mobs adventurers were going to encounter, and arguably tied for the easiest mobs in his dungeon. None of the items Ryan had collected so far were classified as common, so instead he gave his skuirrels the chance to drop a variety of copper coins. He then gave his skrats the same simple coin drops as his skuirrels.

Next, his ratbies. These, he could assign uncommon loot to, so on top of giving them the chance to drop a small range of silver coins, he also gave them the chance to drop silk or the fine iron dagger the mage had been carrying. Both were uncommon items.

For Steve, Ryan had a few items to choose from. Almost everything the mage had been wearing was rare, from his robes down to his boots. There was one item, a 'ring of holding', that was ultra-rare, but aside from that, Ryan could choose from anything. He gave Steve the chance to drop a gold coin like Erin had mentioned and then shuffled around items from the mage. Once he was happy, he opened his eyes, satisfied with his hard work.

"All done." He sent a feeling of happiness through the bond to Erin. "Now what do we do?"

Erin pulled part of the silk cloth up onto him, creating a little bed out of it, and lay down. She sighed with contentment.

"Now, we wait for the adventurers to return."

And with that, she closed her eyes, drifting off to sleep. Ryan was left in silence save for the sounds of his mobs in the dungeon. He prayed for the adventurers to hurry up. He was already growing bored. Maybe he would search for some more skeletal remains while he waited.

Chapter Seventeen

"Is that everything?" Blake and his father stood in front of the head of the Adventurers' Guild, who had been jotting down notes of their recent adventure. She looked young for her position, but Blake knew she was likely the oldest person in Valta, the city that housed the Guild. She was one of the only Diamond-level adventurers alive, meaning she was close to immortal.

"That is everything, Alice. How shall we proceed?" Sean's voice was filled with formality and respect, reminding Blake to straighten his back as he stood there.

Blake knew the Guildmaster was far stronger than his father, meaning Blake was but an ant in the room. To be honest, he wasn't sure why his father had even brought him in for the report. When they teleported back to the city, courtesy of the port stone the cleric had used, Blake had believed that was all for him. Instead, as the cleric went to report to the church, Sean had dragged Blake immediately to the Adventurers' Guild hall.

Alice closed her eyes – which, Blake had noted, continuously shifted colors – before she spoke.

"The information you have provided is interesting to say the least. It is a little-known fact that dungeons can become sentient over time, acting on their own whims and interacting in strange ways. For a brand-new dungeon to not only show sentience but also appear to have made a decision to save an adventurer, it doesn't really add up. Especially since it is a darkness dungeon."

She drummed her fingers on the desk as she paused for thought.

"Are you certain this is what the dungeon produced?" She pulled a chain from around her neck, a glowing feather attached to it. A celestial feather.

"Yes, ma'am. I inspected the item myself. This was not a forgery or some trick by the dungeon. The cleric believes it was a direct sign from the Goddess."

"Pah, I can't see that self-righteous woman aligning with a darkness dungeon." Blake noticed his father wince as the Guildmaster insulted his chosen deity, but his father remained silent, allowing Alice to continue. "But if you swear that is what you saw, I'll believe you." She tucked the feather away, smiling sweetly at the two.

"You wouldn't be hiding anything from me just so your son can have a dungeon to train in, would you?" Her tone said she was joking but her eyes, still swirling with colors, held a serious look.

"No, ma'am. My duty is first and foremost to the Goddess and the Guild. Family has always come second. You know that."

Ouch. Blake had always known his father held his duty highly, but hearing him say it out loud hurt.

"I cannot fathom how anyone ever married you." She leaned back, letting out a laugh.

"I wonder that myself at times." Sean shared in her laugh, leaving Blake standing there awkwardly.

The Guildmaster was not what he had expected. All he ever heard were stories of how she singlehandedly cleared an entire mountain range filled with air dungeons. Her conquest took her from Platinum to Diamond and made her into a legend among adventurers.

"Do you have anything to say, young one?" Alice was staring at him, her face holding a smirk. Blake's eyes were pulled to the shifting colors in her eyes.

"No. No, ma'am." He tried to pull his eyes away, but they

were held, trapped. Her gaze seemed to consume him; he felt as if the room were closing in around him.

"Alice." Sean cleared his throat, and the Guildmaster blinked. The moment she did, the world around Blake stopped spinning and he was able to look away from her eyes.

"Sorry. I was curious what affinity he may acquire once he reaches Silver." She offered Blake an apologetic smile.

"You can see the future?" The words tore from his mouth before he realized he had even spoken. His father's eyes fixed on him in a glare, but Alice simply smiled.

"No one can see into the future. However, with these eyes I can see the potential of all things around me. As such, I was simply delving into your potential, to see perhaps what may be for a brand-new adventurer such as yourself."

"And?" Blake was curious, really curious now. Was he going to be a celestial paladin like his father? Would he wield the holy light of the Goddess of Justice?

"I sought it out for my curiosity, not yours, nor your father's. I do so enjoy knowing things others do not."

So, she wasn't going to tell Blake what she saw. He couldn't help but feel a slight flash of anger, though the moment he felt it, he pushed it away. His fear and admiration for the Guildmaster wouldn't allow him to have an ill thought towards her. At least not in her presence.

"Now I've had my fun, I suppose it is time we get down to business." She pulled out two rolls of parchment, glancing over both quickly before signing them.

"Blake." She held the first piece towards him. "Take this to the clerk. This will start the preparations for an expeditionary settlement at the new darkness dungeon. As I understand it, your father wants you to be a part of this settlement, and so I have authorized it."

Blake almost let out a shout of happiness as his trembling hand reached for the parchment.

"Sean." Alice's voice took on a solemn tone, grounding Blake's emotions. "I know you wanted to be a part of the settlement as well, to help establish and guide it, and to watch Blake grow." She glanced between father and son. "But the guild has a more important task for you." Sean hesitated as he reached for the parchment.

"The necromancer?" His voice was low, serious.

"I have assigned precautions against him." She looked from Sean to Blake. "Don't worry, Sean. The expedition, and your son, will be in good hands."

Sean cleared his throat as he grabbed the parchment. "Understood."

"You will both depart tomorrow, so I will dismiss the two of you for the day. And don't worry about reporting the mage's betrayal to the Mages' Guild. Since I've given you additional tasks, I'll handle that." She shooed them away, pulling out another piece of parchment as they turned to leave. "I expect great things from both of you."

Sean opened the door, leaving the guild office.

"Blake." Alice stopped him just as he stepped after his father, his hand on the door.

"Yes, ma'am?"

"Try not to get killed. I want to see your potential unfold."

∼

????

"My lord." A messenger stood before him, quivering. He looked down upon the messenger, a pathetic, weak thing, and nodded, allowing him to speak.

"The dungeon has been located and confirmed by the Adventurers' Guild."

The messenger paused, eyeing the skeleton that was filling his goblet. He often forgot humans were not used to seeing the undead.

"They are preparing to send a party there on the morrow."

"And?"

He tried to keep his voice stoic, but his excitement broke through. He couldn't remember the last time the Adventurers' Guild had allowed a darkness dungeon to survive. If it were up to him, he would be leaving immediately for the dungeon. However, it wasn't his choice to make. A fact he hated.

"The Exalted One has given you permission to seek out the dungeon

after you have completed your last task, in order to make a pact with it. The Exalted One commends you for your work in the South and is glad to see your undead forces have been growing. With the new darkness dungeon under your command and the town that will be built around it destroyed, we will be able to move the plan forward even sooner."

His mouth turned up in a smile, a rare thing, and he allowed the messenger to exit alive, an even rarer thing. But then again, he had just been given permission to make a pact with the darkness dungeon. Soon, he would have all the minions, all the power, he could ever want.

But first, he had to destroy one more town for the Exalted One. He wasn't sure why he was being ordered to destroy so many towns. Then again, he didn't care. He was never one to complain about free minions.

Chapter Eighteen

The rest of the day passed in a blur for Blake. He remembered handing off the parchment while the Guildmaster's cryptic final words weighed on his mind. After that, his day was a rush of packing his gear and saying his goodbyes. Those goodbyes, filled with a generous amount of liquor, were the reason the day was a blur – and the reason he had such a headache as he stood with the expeditionary group the following morning.

"All set, Blake?"

His father's voice bounced around his head, making him groan. He glanced towards the direction the voice had come and nearly cried out in pain. His father's armor shone brilliantly in the morning sun and sent blinding rays into his bloodshot eyes. Blake silently vowed never to drink again.

"I believe so." He motioned towards one of the wagons, filled with everyone's gear. "I've got my tent and bedroll packed, a few books, spare clothes—"

Sean held up his hand, cutting off Blake's list.

"Are you *ready*, son?" His voice softened and he placed a gauntleted hand gently on Blake's shoulder.

Blake had never seen his father act like that. He sobered up immediately.

"Honestly, I'm... I'm not sure."

His first adventure had been a failure and he was worried

about what was in store for him. He wanted to make his father proud. He wanted to surpass his father. But would he be able to? Blake hated to admit it, but the fact his father wasn't going to be accompanying him was a little unnerving.

His father's grip tightened on his shoulder, which Blake realized had started to shake.

"You'll be fine, son. Just remember what I taught you and find a good team to adventure with. The people you surround yourself with are the ones who will become your family." He stepped back and looked Blake up and down, nodding.

"Do your best, Blake, and make sure to stay safe." His voice cracked, but the paladin quickly reined it in. "I'm not sure when I'll be able to get out there to see your progress, but I expect great things from my son."

Pride swelled within Blake at his father's words, washing away his earlier feelings of doubt.

"I will make you proud." He stood a little straighter, face beaming. His father may put his Goddess before his family, but Blake could feel how much his father cared for him in that moment.

"That you will." He reached into his pocket and pulled out a ring.

It was a ring Blake had seen many times. It was made of pure silver and textured to almost seem like it was made of fur. On it, a wolf's head was open in a howl, eyes shining with a golden light.

"Take this ring, Blake, and treasure it." He held the ring out, and Blake hesitated before accepting it. He slid the cold metal on his finger, surprised at how it fitted perfectly on his finger. "That ring was my father's, and his father's before him. It has been passed down as each generation began their life as adventurers."

"I will keep it safe." He rushed forward and wrapped his father in a hug.

The paladin stiffened for a moment before returning the hug. Sean was not used to showing affection.

"I need to get going, Blake." Sean pushed Blake gently away, breaking their embrace.

"Where are you going?" Blake hadn't spoken with his father

since they left the Guild Hall, and he still didn't know what exactly his father had been tasked to do.

"I'm being sent to investigate some rumors of a growing fanatical group in the remote Northlands. It shouldn't be anything too dangerous. Zealous groups form up periodically, but Alice would rather send a high-level adventurer to deal with the problem than risk lower level adventurers if it does prove to be something that needs taking care of." He turned towards the north, shaking his head. "There are no towns with portal stones up there, so the trek alone is going to take over two months on horseback."

Blake couldn't help but feel sorry for his father. Valta was located in roughly the center of the continent. The dungeon he was going to was about a week's ride west in one of the many forests that populated the land. The Northlands were at the very tip of the continent, and to get to them his father would have to trek through not only dense forest but also treacherous mountain ranges in order to reach the cities up there.

Because of the rough terrain, the lands to the north were all but uncharted and unexplored, with only a few known settlements. The church often sent missionaries to those villages to ensure the people were taken care of, and law and order upheld. What type of trouble could be brewing in the North?

"Don't worry about me, Blake." His father's comment pulled him from his thoughts. Blake guessed his face had betrayed the thoughts running through his mind.

"You just worry about getting stronger. Leave the tough matters to the Guildmaster and myself." He smiled and turned away.

"Be safe, dad—" Blake started as his father's figure moved into the crowd.

He didn't want to make a scene, but his emotions were pushing at him and he felt a moment of panic as his dad walked away. He took a step forward, thinking to rush after the paladin, but stopped. Sean's hand was in the air, waving back at him casually. His father would be all right, Blake decided. He was a Platinum-level paladin, after all.

"Aye, well, that was touching an' all, but you about ready to go?" A hand grabbed his shoulder, and Blake didn't need to turn to know who was talking to him. The gruff voice had been calling out orders all day. It belonged to Marcus, a Platinum-level rogue and the lead adventurer on the expedition.

"Yes, sir." Blake wiped away his tears as he turned, noting a few eyes staring at him from their group. Apparently, they had been waiting for him to finish his goodbyes. He steeled himself and offered everyone a smile. From here on out, he was going to be an adventurer his father could be proud of.

Chapter Nineteen

"Are we there yet?" The question rang out for probably the hundredth time and was met with a mixture of laughs and groans.

The dungeon was a week away from Valta on horseback, Blake knew. But when you had over one hundred people in a caravan, filled with hopeful adventurers, craftsmen, and trainers, as well as all the supplies needed to begin building a small settlement, the trip became a lot longer.

"Next person to ask that is going to make me turn this caravan around!" Marcus called out, his gruff comment met with more laughter.

Though they had been traveling for almost three weeks, spirits among the group remained high. The excitement that came with the news of a new dungeon and the mission of establishing a settlement outside of it was just too infectious. Every day people swapped stories or rumors, speculated on what the dungeon would be like, and made crazy boasts.

Blake spent most of his time listening to the stories and training with a few other adventurers at night when they broke for camp. So far, no one knew he had been part of the group that discovered the dungeon. Well, almost no one.

"How close are we, Blake?" a female voice whispered beside him, pulling him from his thoughts. He had been back in the dungeon, thinking again of the mage's betrayal and the dungeon's actions. A shiver ran through his spine as he turned to answer.

"Another day, maybe two," he whispered back. The woman beside him, Karan, was the only person who knew his father had taken him on the dungeon dive. She was a Gold-level cleric and had apparently been chosen by Blake's father to be his team leader.

By guild rules, five-man parties had to be formed in order to conduct dungeon dives unless you were Platinum or higher. For a low-level dungeon, like the one Blake was heading to, there were additional rules. The team had to have a Silver or Gold-level leader, with the other members falling underneath them in rank.

"Have you found any teammates yet?" Karan had left the task of forming the team to Blake, promising that she would be happy with whoever he chose. Her job, she informed him, was to make sure he and his teammates were properly healed. Being a Gold-level cleric, she was more than capable of that task for a low-level dungeon.

"I think so." Blake had been utilizing his time at nights, when he wasn't training, to observe the other adventurers. A common practice he made note of early on at camp was that individuals looking for a team would leave their level triangles visible on their left palm. This allowed anyone who was recruiting to easily take note of an individual's level.

Blake lifted his left palm and willed his triangle forward. Shimmering golden lines crossed his skin, taking shape into a triangle. Every adventurer had the ability to will their triangle to appear on their palm in order to easily take note of their level as well as their mana capacity.

Blake, being Bronze Eleven, had a single small triangle, on the bottom left of his level triangle, filled in. A number '10' shone lightly, showing his available mana. Bronze Eleven adventurers had fifty mana points to start with. Because Blake was a physical class, eighty percent of his mana was constantly consumed to increase his physical attributes.

The other twenty percent existed for him to utilize skills and abilities. Blake had heard that mages were the opposite, with twenty percent spent towards enhancing their physical attributes, leaving them with eighty percent of their mana for spells. At the Bronze ranks, mana was really only used for the most basic of abilities and spells.

However, once adventurers hit Silver rank, they could choose their next class, and discover their affinity. Silver rank was when Blake could truly start his path to becoming a fully-fledged adventurer.

"I was thinking we could try and recruit Emily and Matt." Karan nodded as he spoke. Emily and Matt were siblings, from what Blake had gained from their earlier conversations. Emily was a Bronze adept, the lowest form of magical class. Her goal was to become a summoner, a special magical class that utilized their chosen affinity to summon familiars to fight for them. Matt, on the other hand, was an archer, a physical class, with the goal of becoming a ranger, a highly skilled and formidable class of archer.

"They would both make good additions to the team, and I believe they are all around your age." Blake was the youngest adventurer in the caravan, having just turned eighteen a few months past. You couldn't join the Adventurers' Guild until you were eighteen, and unless a dungeon appeared, you were then usually stuck simply training and going on small missions to try and gain experience. The fact that a new dungeon had appeared so soon after Blake joined had meant he had little time to actually train or climb the Bronze ranks.

"Yes, Emily is twenty and Matt is twenty-three, I believe." Karan offered him a nod and a smile. Blake wasn't sure what other tasks his father had given Karan, but she had seemed pretty adamant that he try and find fellow adventurers his age as well as of both genders.

"And for your final member?"

"Jack."

Karan winced as he said the name, but quickly hid it with a smile.

"The," she paused as she made a face, "thief?"

"That's the one. He's Silver ranked and he has a wind affinity. I think he can bring a lot to our team."

When you reached Silver rank, you chose your next class. From there, you were set on a path, and your choices of specialization when you became Gold ranked were limited based on your class. Blake was a fighter and intended to become a knight when he hit Silver. From there, he planned to choose paladin as his specialization when he hit Gold rank.

Jack, being a thief, could choose rogue or assassin when he reached Gold. Neither of those classes was looked on kindly by the church, though, which explained Karan's disposition towards him. However, Blake felt a thief could bring some much-needed skills to his team.

"If you think he will be a good match for your team, I will not object." Karan offered him a kind smile.

"Damn straight he thinks I'm a good match." A voice from behind made Karan curse and she turned around, glaring. Jack stood casually behind her, wind blowing gently around him as he offered her a wink. "I'm awesome."

Blake couldn't help but laugh as he offered the thief a smile.

He had a good feeling about his team choices.

Chapter Twenty

The caravan stopped for the night a half-day's travel from the dungeon. At Karan's suggestion, Blake invited Emily, Matt, and Jack to his tent so they could officially form their team and get to know each other. Now he sat nervously waiting for the others to arrive.

"You think they'll all come?" He glanced at Karan, who was patiently waiting with him in the tent. She looked up from the book she was reading and smiled.

"Well, I can't see why they wouldn't. Though I wouldn't be upset if that thief didn't come."

"Aw, now that's just mean." The tent flap opened, revealing a grinning Jack. "If only I had a fire affinity, I could melt that cold heart of yours."

Blake grinned at the comment, feeling some of his previous tension fading.

"If only you'd chosen a proper class, you might actually have been useful," Karan said to Jack.

"Your words, they hurt." Jack feigned pain, grasping at his chest. "Is there a healer nearby? I feel myself dying."

"I hope you're good at dodging. You're going to be the last one I lay my hands on to heal." Karan offered Jack a smile, but her eyes showed she was serious.

"Fine by me. Thieves specialize in being sneaky." He walked

easily to Blake and took a seat, pulling out an apple to eat. "So, who else is coming to the party?"

"Hopefully Matt and Emily." Blake trailed off as the tent flap opened again.

Two forms stepped in and it was immediately evident the two figures were siblings. The brother and sister shared the same blond, almost white hair, as well as icy blue eyes. Matt scanned the room as he stepped in, while Emily seemed hesitant to make eye contact with anyone as she followed.

"Well, it looks like everyone is here." Karan closed her book and motioned for Matt and Emily to take a seat. The two took up positions across from Blake and Jack. Blake offered them both a smile and a nod before turning his attention to Karan. She had asked him to call everyone to the tent to form the team, but he really wasn't sure what that involved.

"Are you going to be the party leader?" Matt looked over Karan, likely taking note of her very plain appearance. Even though Karan was a Gold-level cleric, Blake had noticed she rarely wore anything that would betray her level or her class to others. She dressed in simple cloth robes, the kind that even adepts could afford to purchase.

"Per guild rules, I will be taking that role, yes." She smiled at Matt as she held out her palm, calling forth her level triangle. The triangle blazed to life and filled both the bottom rows, showing the third row partially filled as well. Karan was Gold Four, a fact that seemed to take even Jack by surprise.

"Damn. I knew you were a healer, but Gold Four?" He looked from Blake to Karan. "How did you get a Gold Four cleric to lead the group?"

Blake shrugged. He knew she was strong, but he hadn't thought much of it otherwise. Now that he did, though, healers were rare. Even rarer were clerics, because they needed to have a celestial affinity, which Blake had heard was becoming rarer over the years.

"Is everyone okay with me being the leader?" Karan ignored Jack's comment and looked at the others. Everyone nodded in agreement. "Good, then we can officially form our party and get to know each other a little more."

She pulled five crystal pendants from her robes, one for each of them.

"These pendants will serve to bind our party together. With them, we will be able to communicate with each other if needed, as well as tell if someone is in danger. The crystals will also ensure experience is shared throughout the party when we go dungeon diving."

She handed the crystals around to the group, waiting until each person had one before she put hers over her head, the pendant disappearing into her robes.

Blake and the others followed suit. The moment the pendant hit his skin he felt a strange, almost electric, shock race through his body. It wasn't painful per se, but it definitely made his skin crawl. After a moment, the feeling subsided and he was bombarded with a sudden heightened awareness of those around him.

"So, how do these work?" Jack was holding his pendant up, looking at the white crystal. A faint light glowed within.

"These pendants are created by the Adventurers' Guild to link parties together. Each set contains five specially tuned crystals which are linked via mana to the others in the set. When a party is established and each member equips their pendant, the magic will interact with the wearer's mana as well. We can communicate using the crystal, as it will carry our voices to each other if needed." She held the crystal up to her lips and whispered into it.

"By holding it to your lips and focusing your mana into the crystal, it will project your words to each member of the party."

Her voice rang clear from the crystal at Blake's neck even though he was certain she was whispering too quietly for them to hear normally. *This will make communicating inside the dungeon much easier.*

"The magic in the crystal also links our experience gain and ensures each party member receives an equal amount of experience based on their level. This way, the party should level at the same rate so that we will all grow together." She paused and looked at Jack, then Blake. "This means myself and Jack will be gaining experience at a much lower rate that our three Bronze-ranked members."

"Welp, that's going to suck," Jack mumbled under his breath, just loud enough for Blake to hear. He chuckled, but hated the idea that Jack and Karan would be suffering experience-wise because of the three Bronze members.

"Typical thief, always thinking of himself." It seemed Karan had heard Jack's comment. "Now is the time we want our Bronze members growing the fastest," she said. "Because the dungeon is new, the mobs should be a lower level. While they are low, the experience they provide Silver and Gold-ranked adventurers is negligible.

"As such," she continued, "it is good to take this time to level our lowest ranked members quickly. That way, when the dungeon becomes stronger, we will hopefully have a solid team of at least low Silver-ranked members, aside from myself. At that time, all of you having your chosen class and affinity will be extremely important."

She let her words hang in the air for a moment as everyone took in what she said. It made sense. As Bronze-ranked adventurers, there really was nothing that gave them an advantage in the dungeon.

If they were all Silver, though, they would each be able to bring unique skills and abilities to their fights. For now, they would need to just work on their teamwork, hone what skills they did have, and get used to utilizing mana in the dungeon as they fought against the low-ranked mobs.

"Now that everyone understands the situation, I do have some good news." Karan brought everyone's attention back to her, and she offered Blake a wink, one that made him uneasy. "As a group, we have one advantage the other groups do not. Blake's already been in the dungeon."

All eyes turned immediately on Blake.

"So he can give us an idea of what to expect for our first dungeon dive together." Karan smiled at him wickedly and sat back as Blake decided how best to explain his dungeon dive to the group and prepare them for what they were about to face.

Chapter Twenty-One

"So, I'm guessing that's new?"

Jack's voice was filled with a mixture of awe and humor. The group, along with the caravan, were standing in the woods, staring at a large clearing. It was definitely the location of the dungeon; Blake wouldn't forget the trees surrounding it, having gotten slammed rather painfully into one during his last visit. However, what they were staring at was a lot different from what Blake remembered.

"Yeah, that definitely wasn't there last time," Blake said.

Instead of a hole in the ground leading into darkness, a massive stone wolf skull appeared before them. Moisture clung to the lightly glowing rocks, dripping from the teeth, providing a terrifying yet awesome visual. Blake could see that as you walked into the mouth of the dungeon it began to slightly descend, leading deeper into the darkness.

"Wonder what else has changed, then," Matt whispered, just loud enough for Blake and Jack to hear.

The archer and his sister were normally quiet, and when they did speak, it was in a soft tone. Blake had spent the whole night telling them of the dungeon, its layout, and the different mobs that they should expect – information that would also be shared with other explorers through Sean's report, but not as detailed as Blake's account, he was sure. However, he had to wonder how much the dungeon had changed in the month since his dive.

"It's hard to say," Karan said. "I can't imagine a brand-new Bronze dungeon would be able to evolve that much in the span of a month. Dungeons need to kill adventurers in order to grow in power."

Blake knew Karan had been in a dungeon before, but she'd avoided his questions about her experiences in them. However, her experience did mean she had the most information when it came to what they could expect in the future, and Blake could see why his father had asked her to lead them. With her in their team, he was certain they had nothing to worry about.

"What if—" Blake paused as he shot a glance to Karan, "—the dungeon killed a Gold-level adventurer?" Something Karan had said made him realize a small detail from the first dive might not have been shared to the masses.

"A Gold-level adventurer wouldn't be foolish enough to go solo into an unknown dungeon, and a brand-new dungeon would have little chance of killing one." She glanced at Jack. "It would be more likely for a foolish Silver thief to get himself killed by trying to explore a dungeon before anyone else in the hopes of finding special loot."

"Eh, I prefer to stay alive. No point doing anything foolish and getting myself killed young. There is still a lot I can offer the world." Jack winked at Karan, causing her to scowl.

"I. Um. Can we go talk somewhere privately?" Blake motioned towards the trees away from the group of people.

His party offered him confused looks but nodded and followed him. After they disappeared into the trees, Blake turned towards the group and let out a sigh.

"What's going on, Blake?" Jack leaned against a tree, casually peeling an orange. Blake made a mental note to ask where he kept getting all this fruit.

"Well." Blake swallowed hard.

He had left out the part about the mage's betrayal and the whole nearly killing Blake part. He had also left out any mention of the celestial feather. Blake was certain that information was not supposed to leave the Guildmaster's office.

"What is it, Blake?" Karan placed a hand on his shoulder, offering him a small smile.

He swallowed again and smiled weakly.

"The dungeon killed the Gold-ranked mage that was with us." He let the words hang, and it seemed even the forest went quiet for a moment.

Jack and Matt simply stared at Blake, while Emily let out a small gasp and covered her mouth with her hand.

"How? That's not possible." Karan's grip tightened on Blake's shoulder and he racked his brain on how to explain it without giving away too much information.

He looked at the group and his father's words echoed through his mind. They were his family, and he knew he needed to trust them.

"You all have to promise not to speak a word of what I'm going to tell you." They all nodded, and even Jack, who had been lazily eating his orange, was staring at Blake, giving him his full attention.

"The mage that was with the group really wanted a piece of loot the dungeon had dropped." He cut off Jack before the thief could ask what it was. He trusted his team, his family, but he figured it was best for their protection to not tell them what the loot was.

"He took me hostage, forcing my father to hand the item over." Blake rubbed his neck, remembering the heat of the mage's flames. "When my father gave him the item, he didn't hand me over. He decided to use me as leverage so he could escape the dungeon."

His eyes grew cloudy and he was in the moment again. He could feel the heat, feel the mage's arm around his neck. He drew a ragged breath and shuddered.

"During the commotion, the dungeon respawned its boss mob behind the mage. The boss killed the mage in an instant."

"Why didn't you tell us earlier?" Karan was the first to break the silence from Blake's story. Her words weren't accusatory, but nonetheless, Blake felt like he had betrayed his team.

"I'm not sure. The Guildmaster mentioned she was going to handle that information, and I was afraid of telling you all."

His voice cracked and he looked away, unable to hold eye contact with them. They had been a team for less than a day and he had already betrayed them.

"It's all right."

Emily's soft voice pulled his attention to her. She offered him a small, sad smile.

"That must have been terrifying."

He nodded, unable to speak.

"Yeah, don't sweat it, buddy." Jack shot him a smile and tossed him the orange he had been working on. "But I still want to know what the loot was."

Blake caught the orange, and the juice splashed on his fingers as he shook his head at Jack. "I'm not allowed to say."

"Course not. Just means we're going to need to do a bunch of dungeon diving to get it to drop for us."

"At the very least, this means we will need to be a little more careful on our first dive than I had previously anticipated." Karan smiled at the group. "But even with this new information, the dungeon will still be Bronze ranked, and I am confident we will be fine. If anything, that mage's betrayal just means the rest of you will level up faster, which is definitely a good thing."

Her words lightened the mood and Blake felt himself smiling along with the others. The quicker they hit Silver, the better.

"But first," Karan turned back towards the caravan, where Marcus was calling out orders, "we have to build the settlement."

Chapter Twenty-Two

"Is it me? Did I do something wrong?" Ryan asked Erin as they watched the adventurers settle in for the night. They had arrived a week prior, yet not a single person had stepped foot in his dungeon. Instead, they started cutting down trees in a wide swathe around his entrance.

"No." Erin sat wrapped in her silk blanket, staring at the scene.

The land around them had been changed immensely in a single week. What was once a great forest was now a small settlement, complete with wooden walls and buildings.

"I think they are just establishing a dungeon town before they start allowing adventurers to enter you."

"Psh, they're just teasing me." He sighed and halfheartedly started sifting through his bone collection. "Maybe I should make some new mobs for them."

Ever since he finished his renovations, Ryan had been searching his area for more skeletons. He had met with partial success, finding skeletons in varying degrees for snakes, a fox, an owl, and a bear.

"Are you still mad about that?" asked Erin. Ryan had been pestering her about making new mob types, but Erin kept telling him he should stick to a small number of different mobs for now.

What was the point of collecting bones if he couldn't show off his collection to the adventurers?

"I'm just so bored."

As a dungeon, he couldn't sleep. While he could lose himself to various tasks, such as when he renovated his dungeon, time moved painfully slow if he had nothing to do. Erin at least had the ability to nap to pass time. Ryan just got to amuse himself by occasionally trying to hit his mobs with rocks. Speaking of which:

"Ryan."

Erin's voice was as sharp as the stalactite that dropped from the ceiling, scattering the bones of one of his skuirrels. He quickly absorbed the bones and the loot drop. He knew he had a few minutes before he could summon the skuirrel again, but it didn't matter. No one was coming exploring tonight.

"Hey now, I'm just practicing. I figure I can use those stalactites as another trap." He had been working on a justification for his mob abuse and was rather proud of that explanation. "Also, it's not like it hurts them."

"Yes, but—"

"They don't have nerves, or skin, or even minds. They're pretty much undead, mindless zombies. I mean, the ratbies are actual zombies."

"You still shouldn't kill them pointlessly. The longer your mobs stay alive, the greater chance they have at evolving."

"What?"

This was new information. Erin had a habit of forgetting to share things like this with him. Ryan wondered how much she had actually paid attention when she was being taught how to be a dungeon fairy.

"Well, uh." Yup, she had definitely just remembered. He loved her, but she really made it hard at times. "The longer a mob exists in a dungeon, the higher the chance it has of naturally evolving. What triggers a natural evolution is random and dependent on the mob. So it's best to just let your mobs live out their lives."

"What type of evolution are we talking about? I'm not quite

sure how much a pile of bones can naturally evolve." He dropped another stalactite on another skuirrel without thinking.

"Ryan."

"Sorry. It's kind of become a habit."

He chuckled as he absorbed the skuirrel, summoning another in the room. He had been killing the mobs in his first room quite regularly, though now he thought about it, it seemed the ones he had missed originally had taken to hiding more than the new ones he summoned.

"Well, if mobs evolve, you will be able to create the new version of the mob once it has been absorbed." Welp. That meant dropping stalactites on skuirrels definitely didn't lead to any new evolutions, since the ones he was summoning were all still basic skuirrels.

"Also," Ryan *liked* also, "mobs that have evolved usually cost 1.5 times the amount the normal mob would cost."

"So an evolved skuirrel would cost—" He did quick math. *One times 1.5. Oh, duh.* "1.5 points to summon."

"Well, technically two. It rounds up to the next point." Erin grinned as Ryan's emotions sank. "But if they evolve naturally, the extra cost doesn't count against you until it dies and you have to re-summon it."

Well, that *did* offer him incentive not to kill his mobs. He stopped himself from dropping another stalactite.

"Well, then, I guess you just saved the skuirrels." He shot her a bemused feeling through their bond, causing her to laugh. "Behold Rin, Savior of Skuirrels!" Another chuckle. "Oh, that could be the name of the next boss!"

"If you do that, not even the Goddess would be able to save you from me." The tone of her voice sent chills through Ryan.

Note to self: don't joke about naming a boss after Rin.

"Noted. Though if we don't get some adventurers soon, we won't have to worry about naming another boss for a long time." Seriously, his experience had barely moved since killing the fire mage.

"Speaking of adventurers…"

Erin was looking into his diamond form at the scene outside

the dungeon's entrance. Five figures were slowly approaching, using the darkness to keep their forms hidden.

"Late-night visitors?"

The way they moved suggested they were trying not to be seen, and Ryan wondered if they had snuck out of the town. As they drew nearer, he could hear their frantic, hushed fragments of speech.

"If we get caught, Marcus is going to kill us," one of the figures said.

"Aye, but we aren't going to get caught," the next one whispered, drawing up next to one of the wolf's massive stone teeth.

"How can you be so sure?" the first figure asked.

All five wore dark cloaks with hoods covering their faces, making it impossible for Ryan to differentiate them.

"Because as long as we clear the dungeon quick enough, we can sneak back into town without anyone realizing we were gone," a third one with a deeper voice said.

"Why are we even doing this?" the first one asked as the group started walking through Ryan's entrance into the tunnel leading to his first room. "Marcus is allowing dives to start tomorrow. Why can't we just wait till then?"

"Because," the second one hissed, "I want us to be the first group to clear the dungeon. Then no one can look down on us." The speaker turned and headed deeper into the dungeon with the others following.

The first adventurer paused, watching the group walk away.

"But how will anyone know if they don't know we went diving tonight?"

How, indeed?

Ryan smiled to himself, watching the group venture in. His night had just gotten a lot more entertaining.

Chapter Twenty-Three

Ryan learned a couple of things as the group entered his first room. First, if he focused on adventurers like he did his mobs, he could pull basic information on them. He figured this was a similar skill to what Erin had mentioned the adventurers would have, allowing them to see his mobs' names.

Second, a scared adventurer could jump surprisingly high in the air while screaming at a decibel Ryan hadn't thought humanly possible. The latter part he had learned when the group of adventurers – four Bronze and one Silver – encountered his skuirrels.

"What are those things?" shrieked Todd, a Bronze Ten fighter, his voice still an octave or two too high.

Ryan decided to call this one Squeaker. One of Ryan's skuirrels had flung itself straight at the poor man, managing to scratch his face before it was flung against the wall. The bones scattered from the impact, leaving a copper coin as Ryan absorbed the bones.

"Can I absorb the loot if they don't get it in time?" he asked Erin as they watched the five adventurers. The copper coin was far enough away that their mana didn't stop Ryan from absorbing it.

"Not while they are in the room. That's just rude," Erin said. "Wait until they head to the next room."

"Fiiiine…"

"Don't 'fiiine' me. There is proper etiquette to being a dungeon. It is what keeps dungeons alive. And I'm going to make sure you can grow and become the best dungeon around." She gave him a hug. "Because you are mine."

"Aww, Rin." Ryan glowed a little brighter at her praise before turning back to the group. "So, dropping a stalactite right now…"

"Wouldn't be proper."

"Ugh."

The group were moving cautiously towards the copper coin, their eyes darting around the low-lit cave. Ryan found himself laughing in anticipation before Squeaker even bent down to grab the coin.

"Argh!" There he went again, this time jumping backwards into an adventurer Ryan hadn't examined yet. A quick glance at his stats informed Ryan his name was Adam, and he was a Bronze Five fighter.

"What the hell?" Adam growled as he climbed back to his feet.

Squeaker was on the ground, clutching at a skuirrel that had buried its teeth in his shoulder. Adam grabbed the skeleton and ripped it off the adventurer. Literally – the head was still attached to Squeaker's shoulder.

"That thing leapt from a hole," Squeaker said. He stood, wincing as he pulled the skuirrel's head off and tossed it aside. The skuirrel dropped two copper coins this time.

"It's called a skuirrel," Josh, a Silver Eight thief, said as he scooped up the copper coins. "I'm guessing they're the lowest ranked mobs in the dungeon."

"A squirrel?"

"No, a skuirrel with a 'k'"

Erin broke out into a fit of giggles as Josh spoke. She had said something very similar to Ryan when they had originally named the mobs.

"Whatever they are, they seem pretty easy to kill." The next individual, Leeroy, Bronze Five fighter, had drawn a sword and was looking around.

"Leeroy's right," said Josh. "They have the element of surprise, but they don't seem to do much damage."

"Speak for yourself," Squeaker whined, touching his own shoulder gently and curling the fingers of his other hand around his mace.

"Leeroy is right, they die rather easily,," Josh said. He tossed a dagger towards the wall and the blade sunk into a skuirrel skull. The creature died and dropped three coins. Another dagger – and another dead skuirrel – caused another two coins to drop.

"Let's kill all the mobs in here and keep going. I'm all for easy coin," Josh laughed as he twirled another dagger, flames dancing from this one.

"Why do the fiery ones always insult my dungeon?" Ryan sulked as he watched the group of adventurers search the room for his mobs.

"Who knows. Maybe they're just hot-headed?"

Yes. Ryan loved when Erin tried to make puns.

A scream stopped Ryan from replying. Eight of the skuirrels were dead, but Squeaker – apparently the unlucky one in the group – had gotten his ankle stuck in one of Ryan's traps. Two skuirrels bit at his exposed calf as he frantically swung at them.

"I bet he dies first," Ryan whispered as he watched the man struggle to free himself.

Squeaker's ankle was definitely at least sprained, and the two skuirrels did some good damage before he managed to bat them away with his mace. The blunt weapon seemed rather effective against the skuirrels.

"Really? I was hoping it would be Leeroy. Something about his name." Erin watched as the adventurers regrouped and headed towards the second room. "Though your trap also did some work on Todd."

It seemed Erin was able to observe their names and information, just like Ryan was. Another fact she'd "forgotten" to mention to him, and one which could have been helpful during that first visit from Sean and the gang.

"Squeaker. I named him Squeaker."

Erin raised her eyebrow at Ryan's statement. "Squeaker does seem pretty injured. Good job on the trap."

"Thank you. I let the others keep their actual names, but Squeaker just seemed more appropriate."

"I'm not even going to ask." Erin shook her head at Ryan and turned back to watching the adventurers just in time to see Squeaker land in a pile of bones. If Ryan had to guess, his ankle had given out as he walked along the narrow path, making him fall into one of the pits below.

"He has the worst luck," Ryan said. He was starting to feel sorry for the poor guy now.

The rest of the adventurers paused to glance back at Squeaker, who was struggling to stand, his eyes white with panic.

"We'll be back for you after we clear the dungeon," Josh called to Squeaker, causing him to freeze in shock. "You're probably safer down there anyway."

The others nodded and turned to follow Josh towards the next room. Squeaker sat back on the ground and pulled his knees up to his chest, sobbing. Ryan wasn't sure if the poor man was terrified of the dungeon or upset his friends had left him alone in the hole. Either way, Ryan's psychological warfare was working, though perhaps a little too well. Poor Squeaker.

"Wow. That was just wrong." Erin's eyes were starting to tear up, and Ryan could tell she felt sorry for Squeaker as well.

Ryan couldn't believe the young man's team had just abandoned him. He was certain they would have been able to pull him up easily, but they hadn't even tried.

As he watched the group near the second room, Ryan's pity was replaced by anger, slowly starting to boil within. How could they do that to their friend?

"All right. I'm changing my bet. I want Josh to go first."

"Agreed!"

Chapter Twenty-Four

"What the hell is all this?" Adam asked as he looked around the second room.

The others stood around him, staring at the mass of overgrown plants and fungi. Ryan knew his mobs were watching the adventurers, but the adventurers couldn't see them. The mobs were hidden in the plants and tunnels, just like Ryan had planned.

"The report mentioned the dungeon has three rooms, so let's clear this one quickly so we can get to the boss," Josh called, tossing a burning dagger through the plant life. The blade burned easily through the greenery, leaving a clear path towards the door to the next tunnel.

"Lead the way, Leeroy," Josh said.

Leeroy shot Josh a grin and started forward, sword raised as his eyes darted back and forth. Luke, a Bronze Six fighter, followed next, with Josh and Adam following close behind. If Ryan had to guess, Josh was using the others to keep himself safe.

Not going to work. Ryan urged his mobs to attack, targeting Josh whenever they could. It probably wasn't the proper way to handle the group, but given how they had treated Squeaker, Ryan was certain Erin wouldn't be mad.

"Mobs!" Josh shouted as a skrat burst through a tunnel beside him.

The thief cut the mob down before it could even reach him. But the skrat was just the beginning of the assault, and suddenly the room burst into… *Life? Unlife? Hmm.* Ryan decided now wasn't the proper time to wonder. He watched his mobs attack.

A group of skuirrels leapt at Josh, and though the man managed to cut three of them down, two found purchase on his hands. They sank their teeth deeply into his flesh, making him curse and drop his daggers.

"Yes!" Ryan and Erin cheered the mobs on, watching as more swarmed towards the Silver-ranked adventurer. Leeroy and Luke were busy fighting both skrats and poison ivy, their feet tangled in the vine as they tried to help Josh. Adam, was cursing up a storm as he swatted at skuirrels with his mace.

"What the hell is going on? Why are they rushing us?" Adam said, knocking a skrat into a skuirrel in an explosion of bones. Ryan hated to admit it, but skeletal beasts were rather fragile. Maybe that was why they only cost one point to create.

"Less yelling, more felling," Luke called out, his fists smashing down onto a skuirrel. Ryan noticed he had metal covering his knuckles. *Interesting.*

"This just makes it easier for us to kill them all." Leeroy laughed as he swung his sword downward, severing a skrat with ease.

Ryan winced as his mob died, but Leeroy's cry a second later made the sacrifice worth it. While Leeroy had been focused on the skrat, one of Ryan's ratbies had managed to sink its teeth into his ankle.

"What the—?"

Leeroy's sword swung down, decapitating the ratbie, but the head stayed locked onto his ankle.

"Huh, just like Blake," Ryan remarked as he watched, and soon enough, a fiery dagger burned the severed ratbie head off of Leeroy's ankle.

"Yes, that was rather strange," Erin said.

"But unlike Blake, they don't have a healer," Ryan mused. "And only Josh seems to have any special skills."

Ryan had noticed all the Bronze adventurers were only classified as fighters and didn't seem to have any unique skills.

"They won't. Adventurers don't get their affinity till they are Silver ranked."

"So only Josh has an affinity."

"Yes, fire. Seems a strange affinity for a thief," Erin said, half to herself.

"Remind me to ask you about that later," Ryan mumbled as his mind drifted back to the fight.

The adventurers managed to finish the mobs in the room without any further injuries, and Ryan tried to re-absorb them. However, because most of the mobs had died so close to the adventurers, he found he couldn't just yet.

"Hurry up and go," Ryan hissed as they finished picking up their loot. At first, it seemed like they were going to leave it, because most of it had fallen into the ivy, but Josh burned all the plants away with seemingly no effort. Ryan was really growing to hate fire affinity adventurers.

"All right, let's go take out the boss," Josh said.

He motioned towards the tunnel, and Leeroy once again took the lead. If the ratbie's bite had done anything to him, it wasn't showing.

Ryan sulked, watching the group casually stroll down the winding path towards the boss room. His mobs had managed to inflict some minor wounds on most of the adventurers, and they were definitely showing signs of weariness. But all that remained was Steve.

"Do you think this group is really going to clear the dungeon?" he asked.

"I really hope not," Erin whispered. She wrapped herself in her silk cloth, huddling closer to Ryan's crystal.

"Let's do this." Leeroy's voice echoed through the crystal, the group having reached the boss room. "Leeeeer-rrooooooyyyyyy!!!!"

He rushed in, sword raised, and the rest of the group followed him. However, the adventurer managed two steps into the room before he suddenly collapsed on the ground, his sword flying from nerveless fingers.

"Damn it, Leeroy," Luke managed to shout as he tripped over the fallen adventurer. Josh and Adam paused, their eyes darting from their comrades to the eight-foot skeleton that stood watching the intruders.

Then all hell broke loose.

Chapter Twenty-Five

Luke was fast, Ryan had to give him that. But Steve the Bone Slinger was faster. Even as Luke hopped back to his feet, sharpened bones punched through his chest, easily penetrating the leather armor he was wearing.

The attack happened so quickly, Josh and Adam didn't even have time to react. They simply stood, eyes wide, as Ryan's boss mob reeled in their friend.

"Leeroy, help me," Luke whimpered as he was pulled past the fallen fighter. He struggled uselessly against the black strands of mana bringing him slowly closer to Steve. But the more Luke struggled, the more the bones dug into his flesh, inflicting even more damage. Judging from the placement of the spikes, the wounds weren't immediately fatal. However, Steve's spiked arm was.

Just as Luke came within range of the deadly boss mob, Josh and Adam seemed to remember where they were, and jumped into action. A fiery dagger cut through the black mana, severing Steve's connection to the bones lodged in Luke. The fighter fell to the ground, gasping for air, while Adam rushed towards him.

"What the hell are you doing, Leeroy?" Josh kicked the downed fighter, but Leeroy didn't respond.

"What is going on with Leeroy?" Erin asked.

Luke was crawling back toward the entrance while Adam

held off the eight-foot boss. Josh continued trying to rouse Leeroy.

"Umm." Ryan had just finished absorbing the mobs in his second room and had learned something interesting. "Remember how you mentioned monster evolution to me?"

"Yes."

"Well, my ratbies evolved."

"Really?"

"Yup. It seems the mushrooms in the room started to, well, grow on the ratbies, and they created a new mob."

Ryan paused to admire a vicious slash from Steve, which knocked Adam's mace from his hand. The group really wasn't faring well.

"So the ratbie that bit Leeroy earlier—" Erin began

"—was one of the new ones. An infested ratbie," Ryan finished. He liked that name, and mentally assigned it to his new mob. "It seems they have a slow-acting paralysis toxin which makes their bites rather dangerous. The paralysis kicked in just as they started the boss fight."

"Wow, talk about bad luck." Erin giggled as they turned their attention back to the fight. Adam had recovered his mace but was now bleeding profusely from a variety of cuts. Luke was gasping for air against the wall, his wounds taking their toll. As for Josh… *Wait. Where is Josh?*

"Hey Rin, where did Josh go?" Ryan scanned the room but couldn't find the thief.

"He probably used one of his thief skills. Thieves specialize in stealth. It is possible he used mana to mask his presence."

"Adventurers can use their mana like that?"

Erin let out a deep sigh and looked down at Ryan. "How else do you think he has been throwing flaming daggers around your dungeon?"

"Magic?"

It was a terrible joke, but Ryan couldn't resist. His comment earned him a slap to his hard exterior, which, ironically, coincided with Adam landing a hit on Steve. The mace sent bone chips flying off the skeleton, but Steve's reinforced bones were much stronger than the skeletal beasts.

"You're not wrong. But it's much more complex than that." Erin opened her mouth to continue but stopped as she observed the fight underway. "We can talk more after the fight."

Ryan sent her a mental nod and turned back to the battle at hand. A rush of euphoria filled him, signaling experience gain. One of the adventurers had just died. A quick check on Luke's collapsed form confirmed his suspicion.

For some reason, seeing the fallen adventurer made an unknown feeling arise. Guilt? Killing the mage hadn't bothered him, so why did Luke's death?

"One down." Ryan's voice sounded dull through their bond, and he realized that as much as he wanted Josh dead, he had no ill feelings towards the other adventurers in the dungeon. They hadn't really done anything wrong. Perhaps that was why he was feeling guilty?

"Your boss really is formidable," Erin said.

She had likely sensed his mood drop at the thought of Luke dying, and was trying her best to cheer him back up. Was he going to feel this way after every death? There seemed to be some part of him, perhaps linked with those strange visions he had, that didn't agree with this. Perhaps he wasn't a bad person after all.

"Thanks." He paused and pushed his thoughts from his mind. Ryan knew he couldn't deal with the problem at that moment, and besides, there was a boss fight to watch. With Luke's death and Leeroy still paralyzed, only Adam and Josh remained to fight Steve. Ryan wondered just how long Leeroy's toxin would last.

"Adam's not going to last long." Erin was watching intently, and sure enough, Adam seemed to be slowing down.

He was covered in countless cuts, and while he managed to block most of Steve's attacks, the blocks were coming slower and slower. Clearly, he had given up striking back. He had probably realized that, in a battle of who could take more damage, the skeletal boss had an advantage over the fleshy Bronze adventurer. As such, Adam appeared to have made a new life choice. He was making his way towards Leeroy and the exit.

"He's going to run for it," Ryan guessed, just as Adam made one last block and turned to run.

The adventurer's eyes were filled with fear, and he didn't even glance at Leeroy's motionless form as he ran. He managed three steps before bones suddenly sprouted from his chest. Steve pulled Adam's struggling body closer while simultaneously approaching Leeroy. It seemed the mob planned to finish both adventurers off at the same time.

"Josh, where are you?" Adam was on the ground, holding on to the doorway as he fought against Steve's pull. The dark strands were stretched taut, and even as Steve cut into Leeroy, the spikes ripped deeper into Adam and he lost his grip on the door.

Almost in slow motion, Ryan watched Adam's body slam into Steve, knocking the skeleton to the ground with a clatter. Unlike the skeletal beasts, Steve's body was held together by dark mana, so he didn't shatter apart. That being said, Ryan could tell the combination of Adam's previous attacks, along with the collision, had done a large amount of damage to Steve, weakening the boss. This fact was even more evident as the boss struggled to free itself of Adam's tangled body.

"Josh, help me," Adam groaned. If Steve was in bad shape, Adam was still the worse off of the two.

Josh appeared from the darkness, both daggers glowing with red flames. His eyes were crazed, and Ryan watched as they darted from Adam to Steve. When Adam had smashed into Steve, he had become entangled with Steve's bones, essentially trapping him. Surprisingly enough, the rib cage actually acted as a good cage.

"Oh, I will."

Josh's hands became blurs as they flew towards his belt, and suddenly a string of six flaming daggers were launched towards Steve's skull. The sixth dagger turned out to be the nail in the coffin for Steve, as the moment it impacted, the heavily damaged boss literally fell apart. As Steve died, a golden coin fell to the ground.

"Thank you—"

Another of Josh's daggers flashed forward, ending Adam even as gratitude tumbled from his lips.

Shrugging, Josh stood, the lone survivor of the four adventurers that had attacked Steve the Bone Slinger.

"Sorry, Adam. I've decided you just didn't make the cut."

Chapter Twenty-Six

"Did he just—"

Ryan couldn't even finish the sentence. Josh had just killed one of his own teammates, and for what? How could the adventurer think money was more important than his friend?

"How horrible." Erin's hand was covering her mouth. Ryan could feel her sorrow and disgust through their bond. The celestial fairy may have acted callous towards adventurers dying at the hands of Ryan's boss, but cold-blooded murder was a different story. Or was it hot-blooded, given Josh's fire affinity?

Ryan watched as Josh walked calmly to each of his fallen comrades, taking the time to check their pockets for anything valuable. After the thief pocketed what few coins they had, he picked up the gold coin and calmly left the room. He even had the audacity to whistle as he walked.

Ryan couldn't think, couldn't speak. A feeling, a deep-rooted rage, was growing within him. How could this human do such a horrible thing? All Ryan could think of was how terrible this man's greed must be, and he realized Josh reminded him a lot of the mage that had almost killed Blake.

"We can't." Erin's voice was quiet, defeated. Ryan knew she could sense his rage, and his murderous intent.

"It wouldn't be proper etiquette," she said lamely, even as

Josh cleared the second room and made his way towards the first.

"Josh."

A broken voice called out in the darkness below as the thief walked along the narrow path. Squeaker. How had Ryan forgotten about the poor adventurer trapped in the pit?

"Josh," Squeaker called again as he struggled to stand. Judging from the way he winced, he was in pain.

"Where are the others? Did you beat the boss?"

The thief didn't even pause to look at Squeaker, moving into the first room.

"Are you just going to leave me?" Squeaker's voice grew frantic. "This is why everyone treats you like trash. You're just a good-for-nothing, lowlife—"

Squeaker let out a high-pitched cry as a flaming dagger sprouted from his arm. Josh held up a second blazing blade as he stared at Squeaker from the entrance to the first room.

"Listen here, you filth—"

Squeaker's mouth shut as fear filled his eyes. Josh took a deep breath, as if taking control of himself.

"Sorry, Todd," Josh said, his voice taking on a strangely calm tone. "It's just, you know how I feel about people talking down on thieves."

"I'm… I'm sorry, Josh. I'm in a lot of pain, and I'm scared. Can you help me out?" Squeaker pleaded in a quivering voice.

The thief paused for a moment, glancing down at the trapped adventurer. *Surely he isn't going to just leave him down there?*

"Sorry, man, it's survival of the fittest. And if the others aren't walking out of here with me, you sure as hell aren't." The thief flashed a smile and turned his back on Squeaker.

"So you're just going to leave me?" Squeaker's voice echoed from the pit. "That's just like killing me."

The thief's hand twitched down to his waist as he paused, once again almost into the first room. "I didn't kill anyone. The dungeon was just too dangerous, and you guys were too weak. That's on you, not me." His hand drifted back away from his dagger, and he continued on his way.

To hell with etiquette.

An uncontrollable rage filled Ryan as he watched the thief making his way cheerfully through his first room. Not only had Josh led his teammates to their deaths, now he was going to leave poor Squeaker? That was just too far. The very dungeon began to shake with Ryan's anger.

"What the bloody—" Josh's curse was cut short as a stalactite dropped from the ceiling. Such was its force that the thief's skull caved in, killing him in an instant. The body toppled forward, thudding lifelessly to the ground. The human was much easier to hit with a stalactite than a skittish skuirrel.

"Ryan."

Erin's voice pulled him from his rage, and the satisfaction quickly faded. Erin had explained proper dungeon etiquette to him, and he had failed her. He really was a terrible dungeon. But he couldn't let Josh go unpunished for his crimes. He just couldn't.

"I'm sorry."

He wasn't sorry he killed Josh; he had no qualms about stopping evil people. But he was sorry he had let her down.

"It's okay. You just surprised me is all." Erin's emotions were a jumbled mess, and Ryan couldn't tell if she was happy or upset with him.

"But what about etiquette? I just killed him in exactly the way you told me I shouldn't."

"Yes, but you did it to save an innocent adventurer," Erin said. "That is the very type of justice that my Goddess believes in. You did what was right, what was just. I will never fault you for stopping evil from harming an innocent life."

"Your whole morale code confuses me at times."

Ryan found himself suddenly very tired, and he realized he must have exerted an unexpectedly large amount of mana when he shook his entire dungeon. That, and the confusing morale code being thrown at him.

Seriously, one moment Erin is okay with adventurers dying in the dungeon to my mobs, but then she scolds me for even joking about dropping stalactites on adventurers' heads. And now, when I do that very thing, she's praising me for my action? Are all fairies this confusing?

"Hello?" came a quavering voice.

Ryan had completely forgotten about Squeaker, who was staring out of the pit in the direction of the first room.

"Josh?"

Ryan realized Squeaker couldn't see what had happened to the thief.

"Welp, this is awkward," Ryan muttered.

He fought the exhaustion clouding his mind as he tried to figure out what to do. It was obvious Squeaker would die in the dungeon if Ryan didn't do anything. The poor adventurer could not escape the pit on his own, after all.

And Josh... well, Josh was just dead weight now. With an effort, Ryan pushed his influence into the wall nearest Squeaker, carving out indents to create a makeshift ladder for the adventurer. At the same time, he absorbed Josh's body. Squeaker didn't need to see what he had done.

"Oh, Ryan." Erin wrapped her arms around his crystal form in a hug, a strong feeling rushing through their bond. "You are too kind for this world."

Her emotions seemed a strange mixture of happiness and sorrow, but Ryan's tired mind couldn't be bothered to try and sort through them.

He watched as Squeaker climbed the ladder, his eyes seeking the thief. A flash of sorrow on his face told Ryan the adventurer had realized, to some degree, that Josh had fallen prey to the dungeon. The thief had literally just tried to kill him, yet the man still showed compassion for him.

"*He* is too kind for this world," Ryan muttered.

The wounded adventurer, the only one who had been hesitant about entering the dungeon in the first place, walked slowly through the first room, and out of the dungeon.

The whole time, Ryan and Erin sat in silence. The night had been a long one, and Ryan knew Josh's team was just the first of many that would be coming through very soon. However, he knew he needed to focus and recover his mana before he could deal with what was to come. He sighed mentally and turned his attention back on his dungeon, and Erin.

"So, shall we see what type of loot we got?" he said, half-jokingly.

But he felt little joy as he absorbed the other three adventurers that had fallen to his dungeon.

Chapter Twenty-Seven

The loot from Josh and his gang was rather underwhelming, which wasn't much of a surprise given their levels.

Josh had the best gear on him, which wasn't saying much. Just like the mage, he had a fine iron dagger, which was uncommon. The rest of his gear, just like the others, was common, ranging from basic leather armor to common iron weapons.

Ryan sorted those away without a second glance, deciding he wasn't going to change up his loot drops just yet. The skuirrels and skrats died too quickly, so copper coins still seemed appropriate.

"Anything good?" Erin broke the silence, and Ryan realized he had been lost in his thoughts for quite a while. A glance out of the entrance of his dungeon showed the sun was starting to rise. How long had he been brooding?

"All pretty basic. Nothing worth adding to the current loot drops."

I could always make my skuirrels or skrats drop a single boot or glove, but that just seems wrong.

"How about experience-wise? Josh was a Silver-ranked adventurer; maybe he proved useful in the end?"

Ryan couldn't believe he hadn't considered that. He'd been so caught up in his thoughts. Did all dungeons have the same moral qualms he did? He wasn't sure, but suspected his feelings were really going to make this whole dungeon business a pain.

"Let's check."

He tried to sound cheery, but he was still so drained. He summoned his triangles, and instantly a bit of his exhaustion fled. Sure enough, Josh's group had filled up his experience triangle enough to grant him another level. His level triangle was now filled with darkness all the way to Bronze Six, and a white '75' glowed.

I forgot to summon my mobs back after Squeaker left. Goddess, I'm such a mess right now.

"You know, Ryan, a dungeon isn't any good without its mobs." Erin poked him lightly and laughed. He could tell she was doing her best to cheer him up. "Unless you were planning on killing your adventurers with confusion and boredom?"

She let out her beautiful laugh, and Ryan couldn't help but feel himself smile.

"Yeah, yeah. I've just got a lot on my mind."

He summoned his ten skuirrels in the first room, watching his point total instantly drop to sixty-five. Then he summoned Steve in the boss room, pushing the number down to forty.

"At least you don't have a hundred-pound stone on your mind."

Now she was cracking jokes about dropping stalactites on Josh? *Funny, yet surprisingly dark for a celestial fairy. Then again, Josh deserved it.*

"Hey, it was fifty pounds at most."

Her joking was getting better. Maybe she was using comedy to desensitize him to killing adventurers.

"I'm sure your skuirrels appreciate you dropping a stone on something other than them for once." She paused and looked at his triangle, noticing he hadn't summoned his second room's mobs yet. "Something the matter?"

"Trying to figure out if I summon the same mobs again or try some of these infested ratbies. The regular ratbies cost five points, but the infested ratbies cost eight."

"Maybe you should save those for later," Erin mused, tapping her chin. "You've grown a lot already, and you don't want to make yourself too tough early on. You need the adventurers to want to feel comfortable enough to explore you, and not avoid you."

She sat down on him, legs dangling over his field of vision.

"Yeah, but that group was pretty low level, and they managed to clear the dungeon," Ryan said.

"Barely."

"True."

Ryan wasn't sure why he was arguing with Erin on this point. He wasn't a huge fan of brutally killing adventurers off en masse. He wasn't sure he could handle that emotionally right now.

"Besides, while you do gain experience from killing adventurers, it is proportional to their level compared to yours," Erin said, absently rubbing his surface. "Since you are Bronze Six, I bet you are higher level than a good amount of these new adventurers. Why not hold on to those extra points for now, and let the adventurers have some time to grow and get comfortable with you? Then you can increase the difficulty and catch a few unawares. That will net you more experience than just culling the weak."

Wow, Rin really was brutal. Did his sweet, innocent, kind celestial fairy have a dark side, or was she just trying to help him get stronger?

"Remind me never to get on your bad side," Ryan joked. "You are rather scary, Rin."

She slapped his crystal and gave him a hard stare.

"It's my job to help you grow as powerful as possible. It may be against my celestial nature, but I will do my best to fulfill the Goddess's wishes that you grow strong. She has plans for you."

Well, that's not cryptic at all.

"Great," Ryan muttered. "I'm barely hanging on emotionally as it is, and you decide to let me know a Goddess has plans for me. Thanks a lot for that."

Seriously, what could the Goddess of Justice possibly want from me?

For a moment, he recalled a feminine voice, a whisper in his mind. *"Stay pure to your heart, young man, and I pray you continue to walk the path of righteousness."*

Was he walking the path of righteousness by being a dungeon? Had it been righteous to kill those adventurers?

Well, other than Josh. It was definitely righteous to kill Josh. And hey, Josh – not Ryan – had killed Adam.

"Hello? Ryan?"

Oops. He had gotten caught up in his thoughts again. Erin knocked on his core. "Are you in there?" she called.

"Sorry, all of this is just so much."

When did he become such a depressed dungeon? His mood had definitely gotten rather… dark. *Ha.* Maybe there was hope for him yet.

"I know, hun," Erin said.

Aww, she called me "hun" again. For some reason, that helped him feel a little better.

"Just remember, I will never lead you astray," Erin said. "I don't want to make you do anything that upsets you. We will get through this stage in your growth together. Just trust me."

"I trust you, Rin." As he spoke, he could feel warmth flowing through their bond, a feeling that almost seemed like love.

"I'll keep the second room the same," Ryan said, "save for one small detail." He was going to decrease his ratbie number by one. It wasn't a huge change, but one less mob meant one less danger for adventurers, and right now, his mind told him to make it a little easier. Maybe his depression was making him soft.

He summoned his ten skrats, ten skuirrels, and two ratbies. As his mobs scurried about, he regrew the foliage in the room. Hopefully adventurers wouldn't keep torching his precious plants. It wasn't terribly hard to regrow them, but he felt it was a waste of mana that he would rather hold onto in the event he really needed it.

With those changes made, and his mob points sitting at ten unspent, Ryan unsummoned his triangles, and turned his focus to his dungeon's entrance. In the distance, it looked like the dungeon town was slowly coming to life. He was certain they would have more visitors soon.

Chapter Twenty-Eight

After refilling his mobs in his second room, Erin decided to take a nap. Ryan figured she was just as emotionally drained as he was from the encounter with Josh and his gang. That was fine by Ryan, because the moment she went to sleep, he went to work. He had *plans*.

First, Ryan carved out three small holes under his boss room, spreading his influence down and then covering the incriminating spaces with rock. Erin would not know what he had done. These holes had no entrance or exit, and there was no way anyone would find them. They were roughly three feet in length, width and height. Nice little cubic expanses.

These three rooms were his evolution pits. Ryan had been fascinated by his ratbie's sudden evolution, and while he wasn't making use of these new mobs yet, he knew he would have need for new evolved mobs later on.

As such, Ryan decided he was going to be proactive with his extra points and secretly work to evolve some of his mobs. In particular, his basic, pathetically weak skeletal beasts.

How was he going to do this? It was simple, really, once the idea had come to him. He was going to have his skuirrels and skrats fight each other.

Ryan figured that while his ratbies had evolved naturally with the mushrooms growing on their rotted flesh, he could also try to force his mobs to evolve through experience gain. If humans and dungeons could get stronger from defeating enemies, it only made sense mobs could grow in the same way.

As such, in his first pit, he summoned two skrats. The mobs sprang to life, and quickly inspected their surroundings. Ryan watched them wander around aimlessly for a moment before mentally sending them each an order. They were to fight each other to the death. He did the same in the second pit, but with his skuirrels instead.

While his weak mobs clashed with each other, he created a small tunnel connecting the two occupied rooms to the empty third room. Then he simply waited.

The skuirrels finished their fight first, surprisingly enough, with one finally tearing the other's head off with its little bony claws. Ryan absorbed the fallen skuirrel and opened an entrance to the tunnel he had created.

He pushed his victorious skuirrel into that tunnel and towards the empty third room. The moment the skuirrel reached the third room, Ryan resealed the entrances to his connecting tunnel, and summoned two new skuirrels into the now empty skuirrel pit.

Once his skrats finished fighting, he did the same, sending the champion skrat towards the pit that held the victorious skuirrel, and quickly summoning two more skrats for battle in the now empty skrat pit.

Sealing the skrats in, Ryan ordered all the newly summoned mobs to begin fighting each other and turned his attention to the third room. There, he ordered the skrat and skuirrel to fight, and watched in slight awe as they began their battle.

It was immediately evident that they had learned a little from their previous battle, as instead of jumping into combat at once, they held back and circled each other.

The skuirrel was the first to strike, leaping high at the skrat. Bones clashed against bones, but the skrat, though slower, had a thicker bone structure. The tough little guy absorbed the skuirrel's impact and then bit down against the skuirrel's bony leg, tearing it off.

124

The skuirrel clattered to the ground but wasn't done. He spun and smashed his bony tail into the skrat, knocking him backwards. However, the loss of the skuirrel's leg cost him, and as he completed his tail whip, he fell, off balance, to the side.

The skrat took advantage of this and leapt atop the skuirrel, body slamming the smaller mob. With its skeleton having suffered from the last fight, it shattered easily, bones skittering around the room. The skrat stood victorious.

Ryan sent a small amount of dark mana into the room, watching as it repaired his skrat, making him ready for another battle. It wouldn't do to let it fight again while injured.

Ryan found himself chuckling as the skrat paced around the room, seeming anxious for another fight. Ryan checked the other rooms, and found his two skuirrels were again done fighting, so he sent the next challenger to the champion skrat.

He had, for all intents and purposes, just created a skeletal fight club. He focused his attention back to Erin, noting that she was awake and was looking down at him. She could tell he was doing something, but he knew she wasn't sure what. Rule number one of skeletal fight club: never talk about skeletal fight club.

"My sleeping beauty has awoken," he said with a warm smile. Her inquisitive, questioning look quickly left her face and was replaced by a bright red blush.

"Oh, stop it." She covered her face and flew off of him. He watched, with some amusement, as her foot got tangled in her silk cloth.

"It's true, Rin, you are beautiful."

She wrapped herself in the silk and stared at him. He could tell her emotions were in turmoil, and she was no longer wondering what he had been doing. Ryan sent a small part of his mind back to his fight club, making sure it was operating smoothly, and turned the rest of his attention back to Erin. Rule number two of skeletal fight club: never talk about skeletal fight club.

Between Erin and skeletal fight club, Ryan was almost able to completely keep his mind away from dark thoughts of Josh's group. In fact, for two whole days he simply watched skeletal fight after skeletal fight take place and chatted with Erin when she wasn't taking her naps. It seemed she was handling her own turmoil by sleeping it away. Part of Ryan was jealous that she could sleep and he couldn't.

Oh, well. He lazily dropped a stalactite on a skuirrel, another way he enjoyed passing time. There was something cathartic about trying to hit an object with a rock.

"Seriously, Ryan? Again?"

Skuirrel bones scattered on the ground as rock shards went flying. He quickly reabsorbed them and summoned another skuirrel. A bonus of having his extra points was that he could summon a new mob instantly after he killed one.

If Erin was still upset about his skuirrel target practice, she would be really mad if she knew what he had been doing in skeletal fight club for the past two days. Speaking of, his skeletal fight club was showing some results.

Ryan's original champion skrat had finally fallen after Ryan sent both a skrat and a skuirrel to fight him at the same time. Upon absorbing the champion, Ryan had discovered a new mob. He was going to keep that a secret from Erin for now, though. Rule number three of skeletal fight club: never talk about skeletal fight club.

"What? It's not like there's anything else to do," Ryan said. He turned his attention outwards. "See, once again there's—" He stopped as he took note of a large group of adventurers heading their way from the town. It seemed they were finally going to have more adventurers dungeon diving.

Ryan quickly made a mental change to the fight club, changing it to only skuirrels, before he focused all of his attention on the group advancing. Ryan may not have liked it, but he was going to make sure that when the time came to change his mobs up to make it harder on the adventurers, he would have new skrats and skuirrels to surprise them. He was also looking forward to the day he could surprise Erin with his proactiveness.

"There are so many of them," Ryan whispered.

He was so unsettled by the large group – at least twenty adventurers in all – that he missed a skuirrel with a stalactite. He hadn't missed a skuirrel since before Josh's team had arrived.

"Things are about to get interesting," Erin said. She huddled against him, her excitement garnished by a touch of fear. Ryan was more anxious than excited, but his emotions were high, especially as his latest victorious skuirrel finished off another.

Huzzah for skeletal fight club!

Chapter Twenty-Nine

"It's about time," Jack whispered as he stood next to Blake.

They were waiting outside the dungeon with four other teams. Marcus, the rogue chosen by Guildmaster Alice to head the dungeon town, stood before the twenty-five adventurers, who were all anxious to finally go on a dungeon dive.

"Well, we would have been here two days earlier if not for a selfish thief," Karan whispered loudly from behind Jack, making the thief wince.

The venom in Karan's voice was evident. Two days ago, they were supposed to have started the dungeon dives. However, a thief named Josh had apparently snuck into the dungeon with his team, and all but their lowest ranked member, Todd, had perished.

The poor survivor had been found collapsed and crying outside of the town's makeshift gate, and after reporting his story to Marcus, the dungeon dives had been postponed for two days. Todd had remained permanently drunk in a corner of the tavern ever since, fixing all that came near with a thousand-yard stare. He had *seen* things.

"Yeah, well, Josh was an ass. No one liked him," Jack muttered back, and Blake couldn't help but agree with him.

No one liked Josh and his gang. He really had been a deplorable person; the only nice guy of the group had been Todd.

Blake couldn't help but wonder how Todd had survived while the others had perished. A part of him wondered if the dungeon had let Todd go. It had, after all, saved Blake when he was in trouble.

"Still, I can't believe their whole team was defeated," Emily whispered.

"It just means we need to be careful," Matt said, adjusting the bow over his shoulder. "But don't worry, Emily, I'll keep you safe."

He offered his sister a smile, and she smiled back. Matt was Bronze Two, closest of the three Bronze members to getting Silver. Emily was Bronze Eight. As much as he hated to admit it, Blake was the weakest at Bronze Eleven. Hopefully he wouldn't slow them down too much.

"Just leave it to me, Matt, I'll make sure nothing harms her pretty—" Jack was cut off as Matt swiped his bow at the thief. Before it could connect, a gust of wind pushed it aside. Matt glared at Jack, who simply flashed a wide smile.

"Close, buddy, but remember, I'm just a tad stronger than you are." The thief laughed as the winds around him picked up. His smile was quickly replaced by a wince as Karan's hand clamped down on the thief's shoulder.

"And remember, Jack, I'm a lot stronger than you are." She squeezed his arm tightly before letting go.

Karan offered them all a smile, and Blake felt the tension in the air fade.

"I do love a strong woman," Jack commented before shifting back to Blake's side, noticeably out of Karan's reach. The thief shot the cleric a wink, but even as she opened her mouth to respond, Marcus began to speak.

"I know you are all anxious to enter the dungeon," Marcus said, his voice booming over all of them. "But before we start, I'm going to lay down a few rules."

The rogue was standing in front of the skeletal wolf's maw that was the entrance to the dungeon. From Blake's point of view, it almost seemed like it was watching them, preparing to consume them. He shivered even as everyone else around him cheered at Marcus's words.

"We need to avoid," Marcus paused, eying the adventurers before him, "further unnecessary casualties."

The mood suddenly turned somber.

"First, as per guild rules, every team must have a Silver or Gold leader. Since today is the first day, I will personally be inspecting each team's levels. After today, one of my seconds will be standing guard at the front of the dungeon."

He motioned, and two figures appeared at his side. They were both clad from head to toe in dark cloth, and it almost seemed as if the shadows of the dungeon clung to them.

"These are my seconds."

As they removed their hoods, Blake couldn't help but let out a light gasp. The warriors on either side shared an eerie similarity – they were almost identical, save for their gender.

Blake had heard whispers of these twins. Gold One assassins that specialized as necromancer hunters. The Guildmaster seemed to have carried out her promise to his father.

"Meet Rasha and Sasha," Marcus said. "I trust you will make them feel welcome."

"They ain't human," Jack whispered next to Blake.

"What are they?" Blake asked.

"They're wolfkin," Jack replied.

Both warriors turned their deep emerald eyes towards Jack as the thief spoke. Sasha, the female, smirked, while Rasha's eyes seemed to blaze with anger.

"How can you tell?" As far as Blake knew, wolfkin appeared human, yet could take on a bipedal, wolf-like form at will. They were seen as a neutral race and very rarely interacted with the rest of the world.

"Maybe I'll tell ya sometime." Jack's eyes were still locked on the two wolfkin before him, who continued to hold his gaze.

If Marcus had noticed the tension there, he didn't show it.

"Each day, five teams will be allowed to enter the dungeon," the rogue went on. "Before entering, each team member will touch their pendant to this."

He held up a circular disk, about the size of a plate, for all to see. It was segmented into five pieces, and each piece held a small crystal.

"This disk will allow us to monitor the condition of each team member. If you die in the dungeon, the crystal corresponding to your pendant will turn dark. If all five go dark, we will know your team has fallen. We will then wait thirty minutes before sending the next team in."

Marcus's eyes turned hard as he looked at all the adventurers.

"While the Adventurers' Guild cares for its members, we will not come to your rescue in the dungeon. The strong survive, while the weak perish. If your team is foolish enough to get itself killed in a low-ranked dungeon, it means you would likely have become a hindrance to the guild in the future, and potentially cost the lives of others."

"Wow, that's harsh," Blake whispered to Jack, but the thief didn't respond. His eyes were still locked on the twins.

"Okay, good talk," Blake muttered. He rubbed his hands over his arms, calming the goosebumps that were starting to appear. Marcus wasn't exactly filling him with confidence.

"When you complete your dungeon run, you will meet with the appointed guild representative outside of the dungeon. We will have a cleric on hand to heal any injuries for a discounted price, as well as to collect the twenty percent guild tax on each dive."

"Wait…they tax us?" Blake looked at Karan for confirmation.

"How else do you think the guild can afford all this?" Karan whispered back, motioning at the encampment behind them. "The guild takes a twenty percent cut from every profit adventurers make, be it from tasks around the city, quests for the guild, or dungeon dives. In return, guild members get discounted rates from healers and stores, as well as free class training. It's really quite fair."

Blake figured she was right, but he couldn't believe no one had mentioned there was a tax. Though the more he thought on it, it really wasn't that bad. Besides, the discounts, as well as free training, were worth it.

"Now, then, if there are no questions, we will allow the first team to begin the dive," Marcus said.

Even as he spoke, Rasha and Sasha vanished into darkness from Marcus's side. Unperturbed, the rogue motioned to the first team. Back at camp, all twenty of the adventurer groups had been given the opportunity to select a number from a basket. That number decided their order for dungeon dives.

Blake's team had drawn number five, so while they would get to go the first day, it meant they would be the last team of the evening.

As the first team stepped forward, each member touching their pendant to Marcus's disk, Blake couldn't help but feel excited and nervous.

Waiting for the first four teams to go was going to feel like an eternity.

Chapter Thirty

"Looks like there's just one team left," Ryan called out to Erin as he watched the most recent group of adventurers exit.

Four groups of five had entered his dungeon since the morning, and four groups of five had exited. Now, only a single group of five remained waiting outside.

"Are you going to let this one walk all over you, too?" Erin's voice dripped with sarcasm, making Ryan wince. She had mentioned he shouldn't make the dungeon any harder, but secretly he had made it even easier. He had disabled most of his traps, leaving only one or two, and those were far out of the path of the adventurers. He also may have been holding back his mobs, ordering their attacks in ones or twos to make them easier to pick off.

"I have no idea what you're talking about." Surely she hadn't figured out that he—

"Really?" Erin said, casting a withering look at him. "Then why have they not only reached Steve with minimal damage, but also managed to defeat him with relative ease? Steve has never once missed with his bone shots before, and yet today, somehow, he has missed every shot."

Oops, guess she noticed that as well.

Ryan had ordered every version of Steve to miss his shots. It

133

was his strongest, most deadly attack, and, well, Ryan really wasn't over the carnage of Josh's team.

"Listen, Ryan, I understand, I really do." Erin's voice had taken on a soft, tender tone. "I don't like killing any more than you do, but I've explained it before. This is the way being a dungeon works, and you need to get stronger. I'm not telling you to go out of your way to kill these adventurers, but you can't keep making it easier on them. You heard that man's speech."

It was true. Even the Adventurers' Guild apparently had no qualms about adventurers dying in the dungeon. The way their leader made it sound, Ryan would be doing the guild a favor by taking out those weak enough to fall for his traps and mobs.

"I know, but... I just don't think I can handle more innocent blood on my hands."

"Well, it would be Steve's hands, not yours," Erin retorted. She offered him a sweet smile, likely feeling his invisible glare. "Besides, Ryan, I'm here to go through it all with you. Don't you trust me? You know I wouldn't lead you down the wrong path. I'm a celestial fairy, for goodness' sake."

She had a very good point. She was probably the last being in the world that would try to lead him astray or hurt him. He let out a sigh, letting her know she had won.

"Fine, I won't go easy on this next group."

He pushed his mind throughout his dungeon, reactivating his traps and taking away Steve's previous orders. All of his mobs grew excited as he took away his control over them, allowing them to attack at will the next adventurers that entered. He hoped the next group was stronger than the four before, because if they weren't, he knew someone would be dying.

The fifth group of adventurers stepped inside, and Ryan's heart sank the moment he saw who the first member was. Blake, Bronze Eleven adventurer.

"Oh, his luck really hasn't improved, has it?" Erin whispered as she watched the rest of the group enter. "Hopefully he has some strong friends."

They both held their breath as the rest of Blake's team entered.

"Let's see... Emily, Bronze Eight adept," Ryan said. *That's the first adept I've ever seen. I wonder what she does.*

"Matt, Bronze Two archer," Erin said.

Two of the other teams had archers, and Ryan hadn't been too impressed with them. Their weapons were really weak against Steve.

"Jack, Silver Seven thief, air affinity," Erin observed.

Well, that's impressive. Though the last thief Ryan had seen was Josh, and he secretly hated that class.

"And finally, Karan, Gold Four cleric, celestial." Erin's voice seemed to raise an octave in excitement. "Blake's got a chance."

Her comment eased the tension in the dungeon core room, and both Erin and Ryan broke out in laughter.

"I was really worried for him for a moment," Ryan said. He had saved Blake once before, and he really, really, *really* didn't want to kill the poor guy.

"Me too." Erin pressed her face against Ryan's diamond core, intent on the group as they walked through the wolf's maw and towards the first room. "Now I'm excited to see how his group does against your dungeon when you aren't intentionally making it easier."

She stressed the last part, stopping Ryan before he issued new orders to Steve. The fact she could sense his feelings really was problematic at times.

"Well, let's get ready for a good show, then," Ryan said.

He turned his attention back to Blake and his group as they prepared to enter the first room. Well, almost all of his attention, as he could tell the skuirrel in skeleton fight club was nearing its evolution. He just knew it.

Luckily, even if Erin could feel his excitement there, she would likely think it was because of Blake and his group. He did, after all, have to follow his self-imposed rules of skeletal fight club.

"Here we go," Ryan said as the group of adventurers stepped into the first room.

Let's do this.

Chapter Thirty-One

"Well, I'm glad he has a shield now," Ryan commented as Blake blocked a flying skuirrel. The boney creature smashed against his shield but held on. At the same time, another launched itself at the boy. This time, with the added weight of the skuirrel, Blake wasn't able to get his shield up in time. The attacker latched on to his chest in a flurry of boney claws.

"I hate these things," Blake called out as he flailed at the offending skuirrel. All the while, the other skeletal rodent hung on to his wooden shield for dear unlife.

"At least you don't have to try and shoot them," Matt moaned, letting loose another arrow. The missile whistled harmlessly past a skittering skuirrel before snapping as it hit the wall.

"Annnnnd that's a miss," Ryan laughed, watching. "Keep, trying buddy, you'll get the hang of it."

The adventurers obviously couldn't hear him, but he had taken to commenting on dungeon dives. It was an oddly entertaining habit, he found. And if Ryan could drop a rock on them, he was sure Matt would learn to hit one, eventually.

"That thief seems pretty skilled," Erin commented, pulling Ryan's attention away from the comedy duo.

Sure enough, Jack was walking calmly towards the exit of the first room, blasting away any skuirrel that launched itself at him with a gust of wind. The attacks easily tore Ryan's skuirrels apart, leaving a rain of copper coins in their wake. Jack easily caught the coins before they hit the ground.

"What about the cleric?"

Ryan and Erin both glanced at Karan, but she simply stood back, watching the rest of her team fight. The skuirrels had left her alone, and Ryan had to wonder if they were scared of her.

"Well, it seems even skuirrels have brains." Erin laughed at her own joke.

"Not really. There's nothing there," Ryan responded as dryly as possible, holding in a laugh.

"You know what I—"

Ryan laughed, cutting Erin off. "I really just wanted to see if I could get you to argue whether a skeleton has a brain," he said, in that moment glad that he could still laugh, even telepathically, despite being a sentient rock.

"I wonder at times if you have a brain."

Oh, that one hurt. It seemed he'd made Erin a little upset.

Oops.

He glanced at the group of adventurers. Blake had managed to shake free of his two attackers and was heading towards Jack and the exit. At the same time, Matt seemed to have given up trying to shoot the skuirrels and was instead using his bow like a staff. *Ha, it's a bow-staff.*

"Has Emily done anything yet?"

She still stood by Karan, watching the fight intently. It seemed she was letting the others take all the aggro while she simply watched.

"Nope, nothing yet."

"Darn. I'm curious about what an adept can do." Ryan sighed, then started to chuckle. "I bet Blake finds a trap."

"You're on," Erin giggled.

They both watched as Blake neared Ryan's ankle traps. Sure enough, his foot landed on one, and stone crumbled beneath. He let out a less than manly scream, eliciting a ton of laughter not only from Ryan and Erin, but Matt and Jack as well.

"Shut up and help me," the boy yelled.

Blake didn't seem injured from the trap, just surprised, and with Matt's help he had his foot free in no time. After looking around the room, he motioned towards Karan and Emily.

"It seems it's all clear."

"It's not," Ryan whispered as the two girls made their way across the room.

The men had slain eight skuirrels between them. That meant there were two left, and Ryan was just waiting for them spring into action. He really wanted to see what the adept could do.

"Why aren't they attacking?" Erin asked as the two girls neared the rest of the group. For some reason, Ryan's skuirrels were refusing to attack. Maybe they really were terrified of Karan.

"Not sure. Let me, uh, motivate them." He mentally sent an attack signal to them, and instantly they sprang from their holes. Two white skeletal figures scampered across the floor, flinging themselves at Emily.

Emily shrieked with surprise, then lifted a hand that appeared to be holding a wooden stick. Suddenly, his skuirrels burst into pieces.

"What the chaos was that?" Ryan asked.

"A simple force spell," Erin replied.

"A what?"

"Adepts can use basic, neutral magic," Erin explained. "A force spell is just that: mana condensed into a physical force, launched at an enemy."

She paused as she eyed Emily.

"Given her level, she can probably only cast two spells at a time before her mana needs to recover."

"Oh yeah?" Ryan's interest was piqued, and he remembered this was a conversation that needed continuing from last time. "You've mentioned adventurer mana before. How exactly does it all work?"

Blake was leading his group through the tunnel to the next room. They were taking their time, a wise choice. One of the earlier groups had been rushing and had three members fall in the pits. That had been funny to watch.

"Hmm, the easiest way to explain it would be similar to how you summon mobs."

"All right, explain."

"Well, just like you have a certain amount of points to use on mobs, adventurers also have a set amount of mana to use based on their levels. The physical classes, such as the thief, paladin, fighter, and archer, pump eighty percent of their mana constantly into their body. This reinforces their forms physically, making them stronger, faster, and more durable."

"How durable?"

"Well, if you had dropped a stalactite on Sean, it is likely the stalactite would have broken, and Sean wouldn't even be bruised."

Always back to Sean. I get it, he's awesome.

"And the other twenty percent?"

"They can use that mana to actively utilize skills unique to their class, such as Josh's flaming daggers and Jack's wind gusts."

"How about the magic classes?"

"They are the opposite. They pump twenty percent of their mana into their physical selves, while eighty percent is kept available for spells."

"So does that mean Jack is physically stronger than Karan?" Jack was, after all, a physical class, while Karan was a cleric.

"If they were the same rank, yes. However, Karan is a Gold Four, meaning she has—" Erin started counting on her fingers "—six times as much mana as Jack. That means even at twenty percent of her mana, she can allot more mana to her physical traits than Jack has in his whole body."

"Okay, maybe the skuirrels have a good reason to fear her," Ryan admitted. She was definitely the strongest adventurer to have entered the dungeon since Sean's team.

"Well, nothing says a mob has to have the same intelligence as its creator," Erin said with a mischievous smile.

"Hey!"

"Kidding, hun." Erin started giggling and snuggled closer to his surface. "You know I wouldn't want any dungeon but you."

"Aww. I'm so lucky to have you as my fairy, Rin."

The fairy's face turned red, but she smiled and drew closer to him.

"Enough flattery," she whispered, though a little reluctantly. "They're getting close to the fun room."

Chapter Thirty-Two

The fun room was another term for the dungeon's second room, coined by Erin earlier in the day. Unlike Josh and Sean's groups, no one who had come through the dungeon that day had a fire affinity.

As such, the plants in the room had made the fight much more amusing for Ryan and Erin, and much more difficult for the adventurers. Even with Ryan keeping the mobs reined in, many groups had sustained one or two decent injuries in that room.

"Well, here's the room everyone was complaining about," Blake said. He stood at the entrance to the room, shield raised as he looked around. Unconsciously, the adventurer reached down to his ankle, where the ratbie had gotten him the first time.

"Think he'll get another bite to remember?" Ryan asked Erin, noting where his mobs were in the room. The foliage was doing a great job at keeping his ratbies hidden, and one of the two was even creeping closer to Blake as he shuffled into the room.

"Well, it would be awfully funny."

As if the mob heard Erin's comment – which in a way it *did*, because Ryan had sent it an order – the ratbie leapt out and struck, biting Blake's ankle a second time.

"Seriously?" the adventurer cursed, driving his sword into the ratbie's head.

"Oh, those things look gross," Emily groaned as she stepped into the room, eyeing the oozing, rotting ratbie on the ground.

"Yeah, well, their bites aren't the best either," Blake complained as he looked back towards Karan. "Think you can heal this after we clear the room? Apparently, their bites can be rather dangerous if left unattended."

Karan smiled at Blake, causing the adventurer to blush.

"Not your first time getting a zombie bite?" she asked.

"Guess he didn't tell them about his last trip here," mused Ryan.

"Aw, he's embarrassed," Erin cooed in a playful manner, and Ryan laughed at the poor boy's misfortune.

As far as Ryan could tell, Blake and his group, even Jack, were a likeable sort. He really wished Erin hadn't made him promise to go harder on this latest group. He was secretly cheering Blake's team on. Oh, and he hadn't forgotten his skuirrel in fight club, which was on the verge of evolving.

"Ugh, I hate this room already," Jack, who was already halfway to the exit, called out. "This darned ivy is going to make us itch something fierce."

The thief looked back at Karan, uncaring as a skuirrel came flying towards him. "Think you can lay some healing hands on me later, to stop the itching?"

"If I'm laying hands on you, it's going to be unpleasant for you." Her tone was icy, even as she answered the thief with a smile. "But if you insist."

"No, that's, uh, fine. I think I can buy some salve to cure it."

"Enough for the team?" Karan asked the thief sweetly.

"Yup, salves on me, guys," Jack joked. He turned and hurried towards the exit, easily blasting away any mobs foolish enough to attack him.

"That wind gust trick is really annoying," Ryan said.

"Yeah, but he's wasting a lot of mana doing those bursts," Erin replied. "He's not going to be able to regenerate it fully before Steve."

"Do they regenerate mana just like I do mob points?" Ryan asked.

"Pretty much."

"Oh, well, that's going to suck for him."

Two more skuirrels fell to wind gusts before Jack reached the exit.

The rest of the group took their time walking through the dense plant life, as they had to be more careful of where they stepped. Unlike Jack, they didn't have wind protecting them from flying enemies. As such, by the time the group cleared the room, Blake had three new cuts, along with his ratbie bite, while Matt had a broken skrat fang in his leg. Emily and Karan were untouched.

"Well, that room was definitely not this difficult the last time I came through," Blake moaned as he sat down, holding his leg towards Karan.

The cleric smiled softly at him as her hands glowed with a golden light. "The dungeon has had a good amount of time to make use of the experience it got from killing the mage. Plus, Josh was Silver ranked, so I'm going to guess the dungeon got another level from killing him and his team."

"Oh, she's a smart one," Ryan said. "You know, Rin, I've decided clerics are unfair."

"How so?" Erin asked, flying lazily around the room, bored from the lull in the action.

"She gets to just heal the entire team before they go to fight Steve. It completely undoes all the hard work my mobs put in."

Sure enough, Karan had finished healing Blake, and was working the bone out of Matt's ankle.

"Yes, but usually clerics aren't as strong at fighting as the others," Erin explained. "So, while she can heal the team, she won't be able to aid in a fight as well as another class. That means the team has to trade off damage for healing."

"Hmm, I suppose, but it still seems a bit unfair," Ryan complained. "I'm sure if they were still injured going in to fight Steve, even if there were five of them, their damage would be lower."

"Well, yes, but there are a few other factors at play here," Erin said. "First, clerics are a rare class, so most teams won't have one. Second, when you get stronger, you will start to see just how much of a difference there is. Third, even if she can fully heal a team, her mana reserves will drop lower the more damage they sustain. Spent mana might not be an issue right now for her, but as you get stronger, she will need to use larger spells to keep her team healed, and once she is out of mana, she is practically useless in a fight. She seems unfair right now, because you are Bronze, and she is Gold. Wait until you are a Gold dungeon going against Gold or below adventurers."

"I'll take your word for it."

Ryan realized it was funny he was upset about Karan's abilities. He wanted Blake's team to survive, after all. So why was he upset she was giving them an edge? Was it just because of the unfairness of it all? He figured that was it. After all, if dungeons had proper etiquette, shouldn't adventurers as well? Like, no healing until they'd beaten the boss?

"Just be happy all she is doing is healing the team," Erin said, interrupting his thoughts. She had settled back atop him; Blake's team had healed up and was making its way towards the boss room.

"She could probably clear the dungeon by herself," Erin mused. "Yet she has chosen to stay back, and just watch the rest of the team."

Ryan had a flashback of Sean waltzing through his dungeon with ease, and he found himself suddenly a lot less upset about Karan's healing.

"Now, let's see how they do against our fearsome Steve," Erin said, patting his surface.

She pulled her silk cloth around herself and leaned in to watch the fight. Ryan mentally nodded in agreement and turned all of his attention to Steve's room. Skeletal fight club could wait. Ryan wanted to see how Blake and his team fared against the Bone Slinger.

Chapter Thirty-Three

Blake was first into the room, shield raised. Unlike the other four groups, Blake's team seemed to know exactly what to expect. Ryan figured that made sense, given that Blake had actually seen Steve before.

"Steve? His name is Steve?" Jack erupted in laughter as he followed Blake into the room. "I've got to say; this dungeon has some amusing names for mobs."

And just like that, Ryan decided he didn't like the thief. Ryan was already self-conscious about Steve's name. He didn't need adventurers laughing at him.

"Don't interfere," Erin scolded even as Ryan prepared to order Steve to attack Jack.

Gah, thwarted by etiquette once again.

"You're not allowed to make it easier – or harder – this time around," she went on. "Just let Steve be Steve."

"But—"

"No buts, Ryan."

"Yes, dear."

His comment earned him a slap, but it was playful in nature. Together, they turned their attention back to the boss room.

"Be careful of his spikes," Blake reminded the team as he slowly began advancing on Steve, sword and shield raised.

Matt cocked an arrow and began walking in a wide circle away from Steve, staying on the side of his bladed arm.

"What, you mean he slings bones?" Jack laughed as he sauntered away from Blake and Matt.

Ryan suspected they had discussed a battle plan for Steve prior to entering the room. All the other teams had rushed in, screamed, and then gone into battle in a frantic scramble. Had Steve been fighting at full strength, none of the other teams would have likely survived.

"Yeah, they shoot out—"

At that moment, Steve decided to take action. Five spikes flew from the darkness that hung where his right arm should have been. The spikes flew past Blake's shield and headed towards Emily. Nobody in the room seemed able to react in time, and Ryan was certain, and sad, that Emily was a goner.

"Nope." Jack was suddenly in front of Emily, his daggers moving in a blur as wind whipped around him. He cut the tendrils holding the bones, and Ryan watched, both surprised and impressed, as the spikes fell harmlessly to the ground.

"Did the thief just—" Ryan stuttered.

"Yup," Erin said.

"Huh. Guess I can't hate him now."

Ryan couldn't believe Jack had managed to not only get in front of Emily in time, but also deflect all of Steve's spikes. He was also surprised Jack had put himself in danger; the last thief had simply hidden until the fight was almost over.

"Jack?'

Karan's voice broke the stillness that had filled the room following Steve's attack. The thief was breathing heavily, and Ryan could see blood dripping from his nose.

"May have used a tad too much mana." Jack's daggers dropped from his hands as he fell to the ground, coughing up blood. "Don't mind me, guys. 'tis but a flesh wound." He chuckled and groaned. "Just do something about the boss." He spat more blood as he spoke. "Sooner rather than later," he managed.

His words snapped the rest of the group out of their surprised state, and with a cry, Blake charged Steve. At the same time, Matt began loosing arrow after arrow at Steve. Unfortunately for the archer, basic arrows really did nothing against an eight-foot skeleton that was reinforced with dark mana.

Blake was having a little more success. It seemed he had been practicing his sword work, and Ryan had to admit Blake seemed to know what to do with his shield. He was successfully blocking Steve's blows and landing a few counter blows of his own.

However, his shield was quickly being turned into splinters, and he wasn't chipping bone away fast enough to take Steve down any time soon.

"Any help here?" he called out, breathless as he absorbed another blow from Steve.

The skeleton's bladed arm bit deep into the wood of the shield, and as Steve tried to pull his arm free, he pulled Blake with him.

"Ha," Ryan laughed as Blake was lifted off the ground.

Steve stared down at his arm, which now had a human attached.

"Have you tried sticking it with the pointy end?" Jack gasped.

Ryan noticed now that Karan was at the thief's side, her hands glowing gold as she healed him. It seemed humans took quite a bit of internal damage from using too much mana.

"Not helpful," Blake called back as he kicked Steve. His foot got stuck in Steve's ribcage, making Ryan laugh even harder.

"Emily? Matt?" Blake was a sight to see, his body strangely twisted and held in midair.

Blake's sword flailed about wildly now, and it seemed Matt had finally decided arrows were useless. The archer rushed forward with his bow and smashed it against Steve. That was actually less effective than his arrows, as all it resulted in was his bow cracking in half.

"Seriously? I've had that thing for years." Matt cursed as he let the pieces fall, and started to try and free Blake instead. Blake, in the meantime, worked on keeping Steve's bladed arm away from himself and the archer.

"Em, blast its skull," Matt growled.

"But... I'm not... I can't..." Emily shook her head and stuttered, her wand wavering in the air. "You know I don't have good aim, that's why I just overload the spell with mana."

So Emily had blasted those two skuirrels with brute force, not finesse. That was suddenly a lot less impressive. Ryan started to wonder how this group had made it this far.

"Just fire on three," Matt called out as he braced himself. "One." He tugged at Blake's foot, freeing it. "Two," he grunted as he tried to pull Blake free. "Let go of your shield, you dolt," he cursed.

As realization crossed Blake's face and he let go of his shield, Matt called out, "Three!"

An eruption of force blasted into Steve, sending bone shards flying through the air. Blake and Matt tumbled backwards, crashing against a wall.

"Ha! He's still a bone slinger," Jack called out, wincing as he rose to his feet.

Where Steve's body had been, only thousands of pieces of bone remained, along with a neatly folded silk robe.

"Oh, nice loot." Jack whistled as he walked slowly towards the robe.

Matt and Blake struggled to their feet, groaning as they dusted dirt and bone powder from their clothes.

"I think we need a new plan for that fight," Blake commented as he looked around. His shield had been completely shattered by Emily's spell.

"Same." Matt picked up his broken bow, looking at his sister. "At least no one got injured."

"Hey, I got pretty hurt." Jack was already holding the robes, looking them over and muttering.

"Well, no one that matters," Blake joked halfheartedly, and the group broke out laughing.

Watching them laughing, victorious, Ryan couldn't help but smile to himself. He really was glad to see Blake and his group hadn't fallen to his dungeon, and he had to admit, it seemed they got a lot more enjoyment out of it than the other groups that had been through.

Maybe making the dungeon easier on them wasn't doing them a favor. Maybe he should just let the adventurers test their skills.

"You all did well, and I'm proud of all of you," Karan said, standing near the exit. She smiled brightly at her teammates. They were beaten, and battered, and missing two pieces of gear, but they had all survived. "Now, let's get out of the dungeon and see just how much we gained today."

And with that, the group turned and left Ryan's boss room.

"I like them," Ryan whispered to Erin as they made their way back through his dungeon.

"Me too," Erin said, preparing her silk cloth bed atop him and letting out a yawn. "Hopefully some of the groups tomorrow are just like them."

She stretched and pulled her cloth over herself.

"I had a lot of fun today," she said.

"So did I."

Ryan sat in silence – save for Erin's snoring – for a long while after Blake's team left. With their departure, everyone outside of the dungeon left as well, leaving Ryan's entrance empty.

The night was quickly approaching, casting long shadows and making his dungeon's entrance almost seem to come to life. As he thought back to Blake's team and their dungeon dive, Ryan found himself strangely content and happy.

Maybe, just maybe, he could get used to life as a dungeon.

Chapter Thirty-Four

Spirits were high as the team made their way back to town. They had done it. They had defeated the dungeon.

"You know, Jack, those robes are for a mage class." Karan prodded the thief, who was still clutching the robes, as they neared the town. The robes were the only loot they had gained that wasn't simple coin, and Blake was curious as to how they would split it.

Luckily, the guild tax only applied to the coin they received in the dungeon, so the cost of the robes wasn't taken into account. If they had been, everyone's coin would have gone to the tax, and they still wouldn't have had enough to cover the robes.

"Are you sure?" Jack asked. "I'm sure there has to have been at least one thief that has decided to wear robes instead of leathers." He looked at the group, and everyone knew what he was thinking. He just didn't want to admit it.

"Positive. Robes are mage class armor." Karan shot Jack a wicked smile. "Now, why don't you continue your chivalrous nature, and give them to Emily?"

At her words, Emily suddenly turned bright red, and began looking everywhere other than in Jack's direction.

"It's… no, he… he did enough." She glanced shyly at Jack. Everyone had been surprised at the lengths he had gone to in order to save Emily. Mana exhaustion was a very real risk, and had Karan not been in the group, Jack could have been in grave danger.

"I know it's not much, Jack, but can I buy you a drink? For saving Em?" Matt placed a hand gently on the thief's shoulder and shot him a smile.

Blake could tell Jack's action had changed everyone's perspective of him, even Karan's. Maybe not all thieves were bad. Maybe Jack was an exception.

"Sure, and then perhaps we can discuss how Em can get the robes from me?' He shot her a wink and a grin, causing her to blush even more.

All right, maybe Jack isn't an exception.

"You know, Jack, I didn't want to have to do this." Karan pulled out her pendant, and with a wicked grin, pointed it at Jack. Her pendant glowed red, and Jack fell to the ground, gasping.

"As team leader, I'm able to enforce a few guild laws." She walked over to the gasping Jack. "One of which is the difference between 'need' and 'want' on loot."

Karan knelt down and grabbed the robes from Jack.

"Emily needs these robes. You just want them. Therefore, she gets them."

The glow from her pendant faded, and Jack stood shakily to his feet.

"Do I at least still get a drink, Matt?" he asked the archer, who was glaring at him.

"Not after that comment," Matt said.

"Well, can't fault a thief for trying." Jack shot Blake a smile. "How about you, buddy? Gonna give me any reward for being awesome?"

Blake chuckled as he returned the smile. "I'm Bronze Eleven. I'm pretty sure I have the least amount to offer here."

"Oh ho, my dear friend." The thief draped his arm around Blake's neck. "You have information. How about you tell me about that super awesome item the dungeon dropped?"

"You know I can't." Blake's voice took on a tinge of sorrow. He really liked his teammates and wished he could tell them. And they definitely seemed trustworthy. Jack had literally risked his life to save Emily on their first dive. But Blake knew better.

"I can give you the copper coins I got today, if you want." Blake reached into his pocket and pulled them out. He would already have to wait a month for a new shield; he could give the thief his share for the day. If anyone had earned it, it had been Jack.

"You should save the coin you gained tonight, to begin preparing for class gear." Karan was looking at the two, observing the exchange. "Having full class gear once you hit Silver is really important. Only fools don't save up for their class gear."

Class gear was gear adventurers could get from the guild shops once they reached Silver and chose their class. The armor was infused with neutral mana and served to slightly augment the adventurer who was equipped with it. The more pieces of class gear an adventurer had, the more they would benefit. However, even with the guild discount, the gear was still rather pricey.

"That reminds me, Jack. Why don't you have any class gear?" Karan asked.

Her comment made the thief wince before he answered sheepishly.

"I may have a slight problem."

"Gambling or drinking?" she asked.

"Can you really have just one?" He grinned.

"Typical thief," Karan said, and the rest of the group laughed, even as Jack just shook his head helplessly.

"Tell you what, Jack." Karan paused just outside the gates to the dungeon town. "For saving Emily, I'll buy your gear."

"Wha—"

Karan held up her hand, silencing him.

"But you will need to continue to do your best in the dungeon, and help me keep the team alive and growing."

"Of cour—"

"And, if you keep up your thief-like greedy antics, I may just take the armor back, and charge you interest."

"Deal."

Jack held out a hand to Karan, a genuine smile spread across his face. Karan took his hand and shook it, smiling back at him. Blake could tell Karan really cared about making sure their team not only survived the dungeon but grew together. He couldn't help but wonder why she hadn't been a part of a team or serving as one of the guild's healers before forming their current party.

"Good. As for the rest of you," Karan glanced at Blake and Matt, "I'll replace your shield and bow, just this once."

Blake's mouth dropped open.

How much coin does Karan have?

They had walked away from their dungeon dive with only a handful of copper coins, split among the five of them. Blake had resigned himself to having to fight shieldless for at least a month.

"But please do treat your gear better in the future. Your gear is your life. An adventurer, no matter how strong, is a lot weaker without their gear."

"Thank you," Matt and Blake responded in unison, bowing their heads to Karan.

The cleric smiled at them, though Blake was certain he saw a hint of sadness in her eyes. Now he really was curious to learn more about her.

"All right. With all of that said, how about we go have a celebratory round at the inn? On me."

"Huzzah." Jack jumped up, his fist shooting into the air.

"Except for you, Jack. I'm not going to enable you."

The group laughed as they all walked towards the inn. Even in the torch-lit town, the inn was easy to find. It was the loudest, most populated place. Adventurers really did love to drink.

Chapter Thirty-Five

"So, have you guys checked your experience triangles?" Karan asked.

Blake's team sat around a wooden table, each with a mug of strong liquor in front of them. Except for Jack, who was begrudgingly sipping on a hot chocolate drink. At least Karan had bought him something other than water.

"Oh, I completely forgot," Blake said, holding out his right hand, palm up.

The others all did the same, willing their triangles into existence. Golden lines danced across Blake's hand, forming an inverted triangle. The bottom triangle was filled with golden energy, and the outline of a '3' was visible inside of it.

"Wow, three levels?" Blake had barely gained any experience with his father on the first dungeon dive, likely because they hadn't been linked as he was now, with his team.

"What, you got three levels? Man, I didn't get any experience." Jack, already in a foul mood, took a sip of his hot chocolate. Blake tried to take the thief's anger seriously, but as Jack pulled his mug away, leaving a dark chocolate mustache, Blake couldn't help but snort.

"Hmm, I only gained... maybe a fifth of a level?" Matt said, looking down at his palm.

"I got at least a level," Emily said with a smile.

"As I told all of you before, our experience is going to be split to ensure we all grow at the same rate. That means until you are all Silver, Jack won't get any experience. I won't start gaining experience until all of you are Gold."

"No experience, couldn't even keep my loot, this suc—"

"You're getting free class armor and get the joy of helping train three new adventurers." Jack's comment was met with Karan's hand on his shoulder. Judging by the look on Jack's face, Karan was applying some pressure.

"You're right. Sorry, great for all of you. I can't wait for you guys to grow into Silver, so I can start leveling again." He muttered the last part, but the group laughed at his comment nonetheless.

"Go ahead and pour your experience into your level," Karan urged them all, with a smile on her face.

"Here goes nothing," Blake said.

He had never leveled up before. What would it be like?

He remembered when he first joined the guild and became a Bronze Eleven adventurer. The rush of mana in his body had been exhilarating. He could feel the mana flowing through him, and when he mentally assigned eighty percent of it to his body, as his father instructed, the rush of power had been amazing. Everything had seemed to suddenly enhance: his speed, his strength, even all of his senses. And that was just at Bronze Eleven.

Full of excitement, Blake pulled up his level triangle on his left palm and clasped the two glowing triangles together. Bright light enveloped his fist as his experience pushed into his level triangle. As each level was unlocked, Blake could feel his body pulling more and more mana from the air around him.

When the light faded, he separated his palms, and looked at his left hand. Bronze Eight, which meant he now had sixty-five mana points he could use, instead of his previous fifty. He mentally assigned eighty percent to his body, feeling it surge through him. While it wasn't as large a gain as the first time, he could definitely tell there was an improvement.

"Good, now Blake's Bronze Eight, Emily is Bronze Seven, and Matt is on his way to Bronze One," Karan said, smiling kindly at the team. "In about a month, I'm sure each of you will be ready to ascend to Silver."

"You know, this is so unfair." Jack was back to complaining. "It took me years to reach Silver, just running around town, slaving away for the smallest amount of experience here or there. Now, just because there is a new dungeon, these guys get to jump to Silver in a month. Ugh."

"Don't fault them for your misfortune, Jack. New dungeons are rare, and they prove a great opportunity to quickly grow the members of the Adventurers' Guild. That being said, this dungeon will likely kill more than a few adventurers who are just starting out. Your path may have been slow, but it wasn't a constant life-or-death fight. Their path is more dangerous and difficult than yours has been."

"Yeah, yeah, you're right, as always."

Jack's mood really was sour, and Blake had to wonder if the thief was really mad about the whole situation, or just his lack of liquor. Judging from his longing looks at Blake's drink, he guessed it was the liquor.

"Now, how about we all enjoy the rest of the night, and then get some rest?" Karan said. "We have three days before it is our turn in the dungeon again, and in that time I want all of you fully rested and geared."

Karan smiled at the table and raised her mug in the air.

"Here's to a successful first run, and many more to follow."

They raised their mugs and met hers in the air, even Jack.

"Huzzah!"

The rest of the night devolved into more drinks than Blake could count, and as he stumbled towards his tent from the inn, he was certain he was going to regret it in the morning.

However, even after he got in his tent, world spinning, Blake found himself smiling. Or at least, he thought he was smiling. Maybe he was frowning upside down?

"I'm going to make you proud, Father," he slurred. He closed his eyes, and darkness called to him.

Chapter Thirty-Six

The group stood outside of the dungeon, once again preparing for their dive. The three days of rest had gone by quickly, and everyone seemed in high spirits. They were eager to dive again.

They had met late in the day outside of the dungeon, knowing the other groups would take a while to clear it. While the first day had resulted in zero casualties on the dives, it seemed the later groups had met with more difficulty. Blake wasn't sure what it was, but each day had seen one or two deaths, along with some rather serious injuries. As such, teams were taking longer on each dive, and some weren't even attempting to fight Steve

"Fifty gold pieces," Karan said. "I like to think it was a good investment."

She shared a smile with Jack, who looked down at his new armor. As promised, Karan had bought him his full set of class gear, as well as a new shield for Blake and a new bow for Matt.

"I would have gotten Blake and Matt a class piece as well, but since I don't know their affinity or what class they will choose at Silver, I couldn't."

Class gear started out basic, with neutral mana racing through to help augment an adventurer's class. However, for a little more gold, it was possible to buy gear that was not only class, but also affinity specific. This gear increased the effectiveness of any affinity use, while also decreasing the mana cost to use these skills.

"I knew you were going to get me the class gear, but the wind thief set?" Jack's face was filled with adoration, and were those tears in his eyes? "I really don't know what to say, Karan."

Blake grinned. That was a first. Jack always had something to say.

"'Thank you' is always nice." Karan offered him a smile – a genuine one. She looked the thief up and down. He was clad now in a fine set of leather gear with strange, swirling, wind-like traces of silver throughout. On his chest, as well as the gloves he wore, sat smoky, crystalline stones. The stone was a type of quartz known to boost wind affinity.

"Thank you, Karan." Jack drew his daggers, also brand new. He twirled the blades, each set with a crystal on the pommel. He spun them skillfully, eyes looking lovingly at the blades. "I promise you, I will do my best."

"That's all I ask," Karan said.

Her voice held the faintest hint of sorrow as her eyes once again seemed to skip to the past. Blake wasn't sure if the others had noticed, given how everyone was fawning over Jack's new gear. Just what *had* happened to Karan?

"Now, is everyone ready? Anything else you guys need to do before we begin our dive?" Karan suddenly asked, snapping out of it.

.

"I think we're good." Blake looked at the rest of his team, who all nodded.

"Yup," said Matt, who was stringing his new bow, caressing it lovingly. It was of uncommon quality, with reinforced steel on the limbs, ideal for close range fighting. Karan had likely taken account of Matt's tendency to use his bow as a staff when he couldn't land shots. She had also gotten Blake an uncommon iron shield, which would likely fare much better against the skeletal creatures. It was, however, heavier than Blake was used to.

"Agreed," Emily said. She had switched her basic adept robes for the silk robes that had dropped from Steve. They were a deep crimson, and of rare level. As Karan had mentioned, the robes were part of a mage's class armor, which meant Emily was already better equipped than Matt and Blake. *Talk about lucky.*

"All right, well, the last team should almost be finished," Karan said.

She glanced at the entrance, motioning towards Rasha. The assassin was impatiently tapping his foot, looking down at the sphere in his hand. Even from a distance, Blake could see one of the five crystals had gone dark, and two of the others were dimming and flickering.

"Doesn't look like they fared well," Jack said.

His words were somber, and the rest of the group grew quiet. The cleric standing next to Rasha kept peering into the darkness of the dungeon, worry on her face. She was Gold level, just like Karan.

However, while Karan wore basic robes, the cleric the guild had hired to help heal adventurers was clad in fine white robes. These robes were embroidered with golden silk, depicting the scales of the Goddess of Justice. Blake wasn't sure if her obvious anxious attitude was because she was worried for the adventurers, or discomfort about the dark dungeon.

Apparently, members of the church did not like the fact that a darkness dungeon had been allowed to exist. However, no one dared to challenge Alice's word when it came to what dungeons could and couldn't be left in existence.

"Here they come," Jack said as a light shone from within the dungeon's maw.

The leader of the group, a Silver Five Warrior, was bleeding profusely. His left arm hung limp, while in his right hand he held a torch. Many groups had started bringing torches to help light the dungeon and burn the plant room. That poison ivy caused an extremely irritating rash that lasted for two days. Luckily, as promised, Jack had provided Blake's team with a salve to heal the rash.

"That doesn't look good." Jack motioned past the leader, who was missing both his swords, towards the next figure.

He was a Silver Eight knight, their tank, the member of a party meant to draw the enemies attention, and protect the other, lesser armored members of the party. His armor was dented in countless places, and a bladed piece of bone – one of Steve's – was lodged deep in his arm. Another adventurer, a Bronze warrior, was helping the knight carry their fourth member. He was barely conscious, and dark blood oozed from countless wounds. *Zombie bites.*

"Did they try to fight Steve after being so injured?" Blake wondered aloud.

"Aye, it seems they got a little too confident after their last go-around," Jack mused. "I'm guessing they thought everyone else's stories were exaggerations."

The first four groups had apparently had a much easier time in the dungeon than Blake's group and those that followed. He wasn't sure why, but they had all seemed overly confident about how easy the dungeon was. *Guess this time they found out that isn't the case.*

"Remember, everyone, a dungeon is always evolving," Karan said as she watched the cleric begin healing the group. "Even if you have an easy time on a dive, the dungeon can change before the next one. A dungeon is always figuring out new ways to take down adventurers. It is living, and it will be challenging. Never, ever drop your guard." Her eyes were far away again. "Becoming too relaxed, too confident, will only lead to death."

The group turned away from the scene before them, the very air seeming heavier with Karan's words. Blake looked at each member, noting the looks on their faces, seeing the specter of fear creeping back on the group. The lighthearted excitement they had felt was fading quickly.

"Welp, that was deep." Jack was the first to break the silence, putting a sly smile on his face as he looked at everyone. "But the difference between those groups, and ours," he twirled his blades, small winds whipping up around them, "is that we have the most awesome thief around." He shot a wink at Karan, followed by a sincere smile. "And a leader dumb enough to spend a small fortune on making sure the thief is ready to keep everyone safe."

Jack sheathed his daggers, sending a light blast of air at

everyone around. "Now, how about we go work up a sweat, and cool off tonight with a nice, hearty round of drinks?"

"You're still limited to hot chocolate, to match that hot air of yours," Karan replied, offering Jack a sly smile. Just like that, the mood once again turned around, and Blake could tell everyone was excited to take the dungeon on once again.

Chapter Thirty-Seven

"Ugh, what is with these guys today?" Ryan groaned.

He was in a foul mood. Not even skeletal fight club could improve it. The last four adventurer groups had all been unusually stupid, and as a result, each team had lost at least one adventurer. Ryan appreciated the experience, he really did, but the deaths had been completely avoidable.

"Well, you did make the dungeon really easy on them last time." Erin's voice was quiet, and Ryan knew she was just as upset as he was. While she was a strong advocate for his need to kill adventurers in order to level up, they were both upset over how the deaths had happened.

"Yeah, but still. Even at regular strength, all the rest of the teams over the past four days were at least cautious," Ryan said. "Seriously, that last group just casually walked up to Steve, even with all of those wounds. The guy with the ratbie bites was already showing weakness. Why didn't they just turn back?"

He knew why they hadn't turned back. He had heard their conversation, obviously, before they entered the room.

Their leader had convinced the group to just kill Steve quickly, and then they could get out and treat their injuries. After all, their tank was confident he could block all of Steve's attacks, and the rest of the team would be able to easily just defeat him.

That was how they had managed the fight last time. What they didn't know, though, was last time Ryan had severely limited Steve's fighting powers. The adventurers were completely unprepared for Steve's long-range attack, and with a weakened team member, they were lucky they only lost one person.

"I told you—"

"Don't," Ryan said. "Not now, Rin."

Ryan couldn't stand to hear her say she told him so. He had become used to one or two adventurers falling in his dungeon every day. He understood it was necessary for him to grow stronger, and they knew the risks. But these last four teams, their deaths had seemed pointless.

And Ryan knew he was to blame. Just when he thought he was getting past his moral dilemma, the guilt of setting these teams up for failure and pointless deaths had returned.

"I'm sorry, Ryan."

Erin's emotions flooded into their bond. He could tell she was really beating herself over the latest development. She likely blamed herself for his pain. She was his guide, his teacher, after all.

"It's fine, hun."

He calmed himself. Just one more team today, and then he could try and sort through his emotions.

"On the plus side, we're Bronze Four now." It really wasn't much of a plus side, in Ryan's mind, but he knew telling Erin might help cheer her up a bit. Over four days, he had killed eleven adventurers out of the hundred that had entered. Nine had been Bronze, and two had been Silver. With the last Bronze member he killed from the last team, he had managed to jump to Bronze Four.

Two ranks in less than a week has to be good. Right?

"Well, I guess that does help a little," Erin said begrudgingly.

"Should we do anything with our points?" Ryan asked.

He had eighty-five now, meaning he was currently sitting on twenty spare points. If Erin didn't want him to increase the difficulty anymore, that just meant he might be able to improve his skeletal fight club even more. That thought lifted his mood just a little. He had no qualms killing off his mobs for evolution, after all.

"Not today. Maybe give them another week to get stronger."

"Works for me."

His voice held a little more cheer than he intended, as his mind was already racing towards the possibilities his extra points could mean for skeletal fight club. So far, his evolution pits had given him a new skrat and skuirrel, each costing two points instead of one. He could only imagine what else his pits could provide him with. Maybe he would try with his—

"Oh, look who it is." Erin's voice had taken on an excited tone, and pulled Ryan from his musings. Skeletal fight club could wait just a little longer.

"Who?" He turned his attention to his entrance. He had been purposefully avoiding it, wanting the poor last group to be out of his sight. Seeing their beaten state made him feel guilty.

"Blake." Sure enough, the young fighter was standing with his group next to the strange dark-clad man who was standing outside the dungeon. Ryan knew his name was Rasha thanks to the speech given on the first day the adventurers had begun diving. However, he knew nothing else about the man.

When Ryan had tried to look at Rasha's information earlier, all that had come up were question marks. Maybe he couldn't see his information because Rasha hadn't actually entered his influence? Erin hadn't had an explanation for him either, so it was something he tried not to think about. However, Ryan hated not knowing something.

"Thank the Goddess," Ryan said. "His team makes me smile."

Ryan's mood was improving as he watched Blake's team touch their strange pendants to the disk held by Rasha. He could feel excitement filling him as Blake and his team marched towards the opening of his dungeon.

Something about Blake's team – their comradery, the sense of accomplishment they had given off after their first dive – made Ryan immensely excited. He really liked their team, and maybe they would serve as the distraction he needed.

"Here they come," he said, and through his bond, he could feel Erin's excitement as she settled down to watch their favorite group in action.

Chapter Thirty-Eight

"You can do it," Jack called out to Matt and Emily while he stood back with Karan.

The group had sent the three Bronze members to the center of Ryan's first room, but their two strongest, Karan and Jack, simply stayed back to watch.

"Oh, looks like Matt got a new bow," Erin said, and sure enough, it looked like the archer had replaced the bow he broke. Having absorbed it, Ryan knew his old bow had been a low-quality common item. This new bow looked much better.

"And look at Blake's shield," she went on.

The adventurer was sporting a brand new, metal shield.

Nice.

"Aww, Emily is wearing the robe Steve dropped," Erin said.

Ryan paused in his inspection of the adventurers. The robe was nice quality, a deep crimson silk – a great item for sure. But he still disliked the mage who had owned the original set of robes. Honestly, Ryan was sure Blake had to have remembered those robes as well.

"Just try to focus, Matt," Jack called out.

Jack's encouragement was met with a curse of frustration as Matt let fly another arrow, only to miss a skuirrel. The beast leapt at Matt, but Blake was already moving. The flying skuirrel glanced off of Blake's shield, and clattered onto the floor. The mob was missing a leg and tail now but was still ready to fight.

"Come on, Blake, what type of block was that?" Jack laughed, while Karan watched silently, her eyes taking in the scene around them.

Skuirrels were launching themselves at all different angles. Matt was trying, unsuccessfully, to shoot them. Blake was trying with mixed results to block them all, but wasn't launching his own attacks. Perhaps he was getting used to his new shield? Meanwhile, Emily stood next to the two men, her wooden stick in hand, looking nervous.

"You just going to sit there talking, or you going to help us?" Blake called back, in the middle of blocking another flying skuirrel. This time, he got his shield positioned properly, and the poor mob shattered.

"Eh, you got this. Besides, I'm doing this for you. Helping ya'll get stronger and whatnot." Jack had a wide grin on his face as he stood lazily near the entrance to the first room.

Ryan was curious about the thief's new gear. While the others seemed to have just replaced what had been broken, Jack seemed to have undergone an entire wardrobe change. Unfortunately, Ryan couldn't inspect the gear the adventurer was wearing. While he could see the adventurers' names, ranks, and classes, their mana restricted him from understanding what they were wearing. The only way he could figure out their gear was if they died and he absorbed it.

"Then shut up until we finish, damned thief," Matt yelled across the room, failing once again to hit a skuirrel.

Erin winced as she watched the shot go wide.

"So close," Ryan quipped, watching the arrow land a foot away from the skuirrel.

The archer did seem to be getting a little better at aiming at the mobs, but at this rate, Blake was going to kill them all with his shield before Matt managed a good shot.

"It's your turn, Emily," Karan said in a sweet, firm voice.

Emily, the poor adept, nearly leapt out of her boots at the sound of it.

"But– "

"No buts, Emily," Karan said. "Just believe in yourself."

"You got this, Em," Matt said. He put the arrow he had drawn back in his quiver at his side, motioning towards the adept.

"Don't worry, Em, Blake's a surprisingly good meat shie—"

Jack's words were cut short as Karan punched him in the stomach. Judging by the way he bent over, she had hit him hard.

"Worth it," the thief groaned, before falling to his knees.

"Just focus on the target and envision your mana bursting on it," Karan said. "Your wand will help channel it in the direction you need, but ultimately, your mana will obey your wishes."

"If you say so," Emily muttered. From the tone in her voice, Ryan figured Emily really didn't believe in herself.

"You can do it, Emily," Erin said. The fairy was watching the scene intently, cheering the young girl on.

Seven skuirrels remained in the room, three having been smashed by Blake's shield. One of the remaining seven was still missing a leg and tail, courtesy of Blake's aggressive blocking. Ryan nudged the injured mob forward, and the poor creature stumbled into the open, directly towards Emily.

"Skuirrel," Matt called out, directing his sister's attention to the injured beast.

It was moving fast, but nowhere near as quickly as the others. Emily pointed her wand towards the skuirrel, and without warning, part of the skuirrel burst apart.

"Huzzah!" the entire team cried out as Matt and Blake patted Emily on the back. Ryan held his skuirrels off for a moment, letting them celebrate.

"That was nice of you," Erin whispered, and Ryan could feel her joy through their bond.

"Yeah, well, I want them to get stronger."

Ryan was certain he would be blushing if he had cheeks right now. As it was, he could tell his form was glowing a little brighter than normal.

"You are the perfect dungeon." She gave him a hug, and he glowed even brighter.

"Awww, I'm nothing without you, Rin." The fairy pulled away, face red.

Ha. Ryan hated when his emotions got out of hand, but he really enjoyed making Erin blush.

"Psh, you're just saying that." She hit him lightly and laughed her beautiful laugh.

Ryan didn't trust himself to speak, so gave his mobs the order to resume their attacks on the adventurers. However, he was so caught up he didn't pass the orders right, and all six mobs came out of hiding at once to attack the group.

"Oops," he groaned.

All six were out of their hiding holes before Ryan realized what he had done. *Too late to turn back now.*

"Hey, Em, looks like you got their attention," Jack warned. He was back on his feet, daggers drawn.

"Can I help them out, oh wise and powerful team leader?" he asked.

"Well, you do owe me for the armor," Karan said as she motioned towards the larger group of mobs. "You guys focus on the two to your left. Jack will handle the others."

The three adventurers in the middle turned towards the approaching two mobs, Matt with an arrow drawn, Emily with wand raised, and Blake with his shield at the ready. Ryan was sure they would be fine now. He was more interested in how Jack would—

"What the hell?" Ryan said.

Jack walked casually towards the group, wind swirling around his form, his eyes sparkling with excitement. He was twirling his daggers in his hands, and Ryan noticed the daggers had crystals in them as well.

Silver lines glowed across Jack's armor, with the socketed stones on the daggers, his chest, and his hands seeming to glow as well. Without warning, he stopped spinning his daggers, and made a slashing motion towards the four skuirrels.

A blade of wind cut through the air and covered the distance between Jack and the mobs in an instant. Suddenly, the skuirrels were severed in half, and Jack laughed.

"I freaking love this class gear," he said.

He turned towards Karan as the winds around him began to

fade. The cleric simply put her hand over her mouth as she shook her head.

"You show off way too much, Jack." Her voice was stern, but Ryan could tell she was hiding her smile with her hand. Unfortunately for her, she couldn't hide the smile in her eyes.

"You like it when I show off." Jack offered her a wink and walked back to the fallen skuirrels to grab the coins they had dropped.

"Only in your dreams," Karan responded with a laugh.

The thief grinned and started heading towards the next room.

"Hey, it's good to have dreams," he called back as neared the exit. "Now, let's clear the rest of this dungeon."

Chapter Thirty-Nine

"All right, it seems Steve is weak to magic," Ryan announced.

He and Erin had just watched Blake's team decimate Steve without taking so much as a scratch.

"They've just figured out a good strategy," Erin demurred.

Ryan could tell Erin was trying to build his self-esteem back up. The boss fight had left him in a sour mood.

He loved Blake's team, he really did. But what they just did to Steve, well, it left him feeling a little angry. Their first time against Steve had been so enjoyable, and their cheers and emotions of elation after his defeat had made it seem worth it. This time, they beat him in under a minute. They didn't even look like they were trying.

"Strategy? Blake just taunted Steve into launching his bones at him, and the moment Steve attacked, Emily blasted him to pieces." Ryan would have been tearing out his hair if he had any. Steve was supposed to put up a fight. And Jack and Karan hadn't even participated in the battle. *Seriously, how is this even fair?*

"Wait, aren't you happy none of them died? Why are you so upset?" Erin tried to talk logically, but Ryan could feel her emotions. She was just as upset as he was that the fight hadn't lasted longer.

"They weren't supposed to make it look that easy," Ryan sighed. "Especially after last time."

"Well, Steve really doesn't have the most complex fighting pattern," Erin said, rubbing her tiny chin.

She has a good point there.

Every fight, Steve just stood in the middle of the room, watching the door. When adventurers walked in, he usually targeted the weakest or easiest target with his spikes, and then took advantage of the chaos that ensued.

This time around, after they all entered the room, Blake had simply walked forward, directly in front of Steve, until the boss had attacked him. *Boring.*

"And—" Ryan wasn't just upset about how quickly Steve had died, after all.

"—there's an and?" Erin cut in, which did little more than fuel his frustration.

"Yes, there's an and."

He paused, seeing if she would interrupt him. When she remained quiet, he continued.

"*And*, Steve dropped the ruby amulet."

When Ryan had assigned loot to Steve, he had assigned all the rare pieces the mage had been wearing, along with the chance to drop gold coins. The coins had a much higher percent chance of dropping, followed by the silk robes, then silk boots, then silk gloves, a ruby ring, and finally, the ruby amulet. They had had the quickest fight and gotten the rarest piece of loot off Steve.

"Well, that amulet looks really nice on Emily," Erin said. Her hand was near her own neck, which was bare.

Was Erin jealous of Emily's amulet? Ryan felt his anger subsiding, replaced instead with amusement.

"Would you like a ruby amulet, hun?" His words caused her hand to fly away from her neck surprisingly fast.

"I, uh, no." She looked down sheepishly. "Ruby is the stone of fire. As a celestial, I prefer opal."

Huh, so the stones have something to do with affinities, do they?

"Aw, come on, Karan," Jack was moaning. "The chance of her having a fire affinity—"

Jack's complaining pulled Ryan's attention away from Erin and back to the group of adventurers. They were walking back through the dungeon, and while the others seemed in good spirits, Jack seemed upset.

"Why are you even complaining over this, Jack?" Karan said. "You're a wind affinity, and you have full class gear." Her tone signaled she was already tired of this conversation.

"Yeah, but Emily already got the last big drop from the dungeon," Jack went on, oblivious. "Let's sell the amulet and split the gold. That thing has to be worth ten gold."

Karan's eyes flashed.

"Even after guild tax," she said, "you and the others are making a decent amount of coin—"

"Just coppers and silv—"

Jack stopped as Karan reached around her neck and pulled out a crystal pendant. For some reason Ryan couldn't understand, the thief seemed scared of it. After a moment, Karan put the pendant away before speaking.

"Emily can keep the piece for now. Mages can use amulets to greatly amplify their magical abilities. Amulets on physical classes just offer slight protection in the form of that affinity. If Emily does have a fire affinity when she becomes Silver, she will be the best suited to use the amulet. If she doesn't, but Matt or Blake do, they will get the amulet. If no one has a fire affinity, then, and only then, will we sell it."

Jack was unfazed.

"Ah, but the price on the market will—"

"Jack, keep this up and you leave this dungeon naked." Karan had the crystal pendant from around her neck in her hand again.

"You'd like that," Jack mumbled as he looked away.

"What was that?"

"Nothing, ma'am." He put his hands in his pockets dejectedly and began walking faster towards the exit.

"That's what I thought." Karan had a sly smile on her face. "Just for that, I'll get marshmallows for you in your hot chocolate tonight."

The rest of the party started laughing, while Jack let out a string of curses under his breath. It was quiet enough that the others couldn't hear, but Ryan heard, and was somewhat impressed by the thief's creativeness.

"Well, that was definitely interesting," Ryan said to Erin as the group neared the dungeon's exit.

"They definitely do seem to really get along as a group."

"Though what is this hot chocolate Karan mentioned?" Ryan was really curious. And what were marshmallows? Jack seemed to hate the idea, but the rest of the group thought it was funny. He turned his attention to Erin, hoping she would answer his question, but instead, she was rolling around on the floor, laughing. Well that just wasn't helpful at all.

Ryan let out an internal sigh and watched Blake's group exit. The dark-clad man who had been standing outside all day, as well as the cleric, both seemed mildly impressed that Blake's group was uninjured as they exited. The cleric offered Karan a wide smile before the cleric turned and headed towards the town with them. Rasha remained, staring with a scowl at the group as they walked away.

"Seems the mutt is growing," Rasha whispered, before he melted into the darkness of the night.

"Well, that wasn't ominous at all," Ryan said, before turning his attention back to his dungeon.

Erin seemed to have fallen asleep following her fit of laughter, meaning Ryan could turn his focus towards his favorite pastime. He had one week before he was going to make his dungeon a little tougher, and he needed to optimize that time in skeletal fight club.

Chapter Forty

"Where did these come from?" Erin exclaimed.

Her voice was filled with excitement, and Ryan couldn't help but feel proud. However, he knew he couldn't tell her the truth.

Rule number one: never talk about skeletal fight club.

"I think they just evolved after fighting so many adventurers. One day last week, when I was reabsorbing my fallen mobs, I just had two new types."

That was a terrible lie. But he really wasn't ready to share his skeletal fight club with Erin, nor the fact that over the past week, he had been training his stronger mobs against each other. By the time he hit Silver, he was certain he would have another tier of skrat and skuirrel unlocked.

"Hmm, so you're going to add some of these..." Erin trailed off, unsure of what to call Ryan's new mobs.

He had summoned one of each to show her, following their discussion on how to make the dungeon harder. They had waited just long enough to allow each group to pass through one more time; now that the final team had left for the day, they were beginning the upgrades.

Not only had most of the teams managed to find replacement adventurers, but they had also been much more cautious in his dungeon over the past few days, resulting in only two new casualties. The two deaths had been to Steve, but because they were both low-ranked Bronze, Ryan hadn't really gained much experience from their deaths. He wasn't too upset about that fact, but it had prompted Erin to remind him it was time to make the dungeon a little more difficult, especially since he had twenty points to spend. Twenty points she didn't know he was using to fuel skeletal fight club. Rule number one, after all.

"I call this one a victorious skuirrel." Ryan had the mob stand on its two feet, displaying its new form.

Unlike the original skuirrels, the victorious skuirrel was longer and sleeker looking. Its bones were harder, yet thinner, giving it increased speed and durability. It had also developed sharp edges on all of its bones, which would serve nicely against adventurers.

"That works for me. What about that one?" Erin asked. The only obvious option for Erin to be referencing was of course the skrat variant.

"This is a champion skrat," Ryan said proudly.

The champion skrats stood almost twice as large as a regular skrat and had thicker bones that seemed to be developing almost plate-like qualities. As such, they weren't as fast as a regular skrat, but could take and dish out more damage.

"All right, and since they are evolutions, I'm guessing they cost two mob points apiece?" Erin asked.

"Correct." Ryan wasn't sure if she had forgotten the rules she mentioned to him, or if she was simply confirming the cost. As much as he loved the fairy, he was guessing she had forgotten.

As Erin had explained, mobs that were evolutions cost 1.5 times the cost of the mob they evolved from, rounded up. Since skrats and skuirrels both only cost one point, their new versions were still extremely cheap at two points apiece.

"Are you going to put the infested ratbie back into the dungeon as well?" Erin asked.

Her words pulled Ryan away from his proverbial back patting; he had completely forgotten about that mob. His only mob so far to evolve naturally, the infested ratbies cost eight points, but had a paralyzing toxin.

"Oh yeah," he said. "I was going to replace the two ratbies in the second room with two infested ratbies."

"So, if two ratbies cost five apiece, that's ten points," Erin said, counting on her tiny fingers. "Two infested ratbies, at eight apiece, adds up to sixteen. That means you will be spending six more points and have fourteen points remaining to upgrade some of your skeletal mobs."

Ryan really hated that he was going to lose the ability to spend points freely in his skeletal fight club, but knew he needed to toughen up his dungeon just a little more. If he could keep six points free, he would at least be able to keep three mobs fighting in his evolution pits. Then, if he used the time it took him to refill his mob points after a battle to heal the victor, he should still be able to reach their next level before he hit Bronze One.

"Hello," Erin asked, tapping his surface. "Ryan?"

"Sorry, hun," Ryan said. "I was trying to figure out how best to implement the new mobs. I know I have twenty—"

"Fourteen after the infested ratbies."

"Yes, yes, fourteen after the infested ratbies," Ryan sighed. "Fourteen mob points left. I was thinking I would like to keep at least six points in reserve, to help me re-summon mobs faster after the dungeon is cleared."

That was a partial lie, as his dungeon was large enough that by the time the adventurers made their way from the boss room back to the entrance of his dungeon, he had nearly completely regained his mob points and was able to re-summon most of his mobs. However, he was certain Erin didn't know this.

"All right, so, with six in reserve, you will have eight mob points left to spend upgrading your skrats and skuirrels in your rooms."

Ha, she bought it.

Ryan was excited, but felt somewhat guilty about lying to her. He really wasn't sure why he was keeping it such a secret from her. Frustrated over his dilemma, he dropped a stalactite on his champion skrat.

"RYAN."

Erin's cry of outrage instantly reminded him why skeletal fight club was kept a secret. And, with her outburst, his guilt flew away as well.

"Sorry. Habit. Anyhoo, back to mobs. With those eight

points, I can either add in four of my new mobs, or perhaps add in one new victorious skuirrel in the first room, and upgrade some of the mobs in my second room?"

"What if you upgraded four of your ten skuirrels in your first room?" Erin suggested. "By doing that, you would have four victorious skuirrels and six regular skuirrel for a total of fourteen points. And then you could upgrade two of your ten skuirrels and two of your ten skrats in your second room?"

"See, this is why I love you, Rin. You are so amazingly helpful."

Maybe he was laying on the praise a little thick, but Erin's sudden mood spike through their bond made it all worth it.

"You're just saying that," she said.

"Nope, and watch, I'm going to upgrade it just like you said."

He stopped himself from pulling up his experience triangle until he collapsed his evolution tunnels, killing all the mobs. Their mob refund rushed into him. He had eight of his evolutions going at it, for a total of sixteen points. Killing them gave him eight mob points back instantly, and the remainder would be replaced shortly. His mob point regeneration rate had been steadily increasing as he grew stronger. At the same time, he dropped stalactites on the remaining upgraded mob he had summoned for Erin, as well as on his two ratbies, two skuirrels, two skrats in the second room, and four skuirrels in the first room.

"Ryan." Erin let out an exasperated sigh.

"What?"

"You know you can just absorb your mobs and get a full refund from them, right?" Erin said.

I can what?

"I am pretty sure you never told me that."

"Ugh, I swear I did. I worry sometimes what you would do without me."

Never happened, but I'm not about to argue that point with her.

"Obviously I would fail miserably, since I hate killing adventurers and all that." And with those words, Ryan could tell his mob points were back to max.

He quickly summoned his level triangle, to stop Erin from

replying. The triangle sprang into existence, and Ryan couldn't help but smile as he saw the bottom row. Only three triangles remained empty; he was so close to Silver.

The better part of the bottom of the triangle was filled with dark energy, and the number '38' shone brightly.

"Now, shall we get to work?" Ryan asked.

Erin nodded and Ryan began mentally making his changes. In his second room, he brought forth two infested ratbies. The zombie rats, with their mushroom growths, were even more grotesque and formidable looking than he remembered. As they were summoned, his points dropped down to twenty-two.

Next, he summoned two champion skrats and two victorious skuirrels, assigning them their name mentally as he did. His points dropped to fourteen, leaving him just enough points for his first room and skeletal fight club, as planned. He brought forth four new victorious skuirrels in his first room, watching his points drain to six.

Now, Ryan's first room had six skuirrels and four victorious skuirrels, costing fourteen points in total, while his second room had two infested ratbies, eight skuirrels, eight skrats, two victorious skuirrels, and two champion skrats, for a total of forty points in that room.

Steve still cost him twenty-five points, and Ryan was now using seventy-nine of his eighty-five points. Well, those other six points were going to be used in skeletal fight club. Ryan loved when a plan came together.

"Let's see how these new fights go," Ryan whispered to himself, his attention turning back to skeletal fight club.

"I'm excited to see how Blake's team does tomorrow," Erin replied sleepily as she curled up in the dungeon core room, pulling her silk cloth around her.

Oh, close call. Ryan had been thinking about his skeletal fight club fights, but as Erin fell asleep, he felt excitement filling him as well. He really was interested to see how the groups would do against his new and improved dungeon mobs.

Chapter Forty-One

"Erin!"

Ryan's voice was frantic as he tried to wake the snoring fairy.

"*Erin!*" he said with a little more force.

The fairy mumbled in her sleep and rolled over, pulling the silk tighter around her. Now was not the time for her to be a deep sleeper.

Well, I tried the easy way.

A small rock dropped from inside the dungeon core room, landing directly on Erin's stomach.

"Ouch!" Erin cried out as she woke, and then clutched at her stomach, gasping for air.

Oh, she's being so melodramatic. The rock wasn't that big.

"We might have a little problem," Ryan said.

He was trying to stay calm, but he could tell he was losing his cool. It was more than a little problem. From what he could tell, it might be a big problem.

Erin shook her head, pushing away the last bit of sleep, as she looked down into his core.

"What's going on hun?" she asked.

Knowing he had her attention, Ryan turned his focus back to the problem currently making its way through his dungeon, and pulled up the image for Erin to see as well.

"This… person." Ryan wasn't sure if they were a male or female.

In fact, he really wasn't sure about anything when it came to this invader. Ryan had been minding his own business, watching as a victorious skuirrel wrapped itself around a champion skrat, using its tail to pry away the thicker mob's bones. Then, all of a sudden, a figure had appeared at the entrance to his dungeon.

Over the past few weeks, Ryan had become used to adventurers arriving at his dungeon, and the two twins, Rasha and Sasha, often arrived earlier than most, and left after them.

Ryan was used to that, so when the figure appeared, at first he just figured it was one of those two. However, even as the battle in skeletal fight club reached its climax, Ryan's attention was suddenly jerked away. The strange figure had stepped into Ryan's dungeon.

The moment the figure did this, Ryan knew something was different, and it made him uneasy. First, the twins never set foot in his dungeon. Therefore, Ryan concluded this person was not one of the twins.

Second, this new intruder seemed to be completely cloaked in a swirling darkness, which Ryan couldn't see through. Third, when Ryan tried to pull up information on this figure, nothing came up. That wasn't a good sign. While he hadn't been able to see Rasha's information previously, that was because the dark clad female hadn't stepped foot in his dungeon. He had never not been able to see someone's information once they were inside.

In the time it took Ryan to wake Erin, the intruder had reached the first room.

"Who is he?" Erin asked, and Ryan mentally sent her a blank stare. If he knew that, he wouldn't be so worried.

"No idea. He just kind of showed up, and waltzed right in."

"Has he done anything? Said anything?"

"Nope. Hun, I have no idea about this figure," Ryan said. "I was hoping you might have an idea."

"Oh. Well—" She drew her face closer to Ryan's core, staring intently at the figure.

The shadow-clad form had paused in the middle of the first

room, and was completely still. It really disturbed Ryan. What's more, his mobs seemed afraid to attack. What was going on?

"Ryan, this might be bad." Erin's voice held something he hadn't heard in a while: fear.

"Why do you say—"

Dark projections shot out from the stranger. These tendrils snaked towards Ryan's mobs, and Ryan winced as they struck each of them at the same time. However, they didn't die. Instead, the moment the tendrils hit his mobs, he lost his connection with them.

"What did he just do?" Ryan whispered to Erin, watching as his mobs began to calmly walk towards the shadow-clad form.

"He's a necromancer," Erin hissed. "He can control the undead."

"He stole my mobs?"

That didn't seem right. How could his mobs be stolen? They were his! He made them, and he brought them to life, sort of.

"Yes, he stole your mobs." Erin went silent for a moment, leaving Ryan to watch the figure, and his army of stolen mobs, walk towards the exit of the first room, heading deeper into Ryan's dungeon.

"How?"

"Necromancers are a very rare class," Erin said quietly. "It is a class that is constantly feared and hunted by the church, a class that is viewed as evil."

"Go on."

Ryan could tell Erin really didn't like talking about necromancers, but he needed to know just what was going on. He hated the idea of someone in his dungeon that could steal his mobs.

"The reason the class is so..." Erin shuddered, "...vile, is because they use a darkness affinity to bring back the dead."

"Which is what I do as a darkness dungeon." Ryan remembered how upset Erin had been when he chose his affinity.

"Yes, but you don't bring back the dead. You create your own sets of dungeon bones, and animate those. You're a good darkness dungeon. This vile creature is an evil, disgusting thing."

Okay, Erin really doesn't like necromancers.

"You still haven't covered how he stole my mobs," Ryan said, becoming increasingly worried. The figure had reached the second room, his army of skeletons lined up behind him. He was moving slowly to the center of the room, and Ryan could guess what was about to happen next.

"Because of his darkness affinity, and his class, he can animate the dead," Erin said.

"Yes, you covered that, hun."

Ryan was getting impatient. The necromancer had just shot out his tendrils again, and stolen all of his mobs in the second room.

"Well, the thing about necromancers is that they can steal undead minions from others who are two tiers below them," Erin explained quickly, sensing his fear. "Even though you create your mobs from scratch, the bones are still based off once-living things. Therefore, they are free game for the necromancer."

Well, that's not good.

"So," Ryan thought aloud, "because I'm Bronze, he has to be at least gold to be a necromancer—"

"—who can steal all of your mobs."

The necromancer is at least Gold. Well, that's really not good.

"How can we stop him?" Ryan asked.

"Have you tried your favorite rock method?"

Erin must really hate this guy if she was recommending he dropped a stalactite on the necromancer's head. However, given the fact he was stealing Ryan's mobs, and his class was evil according to Erin, Ryan was happy to oblige.

"Got it."

Ryan didn't need any further prodding. He didn't like evil things, and the necromancer was definitely that. He willed a stalactite into being, and silently dropped the massive stone down onto the necromancer.

"That should—"

Swirling darkness shot from the necromancer to the nearest skeletal mobs, breaking them apart and pulling their bones above the necromancer's form. The bones created a swirling, skeletal shield, which easily blocked the stone spike Ryan had summoned.

Even as Ryan started summoning another, the necromancer started laughing. The sound was dark, and if Ryan could shiver, he would have.

"I see I have gotten your attention, dungeon." The necromancer's voice boomed around the room, coming from deep within the swirling darkness.

Ryan responded by dropping another stalactite, much larger than the first, onto the necromancer. The swirling bones blocked the stone, sending bone shards and rock pieces flying across the room.

"Please, your tricks will not work against me," the necromancer said, unfazed.

Ryan dropped a boulder this time. He was starting to feel the mana drain hitting him. He couldn't keep up this barrage.

Darkness shot out, pulling apart the remaining skeletal mobs the necromancer had stolen. The bones formed into a spike that shattered the boulder, sending its remains cascading harmlessly. The bones appeared to have tendrils of black mana snaking around them. If Ryan had to guess, the necromancer was reinforcing them to preserve them.

Well, that's new.

The necromancer brushed dust from his robe.

"Any ideas, Rin?" Ryan doubted sending Steve after the necromancer would do anything, and he didn't want his boss mob stolen.

"Absorb Steve, and close off the path to the boss room. Maybe he will leave."

That seemed like a good plan, as Ryan doubted they would be able to kill the necromancer. As a Bronze dungeon, he just wasn't that strong. He'd only killed that mage using the element of surprise.

Ryan absorbed Steve, and summoned a stone slab over the exit in the second room. He silently cursed how little mana he had. The necromancer turned towards the now sealed entrance, chuckling darkly.

"I can understand your fear, dungeon," the cruel voice said. "It is good of you to fear me."

The bone spike had joined the rest of the shards, creating a protective, swirling mass of bones around the necromancer's darkness-clad form.

Ryan knew he wouldn't be able to hurt him, but dropped another stalactite for good measure. Small stalactites were the least draining attack he could do. While he wanted to open a pit under the necromancer, he hadn't spread his influence far enough under his own dungeon to kill him with the fall, and he didn't have the time or mana to do so now. A small drop would simply anger the intruder, and Ryan suspected this was not a good idea.

The stalactite shattered against bone, and Ryan heard the necromancer sigh.

"Do you not hear me, dungeon? If you keep that up, I will kill you."

"Can he do that?" Ryan whispered, stopping the stalactite he was about to release.

"Yes," Erin whispered, and Ryan could tell from her swirling emotions that she was extremely scared, and angry, at the intruder.

The necromancer stood in silence for a few moments, waiting to see if Ryan would heed his warning. Ryan, of course, wasn't keen on the thought of dying. He was pretty sure he had done that already, and didn't want to do it again. As such, he made no further attempt to attack.

"Good, it seems you aren't stupid." The necromancer looked around the room, and Ryan wished he had the mana to drop the entire ceiling on him. "I'll keep this short, as I have wasted more time in here than I had planned."

Speaking of time… Ryan turned part of his attention to the entrance to his dungeon. He was certain it was nearing the time for Rasha or Sasha to arrive. Maybe they could help.

"I want to offer you a deal, dungeon." Whatever the deal was, Ryan was certain he wouldn't accept. "I want you to summon an army of skeletons for me to take control of. In return, I won't kill you, and I will bring you sacrifices, to help you grow stronger."

Yeah, like that will ever happen.

Ryan waited in silence. Even if he wanted to respond, he didn't have a way to talk to the necromancer.

After a few minutes, the necromancer cocked his head.

"Is that a no?" he asked. "Are you not excited at the opportunity to gain free strength and spread an army of the undead?"

Ryan decided this was getting nowhere, and he dropped another stalactite on the necromancer. Not a large one, but enough of one to give the necromancer his answer.

"I'm not sure if you are too young to understand this opportunity, or if you are just stupid. Either way," the necromancer said, shaking his head, "I am done with these games."

The darkness in front of the necromancer began to swirl, and the bones around him created a large bone lance. The necromancer turned slowly, aiming the lance until it was pointed directly towards Ryan's core. *Uh oh.*

"I tried to make a deal with you. I was told I would be able to grow even stronger if I worked with you. But now I shall shatter your core, and reassemble your pieces into a perfect mana gem to fuel my own powers."

The bone spear began to spin, and it shot forward, smashing into stone. With some of the last of his mana, Ryan instinctively began reinforcing the stone wall, but slowly, the bone began to bore through it. He wasn't going to be able to stop this weapon.

"You are smart, and capable for a Bronze dungeon, I'll give you that." The necromancer spoke casually as the lance continued to drill towards Ryan.

Ryan was draining his already low mana with each layer of stone he reinforced the wall with. He was silently praying to the Goddess of Justice that someone, anyone, would save him before he ran out of mana and the necromancer's spike made it to his core.

"I especially like the evolution your mobs are taking," the necromancer went on. "I feel we could have created a truly fearsome skeletal army, had we worked together."

The lance was nearing the boss room.

"I'm sorry, Rin, I can't stop him." Ryan's core was vibrating from the exertion, and he felt his power starting to wane. It would only be a minute or two before the bone lance would break into his core room, and into him.

"Oh, Ryan." Erin threw her arms around him, tears streaming

from her eyes. "You were the best dungeon ever. I'm so glad the Goddess sent me to you. I'm just sorry there isn't more I can do for you."

She sobbed, her emotions awash in pain and sorrow, and Ryan felt a renewed sense of energy. He pushed even more mana, all he could muster, into reinforcing the wall between him and the lance, slowing its approach even more. The spinning weapon slowed, but still it inched towards him.

"Get out while you can, Rin," Ryan whispered, feeling his vision waver. Erin had explained to him mana was life. She had never said it out loud, but he was starting to realize the dangers of using it all up.

The light in his core started to flicker. *Am I going to die if I use all my mana?*

"I live – and die – with you, Ryan." She held him tighter and closed her eyes.

The spike was inches away from breaking into the core room.

"You were the best thing to happen to me," Ryan said.

The lance broke through, shooting towards Ryan's core. He closed his eyes, waiting for the inevitable darkness of death. He wondered if he would feel pain when the lance struck him.

A moment passed, then two. Nothing.

Hesitantly, Ryan opened his eyes, looking around. Bones lay scattered in his room and in the tunnel that the lance had created, but the weapon was gone. He sent his attention back to where the necromancer had been, and for a second, he was certain he was dreaming.

Sasha stood in the room, darkness swirling around her form, a bloody dagger in her hand. A small splash of blood was noticeable where the necromancer had stood, but there was no sign of him.

The woman shook her head, wiping the bloody weapon on her leather armor before sheathing it. She pulled a crystal out of her armor and whispered into it.

"The necromancer got away, but I saved the dungeon."

"And our suspicion?" Ryan recognized the voice as Marcus's.

What was their suspicion? What was going on?

"It was Viktor," Sasha said, her voice filled with disgust. Ryan wondered just who this necromancer, this Viktor, was.

"I'll report back to the Guildmaster. Good job, Sasha," Marcus's voice said.

At these words, Sasha put the crystal away, and simply faded back into the shadows, leaving no trace of her presence.

Ryan wasn't sure what had just happened, but all he could guess was that Sasha had saved him. He closed his eyes, letting out a shaky sigh of relief, before he looked at Erin. The fairy was wiping tears from her eyes, and sat trembling, her silk cloth wrapped around her.

"So, I think we need to get a lot stronger," Ryan whispered, doing his best to try and shake the overwhelming fear that had filled him. He had been seconds away from death, and he never wanted to experience that again.

Erin offered him a small smile, even though her emotions were still a mess.

"I've been telling you that the whole time." She let out a laugh and wrapped her arms around him. "Grow stronger, so I never have to lose you."

Ryan sent her a mental nod and turned his attention to the entrance of his dungeon. He had an hour or two before the first group of adventurers arrived. That should be enough time for him to refresh his mana enough to fix the damage to his dungeon and prepare for the adventurers.

He was looking forward to the dives, and the chance to grow stronger. The necromancer's visit had just given him incentive to reach Silver as quickly as possible.

∾

Viktor

He let out a gasp as he fell to the floor, safe in his castle. His hand left his side, and he was happy to note the wound had already begun to close. Still, the pain was excruciating. He clutched at the cord around his neck, pulling his pendant out.

"Is it done?" a voice asked through it, and it took everything Viktor had not to throw the stone away.

"The dungeon turned me down," he said.

"A pity." The voice on the other end seemed bored.

"The twins were there. I could have been killed."

Viktor regretted his tone as soon as the remonstrative words had left his mouth. He knew it was dangerous to speak that way to the Exalted One.

"We both know you cannot be killed that easily." Dark laughter echoed from the crystal. It sent shivers down the necromancer's spine.

"I am surprised, though," the voice said, *"that she sent Marcus and the twins to that dungeon. I wonder what is so important about it."*

The voice trailed off, as if lost in thought.

"What shall I do?" Viktor asked. He had not only failed to make a deal with the dungeon, but to destroy the town. Failure was not taken lightly by the Exalted One.

"Rest and heal, Viktor. I will send a messenger to you after I deal with another inconvenience the Guildmaster has thrown my way."

With that, Viktor was left in silence. Groaning, he rose to his feet, pulling more darkness around him to heal his wounds. Next time, he would get his revenge.

Chapter Forty-Two

"If this keeps up, we should hit Bronze One this week," Ryan said

It had taken the remainder of the night for Ryan to shake the dark shadow the necromancer had left over him. He and Erin had been unusually subdued following their near-death experience, and rightly so.

However, looking at his experience triangle, Ryan was cheerful as the fourth group of the day departed the dungeon. His improved mobs had definitely increased the challenge to the groups, and two adventurers had fallen out of the twenty that had entered so far. Both had been high Bronze, and Ryan knew he was close to reaching Bronze Rank Three.

"Mm-hmm," Erin agreed. "Those infested ratbies really are deadly."

The first group of the day had managed to clear the first room with only a few extra scratches, but it was the second room that really cost them. While they had been struggling against the much faster victorious skuirrels and the sturdier champion skrats, the infested ratbies had managed to bite two different adventurers.

The group, used to receiving ratbie bites, rushed towards the boss room. Ryan knew they planned to beat Steve as quickly as they could so they could get the bites healed outside of the dungeon. A perfectly sound strategy for regular ratbie bites, but a fatal mistake for infested ratbie bites.

Seconds into the fight against Steve, the group's tank and one of their fighters fell to the ground, paralyzed. The moment of panic, along with the sudden incapacitation of the tank, allowed Steve to send his bone spikes into their other Bronze One fighter.

The rush of experience Ryan felt had lifted some of the exhaustion hanging over him following his long night and brought him one step closer to Silver. It was amazing how a near-death experience could put things into perspective. Ryan found himself caring less about the death of an adventurer, as it meant a greater chance at life for him and Erin.

With two members paralyzed and another dead, Ryan had thought the adventuring group finished. However, their Silver leader had surprised him, unleashing an earthen attack that managed to shatter one of Steve's legs, allowing the Silver and his companion to finish off the boss mob. A few minutes later, the ratbie paralysis wore off, and the group, now a member down, limped out of the dungeon.

"You think I should offer the antidote mushroom as a loot drop?" Ryan asked.

While Ryan was resolved not to pass up deaths, he was still hesitant about there being too many. He wanted to grow strong, but couldn't get too carried away, lest the guild decide his dungeon was no longer suited for training in. Even if he wanted to grow strong enough to survive the necromancer, it wouldn't mean anything if he scared away the adventurers, or worse, brought the wrath of the Adventurers' Guild down upon himself. Ryan was suddenly curious as to who was stronger: the necromancer or Sean?

"You have a mushroom that cures paralysis?" Erin's eyes were still bloodshot from the sleepless night, but Ryan noticed she was relaxing more as time went on.

"Yup, yup," Ryan said. "That room is actually full of herbs that have healing properties, mushrooms that can cause, or cure, paralysis, a few mushrooms that I think are edible, and of course, my poison ivy."

The paralysis lasted under a minute, and even less for stronger adventurers. As such, the only adventurers who seemed to fall as a result of the paralysis, weren't giving him much experience. For that reason, he figured he could throw the adventurers a bone, and help them figure out a way to cure it. The stronger they grew, the more he benefited, after all.

He ran through the list in his mind, noting that some of the mushrooms had differing types of toxicity to them. Ryan wondered what types of effects they would have on adventurers.

"I mean, if you want to, why not?" Erin was definitely not fully herself, judging by the way she didn't try to talk him out of helping the adventurers. He paused for a moment, trying to think of a way to cheer her up.

"How about I add all the plants and mushrooms as possible drops?" he asked. "That way, sometimes adventurers will get drops that can be used to heal, and others that can be used to harm?"

Part of Ryan just wanted to direct the adventurers' attention to the plants in the room. Most of the time, groups just burned them away, and he had spent a lot of time deciding what to grow in there. Maybe if the plants started showing up as drops, adventurers would appreciate the room a little more.

Erin offered him a smile, and he could feel her mood perk up a little.

"That could work. It would be funny if they ate the wrong ones." She let out a giggle, and Ryan smiled all the more. It had taken most of the day, but they were casting off the feelings of dread left by the necromancer.

"Deal," Ryan said.

Ryan mentally assigned the plants to his skrat and skuirrel mobs in the room, increasing their loot pool from just copper coins to include the different plants. Since they were growing in the room already, the plants had a common loot level.

"Next up is Blake's team, right?" Erin pulled her silk cloth around herself as she stifled a yawn.

Ryan turned his attention to the entrance of the dungeon, looking for signs of the next group. At first, all he saw was

Sasha, the female twin who had saved his life, and a cleric standing outside his entrance.

As he continued his search, he saw a group of five breaking from the trees. Even from a distance, he could hear laughter, and something about turkey wings. It was a laugh he had gotten used to; the laugh of the Silver thief, Jack, which meant Blake's team had arrived.

Ryan hoped Blake and his friends could help them forget the necromancer, if only for a little while. He always found Blake's team's presence therapeutic.

"They're here," he said, excitedly ensuring all his mobs had been summoned and the rooms were ready. Ryan even paused the fight that was currently ongoing in skeletal fight club. In the chaos of the necromancer's arrival, Ryan had missed what he could only imagine was an impressive turn of events, because when he finally had enough energy to check back in on his mobs, the victorious skuirrel was scattered about and the champion skrat was, well, victorious.

Ryan wasn't going to miss any more of this impressive skrat's battles, and he wanted to devote all of his attention to Blake's team.

"Want to bet on who gets bitten by an infested ratbie?" Erin asked as Blake and his team reached Sasha. The fairy's mood had definitely picked up.

Ryan found himself chuckling, remembering Blake's past encounters with the regular ratbies.

"We both know it's going to be Blake," he joked.

Erin's laughter at his remark chased the remaining darkness from his core room as Blake and his team stepped into Ryan's dungeon for another dive.

Chapter Forty-Three

"All right, that paralysis sucked," Blake said.

His group laughed, and he couldn't help but smile. They all sat at their usual table in the inn sharing a round of drinks. It had become a tradition of sorts over the past few weeks.

"Well, those new victorious skuirrels aren't much fun either." Matt offered Blake a smile as he took a drink. Blake returned it with a knowing grin. Matt had finally managed to land shots on normal skuirrels, but the new victorious versions were too fast for him to shoot, so he was back to square one.

"What type of archer runs out of arrows?" Jack asked, holding a mug of hot chocolate in his hand. Blake had to hold back a laugh as Jack sprinkled a handful of marshmallows into his drink.

"Hey, archers don't have infinite arrows, you know. Sheesh. And I was certain I would be able to hit at least one of them." Matt took another sip. "Though if I become an arcane archer..."

He let the thought hang in the air.

"I thought you wanted to be a ranger?" Blake asked.

When Blake had first met Matt, the archer had told him his dream was to become a ranger, a specialized version of archer that specialized in hunting and tracking. Gold and Platinum-ranked rangers often worked with the elven nations to track down enemies of the light and dangerous beasts.

"I did," Matt mused, half to himself. "But the more I think on it, an arcane archer would probably help our group more."

Blake knew arcane archers were a special archer class that allowed the archer to utilize their affinity to create various arrows and effects. Because physical classes only allotted twenty percent of their mana to class skills and abilities, very few archers chose the arcane path.

"You should choose the class you feel best suits you and your dreams for your future," Karan said, looking at Matt with a small smile on her face. "Don't just look at just the short term, because once you choose your class, you can't choose another."

"I know. I won't make the choice carelessly, but the more I think about it, the more I believe it will be the right path for me." Matt offered her a smile, holding out his glowing palm. "Besides, after today, I can officially pass into the Silver ranks."

Matt had filled his experience triangle enough to break into Silver. Emily was about halfway through Bronze One, and Blake had just reached Bronze One.

"Well," Karan said, "we have one more dive before the three of you will be ready to progress, so please spend a few more nights thinking on it."

To pass into Silver, they would need to go to their class trainer, who would help them break into the Silver ranks as well as discover their affinity. From what Karan and Jack told them, it would be about a month before they would be ready to return to dungeon dives as Silver-ranked adventurers. As such, they had agreed to hold off on ranking up until all three Bronze members could do so at the same time.

"I can't wait to rank up," Emily said as she stared at her glowing palm.

Blake found himself doing the same, dreaming about how close he was. He could already imagine how proud his father would be when the paladin finally returned from his mission to the north.

"Are you still set on becoming a summoner?" Blake asked, and Emily nodded in return, a huge smile on her face.

"What about you, Blake? Still planning on becoming an even better meat shield?" Jack asked. He flashed him a grin as he took a sip of his chocolate. If Blake didn't know any better, he would have thought the thief was starting to enjoy the sweet drink.

"I'm not a meat shield," Blake replied, a little testily. "I'm the tank. And yes, I'm going to become a knight, and grow one step closer to becoming a paladin."

He could already see himself as a paladin, clad in shining armor, holding a shield emblazoned with the scales of the Goddess of Justice, standing proudly besides his—

"What happens if you don't get a celestial affinity?" Jack's words pulled Blake back to reality and instantly killed the slight buzz he was getting from his liquor.

"Well, my father has a celestial affinity," Blake said.

No one knew how affinities were decided; merely that for some reason, when adventurers hit Silver rank, they would awaken to one of seven kinds of mana. These seven types – celestial, earth, fire, wind, water, darkness, and chaos – were said to stem from the seven deities that ruled over the land.

An adventurer's affinity dictated the types of abilities they could use, and sometimes restricted the types of classes they could become. Paladins to the Goddess of Justice, for instance, had to have a celestial affinity, which was the affinity said to stem from the Goddess herself.

"Doesn't mean that's what you'll get. According to my mother, my father's affinity was darkness." Jack stared into his mug as he summoned a small amount of wind to make the steam coming from his drink dance. "But, as we all know, I got wind."

"That's just because you're filled with so much hot air," Karan chimed in, placing a hand on Jack's shoulder. She passed him a look and turned towards Blake.

"Don't listen to the lowly thief, Blake. I am sure the Goddess has plans for you and will choose you to inherit a celestial affinity."

She gave Blake a smile, which he returned. However, his mind was racing, filling with dark thoughts. What would he do if he didn't have a celestial affinity? All he wanted was to become a paladin like his father.

"And no matter what your affinity, Blake," she went on, "remember that you are a valuable member of our family."

Karan's words and her smile helped calm his fears a little, and he took another drink. Surely everything would work out. He couldn't see any reason why the Goddess wouldn't choose him.

"Enough talk of gods and goddess and affinities and whatnot," Jack said. His hand shot into his pocket, and the thief pulled out a deck of cards. Another tradition the group had started was playing cards every night together. Karan wouldn't let the group gamble away their coin, reminding the Bronze members they had save for their class gear.

She would, however, let them gamble in dares, with the loser of each round having to complete some sort of usually embarrassing dare.

"Who's feeling lucky tonight?" Jack asked, his eyes twinkling.

"Count me in," Blake said, and offered the thief an evil grin.

He was going to get Jack back for that turkey wing dare.

Chapter Forty-Four

Ryan stared at his experience triangle with hunger in his eyes. Another adventurer, the Silver Four leader of the group, had just fallen, and the resulting experience had filled the bottom triangle. The difference this time, though, was that Ryan was currently Bronze One, and with this experience, he was ready to climb into the Silver ranks.

"Tell me again why we have to wait?" Ryan asked.

"Because proper etiquette is to at least wait until the end of the day to ascend into the next rank," Erin said. She acted annoyed, but Ryan could tell from her emotions that she was just as excited as he was.

I hate etiquette. He really did at times, though Erin had explained to him countless times that dungeons that broke etiquette rarely survived long. The Adventurers' Guild apparently had a reputation for eliminating dungeons they deemed too dangerous or out of control.

"How many groups are left?" Ryan asked.

He really wasn't paying much attention to the groups now. Blake's team had come and gone for a fifth time the day before, and they were really the only team he cared much about. They had seemed especially happy after their last dive, and Ryan felt proud of both their group and himself. They had all grown so much since Blake's first dungeon dive, and Ryan felt he had played a large part in helping Blake grow.

"Two more groups today and then we can begin your ascension."

"Fiiiine." He let out a long sigh and turned part of his attention back to the entrance, watching as the next group prepared to enter.

They presented their crystals to the male twin, Rasha, and stepped into the dungeon. This group consisted of four Bronze One fighters and a Silver Five warrior. Judging by their ranks, it was going to be a rather uneventful dive. That just meant Ryan could turn his attention back to his favorite pastime: skeletal fight club.

Having reached Bronze One, Ryan had access to a total of one hundred mob points. Steve cost him twenty-five. His second room, with its two infested ratbies, eight skuirrels, eight skrats, two victorious skuirrels, and two champion skrats, cost him forty points.

His first room, with six skuirrels and four victorious skuirrels, cost another fourteen points. Altogether, he was spending seventy-nine points on mobs in his dungeon, which left him twenty-one points for skeletal fight club. Ryan had not wasted any of his time and points, and he had results to prove it.

His champion skrat had finally evolved two days prior, creating a new version that cost three total mob points. Ryan could tell the new mob would be worth that extra point. It was covered in plate-like bones, giving it extremely strong defense. Atop its head was a bone spike. Additionally, the new mob had grown larger, nearly knee height on the average adventurer. Ryan had decided to call this mob a plated skrat.

Because he had reached another evolution with his skrat, Ryan was now working on getting his skuirrel to its third evolution. For the past two days, Ryan had been running his evolution pits at full steam for a total of 20 points.

After each battle, the surviving skuirrel was healed with dark mana, and once healed, a new victorious skuirrel was summoned to fight. It was a rather repetitive process, but one that Ryan had found effective. Generally, once a victorious skuirrel began winning, it would keep winning. This ensured it would continue to gain the most experience and draw ever closer to evolving.

In fact, as Ryan looked over his pits, he was pleased to see signs indicating an evolution was near. The victorious skuirrels in each pit that had been continually winning had dark mana constantly swirling around their bones. Ryan found that when his mobs became close to evolving, his mana would begin to cling to them, slowly preparing to make a change. It was almost reminiscent of how Steve had been created, though a much slower process.

Perhaps creating a boss mob is just advancing a mob's evolution multiple times? Ryan wanted to ask Erin about this, but his skeletal fight club rules were absolute.

Internally sighing, both at his inability to share skeletal fight club with Erin and at the fact one of the adventurers had just eaten a paralysis mushroom by mistake, meaning they were going to waste his time even longer, Ryan turned back to his precious mobs.

He waited for each one to finish off its opponent, but mentally stopped the process that would summon another. He had an idea on how to get his next evolution before he ascended into the Silver ranks.

"Oh, look, Ryan." Erin's voice pulled him away from his task, sending a slight hint of irritation through Ryan.

What now?

"Huh? What is it, hun?" he asked, trying to hide his irritation. He was so close to an evolution; what could she possibly be pulling him away for?

"They're harvesting your plants," she said.

Wait, what?

Even though Ryan had implemented the plants as drops a rotation ago, no one had shown much interest in them. A few had tried the mushrooms, which occasionally resulted in rather amusing events. Ryan's favorite was when one of the adventurers ate a toxic mushroom that made him hallucinate. His team had to drag him out of the dungeon, as he was sobbing about how a dingo – whatever that was – had eaten his baby. Otherwise, though, most adventurers just shoved the drops in their packs and moved on to fight Steve.

"That is interesting," Ryan said. His irritation faded by a fraction, and he was mildly intrigued. Still, he really wanted to get back to skeletal fight club.

"Looks like you finally made them realize how important those plants of yours are," Erin said.

Ryan could feel that she was happy and proud of him. Normally, he would be thrilled. Now, though, he had mobs to evolve.

"Let's see if the next group shows an interest in them as well. Maybe this group is just strange," Ryan chuckled. Seeing Erin nod and go back to watching the group, he let out an internal sigh. He was finally able to get back to his task at hand.

Ryan created small tunnels leading from each of the evolution chambers into a single, much larger pit. The pit had a small haze of dark mana floating in the room and was where Ryan generally held his most exciting battles.

It was here that he had pitted so many victorious skuirrels against the skrat that finally became his plated skrat. And now, in the grandest spectacle to date for skeletal fight club, ten victorious skuirrels, all on the brink of evolution, would fight. Ten would enter, and only one – hopefully evolved – would remain.

Ryan was practically shaking with excitement as he finished carving out the tunnels and opened them up to the victorious skuirrels. With a mental push, each victorious skuirrel, now fully healed, marched into the tunnel and towards their final fight.

He watched as their little forms scampered through the tunnel, admiring their sharp boney protrusions. This evolution had proven to be quite dangerous for adventurers, especially those with only leather armor. He couldn't wait to see what the skuirrels' next form brought.

"Hey, Ryan?"

Again?

"Yes, hun?" She flinched, sensing his irritation.

"Did I... did I upset you?" she asked. Her emotions started on a downward spiral, and Ryan knew he had to fix this, fast.

"No... I just... well, you see," Ryan scrambled, trying to find an answer. He glanced through his dungeon, noting the fourth adventurer group had beaten Steve, and was nearing the exit. Ryan watched for a split second as the group easily maneuvered around one of the traps he had laid in the first room.

That's it!

"I'm sorry, hun," he ventured. "It's just I've been secretly trying to plan out new traps."

New mobs, new traps. Same thing, right?

"And you interrupted me as I was working on one."

He waited silently, praying to the Goddess that Erin believed him.

The fairy looked down at him, her emotions unreadable for a moment, before she broke into a large smile and wrapped her arms around him.

"Oh Ryan, I'm so proud of you."

Crisis averted.

"I'm sorry I didn't tell you earlier, sweetheart," he lied, feeling only a little guilty. "I just wanted to surprise you."

Erin pulled away, shaking her head as she stared at him. He could feel through their bond just how proud she was. Now he felt a little worse about lying to her.

"Don't be sorry, Ryan," Erin said. "Every dungeon fairy dreams of the day their dungeon becomes more engrossed in bettering themselves. I'm really excited to see what new traps you've made. What have you been working on?"

Crap.

"Uh, well, I want it to be a surprise. After I reach Silver."

"Oh." Erin's eager demeanor dimmed by a small degree, but she offered him a smile. "That's okay."

Her mood was slowly evening out, and Ryan could detect a touch of sadness. Did she feel left out? Ryan made a mental note to try and include her in the future. Especially since now he apparently needed to plan out some new traps for his dungeon.

"Don't worry, hun," Ryan said. "Maybe we can come up with a trap together after I finish what I'm working on?"

"Deal."

She zipped around the room excitedly, and Ryan couldn't help but smile. Her mood was infectious, and he really did like making her happy. However, he also wanted to get back to what was going to make *him* happy: evolving his mobs.

"All right, well, I'm going to go back to my experimenting," Ryan said. "Will you let me know when the final group finishes?"

His victorious skuirrels were all at the end of their tunnels, just waiting for Ryan to open them up into the fighting pit.

"Sure thing, hun." She gave him another hug, and then turned her attention to the group preparing to dive.

With that, Ryan threw his full attention back to his fighting pit, and with a silent cry of glee, opened up the tunnels. In a rush, ten boney forms clashed against each other in the center of the large pit, and Ryan knew he would have a new mob at the end of it all.

Oh, how he loved skeletal fight club.

Chapter Forty-Five

Erin sat atop Ryan, guiding him.

"All right, now that you've sealed off the dungeon, absorb all your mobs," she said.

The final group of adventurers had departed, Ryan's victorious skuirrel had evolved, and now it was time to break into Silver. The first task Erin had for him was to seal his dungeon.

"As you wish."

He could have simply blocked the entrance, but Ryan liked to be a little more… theatrical. As such, he had lowered the top part of his wolf skull entrance onto itself, given the appearance that the dungeon had closed its mouth.

Ryan absorbed all of his mobs, smiling as he absorbed his new skuirrel. He was going to call it a bladed skuirrel.

"Next, call forth your triangles," Erin instructed.

Ryan complied, and the two triangles appeared. His level triangle showed the entire bottom covered in darkness, with a '100' showing. His experience triangle shimmered, with the bottom triangle filled and ready.

Erin flew down to look at both triangles before nodding to herself.

"Now, push the two triangles together."

Ryan did as he was told, interlaying the two triangles on each other. The golden shapes flashed with light as they neared, and then suddenly combined, creating a six-sided star. The star began to spin as dark mana swirled around it.

He could feel energy crackling in the air around him, and the spinning star seemed to be growing in size. Dark mana condensed around it, creating a dark, swirling void of pure energy. Ryan couldn't help but stare into it, a black abyss that seemed infinite.

"Get ready," Erin whispered, but Ryan, so enthralled with the darkness, barely heard her.

Suddenly, a single light seemed to grow from within the darkness, and Ryan felt himself being pulled towards it. Like a moth to a flame, Ryan's consciousness reached out, and as he touched that light, it was as if he had unleashed a dam.

Dark energy blasted into him from the spinning star, attacking him, rushing over him. He fought against the torrential energy, his mind swimming upon tumultuous waves of energy. Images flashed through his mind, faster than he could comprehend, and he felt something within him unlock. The mass of energy continued to pour into him, until all the darkness surrounding the six-sided star had faded, absorbed by Ryan. Then, as the star came to a stop, the triangles once again separated.

As his mind stopped spinning and he got over the intoxicating new levels of power he could feel, he looked at his experience triangle. The line that had signaled a Bronze level worth of experience was gone, and now the amount of experience needed for a single level seemed to have increased fourfold. That was going to take a while.

Next, his level triangle. The entire bottom was black, and the next row showed a single triangle, on the far left, filled in. Within it, the number '200.'

"My mob points doubled?" Ryan exclaimed.

Even if Erin couldn't feel his excitement, his voice practically crackled with the emotion.

"Mm-hmm," she said. "And from now on, each level you gain will give you many more mob points than before. And that's not all."

Erin hovered in front of Ryan, a wide smile on her face.

"Look at yourself," she said with a smile.

Ryan pulled up a mental image of his core room, and nearly lost it. His diamond core was now the size of a human skull.

Guess it's time to make the core room bigger.

"Every time you climb a tier, your core will grow larger," Erin said, "to accommodate the amount of mana you can hold."

"This. Is. Awesome!"

He hadn't noticed it before, but at Bronze One, he had felt full. Now, at Silver Nine, with double the mob points and mana capacity he had previously had, he felt empty. Ryan couldn't wait to begin climbing the Silver ranks, wondering just what powers he might unlock.

"Also—" Erin began.

There's an also?

"—now that you have reached Silver tier, you should have the ability to summon new types of mobs."

New mobs? I like the sound of that!

Ryan mentally pulled up his list of mobs, only pausing for a second to admire his bladed skuirrel, before flipping towards his wolf skeleton. Before, the mob had been out of his ability to summon, but now, he could tell, he would be able to utilize it.

Medium beasts had been unlocked. But that wasn't all. As he flipped through to his human skeletons, he nearly gasped in surprise. He mentally looked at his first full skeleton, the fire mage he had killed to save Blake, and noted two things.

First, the bones now had an affinity. Second, his newfound knowledge told him he could summon a hardened skeleton out of these bones, or a skeletal mage.

"What's a skeletal mage?" Ryan asked.

He was really curious, but even as he spoke, he nearly choked.

"It costs fifty mob points?" he exclaimed.

Erin broke into a fit of laughter, obviously enjoying his reaction to becoming Silver.

"Skeletal mages are a powerful mob type that can utilize basic spells depending on the affinity of the individual whose bones are used," she said. "A fire affinity skeletal mage can use basic fire spells, a water mage, water spells, and so on."

Ryan's mind immediately rushed through his human skeletons. He had fire, water, earth, and wind affinities. Not bad, but the collector in him wanted to get them all. He had to pause, though, as a thought crossed his mind.

"So, would a celestial set of bones allow my mobs to heal each other?" he asked.

Erin grimaced at his question and shook her head.

"As a darkness dungeon, it is against nature for you to be able to create a celestial skeletal mage. There are stories of necromancers attempting to resurrect clerics and paladins, which resulted in an explosion of celestial energy. So please, don't try."

Okay, note to self: never try that. Ryan really didn't want to blow up his own dungeon.

"Besides," Erin went on. "As a darkness dungeon, you can naturally create dark skeletal mages, which will have the ability to heal your other mobs with dark mana."

Oh, that's neat. That only covers six of the seven mana types, though.
"What about—"

"If you're going to ask about chaos, don't," Erin interrupted. "While you could summon a chaos skeletal mage, as a celestial being, I could not allow such an atrocity to ever take place."

Oh, right. Celestial and chaos are apparently lifelong enemies.

"It's like you read my mind," Ryan chuckled as he spoke. He knew she could feel his emotions, but luckily, she couldn't read his mind. Otherwise, she would have found out about skeletal fight club long ago.

"So, anything else new with Silver?" he asked. He wanted to make sure he thoroughly understood what came with his new tier. He also wanted to give Erin a chance to explain anything she could to him. He knew she really enjoyed teaching him.

Erin tapped her chin. "Hmm. I think as a Silver darkness dungeon, you can combine skeletons to create new types of creatures."

"I can what?" Ryan was surprised.

The level of possibilities that fact opened up! What if he combined a human and a beast? Could he combine his skuirrels' and skrats' evolutions to create something even more powerful?

Ryan might have just found something new to do during his long nights.

Erin thought for a moment.

"From my understanding, you can try and create new skeletal... creations. I'm not sure how it works, so that's up to you to figure out," she said. "I just know you can combine different skeletons together to try and create new combinations. Whether or not they work comes down to magic."

She smiled slyly at her last statement. So, they were back to making those terrible, magic being vague, jokes.

"You know you're going to regret opening that line of jokes back up," Ryan warned, only half-jokingly.

"I'm looking forward to it." She landed easily atop his now much larger core. "But first, I think I'm going to take a nap while you create the next floor of your dungeon." She pulled her silk cloth around herself like a blanket.

"Any suggestions?" Ryan asked.

Erin stifled a yawn as she snuggled into her blanket.

"Generally, the second floor has at least five rooms," she said, stretching her arms. "Four basic rooms with mobs, and a boss room. Other than that, surprise me."

Ryan sent her a mental grin as she closed her eyes.

"Oh, you know I love surprising you."

Chapter Forty-Six

"Now, where to start?" Ryan thought out loud, turning his focus away from the quietly snoring Erin to the task at hand.

When it came to dungeon design, he was still rather inexperienced. He wasn't unhappy with his first floor, but he definitely felt he could do much better.

First, I suppose I should find out what's underneath us. He spread his mind to every corner of his current dungeon, and slowly pushed his influence downward.

When he had last built out his dungeon, he had been Bronze Eleven. Immediately, the capacity difference from Bronze Eleven to Silver Nine made itself evident. Ryan was able to quickly excavate the earth beneath him, spreading his influence, gaining more ground. It was simple enough to eat away at the rock, and he did have practice in quickly filling the areas he excavated.

It was monotonous, and even with his increased capacity, he was certain the task would take him quite some time. As he went to work, Ryan made the mental note to begin spreading his influence more, even when he wasn't building. It would make this a much quicker process in the future.

The first two rooms on Ryan's first floor were nearly thirty feet high, while his boss room was fifteen feet. For his second floor, Ryan wanted to do something different.

A few of the adventurers Ryan had killed had been carrying

books, and once absorbed, Ryan had gained all the knowledge in these books. One in particular detailed a variety of different types of architecture, and Ryan wanted to begin creating an underground castle of sorts. As such, his second floor was going to be much more uniform. He really felt it would help elevate adventurers' perception of him.

Ryan let his influence spread thirty feet below his first floor before he started getting serious. At thirty feet, he sent his influence down another ten feet, but as he did, he absorbed all the rock and material he could, completely hollowing the area out.

This labor came with the added bonus of netting him a few more skeletons for his collection. Always a plus, and another reason he should be continually spreading his influence, even when he wasn't building new floors.

Now to begin building.

Below his first floor, Ryan had created an expanse twice the size of his first floor, not only in length, but also in width. Erin had told him to create five rooms with mobs, and he intended to do so. However, he also felt he should make his dungeon a little more complex. A straight path from start to finish seemed rather boring. His second floor was going to surprise Erin. She was going to be proud of him.

First, he created his starting room. He decided this room was going to be directly under the first room on his first floor. It made things easier in his mind. This room, just like all the other rooms on the second floor, was going to be fifteen feet wide, and fifteen feet long, with a ten-foot ceiling.

He also decided this would be the first room to have new mobs on his second floor. He wasn't sure what type yet, but he wanted to welcome the adventurers to his second floor with not only new architecture, but new challenges.

Once the expanse was created to his desired shape, Ryan created an arched doorway leading down a single hallway. This hall led to his next room, which he quickly crafted. He paused after his second room, smiling. Oh, how proud Erin was going to be.

Ryan lost himself to building his second floor, working as long as he could before resting to let his mana refresh. Even with his drastic increase in capacity, as well as the influx of mana gained over time by his increased area of influence, he was expending quite a bit of it. Clearing away all of the rock may not have been the most efficient building process, because now he had to replace the rock where he wanted his walls and tunnels.

He wasn't just dumping rock back into the expanses, though. Instead, he was creating uniform blocks, as he had seen in the book he absorbed. He lined the walls of the tunnels and rooms with these bricks, which shone with a dim light. It was eerie, giving off the feeling of a long-forgotten castle, and Ryan liked it, even if it used a lot more mana to make them.

Thanks to the book – as well as the different woods he had absorbed through weapons and materials dropped by adventurers – Ryan was able to finally create doors. He spent a lot more time working on these than he probably should have, but the devil was in the detail.

One wood Ryan had in his inventory, courtesy of a rather fancy dagger an adventurer once dropped, was a black and white ebony. He chose that wood for his door, and it created a stunning mixture of white and dark patterns. Ryan found that with some concentration and the help of mana, he was able to craft the patterns as he saw fit. The end result: bone-white doors, lightly glowing, with a dark wolf skull outline on them. The handles on these doors were skeletal hands. He was really embracing his bone theme.

When Ryan was done with the initial layout and his intricate doors, he paused to admire his work. His first room had a single exit, which led down a narrow hallway into his next room. This room had exits in all directions, leading to three different rooms. The room on the left was the correct path towards the boss.

However, Ryan wasn't about to let adventurers just waltz towards his boss; oh, no. Especially not if they meant him harm, like that necromancer. Never again would Ryan make it so easy to reach his boss room. He was working on plans to stop that necromancer if he ever reappeared. Many plans.

The door leading to the correct path had three different keyholes locking it shut. This door was also reinforced with steel and spikes, inspired by the design of a portcullis. For good measure, Ryan reinforced the door with dark mana as well.

After the necromancer attack, Erin had mentioned that objects infused with a dungeon's mana could become impossibly strong. Ryan's door, now completely reinforced, would likely be impossible to destroy unless attacked by a Platinum-level adventurer or higher. Unless the adventurers had all three keys, that door wasn't opening.

In order to get these keys, adventurers would need to explore the rest of Ryan's dungeon. The door on the right led to a room which held the first key. This key rested atop a pillar of bones sitting in the middle of the room. Some of these bones were harmless, but Ryan was already planning on having mobs in that room, several of which would blend in with his pile. He could already imagine the surprise of the first group to enter that room.

The door opposite to the adventurers once they entered the first pillar room would be filled with mobs and another key pillar. Once adventurers defeated those mobs and grabbed their key, they would have to make a choice between another two doors leading from that room. One, directly across from the door they entered into, led down a hallway and ended in a dead end. The other, on the left-hand wall as they entered the room, led adventurers on a winding route that eventually reached the third key room.

This room wouldn't have mobs, but was going to be a trap room, again with the key in the center atop a pile of bones. The exit from this room was actually a hidden door that led directly back to the room with the triple-locked door,. In essence, Ryan had them doing a large loop to get back to where they started.

Once they had all three keys, they would be able to open the door leading to the boss room. However, Ryan wasn't about to hide the boss room directly behind that door. No, instead, the portcullis door opened onto a path that led to another room, which Ryan decided he would also trap. The next room after that would be a mob room, and only after that room was cleared would adventurers be able to enter the boss room.

All in all, Ryan felt this setup was much more dungeon and

adventure like, and he really was excited for the first set of adventurers to dive into it. Before that could be allowed, though, Ryan had many more steps to prepare for his visitors.

First, he needed to actually set up his traps. Had he actually been working on those, instead of skeletal fight club, this part would be easy. But he hadn't. So, while he had some really cool new mobs, he had zilch for new traps. Not to mention the fact that he would have to decide on mobs for his second floor, assign their loot, and create his new boss.

Being a dungeon was a lot of work.

Chapter Forty-Seven

Traps, it turned out, were a lot of fun to design. The first new trap Ryan designed was a basic one that he quickly spread throughout his second floor. It was extremely simple, and as much as Ryan hated to admit it, it had been slightly inspired by the necromancer's attack.

After watching the necromancer create a bone spear, Ryan had decided to try the same. He found that not only could he create a bone spear, he could also set it up to be triggered quite easily. Thanks to the books he had absorbed, Ryan had learned of a simple device that he felt would act as a great trigger for these new bone spears: pressure plates.

By creating hidden pressure plates in various points on the floor, he was able to hide his bone spikes in the walls or floors. Whenever one of the plates was stepped on, it would trigger the tendril of dark mana that was attached to the spear, driving the spikes from the hiding space to likely impale the poor soul that had triggered the trap. The spikes weren't too large, though; they were unlikely to instantly kill an adventurer but would create quite the painful wound. As much as Ryan knew he needed to grow strong, he also remembered Erin's warning against creating too difficult a dungeon.

While those spike traps were simple, and more likely to injure than kill, the next trap Ryan created was much more potent. This one was reserved for the trap room that held the third key and would present a much larger problem for adventurers. Ryan was Silver, and the second floor needed to be dangerous for Silver adventurers.

However, heeding Erin's warning, Ryan knew he shouldn't just make a trap that would instantly kill. There wouldn't be any sense of excitement in that, and Ryan really didn't want to scare off the adventurers. He needed to grow stronger.

The trap for the room with the third key was a multi-part trap, one that would be both triggered by adventurer actions and controlled by Ryan. First, Ryan hollowed out the floor beneath his trap room, creating darkness-lined pits all throughout the floor.

Second, he lined these pits with bone spikes that could ever so slowly completely pierce the pit. He had stolen this design from a torture tool he had read about called the iron maiden. He decided to call them bone maidens.

Once he littered the floor beneath the room with bone maidens, he went to work truly creating his trap. His idea for the room was to force adventurers to choose between the key and the way out, or saving one of their friends. In his mind, he felt it was his goal, as a dungeon chosen by the Goddess of Justice, to see that adventurers were just.

In his mind, he was already playing out how the room would work. He set a small, nearly invisible tendril of dark mana directly across the path adventurers would need to take toward the key. When an adventurer hit this tendril, the door they had come from would be suddenly sealed shut with mana-infused rock. At the same time, the door leading out of the room would open.

From there, the trap got fun. The moment an adventurer pulled the key off the pillar, Ryan would drop part of the floor away from underneath another unsuspecting adventurer in the room. That adventurer would fall into one of the bone maidens.

Over the now-trapped adventurer a key-shaped hole would appear, matching the skeletal key in the room. Ryan had decided to add a hint for the adventurers at this part and set up dark tendrils of mana to spell out a cryptic message: "A key for a life."

The spikes would begin closing in on the trapped adventurer, and at the same time, the exit would begin to close. Adventurers would have to choose to save their friend or leave the room with the key. If they left their friend, the adventurer would die, giving Ryan a boost of experience, and the party would be down a member.

Even with all three keys, he wasn't sure a group would choose to take on the rest of the dungeon. If they did, it would probably signal more experience for Ryan, but he wouldn't mind. Those who would leave their friends didn't deserve to conquer his dungeon.

Unknown to the adventurers, if they rescued their friend, Ryan would open the door back to the second pillar room, and when adventurers returned there, they would be greeted with more mobs, and the third key. This meant adventurers who chose to save their ally would be rewarded not only with a key, but more loot and experience. He was rather proud of his trap.

With his trap room established, and his spike traps spread throughout his dungeon, Ryan took a pause to catch his breath. He was nearing the completion of his dungeon and knew his next step should be his mobs. But that step was also going to be the most exciting, yet draining process, so he decided he should finish any and all other aspects of his dungeon before moving on to mobs and loot.

As he looked around at his stone-brick walls, he found they were rather boring compared to his wonderfully artistic and intimidating doors. That just wouldn't do, and he really did feel he needed to try and offer a little more light in the dungeon other than the faint white glow everything he influenced projected.

Ryan sifted through all the items he had collected so far, racking his brain for any way to improve visibility. After what felt like an eternity, and perhaps one or two skuirrel fights to help him think, an idea finally came to him.

Everything Ryan created glowed with a faint, white light. He knew that, and it did provide an eerie level of light. However, if Ryan's idea worked, he would be able to fill his second level with an even more ominous effect.

In his first room, Ryan turned his attention to the ceiling, preparing to give his idea a go. He hollowed out a large portion of the roof and filled the empty expanse with a massive human skull, looking down onto the room.

Then, in the empty eye sockets, he grew two massive rubies, which he secured tightly with a web of dark mana. *No stealing my gems.* The brilliant red gems enhanced the white light provided by Ryan's glow, refracting it and bathing the room in an eerie, blood-red glow. *Oh, yes.*

Ryan quickly proceeded to create a massive skull in every room, looking down on the adventurers as if watching them. It would give the feeling that they were being watched, which they were. With the rubies grown, each and every room took on the eerie, ominous glow. Ryan figured his fear factor must have increased by at least ten thanks to the latest idea.

Next, my hallways.

He decided to leave these in the soft white glow, not wanting to overplay the red. Instead, he took a more artistic approach, using his newfound ability to craft weapons from bones. He lined his hallways with crisscrossed bone swords and shields.

He also decided to construct Steve-sized skeletons – with both arms – to stand silently along the hallways. Ryan had no intention of animating these skeletons, but felt they added to the overall feel. As a precaution against necromancer attacks, he made sure the skeletons were secured firmly to the ground. The last thing he needed was a necromancer animating his decorations.

With his rooms cast in an eerie red glow, and his hallways properly decorated, Ryan knew the time was coming for his final step. Nearly buzzing with excitement, Ryan closed his eyes and began browsing his skeleton collection. It was time to decide on his boss and mobs.

Chapter Forty-Eight

"Boss, boss, boss, boss, boss."

Ryan repeated the word over and over, flipping through the collection of skeletons he had acquired. He had human skeletons of all shapes and sizes, with water, fire, wind, and earth affinities. He also had his various skrat and skuirrel evolutions, but none of those seemed boss-worthy. Also, he *really* wanted to try out some of the new mob types he had unlocked.

During his excavation, Ryan had completed two new skeleton types: a snake skeleton and an owl skeleton. Both constituted small beasts, though, and so didn't immediately pull at Ryan's attention for boss mob. He did have plans for those snake mobs, though.

What did scream "boss material" were his wolf and deer skeletons. Both constituted medium beasts, but frustratingly, both were incomplete.

"Ugh." Ryan let out a cry of frustration. Why hadn't he continued searching for skeletons? He had wasted so much time at his Bronze levels. *Never again.*

"Everything all right, hun?" Erin's sleepy mumble, after what Ryan figured had been days of silence, made him nearly jump out of his core.

"Oh, sorry, Rin. I didn't mean to wake you."

He really hadn't, and he was upset he had. He had wanted to

surprise her with a completed second floor. But now that she was awake, maybe she could help him.

The fairy yawned as she sat up to stretch. Ryan couldn't help but admire her as her feathery wings spread out behind her. She was beautiful.

What's the matter?" she asked.

"I wanted to create my boss from a medium beast, since it's my new mob type. But both my wolf and deer skeletons are incomplete."

"Have you tried combining them?"

She asked it so innocently, as if it was a simple matter. The fact Ryan hadn't thought of that himself left him feeling extremely ashamed. *Stupid, stupid, stupid.*

"Uh, I... hadn't thought of that," he mumbled, continuing to silently berate himself. After all the innovation he had been doing, how had he not thought of something so simple?

"So, since it was my idea, do I get to name the boss?" Erin asked mischievously.

Crap.

"I... I guess so, hun," Ryan mumbled.

He could already tell this was not going to end well. However, his excitement at creating a new boss mob quickly overcame his apprehension of letting the fairy name it. It couldn't be worse than Steve, could it?

"Hooray!" Erin cried, twirling in the air. A flood of happiness rushed across their bond, and that was worth whatever terrible name she came up with. As long as it wasn't as bad as Steve.

"All right, so how do we do this combination trick?" Ryan asked.

Erin shrugged, making her wings shake, as she shot him a sly smile.

"Magic?" She winked.

Ugh, he walked right into that one.

"Thanks for the brilliant suggestion," he muttered under his breath.

"What was that?" she asked.

"You're so pretty."

Ryan reverted to his normal go-to distraction phrase and

turned his attention back to the wolf and deer skeletons. As he focused on the two with the intention of combining them, knowledge flooded him. He suddenly knew what to do.

"Rin, watch this."

Ryan turned his attention to his first-floor boss room, which currently stood empty, and was still connected to his core room. The image of the room projected in his diamond core, allowing Erin to watch.

"This is Steve's room," she said, confused.

So perceptive.

"Well, you don't get to see the second floor until I'm done with it," Ryan teased.

"Fiiiine." She let out a long sigh, but settled in. Her emotions showed she was just as excited as Ryan was.

He summoned his incomplete wolf and deer skeletons in Steve's room, and quickly animated them. The incomplete mobs stumbled and clattered about less than gracefully. It was a bit underwhelming. At ten points apiece, these two mobs were nearly equal to Steve's cost.

"So, first I summon the mobs to be combined." Ryan figured he would explain the process for Erin, who was watching intently. "Then I push my mana into both of them, preparing them to combine."

He acted as he spoke, and dark mana swirled around the skeletons, enveloping each in a black egg-like shape – just like when he had created Steve.

"Next, I imagine the two mobs combining."

As he pictured the two coming together, the two dark eggs drifted towards each other. Upon contact, the dark mass grew outwards, creating a single, large black egg.

"Ohhhhh." Erin was clinging to his surface, and Ryan grinned internally. She had come so far since the fairy who had been repulsed by his becoming a dark dungeon. They had both grown.

"Now, let's see what hatches," Ryan said.

Silence filled the dungeon as they sat and stared at the dark egg. Ryan could feel mana swirling within, but until the combination was complete, not even he knew what would emerge.

"I want to go look. Have you fixed the tunnels?" Erin asked after a long moment.

She was met with silence as Ryan realized he had yet to fix the zigzagging pattern that was the path from the core room to Steve's room.

"Um..."

He silently made a note to make the path from his core room to his second boss room a lot simpler, for his own sake. An irritated Erin led to an unpleasant situation for Ryan.

"I hate you," Erin muttered before taking off and flying through the tunnel system.

"Love you too, hun," Ryan called, turning his attention back to the dark mass. He silently prayed to the Goddess that it didn't finish before Erin reached Steve's room. Otherwise he would be in even more trouble.

Thankfully, in the minutes it took Erin to fly into Steve's room, the egg hadn't hatched. However, silver lines had begun to form on its surface.

"Any moment now," he said, even as a large crack formed in the egg.

Erin squealed with joy, and flew over the dark receptacle, trying to peek inside. More light erupted as larger cracks appeared, and suddenly the dark egg erupted outwards, causing Erin to cry out as dark mana flew past her. It couldn't harm her, but it startled her enough that she fell to the ground.

"Don't," Erin warned.

The threat in her voice was enough to stifle his laughter as she dusted herself off. Well, that and the creature that now stood before Erin.

"Oh, my." Ryan let out a breathless whisper as he took in the new mob, pride and awe filling him.

The creature was terrifying. Magnificent. And perfectly suited to become his boss mob.

Chapter Forty-Nine

From head to foot, the creature was roughly four feet tall. From nose to tail, perhaps six feet in length. Its body was long and lanky, similar to a wolf, and even ended in a wolf-like boney tail.

However, its leg had the structure of a deer, giving it the added height, and each leg ended in a hoof. The head was comprised of a wolf's skull, but sprouting from it was a massive set of curved antlers. Those antlers had to have been close to two feet in height and sprouted a foot in either direction. Ryan *loved* this new mob.

"Welp, I just found a new hobby," Ryan said carelessly, drawing Erin's attention away from his new mob.

"A new hobby? What was your old hobby?"

Oh, crap.

"Uh. Bone collecting?" Ryan had almost given away skeletal fight club once again. He really was terrible at keeping secrets when he got excited.

"Gross," Erin huffed as she continued looking over the new mob.

Despite her reaction, he knew she secretly had a soft spot for his bone collection. After all, it was the reason he'd been able to create the amazing mob that stood before them.

"So, what should we name it?" Erin asked as she landed gently atop one of the antlers.

"We aren't done yet."

A quick glance at his level triangle, which he had summoned to confirm a suspicion, showed 190. The combined mob still counted as a single medium beast, meaning it only cost him ten points.

"What do you—"

"We're turning this into a boss mob."

Ryan quickly absorbed the skeletal creature, gaining its bone pattern and mentally setting a reminder to name it later on. Ryan figured he had time, because he had already decided he was going to populate his second floor with human skeletons, not beasts.

Well, mostly humans. He still had an idea for his bone pillars that called for a certain skeletal beast.

"Hey," Erin called out. She flapped her wings, finding she suddenly no longer had a seat as the mob disappeared.

"Sorry, hun, but trust me, this is going to be amazing."

Ryan summoned a new copy of his skeletal hybrid and quickly animated it. Then, with his eyes on his level triangle, he calmed his nerves. He was so excited.

"You might want to get a little distance, hun," Ryan said. "Who knows what's about to happen?"

That was what made being a dungeon so much fun. Ever since he created Steve, Ryan had wanted to see what would happen if he tried to make another boss mob. Now, he had gotten that chance.

"I've created a monster," Erin called out, laughing as she flew closer to the ceiling. She could clearly feel his nearly uncontainable level of excitement.

"Nope, I'm creating a monster," Ryan said.

And with that, he flooded his dark mana into his creation. The dark energy rushed around his hybrid, creating a dark egg once again, which grew larger and denser until Ryan's level triangle showed 150. His new boss mob was going to cost twice as much as Steve, but he felt that was fitting for his second floor. He was, after all, twice as strong as he had been.

The wait was nearly unbearable, and if Ryan could, he would

have been bouncing around his room. His attention was fully fixed on the dark egg.

"Come on, hatch already," he whispered, and he could tell Erin was just as impatient.

Already, Ryan was planning out an addition to skeletal fight club. He decided he would keep the matches going when he had the mana. But he would also create a combination room, where he could see just what exactly he could create with this new technique.

Oh, the possibilities.

"Here it comes," Erin called out, her wings flapping excitedly.

The dark egg was cracking, the tell-tale silver lines and white light appearing.

"Don't fall, hun," Ryan replied, earning him a dark look from the fairy.

Worth it.

Before Erin could respond, the egg erupted once again, and for the second time in roughly an hour, Ryan got to see a new mob be born.

If his previous hybrid had been perfect, this new mob transcended even that. The creature that stood in the room was amazing. It had grown to nearly six feet in height, and nine feet in length. Its antlers had widened and grown even more, making it stand closer to a magnificent eight foot. In addition, dark mana seemed to cling and swirl around its antlers, very similar to how the necromancer had shrouded himself in mana.

To Ryan's eyes, he had just created a god. This was a creature to be worshipped and feared. The adventurers would run in—

"Buttercup." Erin's voice pulled him from his thoughts before he could even fully admire his new creation.

"What?" Ryan asked.

"Its name is Buttercup."

Oh, no.

"I don't think—" Ryan began.

"You promised I could name him." Erin had a pout on her face, and he could see her eyes starting to tear up.

Oh, no, you don't.

"Come on, Rin," Ryan pleaded. "Can't you think of something a little more boss-like? That name sounds like something you would name a pet."

Seriously, his boss needed to be feared. With a name like Buttercup, he could already hear Jack laughing.

"You promised I could name him." Erin crossed her arms, glaring at him as tears filled her eyes. "And I'm naming him Buttercup."

Ryan could tell she was on the verge of breaking down. He let out a sigh, defeated.

"Just Buttercup?" he asked.

"Nope, you can choose the second part of the name," Erin said, placated. "I want us both to have a part in naming Buttercup."

Ryan resigned himself to the ridicule he would receive over the name and took a long look at his boss. How could he help make the name a little better? He needed to see what the creature could do.

"Erin, back away from—" Ryan sighed before he spoke the next word. "—Buttercup."

"What are you going to do to him?" she asked, flying back even as she spoke. Ugh, she didn't trust him at all.

"Just going to test something," he mumbled as he grew a stalactite above Buttercup's head. Without warning, he dropped the missile on it.

"RYAN!" Erin's scream filled the room, but quickly died as Ryan's suspicions were confirmed. Before the stalactite could crush Buttercup's skull, the dark mana pulled the antlers from the wolf's skull, spinning them rapidly, creating a swirling blockade of bones that easily blocked the rock. The moment the threat was gone, the antlers returned to Buttercup's head. Oh, how he loved Buttercup.

Aside from that impressive feature, Ryan took in the two additional changes that had taken place on his hybrid. Buttercup's bones had grown larger and denser, while also growing plate-like bone armor, similar to the plated skrat.

A fine layer of dark mana covered Buttercup from head to hoof, almost like black fur. In fact, the mana seemed to create a full wolf tail out of darkness. In that dark mana tail, the wolf-tail bones floated lazily, just like Steve's arm.

With a mental command to Buttercup, the boss mob's tail flicked to the side, shooting a bone spike out at a rapid speed.

Oh yes, Buttercup could sling bones as well. Ryan watched lovingly as Buttercup opened its wolf-like maw, revealing rows of sharp bone teeth, and let out a long, monstrous howl. His heart swelled at his amazing creation.

"All right, I think I've come up with the rest of Buttercup's name." Ryan knew he couldn't change the first part, but he could sure make the second part reflected just how dangerous Buttercup was.

"Let's hear it." Erin's voice was filled with excitement as she admired Buttercup's form.

"Buttercup: Adventurer's Doom."

Maybe it was a bit too ominous, but given what Ryan had just seen, it seemed fitting. Buttercup was bound to give the adventurers a challenge, and he hoped for their sake they were ready for it.

"I love it," Erin said, flying down to look Buttercup over as Ryan assigned the name to his new boss mob.

"Good. Now, let's send Buttercup away and get the rest of the mobs sorted out." Ryan absorbed Buttercup and quickly closed off Erin's tunnel, leaving her cut off from the core room.

"What?!" she shrieked, staring at the entrance that had just closed before her.

"You stay right there, hun," Ryan said. "I want this to be a surprise."

And with that, Ryan blocked out her sputtering outrage as he turned his attention to his second floor. Hopefully, Erin would be so impressed with his second floor – once it was fully filled with mobs – to forgive him.

If not, well, he did tell her he was going to get her back for those "magic" comments.

Chapter Fifty

Following the excitement of Buttercup's creation and the construction of his second floor, Ryan was drained. His mind just wasn't working, and he couldn't figure out how he wanted to fill his second floor.

"I have no idea what to do," Ryan said out loud to no one. It had been roughly an hour since he locked Erin out of his core room, and he was still staring blankly at his second floor.

Maybe I shouldn't have locked her out.

Ryan checked in on Erin, noting the fairy was angrily kicking apart the plants. On second thought, he couldn't ask her for help now. If he didn't impress her with his new floor, he was going to have to deal with her anger for a while. Ryan did not want to go through that.

He had a basic idea but couldn't work out how to make it fit.

"You can do this," he told himself. "You're a strong, independent darkness dungeon core."

Saying the words made him feel a little better, and he started to calm himself.

"First, Buttercup." He summoned his glorious, though ill-named, boss mob into its new room. The creature stamped a dark hoof against the ground and let out an annoyed snort.

"All right, that's fifty points."

Ryan pulled up his level triangle, confirming his thought. A '150' greeted him, showing him his math was correct.

"Perhaps I should fill the first floor again, so I know what I'm working with."

He summoned Steve, watching his count drop to 125. Then, his two infested ratbies, eight skuirrels, eight skrats, two victorious skuirrels, and two champion skrats in his second room. His mob points dropped to eighty-five, making him wince.

Even though his mob points had doubled from Bronze One to Silver Nine, he knew eighty-five points wouldn't go a long way. And he still had to fill the first room on his first floor.

"Well, guess I'll just need to level up even more," Ryan whispered, summoning the six skuirrels and four victorious skuirrels into his first room. He had seventy-one mob points left to spread across four rooms on his second level.

That's not going to do.

Ryan scanned his first floor, mind racing. He really wanted one hundred points to spread across the four rooms, but he knew he couldn't weaken his first floor too much. Sighing, he settled on removing a few mobs from his second room. It had the largest amount of points allotted to it on the first floor, after all.

"So, if I take away one infested ratbie, three skuirrels, and three skrats, that will give me..." He mentally started counting, then stopped.

There was an easier way to do this math. Without a second thought, he reabsorbed an infested ratbie, three skuirrels, and three skrats from his second room. His mob points jumped up to eighty-five. It wasn't perfect, but he could work with that.

His second room now had one infested ratbie, five skuirrels, five skrats, two victorious skuirrels, and two champion skrats, for a total of twenty-six mob points. Now, his first room cost fourteen points, his second room cost twenty-six, and his third, with Steve, cost twenty-five. That was a total of sixty-five points spread across his first floor. Ryan was okay with that.

Now, what do I do with these mobs for my second floor?

Since creating his second floor, Ryan had known he wanted to use his human skeletons. However, he had never actually summoned any, other than Steve, so had no idea how to implement them.

Looking at his mob collection, Ryan technically had three options for his human skeletons. Basic, which cost five points; hardened, which cost fifteen; and then the skeletal mage, at fifty.

Who thought of giving me a mob at Silver Nine that costs a quarter of my points? That's just rude.

Considering he only had eighty-five points to spread across four rooms, the skeletal mage was out of the question. Ryan had to wonder if there had been any dungeons that just used their most expensive mob on the second floor right at Silver Nine. He did remember Erin mentioned most darkness dungeons didn't really rely on their mob points, instead reanimating adventurers and anything else foolish enough to enter the dungeon.

Did that mean those dungeons could reanimate mages upon death, and instantly use them at Silver Nine? That was definitely a way around the high cost, albeit a way Ryan would never use. He was again reminded of just how powerful darkness dungeons could become if they didn't worry about etiquette.

Back to mob summoning. He chased such thoughts from his mind and turned back to his task at hand. He would never cross that line, so no use thinking about it.

Ryan could use a mixture of the hardened and basic skeletons. He flipped through his mobs one more time, doing a little mental math. He knew he still had one more mob to summon on his second floor for his surprise and needed to make sure his math was correct. This floor was going to be much more challenging than his first, but it was meant to be.

"Now, let's see what these human skeletons can do."

To test them, he summoned two human skeletons in the first room on his second floor. He grinned as he did. Nothing like an impromptu skeletal fight club match to help him destress.

Round one. Fight!

The two skeletons turned and faced each other. The red light from above cast an eerie glow on them, as if their bones were stained with blood. Upon receiving Ryan's mental command, the two creatures lunged at each other, quickly meeting in a clatter of bone on bone.

They scratched, they punched, they tore at each other. Entertaining, but Ryan doubted they would prove much of a challenge against the adventurers. Adventurers had swords, and shields, and armor, and—

Oh.

Ryan stopped the two mobs, deciding the round was a draw, and healed them both.

I wonder…

He quickly summoned a set of bone swords and shields on the ground, mentally instructing the skeletons to pick them up. The two mobs grabbed the weapons and turned to face each other again.

Round two. Fight!

The first skeleton went on the offense, while the second skeleton watched the first one warily, shield raised. It seemed, just like Ryan's other mobs, these mobs could quickly learn and develop different habits. The aggressor swung his bone sword down in a slash that the second easily blocked. Having blocked the sword, he swung his own blade, only to be met by the shield.

They may have been developing different fighting tendencies, but they were both still new to fighting with sword and shield. Neither was going to overpower the other in such a short amount of time, and Ryan wanted to try one more thing before he committed to his dungeon mobs.

"Good fight, guys. This next one will be to the death." He ordered the aggressive mob to drop its sword and shield. Ryan had one last test that might give his mobs an even larger edge against adventurers.

The moment he absorbed the bone weapons, Ryan summoned a bow for his mob, giving it a quiver full of arrows. To keep the theme, everything was made from bone, except the string. That Ryan formed from sinew.

Let's see how this goes.

He ordered the mob to pick up the weapons, and then sent each skeleton to a different corner of the room.

Round three. Fight!

The aggressive skeleton, now armed with a bow, tried to launch the first attack. However, as it nocked its arrow and tried to let it fly, the bone missile fell after a few feet of flight. Its second arrow had a similar result, and the defensive skeleton was slowly approaching, shield raised protectively.

Maybe that weapon is too complex?

The skeleton was pulling back on his bow for a third time, arrow nocked, and this time, when he released, the missile flew true. It clattered against the bone shield, causing the defensive skeleton to stop for a second.

Oh, they learn quickly.

Ryan had noticed his skrats and skuirrels developed new tactics the longer they lived and fought, which was what made skeletal fight club so beneficial. Watching these two skeletons fight, countless thoughts and plans started to fill his mind.

Could he make his mobs masters in the countless weapons he had collected? It would definitely create a challenge for adventurers if he could.

The sound of bones crunching pulled him from his thoughts, and he watched as the defensive skeleton smashed his shield into the aggressive one's face.

Welp, this fight is over.

But even as the thought crossed Ryan's mind, the skeleton armed with the bow did the unexpected. Even as the shield came towards its face again, the aggressive skeleton pulled an arrow from his quiver and smashed it into the skull of the defensive one.

Fatality.

Ryan cheered as the defensive skeleton's skull cracked and it collapsed into a pile of bones. He was really looking forward to Silver skeletal fight club.

A sudden wave of anger washed over Ryan, drowning out his joy.

Oh yeah. Erin.

He had forgotten about her during his little skeletal fight, and he could tell she was not amused with his happy emotions. Time to finish, before she got any ideas. Ryan could only imagine how Erin could torture him if she really wanted to.

Guess I should hurry up.

Ryan reabsorbed both skeletons and was pleasantly surprised

to find he had unlocked two new variants of basic skeleton: skeletal archer and skeletal fighter, both at five points. It seemed that even though they had gained the skills to use weapons, they still only cost the basic cost of a skeleton.

If Ryan had to guess, that went back to Erin's belief that the God of Death wanted human skeletons to be used. Ryan, with only eighty-five mob points, wasn't about to complain about cheap and efficient mobs.

For Ryan's first room, he summoned two skeletal fighters, leaving him with seventy-five remaining points. In the second room, he also summoned two skeletal fighters. He wanted adventurers to get used to them, so that the third room would come as a surprise. He had sixty-five mob points left.

In the third room, which was the first room to have a bone pillar and one of the three keys, Ryan summoned two skeletal archers. He sent them each to one of the corners, facing the entrance adventurers would take. These skeletal archers should prove quite the surprise for adventurers and would make them a little warier for the rest of his dungeon. The other surprise for this room would be at his bone pillar with his other new mob.

Grinning to himself, he summoned five of them. They were, after all, considered small beasts. He watched as the five bony forms, well, formed on the floor. They were long and slender, with small amounts of dark mana holding them together. In each of their mouths were two dangerous fangs.

Ryan had to admit that finding the snake skeleton had excited him more than he expected. And now, as they slithered into the pile of bones, waiting to strike the first adventurer to reach for the key, he grinned even more. These were his sneaky snakes. He decided to call them sneks.

Fifty points left.

In the next room, Ryan assigned two skeletal archers and two skeletal fighters, costing him twenty points and leaving him with thirty left for his final room. He had decided to make the rooms increasingly harder as adventurers conducted their dive. He wanted to wear them down to their bones before they reached Buttercup.

Ha. If only Erin had been around for that pun.

The final room for his mobs – the room right before his boss room, and right after a trap room filled with bone spikes – was going to be the most difficult. He summoned two skeletal archers, two skeletal fighters, and ten sneks.

He created a tunnel system that snaked through the room, allowing the sneks to pop up and attack from countless angles and areas. Hopefully, while adventurers focused on the human skeletons, his sneks could do some good damage.

This way, maybe we can prevent some pointless deaths, too.

Ryan purposefully made the room before his boss room the hardest. He had learned from Erin, and from his own observations, that the weaker adventurers gave him less experience when they died.

As such, he wanted adventurers to be as strong as possible before they died. No need for pointless deaths of low-ranking adventurers; those didn't gain him anything. And he needed to get stronger, because that necromancer still scared him.

Because of this, Ryan wanted the room before the boss to do its best to scare the adventurers off. If they took too much damage before Buttercup's room, hopefully they would turn back. That would allow them to continue to live, and dive, another day, which meant when they did face Buttercup, and likely failed, Ryan would benefit even more.

He smiled at the thought and scanned his second floor one last time. It was ready.

Chapter Fifty-One

Erin glared at him, rage flowing through their bond as she tapped her foot impatiently.

"How am I supposed to get down there, bonehead?" she demanded.

Ryan had let her back into the core room, excited to show her the second floor, but he had apparently forgotten one small detail. He hadn't connected his core room to the second floor. In fact, he hadn't connected the first floor to the second floor either. *Oops.*

"Well, I, uh—"

Think.

"I wanted your suggestion for that part," he said lamely.

"Hmph." Erin crossed her arms and stared at him. He knew she knew he was lying. But Ryan could also tell she was excited to see his second floor, making her more willing to let go of her anger to help him.

"Well, hun?" he asked.

Erin sighed and flew on top of him.

"Most dungeons put a door or passage at the end of their first boss room that leads down into the start of their second level."

Oh, that made sense. Only one problem.

"So, if the first room of my second floor is below the first room of the first floor—"

"Seriously?" Erin let out an exasperated sigh. "This is why you should have let me help."

"I wanted to surprise you." Ryan's voice was quiet.

He had been so proud, but now he realized he may have made a few mistakes. He was definitely still learning.

"Well, create a tunnel that leads back underneath the first floor," she said, "down to the start of the second floor."

She spoke as if it were easy. Well, technically, with his increased mana, it was. He had found, thanks to his new mana reserves, he could build and destroy things within his dungeon a lot faster than before. However, such a large tunnel would still take him some time.

"And then?" Ryan asked.

He mentally began clearing out a tunnel. He started it as rough and cavernous, but mentally began to improve upon it as he went. He wanted adventurers to feel they were transitioning from a rough cave to an underground castle. Looks mattered, after all.

"And then you need to drop the core room down, so that it connects easily to the second boss room. Your core needs to always be connected in some way to each floor. Otherwise, you won't get experience from the floor."

Really? That's a thing?

Ryan couldn't believe she had never mentioned that important fact before. He would have hated to lose out on the potential experience his second floor would give him.

"Well, thanks for letting me know now." His tone betrayed a bit of his annoyance, earning him a slap from Erin.

He deserved that. She was just trying to help him, even if she was rather forgetful when it came to the important facts. Ryan could only wonder what else she had forgotten.

"Don't give me attitude, especially after you locked me away from the core room for so long."

How long had it been? Ryan had a bad habit of losing track of time when he was doing things in his dungeon. How long had he been working on his second floor?

"Sorry, hun," Ryan said, a little regretfully. "But trust me, you're going to love the new floor."

He was nearly done with the tunnel connecting the first floor to the second and had begun moving his core room lower in the dungeon. Unlike the rest of the dungeon, he found he was able to easily move his core room through the rock and stone that held his influence. Perhaps it was because the room contained his core and physical being?

Regardless, as he finished connecting his two floors, he had also finished placing his core room behind Buttercup's room. He connected a tiny, fairy-sized tunnel from the core room to Buttercup's and straightened the tunnel connecting his core room to Steve's room. No more twisting tunnels to annoy Erin.

"Are you ready?" Erin was hovering now, wings fluttering quickly. Her anger was giving way to impatience and excitement.

"Yes—"

Erin let out a squeal of joy and shot towards the tunnel leading to Buttercup's room.

"Wait." Ryan's exclamation caused the fairy to pause. "Can you start at the start of the second floor? I want you to see it how adventurers will."

Erin stared at him for a moment before nodding

"I suppose." She looked with disgust at the tunnel leading towards Steve's room. Ryan knew she really hated the snaking tunnel. Little did she know he had fixed it.

"Well, get going." He nudged her mentally, sending a burst of excitement through their bond, and with a sigh she took off.

Ryan nearly broke out in laughter as he felt her mood shift from trepidation to excitement as she realized the tunnel was a straight shot now to Steve's room. He couldn't wait for her to see his second floor. And once she was done touring the second floor, he could finally open his dungeon again.

Speaking of opening the dungeon...

As Erin zipped through the door from Steve's room, down the tunnel that led towards the second floor, Ryan realized he had forgotten to do one thing. He needed to assign loot to his new mobs. As Erin had told him, loot was one of the main reasons adventurers risked their lives in a dungeon.

Let's see what we can do here.

His basic skeletons were technically Bronze mobs. However,

since they cost five points, just like his ratbies, he assigned silver coins to them, as well as the occasional uncommon loot drop, such as the fine silk cloth and fine iron dagger. His sneks were one-point mobs, and as such, copper and common items.

"Hey, Rin." She was just about to reach the second floor, and Ryan's voice made her pause.

"Yes?"

Her voice held a tinge of irritation, but Ryan decided to ignore that. He couldn't be mad that she was excited to see his new floor.

"For Buttercup, should we stick to rare item drops like Steve, or can we do ultra-rare?"

"Hmmm. We need to stick with rare items still. Usually ultra-rare items aren't dropped until Gold-level dungeons. Legendary items aren't supposed to drop until a dungeon is Diamond level. Remember, if you start dropping too-good loot early on, you're going to be swarmed by powerful adventurers who will walk all over you."

Ryan was once again reminded of why he shouldn't have dropped that celestial feather.

"Rare drops it is," he said.

Ryan began mentally assigning loot drops to Buttercup. While he needed to stick with rare items, because of Buttercup's higher mob cost and difficulty, he increased the amount of gold or items it could drop. While Steve dropped one or two pieces of gold, or a single item, Buttercup could drop up to three items if the group was lucky, and had the ability to drop anywhere from five to fifteen gold. For good measure, he increased the amount of silver and copper coins his mobs could drop throughout the second floor. More risk, more reward.

Erin was at the door to his second floor now, and having just finished his mob loot, Ryan was ready for her to begin exploring. The moment she gave him the okay, he would be able to open his dungeon again.

And with his dungeon open, Ryan could begin gaining experience once again. Skeletal fight club was calling, and he needed to hit Silver Eight to get more mob points to start it back up.

Chapter Fifty-Two

"Who are these people?' Ryan asked.

He had opened his dungeon during the night, raising his wolf skull mouth back from the ground, opening his maw once again. The moment he had, a dark form had walked from the shadows of the trees to look him over.

Ryan grew tense for a moment, fearing it was the necromancer, until he recognized the figure as Rasha. The male glanced at Ryan's entrance, his eyes seeming disinterested, before he simply vanished again.

However, in the morning, a mass of people began to gather outside of Ryan's dungeon. People Ryan didn't know.

"Who knows?" Erin replied. "But I hope they're ready."

Erin was sitting atop his core, practically shaking with excitement. She had showered him with praise over his second floor, which had earned him forgiveness for locking her out of the core room. But now they both wanted adventurers to begin diving to see just how the second floor would play out.

Ryan scanned the crowd, frustrated that he couldn't pull up their information unless they entered his dungeon. He was looking for the familiar faces of adventurers he knew to be strong. He was looking for Blake and his team.

"Ugh, where is he?" Ryan asked aloud.

He noticed a few of the old teams milling about, but most of the people were new to him. What's more, he couldn't find Blake or any of his members.

"Maybe they got bored of waiting?" Erin guessed.

Since she had been asleep most of his dungeon building, and since Ryan had lost track of time, neither of them knew just how long the dungeon had been closed off for.

"I wasn't closed that long."

It couldn't have been more than a week. Maybe two. Even though his second floor was much bigger than his first, his increased mana made the work much faster. However, he had no idea how much time he had wasted on interior design, and then of course mob building. Maybe three weeks, tops.

"Well, it looks like Marcus is back. Maybe he will tell us something," Erin suggested.

The man in charge of the adventurers was making his way calmly through the crowds. He didn't seem an impressive figure, but the way people moved out of his way made it clear he was important. As he stepped forward, he took a single step inside the dungeon, allowing Ryan to pull up information on the adventurer.

"He's Platinum?" Ryan was impressed.

Marcus was a Platinum Two rogue with an air affinity. For a moment, Ryan wondered just how much experience Marcus would give him if the rogue fell in his dungeon. Then he remembered what Erin had said about Sean and knew even with his new Silver tier he wouldn't be able to scratch the rogue.

"Guess there is a reason he's in charge." Erin seemed a little less impressed. The only Platinum adventurer she had eyes for was Sean.

For just a moment, Ryan felt his jealousy flare, and he had to stop himself from summoning a stalactite to drop on a skuirrel. He was working on his impulse control.

"Wonder if he can keep the necromancer away," Ryan mumbled.

He knew the necromancer was Gold One; the man had said it himself. Marcus had to be more than a match for him. So where had Marcus been when the necromancer attacked? Ryan had taken precautions against a future attack, but if he knew Marcus was guarding him, it would make him feel a lot better.

"Sasha seemed to have at least injured him." The fairy had her arms around herself, holding back a slight shudder. The shadow of the necromancer still hung over them, a very real threat that pushed Ryan to grow stronger.

"But she didn't kill him." Ryan would have noticed if the necromancer had died. For one, the experience gain would have been amazing, and for two, there would have been a body. No matter how strong Sasha was, she had failed to kill the necromancer. Meaning he was still out there, meaning Ryan was still in danger.

"Well, we are more prepared now," Erin said, "and he can't take control of our mobs this time."

Unless, of course, he had become Platinum. If that was the case, Ryan was sure the next time the necromancer appeared, he would die. He didn't like that fact.

"Maybe you should focus on reaching Gold, just to be sure?" said Erin.

"Don't worry, hun, I've learned my lesson," Ryan said. "These adventurers are in for a big surprise. As Marcus said, only the strong shall survive."

"That's my dungeon." Erin gave him a big hug, causing him to glow a little brighter. He really liked it when she called him hers. Ryan loved making her proud.

"Looks like Marcus is about to speak." Ryan's words made Erin pull away, watching intently through Ryan's core. They were both curious what the man would say.

"I'm going to keep this short, as I'm sure most of you are eager to begin your dives." Marcus's voice was deep and strong, washing over the adventurers. "The dungeon has been closed off for almost a month."

"Whoops," Ryan groaned as the adventurers cheered. "Guess I really lost track of time."

"You think?" Erin hit him lightly and laughed, but quickly grew silent as Marcus continued.

"During that time, it is likely the dungeon transitioned to Silver."

More cheers.

"As you know, when a dungeon transitions, a new floor appears."

Even more cheers. Marcus held up a hand, silencing the group.

"Are you all going to let me speak? Or shall we stand out here all day?"

Marcus's tone was light, but by the way the crowd reacted, his threat must have been a serious one.

"Thank you." The rogue dropped his hand and continued. "Obviously, while we can inspect the ranks of your team before you enter the dungeon, we cannot dictate how far you go during your dive. That being said, I highly encourage teams that still have Bronze members to avoid beginning the second floor."

The mood around the crowd seemed to darken, and Ryan could just barely make out some murmuring.

"If," Marcus stared hard at the crowd, "you do not heed my warning, the Adventurers' Guild will consider your deaths deserved, and I will personally be thanking the dungeon for clearing out weak fools who can't follow my advice."

"Oh, he's harsh," Erin said in a hushed voice.

"But he does have a point," Ryan said.

He secretly hoped the adventurers would listen. He didn't want any Bronze fools dying; they hardly offered him much experience. The Silver adventurers, though, would help him level up quickly.

"As such," Marcus went on, "if you wish to heed my warning, I suggest teams embarking on the second floor are at least all Silver, preferably with a Gold member, or two high Silver members. The dungeon is going to be dangerous. It has likely developed new mobs to challenge you, and from my experience with dungeons, you can expect more traps than before."

"Uh, how predictable are we?" Ryan didn't like that Marcus had essentially just pegged exactly what Ryan had done.

"Well, fairies are all taught the same thing when it comes to dungeon development." Erin was looking sheepish. "So, if Marcus has seen a lot of dungeons, there's a good chance they all followed the book."

"There's a book on dungeon development?" If Erin had a book, she could just give it to him, and Ryan would know everything.

"Mm-hmm. It's called the Dungeon Master's Guide," Erin said. "No one knows who developed it, but all dungeon fairies are taught from it. The book itself has been lost for a long time, though, so the elders only have notes pulled from it."

That explained why she seemed uncertain about a lot of things. If Ryan had to guess, his sweet loveable airheaded Erin hadn't been the best student. And he doubted she took notes of her own.

"Well, I guess next time I'll try not to play by the book," Ryan said. "It's no fun if I can't surprise them."

Marcus started to speak again.

"Now, there are a few other things to address before I let the dives begin." Marcus pulled out a pendant. "As you all know, the dungeon town has now established its own teleportation crystal. As such, when you have gone as far as you wish in the dungeon, please use your pendants to teleport back to town. The clerics will establish a healing tent next to the crystal, to tend to your wounds."

He pulled out the disc that was used to track adventurers.

"The moment your team teleports out, the crystals will flash blue, letting us know you have left, before they dim. That way, we can send more teams through on a faster schedule."

The crowd broke out in cheers. Ryan couldn't help but cheer as well. More teams each day meant more opportunities to level up. He really wanted more mob points so he could begin skeletal fight club once again.

Marcus looked at the crowd of adventurers, and as he scanned the group, his lip curled up and his eyes seemed to fill with distaste.

"I also see, with the implementation of our own teleportation crystal, the kingdoms have begun sending in nobles to train."

A few of the more well-dressed members in the crowd frowned at this statement.

"Just know this," Marcus went on. "The Adventurers' Guild is not to be held responsible for any of your deaths. Dungeons are dangerous places, and accidents happen. The kingdoms understand this and have likely provided strong enough guards to protect the nobles as they conduct their dives. However, I don't doubt one or two of you will be foolish enough to get yourselves killed in the dungeon. Just know if that happens, no one will cry, and no one will come and avenge you. You've been warned."

The well-dressed individuals' faces had taken on a mask of rage, while Marcus seemed to be smirking.

"Guess he really doesn't like nobles, whatever those are," Ryan whispered.

"I wonder why?" Erin peered at the groups through Ryan's crystal.

Other than being dressed in much finer clothes than the other adventurers, Ryan couldn't see anything that would make the rogue dislike the nobles as much as he seemed to. Guess he would just have to wait till they dove into the dungeon to make his own opinion.

"All right, with that done," Marcus said, rubbing his hands. "Each group will once again draw lots to choose dive order. You are allowed to wait in town, but know that if you are more than fifteen minutes late when your number is called, you will be skipped."

He stepped out of Ryan's wolf skull, and Rasha and Sasha appeared at his side.

"Now," Marcus announced, spreading his arms wide. "Let's begin!"

Ryan was certain he and Erin cheered louder than the adventurers.

Chapter Fifty-Three

Ryan watched another group of adventurers teleport out of his dungeon, having barely managed to defeat Steve. So far, three groups of adventurers had entered, all new to Ryan, all with members in Bronze, and all barely able to clear his first floor. Three adventurers had fallen so far, courtesy of his single infested ratbie's paralysis poison. It was like they were surprised when the paralysis kicked in during the fight against Steve.

"What in the name of the Goddess is going on?" Ryan groaned.

"I'm not sure. Where are the regular groups?" Erin shook her head, and Ryan could tell she was disappointed.

They both wanted adventurers to test out their second floor. But so far, it had only been these noobs – a term Ryan remembered the fire mage using to describe Blake during the initial exploration dive. He knew it was derogatory, but it described these weak adventurers so well.

"I see one regular group waiting outside, but they haven't stepped up yet." Ryan was secretly starting to hate the selection process. He wanted an advanced group, and he wanted them now.

"Oh, one of the noble groups is up next," Ryan said.

As he spoke, a group consisting of four impressively armored soldiers and a well-dressed man stepped towards Marcus.

"It's about time," the noble said, shoving his pendant against the disc in Marcus's hands. "How dare you make me wait for a bunch of second-rate commoners?"

Ryan was pretty sure he saw a vein twitch in the rogue's eye.

"Baron Aaron, is it?" Marcus's voice was cold.

"It is actually pronounced A-a-ron," the noble replied haughtily. "My family has elven blood in our lineage, from my great-grandfather's line. As such, we choose to adopt their noble naming convention, and emphasize our vowels. Though I wouldn't expect a commoner like you to understand."

Marcus's eye twitched again, and his knuckles grew white on the disc. Ryan was starting to see why the rogue disliked nobility.

"Very well, A-a-ron," Marcus said through gritted teeth. "I would love to see how your guards carry your sorry self through the dungeon. Please do try not to get killed just yet."

The noble turned his chin up towards Marcus, fingers on his sword. "Are you implying that I cannot take care of myself?"

"I'm implying that you're going to get good men killed with that attitude." Marcus's tone was cold, and Ryan was certain if looks could kill, A-a-ron would have died right there.

"My lord, please." One of the guards stepped forward, bowing towards the baron. "Do not allow this lowly rogue to waste your time."

"Good point." The baron motioned for the four men surrounding him to step forward. As one, they marched into Ryan's dungeon, the noble safely positioned in between his guards.

"Now, let's see just how strong they—" Ryan pulled up the stats on the noble's group. "—well, that's just not fair."

All four of the guards were Gold, while A-a-ron was high Silver.

"Hmm, well, you wanted a strong group to clear the first floor." Erin had perked up, and was watching the group as they advanced.

As they neared the first room, A-a-ron stopped at the entrance, and the four Gold guards stepped forward. With practiced ease, they eliminated all the mobs in the room, and once again took up their protective formation around the noble as they started towards his second room.

"Yeah, but this just seems like cheating," Ryan complained. "That noble is getting all the experience, while doing none of the work."

I wonder if the noble even knows how to fight?

Ryan started to formulate a plan.

"Ugh. Guards, I will not walk through these filthy plants." A-a-ron's voice pulled Ryan from his scheme, and he watched as one of the guards stepped forward. A quick glance at his class told Ryan all he needed to know, and a second later, all the greenery in his second room burst into flames, instantly turning everything to ash. Ryan hated it when adventurers did that.

"I'm really starting to dislike this guy," Ryan muttered.

"Me too," Erin sighed as the group marched easily towards Steve's room. Ryan's poor first-floor boss didn't stand a chance.

Sure enough, the four guards killed Steve before the boss mob could even launch his attack at A-a-ron, as Ryan had been planning.

"This dungeon is pathetic." The noble flicked a small piece of bone off his clothes, the closest he had gotten to a skeleton yet. "Like, seriously, why must Father send me to such a drab place?"

"Sir, you know nobles need to reach Platinum before they can be deemed a worthy successor," the first guard – named Frank – said as he picked up the gold coin Steve had dropped.

"Yes, yes," the noble said. "But why this dungeon? It's in the middle of nowhere, the town is pathetic, and the dungeon is only Silver tiered." A-a-ron let out a sigh as the guards surrounded him and began towards the door at the end of Steve's room. They were the first group to reach the door and actually choose to move on.

"Well, sir, it's common practice to send nobles to Silver-tiered dungeons so that there is less of a chance of an accident occurring." Frank cleared his throat. "We can keep you safe in this dungeon. The next lowest dungeon in existence is a high Gold fire dungeon, which has been known to wipe out entire parties of Gold—"

"Are you implying I cannot pull my own weight?" The noble

pulled out a finely crafted sword, waving it at the guard. Ryan was sure A-a-ron intended it to be threatening, but the noble didn't seem to know how to actually use his weapon. Ryan saw the guards behind the noble smirk.

"No, sir. It's just... we would never wish to burden you with having to fight in the dungeon. Please, allow us to keep you safe as we level you up."

A-a-ron huffed, and after three attempts, managed to sheathe his sword.

"Very well. Just know: the noble blood running through my veins means that even at Silver, I am much stronger than all of you. Never forget that."

"I don't like him," Ryan repeated as the group walked through the long tunnel towards the second floor.

"He is rather dislikable, isn't he?" The fairy frowned at the noble.

"Can we—"

"No." Erin stopped him before he even finished his thought. "You know it's not proper dungeon etiquette."

"I'm getting really tired of this etiquette at times," Ryan moaned. "Besides, he's high Silver. I'm sure that would give us enough to reach Silver Eight."

Three Bronze adventurers had barely filled a third of his experience triangle, but Ryan was sure a high Silver would do the trick. Then he would have enough points to start up skeletal fight club again.

"You know I want you to get stronger, Ryan," Erin said. "But we can't go around dropping boulders on people's heads, no matter how dislikable they are. Dungeon etiquette is in place to keep you safe. I don't know how many times I've had to tell you now, dungeons that break etiquette do not live for long. The Adventurers' Guild has no qualms closing off dungeons that grow too dangerous. And, if that doesn't stop you, or they view you as an even graver threat, the guild will destroy you. Everyone out there knows that, which is why so many adventurers are flocking to you. They don't know how long you will be around."

She had already told him these very facts many times. Ryan

knew etiquette was important, and he had no intention of angering the guild. But still; this noble really deserved a good stoning.

"But we did it to Josh," Ryan grumbled.

"Josh was evil. A-a-ron is just, well, a spoiled brat. That's not a crime in the eyes of the Goddess."

"Fiiiine," Ryan moaned, watching as the group neared his second floor.

Sure, Erin said he couldn't just flat-out kill A-a-ron. But Ryan was sure he could at least have some fun with the noble. Especially on his second floor.

Chapter Fifty-Four

"Break down the door." A-a-ron stood with his arms crossed, staring at his guards.

They had reached the second room of the second floor and had discovered the locked door. *Good luck with that.* Ryan pushed a little more mana into the door's reinforcements just in case the guards decided to give it a try.

"Sir, generally, attempting to force open a locked door in a dungeon is ill-advised." As Frank spoke, the other guards nodded in agreement. Given their ranks, Ryan was sure they had all spent a good amount of time either in dungeons, or in extensive training.

"Bah! Are you implying we have to play this dungeon's little game and search for the three keys?" A-a-ron aimed a petulant kick at the door. He missed.

"Yes," Ryan snapped. "That's exactly what you have to do, you pretentious little—"

"Ryan." Erin shot him a look. "Language."

"Sorry, hun," Ryan said sheepishly. He turned back to the group. A-a-ron was really starting to irritate him.

"Trust me, Ryan, if it wasn't so dangerous, I would be asking you to drop a rock on his head right now." Erin gave Ryan's core a comforting touch.

A-a-ron had insulted every aspect of Ryan's dungeon so far.

He really wasn't looking forward to the baron reaching Buttercup.

"Ugh, it's so hard being good sometimes."

The noble's words interrupted them.

"Let's get this over with, then," the spoiled man said. "Hopefully this dungeon's next boss isn't as pathetic as the first. I would rather rank up as fast as possible."

A-a-ron motioned to the guards, and the group headed towards the next room. Sure, Ryan couldn't purposefully drop a rock on A-a-ron, but that didn't mean he couldn't have his mobs target the noble.

"Let's see how well he—" Ryan stopped as the guards opened the door and quickly stepped in front of the noble, blocking any chance Ryan's skeletal archers had of hitting him. With ease, the Gold guards destroyed his two mobs.

"Would you like to grab the first key, sir?" Frank motioned towards the tower of bones.

Ryan had made his keys out of bones and had named this one the skeleton key.

"I hate your sense of humor at times," Erin commented as Ryan started chuckling. He could only imagine the looks the guards were giving each other was because of the name on the key.

The noble spoke. "Psh, like I would soil my hands with such a filthy thing," he said.

"Very well, sire." Frank stepped forward, reaching towards the skeleton key.

Ryan held his nonexistent breath, waiting.

As Frank's hand brushed against the key, the pile of bones erupted in motion. *Huzzah, sneks!*

"Yes!"

Ryan's cheer faded as Frank's skin seemed to turn to metal. The sneks that lunged at him slammed against his metallic exterior, shattering into tiny bone fragments.

Right. Frank was a centurion, an elemental knight with an earth affinity.

"Well, that's just no fun." Ryan pouted, silently mourning the death of his newest mobs. At least he knew the sneks would surprise the other adventurers if they had managed to catch Frank by surprise.

"Maybe next time, hun," Erin comforted him, though she seemed just as disappointed as he was.

"You know, I really hate the idea of this group being the first to face Buttercup," Ryan said.

The group headed towards the next room, again leaving A-a-ron at the entrance while the guards easily dispatched the four mobs within. Ryan hated to admit it, but the guards were definitely well trained. If only A-a-ron wasn't with them.

"At least there aren't many noble groups out there," Erin said.

"Yeah, but those other adventurers weren't prepared at all." Ryan wanted the original groups back.

The new adventurer groups were too weak, the noble groups too strong, but the original groups – Blake's group – were just right.

"They will learn, hun," Erin said. "They will grow stronger. It's not like they have a guide to tell them what to expect. How would they have known your infested ratbies cause paralysis? All the original groups had to learn on their own as well. You just got used to them knowing what your mobs could do."

She was right. Ryan had become used to his original groups. They had been just as clumsy as these new groups in the beginning, and Ryan had got to watch them grow stronger over time.

However, he wanted these new groups to be just as prepared now, without weeks of trial and error. Otherwise, it was going to be a while before Ryan could gain a significant amount of experience, and level up. Perhaps he could come up with a way to help prepare these new groups, to prevent pointless Bronze deaths. Then he could benefit from the Silver experience.

Hmm.

"What are you thinking?" Erin's voice pulled him out of his musings.

Ryan had come up with a new plan, and he was certain he would be able to implement it in a few days. He just needed to try a few things out.

"Nothing, hun. How's our super powerful baron doing?"

Ryan's voice was filled with sarcasm as he watched the group head towards the room with the third key. At least Ryan would get to see his new trap in action.

"The Baron of Complaints has just been complaining about the state of your dungeon so far," Erin said. "It seems the guards, other than Frank, are just doing their best to ignore him."

"I don't blame them," Ryan said.

He watched as Frank pushed open the door to the third pillar room, the guards stepping forward cautiously as they scanned for enemies.

"Oh," Erin said, clapping her hands. "This room should be amusing, at least."

The fairy's wings fluttered excitedly as she looked into his core. According to Erin, only adventurers with a thief class, a ranger class, or certain mages, were able to detect traps proficiently.

That meant the four guards, who were all elemental knights, wouldn't be able to detect Ryan's traps. That could be amusing indeed.

"Well, what are you waiting for?" A-a-ron's voice came across in an irritated whine. His foot was tapping as he stared at the backs of the stationary guards.

"There aren't any mobs in here, sir," Frank explained. "It is likely the room is trapped."

The four guards were carefully walking towards the pillar, taking slow, measured steps. They couldn't detect traps, but Ryan was sure they had experience with a plethora of different types. He hoped his could at least surprise them.

"The dungeon hasn't had any advanced traps so far." A-a-ron pushed past Frank. "What makes you think it would have any—"

He triggered the tripwire. The door behind the group closed, causing the noble to jump with fright as the other guards winced. Ryan was certain a few of them were thinking nasty thoughts about the noble.

"I've had it with this dungeon," A-a-ron yelled as he regained his composure. He reached the bone pillar and grabbed at the key.

"Yes!" Ryan cried out gleefully, opening the ground up beneath A-a-ron.

Initially, he had planned for the trap to open a hole underneath a different adventurer in the party, to force the group to use the key to save that member. But this group didn't know that, and this was a perfectly fine way to kill this annoying—

Faster than Ryan could anticipate, one of the guards, a knight with a wind affinity, called a Tempest Knight, rushed to A-a-ron, shoving him out of the way as the floor opened up. Unfortunately, that meant the knight fell through the hole and into the bone maiden instead.

"Alex," Frank called out, lunging towards the now-sealed hole. Ryan watched Alex take in his new surroundings. Wind began swirling around the knight, trying to protect him, but Ryan's bone spikes were lined with dark mana.

Slowly, they began cutting through the wind toward the knight. Frank looked at the cryptic message that appeared on the ground and turned towards the baron.

"Sir, we need the key."

"Nonsense." A-a-ron's voice echoed out in the room. "Alex has done his job and preserved my life. Now, let us be on our way."

The baron hastily exited the room, leaving the guards staring from Alex to the baron. With a growl of frustration, the three guards left the room before the door closed. The door may have been closed, but it couldn't block out Alex's cry as the bone maiden completed its task.

"You killed him," Frank growled as he grabbed the baron's collar, lifting him easily into the air.

"I don't care. I want to be done with this dungeon now." A-a-ron's voice was cold as he pulled a pendant from his shirt, causing the guards to flinch. "Besides, if he was strong enough, he wouldn't have died."

Frank's eyes flashed with anger.

"He was only in that trap because of—"

The knight bit his tongue as the pendant around A-a-ron's neck began to take on a red hue. Gingerly, the guard set the baron down.

"I'm leaving." With that, the baron simply disappeared, leaving the guards standing alone in the room.

"Did he just leave us?" one of the remaining guards asked Frank.

"I'm pretty sure that idiot forgot he had to mentally focus on teleporting us out as well." Frank sighed as he stood. "Had the coward thought of that port ability sooner, Alex would still be alive."

The group turned back towards the closed door, towards their fallen friend.

"We'd better get out of here before the baron gets himself killed in town." Frank offered a sad smile at the others. "I really wish Alex had let that fool fall into the trap."

"Me too," Ryan whispered, feeling bad for the guards as they headed towards the exit. The guards seemed a good bunch, but that noble was something else.

However, even as the group walked quietly out of the dungeon, Ryan silently vowed to them that Alex's death wouldn't be in vain.

The Gold guard had given Ryan enough experience to level up, meaning skeletal fight club was back in business, and had also given Ryan a new idea on how to avenge the poor guard. He was going to come up with something extra special for the next time A-a-ron appeared.

Leaving his guard to die was, after all, something Ryan was sure the Goddess of Justice wouldn't approve of.

Chapter Fifty-Five

"It seems you have mastered the basics of being a knight, Blake." A grizzled man stood before him, offering him a gauntleted hand.

Blake took the knight trainer's offered hand, smiling as he shook it.

"Thank you for everything, sir," he replied.

Blake had spent the past month training with the knight class trainer, Gerald, who was a Gold sentinel with the Adventurers' Guild. A sentinel was the purest form of knight, and Gerald had been able to teach Blake all the basic skills and abilities needed to be a knight. He had also helped Blake get used to the influx of power he had received when he became Silver.

Over the month, the knight trainer had not only helped Blake learn to infuse his mana into his equipment, and create various forms from his mana, but also taught him how to utilize all of the abilities he now had as a knight. Most of these abilities included defense techniques as well as taunts, skills that drew the full attention of an enemy, and were focused on allowing the knight to better protect those around him.

The thing that had most surprised Blake during his training was that many of the skills scaled with mana use. That meant that while a Silver Nine and Silver One knight had the same skillset, the Silver One knight could activate much more powerful forms of the skills. The skills also seemed to change depending on the mana type used.

For example, a knight with a fire affinity had a taunt that would send out waves of flame that could burn enemies, while a knight with a water affinity sent out a chilling wind that could slow enemies as well as taunt them. Blake had been taught over the past month that the key to growing as a knight was to learn how best to apply his mana to his skills, to utilize them to their full potential. There was only one problem with that train of thought.

"Just remember to be careful, Blake. The church might not take kindly to you now." The knight's eyes grew sad before he turned away. "And remember, boy: you've been blessed, not cursed. If you keep holding yourself back, you will die."

"I won't die, and I will still become a paladin," Blake replied, even as the knight walked away. If the knight trainer had heard him, he didn't stop to respond.

"I will," Blake whispered to himself.

The past month had been hard on him, and he knew his future would be much harder – all because of his ascension a month ago. He turned and headed towards the guild hall at the center of town, losing himself to his memories.

After their last dive, Blake, along with Matt and Emily, finally had enough experience to ascend to the Silver tier. After a final meeting at the inn, Karan had tasked each of the Bronze One adventurers with seeking out their class trainer and ascending to the Silver ranks. They agreed to meet back after their training, which would take roughly a month for each class.

That night, Blake had barely been able to sleep, and he practically ran out of his tent at first light, nearly forgetting to grab his sword as he went. He was finally going to discover his affinity and take the next step towards becoming a paladin. It was going to be the greatest moment of his life. Or so he had thought.

Once he reached the trainer, he was teleported to the knight headquarters, along with the other hopefuls. It seemed most of the adventurers that had started with the original expedition were all choosing to ascend at the same time.

After arriving at the knights' headquarters, Blake was sent to wait, along with the others, outside the quartermaster's room. There, after what seemed like hours of waiting, Blake was assigned a room and given a time to report to the knight-commander. The knight-commander was the ranking official at the headquarters and was going to help each adventurer ascend to Silver.

Blake dropped his extra gear off at his room, and then, because he couldn't wait, rushed to the training yard. He spent the whole afternoon training until it came close to his time to meet the knight-commander. He reported promptly to the great hall, where the ascensions were taking place, uncertain yet excited for his next step.

The knight-commander called him in when it was his time and had him sit in the middle of the great hall, within a small circle. Blake couldn't ignore the fact that the ground was blackened and scored, and also ripped apart in a few areas. Just what did ascension to Silver involve?

After he was seated, the knight-commander had Blake bring forth his level triangle and experience triangle. Both shimmered golden on Blake's palms, and he promised the knight-commander he was ready and willing to ascend. The knight-commander placed a golden shield on the ground before Blake, and the beauty of the shield had caused Blake to pause.

The shield had four gems, representing fire, earth, wind, and water in four points, creating what appeared to be a plus sign. In the middle, running in a line, were three more gems: an opal for celestial, an onyx for darkness, and a strange stone that was a darkly colored with specks of red crisscrossing through it – a bloodstone, for chaos.

On either side of the shield, outside of the gemstones, strange silver markings swirled, and there were two spots for a hand to be placed. Blake was instructed to place his hands on those spots, and to channel his mana through his hands, into the shield.

The shield would serve as the conduit, locking his class as

that of a knight, and unlocking in him the inherent skills and traits a knight would have. At the same time, his mana would flow freely through the shield until his affinity awoke within him.

~

At least I didn't awake to chaos, Blake thought cynically, replaying the rest of his ascension through his mind as he neared the Adventurers' Guild. He was to meet with the Guildmaster before he returned to his team. *If they'll still have me*, he thought gloomily.

~

The moment his mana flowed into the shield, Blake's body erupted in pain. Strange visions flashed through his mind, faster than he could track, and it felt as if every muscle in his body was being torn apart. His mouth opened in a scream, but no sound came out, as the mana paralyzed even his vocal cords. Still more mana poured out of him, into the shield, before it rushed back into him. Each time it passed through the shield, the amount of mana seemed to increase, as did the pain it brought with it.

As his mind fought to stay conscious, Blake could also tell that the mana was growing stronger, and so was he. The pain was from his body being torn apart from the inside, and then repaired just as fast. While mana at Bronze tier had amplified his physical skills, he could tell Silver tier mana was changing him, improving him.

He also began to comprehend the images flashing through his mind. Countless abilities, all with their accompanying mana cost, flooded into him, along with years of training, skills honed and passed down by the original knights.

The shield was a medium, to pass on the knowledge and skills unlocked through generations of training. However, as the ritual reached its peak, Blake realized he still hadn't had an affinity appear.

～

Would it have been better? To be without an affinity?

Blake wasn't sure if such a thing existed, but surely that would have been preferable to what had happened.

"I'm here to see the Guildmaster." Blake spoke calmly to the receptionist at the Adventurers' Guild, who nodded as she reached up the crystal pendant around her neck. She whispered quietly into it, and then nodded.

"The Guildmaster is ready to see you." She motioned towards the stairs, and Blake nodded, walking slowly towards them.

What could the Guildmaster possibly want with him?

His mind drifted back to the ceremony.

～

The mana flowing through him slowed, the pain and images subsided, and Blake was able to focus on the shield. His hands were white from the pain he had been enduring. Sweat dripped onto the shield, sizzling as it landed. The amount of mana circulating through the shield, and Blake's body, was creating an immense heat.

Blake grasped the mana that flowed inside him, marveling at how much he had. He was certain it was double the 100 he had held at Bronze One, but he couldn't confirm until he looked at his level triangle. However, none of the gems on the shield had begun to glow yet, meaning he still didn't have his affinity.

Angrily, he pushed his mana into his palms, urging it to once again rush through the shield. Blake starred at the opal on the shield, his vision narrowing solely on to that gem. Silently, he prayed to the Goddess of Justice, begging her to give him a celestial affinity.

Slowly, the shield began to draw in the mana he was pushing into it. It started as a trickle, but then the shield began to drink his mana in fully, and suddenly Blake found himself empty, his vision wavering. He could feel his organs protesting, feel his body screaming out.

The shield still pulled at more, tugging at his very essence. Blake fought, urging his mana to flow back into his body, refusing the hungering of the shield. He would not let his journey end here. He would not die from mana depletion. In his mind, he felt something give, as if he had broken past a barrier deep within his body, and suddenly, a bright light erupted around him.

Life rushed into him, and as his vision cleared, he could see the opal glowing. Golden light, just like his father's, rushed around his body. He had done it. He had a celestial affinity. But then—

Blake's hand was cold as he pushed open the Guildmaster's door, and he stepped slowly in. Alice glanced up, a smile on her face as she looked at him. Her eyes swirled with colors, drawing him in.

"So nice of you to join me, Blake." She stood from the desk and walked slowly towards him.

The woman looked no older than thirty, but Blake knew she was ancient. As a Diamond Two, she was one of the strongest humans alive, after all.

Alice came to stand before Blake, her swirling eyes holding him captive. No matter how hard he fought, he couldn't move. The Guildmaster reached down and took his left hand, twisting it over so she could see his palm. She held her hand over his, and he could feel an unimaginably strong pull from her hand. Try as he might, he couldn't stop as his mana responded to her strange pull, and his hand began to glow.

Golden lines crisscrossed his hand, calling forth his level triangle, even as golden, celestial energy flowed from his hand into Alice's. Then, as his level triangle finished forming, a pitch-black energy meshed with his golden energy, swirling violently between the golden celestial energy.

His darkness energy.

"So, it is true." Alice smiled as she stepped back.

The moment she took her hand away from Blake's, his energy

dissipated into the air. Alice raised her left hand towards him, calling forth her own level triangle. Red energy flared across her hand, creating a triangle that was nearly full.

Then, to Blake's surprise, blue energy surged around her hand, intermingling with her red energy, creating a beautiful contrast of colors.

"You have two affinities, Blake. Just like me."

Chapter Fifty-Six

Blake had never heard of anyone having two affinities, and he really didn't know what it meant. In fact, he probably would have been ecstatic about it, had it not been for the darkness affinity. The church viewed dark mana users nearly in the same light as chaos users. Dark mana users had a reputation for evil, usually becoming classes such as necromancers and death knights.

People generally tended to avoid those who had dark affinity. Blake had even refused to use it during his month of training. He had secretly hoped that if he didn't use it, it would simply go away.

"You have no idea how long I've waited for another." Alice's mana, taking on the shape of two serpents, one red and one blue, dropped to the floor, slithering towards Blake.

He tried to speak, tried to break her gaze, but she held him trapped. Her mana reached him, and each snake began to wrap itself around his legs, climbing up his body till the two snakes were positioned on either side of his face.

"I'm sure you are wondering what is going on." Alice must have let her control over him lessen as she spoke, because Blake found himself able to move his head. However, he still couldn't speak. Hesitantly, he nodded. She smiled at him as her eyes danced.

"First, I have a test for you, Blake." Her eyes began to shift colors, faster and faster, and Blake felt as if they were staring directly into his soul. All the while, Alice's smile continued to grow.

"At this moment, you stand at the very precipice of your future," she said. "Before you are two paths. One is the path of potential greatness, though I am sure it would be filled with hardship and struggle."

The red snake hissed, and Blake felt a rush of heat race across his body.

"Your other path will see you fulfilling your dreams, though your potential will be ruined."

The blue snake hissed, and Blake nearly shivered from the rush of cold he felt.

"Tell me, Blake: what is it you want in life?" she asked.

Blake again felt her hold over him weaken, and he knew she was permitting him to speak. So he did.

"What do I want?"

His entire life, he wanted to become a paladin, just like his father. He wanted to serve the Goddess of Justice and make his father proud. However, Blake knew with a darkness affinity, he would never be allowed to become a paladin.

In fact, the church wouldn't even allow those with dark affinity into their facilities. Blake's dreams had been ruined the moment his dark affinity had appeared.

"I want to become a paladin. I want to serve the Goddess of Justice, just like my father." As he spoke, Alice yawned, waving a hand dismissively towards him.

"Is that all, Blake?" she asked. "Do you want to become just like your father? Serving the Goddess of Light fully, putting the church before everything else?" Her eyes hardened, and her voice grew cold. "Think hard before you answer."

Was that all he wanted? He knew his father was well respected, idolized even, amongst adventurers. But the more he thought about it, he wondered if he could become like his father. Did he want to be the cold, calculating paladin that his father was?

Blake wanted to get strong, to serve the Goddess, and to

protect those he cared about. His father was strong, but his duties kept him from his family, and Blake realized he had never seen his father form a permanent team. If Blake became like his father, would he have to leave his team?

The more he thought about it, he realized what he really wanted was to have the power to protect his team. He wanted to stay with them, adventuring, as long as he could. He would keep them safe and serve the Goddess of Justice at the same time, regardless of his affinity. Even if the church wouldn't allow him to become a paladin, he would make the Goddess, and his father, proud through his actions.

"I want to keep those I care about safe," he said, his words measured. "I want to keep adventuring with my team, while living in a way that will serve the Goddess. I want to grow strong enough in my own way, and still make my father proud."

Alice's eyes softened, and a small smile crept onto her face.

"That is the answer I wanted to hear," she said.

The blue snake disappeared as the red snake struck, sinking fiery fangs into Blake's neck. Fire roared through his veins, and Blake's vision wavered as the fire threatened to overwhelm him.

He called upon his celestial energy and felt the gold glow rushing through his body. The mana could heal him; he had learned that during his month of training, and now the golden glow encompassing his body tried to do just that. But the fire was stronger, and he could tell his celestial mana wouldn't be able to keep him conscious for long.

"You want to be strong enough to protect those you love?" Alice demanded. "Then you must be willing to use all the power at your disposal."

The way Alice smiled as she spoke, Blake was certain she was enjoying this. He also had the sinking suspicion that she had been informed of his refusal to use his dark mana through his entire set of training.

Blake pulled at his celestial mana, channeling it through his body, but no matter how much he pulled, the fire within kept burning his light away. Gritting his teeth against the pain, he closed his eyes, seeking out the darkness that he held trapped within.

With a growl, he called it forth, and the mana answered. While his celestial mana was warm and soothing, the darkness mana was heavy and cold. He grasped the energy with his mind and pushed it through his veins.

The dark mana oozed throughout his body, and to Blake's surprise, the darkness smothered the fire burning through him. With his two mana types, he was able to extinguish the flames Alice's fire serpent had injected into his body.

He opened his eyes, noting how his body seemed clad in a dark armor, with flashes of light cracking through. His glanced at Alice, and the Guildmaster flashed him a large smile, her eyes dancing with excitement.

"You have taken the first step to greatness, Blake," Alice said. "Now, allow me to enlighten you as to what your future holds."

She walked back to her desk, and Blake let go of his mana. Exhaustion rushed through him, and for a second, he was afraid he was going to faint. As quickly as he felt it, though, his exhaustion was gone. Blake marveled as he felt mana rushing into him. What was going on?

"I'm sure, by the expression on your face, that you are currently experiencing a rush of mana?" Alice sat in her chair, holding a small, ancient-looking book in her hand.

Blake nodded in response, afraid to speak.

"That is normal, and is the result of you drawing upon both of your affinities to their maximum." She opened the small book and began sifting through it. "As you know, Blake, adventurers have a set capacity for mana, dependent on their level."

"Yes, ma'am."

"So, in theory, as a Silver Nine adventurer, you should have two hundred mana points available to you."

That was correct. Blake had confirmed his mana points the moment he finished awakening to Silver. Because eighty percent of his mana went to strengthening his body, he had been left with forty mana points for skills.

"Please, Blake, open your level triangle again for me."

He walked shakily to Alice's desk and presented his left hand to her. The rush of power filling him had subsided, and Blake gasped as he summoned his level triangle. He was Silver Nine, but his mana points, which earlier had been forty, now showed 240.

"How?" he breathed. That couldn't be right. His maximum had been 200, with 160 points allocated to his physical attributes, and forty points for skills. How could he have 240 points of spare mana now?

Alice smiled.

"When you awakened to Silver, your body drew in the normal 200 points of mana, because that is how the medium you used to ascend is calibrated." She let go of his palm and turned back to the small book she was leafing through. "With dual affinities, you are able to pull in 200 points of each mana type. However, in order to awaken fully to your affinities, and gain that extra mana, you must draw upon both types of mana at the same time till you are empty."

She stopped flipping through the book, marking a page with her finger as she looked up at him.

"Hence I forced you to not only heal yourself with your celestial mana, but also use your darkness mana to block my attack."

"How come I've never heard of anyone with two affinities before?" Blake asked as he willed his triangle away, mentally assigning his open mana to his body.

He had entered the Guildmaster's room with 160 points of mana strengthening his body, with forty points free for skills. Now, as he reassigned his mana to fit the eighty to twenty ratio, he had 320 points assigned to his body, and eighty points free for skills.

"That is because it is extremely rare. . Until you came along, I was the youngest living adventurer with dual affinities, and I'm a few hundred years old."

"So how many are there?" he asked. His head was spinning with the knowledge. What did it all mean? Why him?

"Currently, I know of three others living with dual affinities," Alice replied. "Our records show only a few dozen have ever existed, and our records are over a thousand years old."

What?

"What does this all mean?" he asked.

"For you, right now? Not much, really. You will gain power at a faster rate, because every time you level, the mana you gain will be doubled." She turned the book towards him. "As for your future... you are the first person to ever have an affinity for celestial and darkness. The old scholars who developed this book, who truly understood the secrets of mana, gave your type of affinity the name 'ethereal.' However, it is up to you to learn how to wield these powers together."

"Ethereal?"

Blake had to admit he liked the way it sounded. But he really had no idea how he would use the two mana types together. Also, and more importantly, Blake wanted to know what it meant for his specialization.

"Can I become a paladin with an ethereal affinity?" he asked.

Alice smiled at him, a mischievous smile, as she closed the book.

"Normally, I would say no. As you know, the church will not allow darkness users into their ranks."

Blake felt his heart sink, and opened his mouth to speak. Alice raised a finger, stopping him.

"However, if my theory is true, there is a way for you to become a paladin still."

"How?" Blake forgot himself in his excitement, and leaned forward excitedly on Alice's desk, bringing him uncomfortably close to the Guildmaster.

She simply smirked at him and leaned back, reaching into her shirt. The movement made Blake realize just how close he was to her, and he jerked back away from her, his face growing red. She pulled out her celestial feather and winked at him.

"As you know, a paladin is an elemental knight who has a celestial affinity," she said. "To become a paladin, a knight with a celestial affinity is taken by the church to the God-tier celestial dungeon, where the knight pledges allegiance to the Goddess. If she deems him worthy, she gives the knight her praise, and a bond is created between the dungeon and the knight. Through that bond, the celestial elemental knight is able to access the skills and talents of a paladin."

Blake nodded. He had heard all of this from his father. Elemental knights had to bind themselves to a dungeon that held their affinity, and in doing so they unlocked the skills and talents related to their affinity. But Blake knew the church controlled all access to the celestial dungeon, and he would never be allowed near it with a darkness affinity.

"Well, in your case," Alice went on, "you would have to find a dungeon that not only had a link to the celestial affinity, but also to the darkness affinity."

"No such dungeon exists," Blake said.

The Adventurers' Guild kept a list of all the dungeons in existence. Only one celestial dungeon existed, and Blake knew of just two darkness dungeons. One was the God-tiered darkness dungeon that served as the home to the God of Death. The other was the dungeon he and his team explored.

"That is where you are wrong." Alice's eyes sparkled as she put her celestial feather away. "The dungeon you currently dive in – if it is still around when you reach Gold tier – will serve as your path to becoming an ethereal paladin."

"What do you mean?" he asked.

Alice wasn't making sense. First, how could a dungeon have two affinities? And second, what did she mean 'if it was still around when he reached Gold tier'?

Alice waved a hand dismissively.

"I've said too much. I swore I wouldn't affect the world too much after I got these eyes. Just know there is a threat in the shadows that wants to destroy the darkness dungeon. If you want to become a paladin, you must do all you can to grow as strong as you can, as fast as you can, and do your best to protect the dungeon and its town."

"I promise." Blake stood tall, pride flowing through him. He didn't know what she was talking about, but if the dungeon was the key to his dreams, he would do what Alice said.

"Good." She smiled and nodded towards the door. "Now, I believe your team is supposed to be gathering back at the dungeon town soon, to resume your dives. I wish you the best of luck."

Blake turned, heading towards the door.

"And one more thing." Alice's voice caused him to pause, one foot out of the room already.

"Ma'am?"

"Tell Karan I miss her."

Chapter Fifty-Seven

"What type of odds are they giving this group?" Ryan asked Erin. It had been a week since he reopened his dungeon, and still no one had made it to Buttercup.

The furthest a group had gone was to the room before Buttercup's. That had been one of the original groups, who had all become Silver during the time Ryan was improving himself.

They had cleared his first floor with practiced ease, but after struggling against his final mob room, had made the decision to head out without challenging Buttercup. It was the right choice, as Ryan had been certain his new boss would have taken them down.

The adventurers had begun placing bets outside of Ryan's entrance on which team would be the first to clear his second floor. A one hundred-gold bounty had been placed on his unknown boss.

"Sounds like the bet is eight-to-one odds; nobody thinks this group can even make it to the second level," Erin said in a bored voice.

That bounty was in part due to A-a-ron's group. It seemed word had spread about Alex's death, and Ryan had overheard the other groups of nobles mentioning they would not venture down to the second floor until the boss was defeated and information made available to their guards.

"I wonder when Blake's group is going to show back up," Ryan mused.

Ryan had been scanning the crowds of adventurers for any sign of his favorite team. He was confident Blake's group could make their way to Buttercup's room and give his boss a challenge.

"It must take them some time to level up to Silver, judging by the absence of many of the other groups as well," Erin said. "A few have started to reappear as Silver though, so hopefully he will be here soon."

She let out a sigh and laid down on Ryan's core.

"I'm so bored," she groaned, kicking her feet.

"Me too, hun."

Well, technically, Ryan wasn't too bored. He was watching multiple skeletal fight club matches at that exact moment. A week of adventuring, Alex's death, and the death of a handful of Silver adventures meant Ryan was now Silver Seven.

Since no one had been able to clear Ryan's second floor yet, Erin had agreed that he should hold off on adding more mobs to it. That meant Ryan could use all 100 points he had gained from Silver Nine to Silver Seven for… other tasks. In other words, skeletal fight club had gotten an upgrade.

The first thing Ryan did when he hit Silver Eight was resume his skrat and skuirrel fight club. He decided to refer to this as level one of skeletal fight club and created a large arena underneath his first floor. With fifty mob points, Ryan could summon sixteen plated skrats, given that each of the mobs cost him three points each.

He separated the arena into four sections, ordering four of the skrats into each room, and once again started the battles. Ryan's plan was to later use the next evolution of his skrats and skuirrels as their final evolution. He had spent plenty of time on them, and wanted to start evolving other mobs, after all.

Once they evolved once more, he intended to use those forms to roam his second floor. But first, he wanted one more evolution, and the adventurers needed to grow stronger. There was no reason to make his dungeon more difficult if adventurers couldn't even clear it as it was now.

When Ryan hit Silver Seven, he gained another fifty points, and seeing his plated skrats were progressing nicely, had decided to start level two of skeletal fight club

This club was established underneath his second floor, which Ryan had conveniently already excavated. He had been using his free time to gain as much influence on the land around him as possible, to allow for a faster transition once he hit Gold.

The arena he created under his second floor – level two of skeletal fight club – was for his human skeletons. Given the mobs cost him five points each, Ryan decided to spend forty points to summon eight of them. He decided level two would focus on training his human skeletons up in different weapons, so he summoned two archer skeletons, and six fighter skeletons.

These fighter skeletons he broke into three pairs, arming one group with a basic sword and shield, one group with axes, and one group with shields and spears. Ryan wanted variety in his future mobs.

Between level one and two of skeletal fight club, Ryan was left with twelve mob points. Not enough to do much, but he had decided to utilize these points for mob evolutions. While skeletal fight club had strict rules that kept him from talking about it, his mob evolution chamber did not. That was something he could share with Erin, to ease their boredom at times such as now.

"Want to try another fusion?" he asked suddenly.

Erin's emotions jumped at his suggestion, and the fairy quickly sat up, eyes filled with excitement. So far, ever since the creation of the wolf-deer hybrid, they hadn't had much success on combinations. But even if the combination didn't take, the suspense, and the usually colorful shower of bones and mana, made the effort good for wasting time.

"As long as you don't try another zombie fusion," Erin warned.

Ryan had tried to combine a ratbie with a skuirrel zombie, and that had resulted in a rather repulsive explosion of – well, everything.

"I think I'm going to stick to mostly bone creatures in my dungeon." He had noticed adventurers were referring to him as the bone dungeon, and he quite liked the name. Ryan figured he would only create zombie mobs if he was trying to get effects such as the infested ratbie's paralysis. In fact, he was planning just that with a zombie snake, and had already seen the beginning of a combination of the paralysis mushrooms with the snake's rotting flesh.

It was only a matter of time before he could add the zombie snakes into his dungeon, though he was currently unsure as to where.

"I would prefer if you did stick to bones." Erin glared at Ryan as she spoke, and he knew what came next. "Skeletons are creepy and all, but zombies are disgusting. Plus, they smell. Do you know how long it took me to get rid of that smell?"

"A week. I remember, Rin."

She had been in the fusion chamber when his zombie fusion had failed. As a result, she had been covered in zombie bits, which she informed him had left her smelling like death for a week straight. Ryan assumed that was a bad thing, but he couldn't smell anything. All in all, he had found the experience rather amusing. A fact that had gotten him yelled at more than once since the incident.

"Hey, Rin." A thought had crossed his mind.

"Yes?"

"Can we combine two of the same mob?" Ryan asked. He took a look at his sneks, his mind racing.

"Umm, maybe?" came her reply.

That's insightful. Not.

"Want to give it a try?" he asked.

He was already summoning two sneks in the fusion room before Erin could answer. What was the worst that could happen?

"It's not like there's anything better to do." Erin glanced at the group making their way to Steve. It was a new group of mostly Bronze adventurers. They weren't putting on much of an interesting show.

"Welp, here goes nothing, then," Ryan announced.

Ryan poured his mana into the two sneks, creating the dark mana eggs around them. The eggs drew together, creating a large black egg. So far, so good.

"Moment of truth," Ryan whispered to Erin, both for his snek evolution, and the group of adventurers who had opened the door into Steve's room, and were staring inside.

He wondered for a moment which would come first: the team chickening out against Steve, or the egg hatching.

"They teleported out," Erin observed, just as the dark mana egg started to crack.

Both at the same time. Drat. Oh, well.

The team leaving meant Ryan and Erin could fully watch the fusion. Bright light flashed out of the egg, and Erin looked away. Ryan knew she didn't enjoy watching the rain of bones that happened after a failure.

"Rin, look."

Ryan flooded their bond with excitement as he watched a skeletal form begin moving across the floor. Where before two sneks had been, now a single snek remained. The difference, though, was that this snek had two heads splitting off from a thicker body and was nearly twice as large as the individual sneks.

"Two heads are better than one?" the fairy said, and Ryan realized she was trying to make a joke.

Her puns really needed work.

"Perhaps," Ryan said. "I wonder how many times we can do this."

Ryan absorbed his mob and was surprised to find his two-headed snek now cost two points instead of one. That was strange, given that the combination of his wolf and deer had resulted in a mob that cost ten. Perhaps combining the two sneks had created an evolution and not a proper fusion?

Just how large and powerful can I make this new mob?

Before Ryan could ponder this new mystery, commotion outside his dungeon drew his attention. He glanced outside and saw a sight that both excited and confused him.

The part that excited him was that Emily was standing outside his dungeon. If Emily was outside, that had to mean Blake and the rest of his team would show up. What confused Ryan, and what was causing the commotion, was the little red creature sitting on top of Emily's shoulder.

"Hey, Rin, what is that?"

The fairy turned her attention from the fusion room to the image Ryan had pulled up, focusing directly on the little creature, which was now blowing out small flames to the cheers of the crowd.

Before Erin could respond, a loud voice – Jack's voice – called out from the crowd.

"Seriously, Em, a dragon?"

Chapter Fifty-Eight

Ryan was practically vibrating with excitement as Blake and his team presented their pendants to Sasha. It had taken a few minutes for the rest of the team to show up, and Ryan had been impatiently checking over his entire dungeon, making sure everything was ready for his favorite group.

By the time the last member, Blake, had arrived, Ryan had paused all of his fight club battles, and had all his attention focused on his dungeon's entrance. He had been waiting for this.

"Here they come," he announced.

"I'm really interested to see what classes everyone is." Erin was just as excited and was zipping around Ryan's core room.

She brought up a good point, as they had noticed the returning veteran adventurers had all come back as Silver, and with new classes.

"What do you think everyone's affinities are?" Ryan asked. He eyed the group, silently urging them to step into his dungeon. They sure were taking their sweet time.

"Well, Emily has to be fire, based on her dragon," Erin mused aloud.

That made sense, and also meant all the fire-related gear that had dropped for their team was now enhancing Emily even more.

Lucky her.

"What about Matt?" Ryan asked.

The archer had arrived with no telling hints, wearing his same old gear. Ryan had been hoping he would be wearing a gem or two, to give them a hint.

"Hmm. Fire as well, like Emily?" Erin replied.

"I'm guessing wind." Ryan felt wind for an archer would be the most beneficial. "Why would he choose any other element?"

"Oh, living beings don't choose their affinities like you did." Erin slowed her flight, landing gently on Ryan's diamond core. "Didn't I tell you that?"

"Uh, nope."

Really, not being able to choose your own affinity seemed a bit unfair. Then again, he had the chance to choose his, and he had messed it up. For a second, Ryan stared longingly at Emily's dragon. He wanted one.

Erin's voice broke into his thoughts.

"Well, races not created in dungeons *awaken* to affinities. They aren't born or created with one, and they can't choose their affinities like dungeons can. I'm not really sure how their affinity is decided. I just know it is outside of their control."

"So, Emily got lucky with becoming a fire affinity?" Ryan had assumed she had chosen her affinity based off the gear she had been earning.

"Exactly. So it's hard to tell what the others will get."

"Well, I'm still guessing wind for Matt," Ryan said. "And I will say earth for Blake." After watching Frank turn himself to metal, Ryan figured earth affinity would be great for Blake's class. Especially since Blake seemed to favor being the team's tank.

"Hmm," Erin said, biting her lip. "I would like to see Blake have a celestial affinity, just like Sean."

Uh-oh. Erin's eyes had that dreamy look in them again.

"Focus, hun," Ryan said. "You can't develop a crush on Blake." Besides, Ryan secretly had become quite fond of Blake and his team already.

"You're one to talk." Erin hit his core, laughing. "You have a soft spot for him too."

"I have no idea what you're talking about," Ryan said sheepishly, noting that Karan had finished presenting her crystal to Sasha. The disc the dark-clad woman was holding now showed five glowing lights. They were ready.

"Uh-huh. You are *so* team Blake," Erin giggled as she drew closer to Ryan's core.

The group of adventurers had all turned towards the entrance.

"Does Blake look nervous to you?" Ryan asked.

Most of the group were smiling. However, Blake seemed to hesitate as Jack stepped into the dungeon. Instead of being the first in, like he normally was, Blake was the last.

"I wonder why?" Ryan began scanning the members as they walked forward. He saw Jack was a Silver Seven thief, and Karan was a Gold Four cleric.

"Emily is now a Silver Nine summoner," Erin said.

A summoner?

"That explains the baby dragon," Erin went on. "Summoners create a pact with a God-tier dungeon dependent upon their affinity. Having done so, they gain the ability to summon a single familiar from that dungeon. I'm surprised she got a baby dragon. They're supposed to be capable of turning into the strongest mobs a fire dungeon has at its disposal."

Ok, Ryan was even more jealous now.

"Matt's a Silver Nine marksman," Ryan noted. Every archer so far that had become Silver was a marksman. Ryan wondered if there were other classes for them later on.

"He has a water affinity," Erin said gleefully.

Well, Ryan lost that bet.

"How about Blake?"

Erin's wings were starting to tremble with excitement, and Ryan turned his attention to his favorite adventurer. Uncharacteristically, Blake was still trailing slowly behind the group, his eyes shifting from his companions' backs to the ground. Something was wrong.

"Hmmm, Silver Nine knight," Ryan said.

That was the tank class he had noted Bronze fighters could become.

"And—" Oh, something was definitely up. "—Celestial—"

"Yes…"

"—and darkness affinity?" Ryan trailed off, starring hard at Ryan's information.

He had definitely read that right. Was that even possible?

Viktor

He leaned against his bone throne, letting out a sigh as he took a sip from his chalice. It was a hundred-year-old wine, one of the few treasures he had from his childhood. As the sweet liquor filled his mouth, he slowly opened his eyes, and turned towards the messenger before him.

"My lord." The young man, a lowly Bronze mage, spoke with a trembling voice. "I have a new request for you."

The mage kept his eyes turned down as he spoke, not daring to look Viktor in the eyes. It was probably for the best.

"The last request – to make a pact with the darkness dungeon and destroy the town – nearly resulted in my death." Viktor's voice was soft, devoid of emotion.

His side flared as it remembered the pain of that assassin's dagger. The higher-ups had failed to mention those disgusting twins would be guarding the dungeon.

"I, uh, I—" The man started trembling, stumbling over his words.

With a snap of his fingers, Viktor sent an arrow of bone into the man, killing him. With another snap, he reanimated the man's body. A Bronze-level zombie was still helpful fodder, after all.

"I do wish you would stop shooting my messengers." A bored voice came through the pendant around Viktor's neck. "I am running out of souls I dislike."

Viktor shrugged.

"And if you kill every messenger," the voice went on, "just because you don't like their message, I may stop sending you gifts."

The messenger had indeed come with gifts; more dungeon core fragments for Viktor. Very difficult objects to come by, but ones that Viktor needed dearly to grow stronger.

It seemed the Exalted One had sent the fragments as a way to appease Viktor over his run-in with the twins. The gift had done just that.

"He was wasting my time." Viktor spoke into the pendant, but

knowing who was on the other end, quickly changed his tone. "It is my understanding, Exalted One, that you have another task for me?"

"Yes, a simple matter for you."

We'll see about that, *Victor thought, but he remained silent.*

"There is a young boy who has returned to the dungeon town," the voice said. "He wears a ring in the shape of a wolf's head. I would ask that you kill him, preferably in the dungeon, and retrieve that ring."

"And the reward?" Viktor asked.

He was confident he could complete the task. However, even with his overwhelming power, he would rather not risk simultaneously fighting the twins and the Platinum rogue the Adventurers' Guild had sent to the town.

"The Adventurers' Guild has guarded that dungeon with skilled necro-mancer slayers." *Viktor went on. For a task that posed at least a hint of danger to him, he expected a good reward.*

"Your reward, Viktor, will be the Crown of Sorrows," the voice said.

Viktor's chalice dropped from his hand at the words. With that crown, he would be able to decimate both the dungeon and its town, a fitting revenge for the wound he had received.

"Consider it done," he said.

Chapter Fifty-Nine

"Come on, Blake, aren't you supposed to be our meat shield?" Jack walked backwards, staring at Blake as they headed towards Ryan's second room on the first floor.

In the first room, much to Ryan's entertainment, Emily's dragon had hunted down his mobs like a puppy chasing butterflies.

"Cynder is sooo cute," Erin cooed to Ryan, her eyes lovingly on the baby dragon that was riding on Emily's shoulder. The little dragon, which Emily had named Cynder, was chewing contentedly on a skuirrel bone.

"Yeah, but what is going on with Blake?" Ryan asked.

During the entire fight in the first room, the knight had stood by Karan, not saying a single word. It wasn't until they cleared the room, and started heading towards the second room, that Jack decided to break the odd silence.

"I—" Blake started to speak, then turned away.

"Dragon got your tongue, man?" Jack flashed a smile at Emily. "What's the matter, did you get a terrible affinity? Are you a wind knight?"

The thief pulled out his dagger and spun it, creating a small whirlwind on the blade.

"Wind isn't bad, man," he went on.

Ryan could tell Blake wanted to say something, but the knight just couldn't bring himself to.

"Leave him alone, Jack," Karan snapped. She said it so forcefully that Jack was startled, tripping and falling off the ledge and into one of the pits below. He caught himself with his wind, softening the blow, but the group burst out in laughter nonetheless.

"Sorry, Karan." Jack's voice dropped an octave. "I'm just curious why Blake's not taking the lead. He was so excited about becoming Silver, but now he hasn't said more than three words to us."

Jack ran his fingers along the wall, seeking purchase, but it was smooth as polished marble. Shrugging, the thief ran up the wall, pulling himself back on the ledge, and somersaulted to land in front of Blake. Ryan had to admit that was cool.

"You know we're here for you, right, man?" The thief put his hand on Blake's shoulder and offered him a smile.

This was why Ryan loved this team.

Blake looked Jack in the eyes, and Ryan noticed the knight had tears starting to form. That was so outside of Blake's character.

"Snap out of it," Ryan whispered, straining to hear what the knight would say next. This situation was intense, and he really wanted to know what had Blake so messed up.

"Thanks, Jack." Blake put a hand on Jack's shoulder and smiled back at him.

"We are a team, Blake. A family," Karan said, walking over and giving the boy a hug. "No matter what, you are one of us, and we are always here for you."

The knight looked to Emily and Matt, both of whom gave him a smile. The scene would have been perfect had Cynder not accidentally dropped the bone she held in her mouth at that moment. The scorched bone clattered on to the floor, and the group laughed at the little creature.

"You guys promise not to hate me, no matter what?" Blake asked as he freed himself from Karan's embrace and walked over to the fallen bone. He picked it up and offered it to the baby dragon, who quickly took it and returned to chewing on it. Emily offered him a grateful smile.

"Well, I won't hate you, buddy. But I think Matt might, if you try anything with Em." Jack's comment earned him a hit from Karan.

"Worth it," the thief wheezed. Karan's punch had knocked the wind out of him.

"All right." Blake walked past the group to the entrance of the second room. "I guess I'll show you."

Blake closed his eyes, furrowing his brow in concentration. A moment later, golden light flowed from his right hand, enveloping his sword.

"You're ashamed that you got celestial?" Jack started forward, but stopped a moment later.

Dark energy flowed around Blake's left arm, enshrouding his shield.

"What in the name of the Goddess?" Jack cried, alarmed. The thief stumbled back, his eyes wide with fear.

"So, he really does have two affinities," Ryan gasped. His mind was racing as he looked on the young knight. Glowing sword in one hand, pitch-black shield in the other. What else could he do? What did his dual affinities mean?

"I've never heard of this," Erin said.

Her emotions were filled with confusion and excitement. It was rare that something happened that she hadn't even heard about. Apparently, the pages of the Dungeon Master's Guide didn't cover everything. If Erin had never heard of dual affinities, Blake must be something really rare.

"Well, Blake's group just got even more exciting," Ryan said.

With this new revelation, he was certain Blake's group would reach Buttercup. And he silently prayed to the Goddess that they would *beat* Buttercup. If Blake's group was this interesting at Silver, what would happen later on?

"This is so unfair," Jack's voice echoed.

The group of adventurers had entered the second room, with Blake and Matt taking out the mobs. The thief leaned against the wall, shifting his gaze from Blake to Emily.

"First, Emily gets fire affinity, meaning she is practically in full class gear now," Jack said.

He gestured at Cynder.

"Then she gets a baby dragon, literally the rarest summon for a fire summoner."

He picked up a rock and surrounded it with wind.

"And finally, Blake has not one, but two affinities!"

Jack threw the rock into the foliage. Propelled by the wind surrounding it, it cut through the plants and impacted into the skull of a champion skrat that had been sneaking up on Matt.

Darn it. Ryan had been cheering the little guy on.

"Anything special about you, Matt?" Jack grumbled, continuing his tirade. "Did you secretly get gifted, like, a legendary bow, or maybe a quiver of infinite arrows? Are you secretly a half-elf?"

Matt loosed an arrow into a skuirrel before he answered Jack's comment.

"Nope, just me and my bow." He nocked another arrow. "Though I suppose I'm special because unlike you, I can enjoy a nice alcoholic beverage after this dive."

The marksman let out a laugh that was joined by the others. Even Jack cracked a grin.

"Speaking of clearing the dungeon." Karan stepped away from the wall, smiling at her team. "How about we go beat Steve and get to the second floor?" The cleric turned back to Jack and offered the thief a grin. "If you didn't notice, there is quite the bounty on the head of the second-floor boss mob," she said.

Karan turned and headed towards the exit that led to Steve's room. The rest of the group followed her, leaving Jack standing, mouth agape, as he watched the cleric walk away.

"Darned cleric knows the way to a thief's heart," he whispered, quiet enough that Ryan was sure the group couldn't hear, but not quiet enough that Ryan and Erin couldn't.

"Bet they become a couple," Ryan whispered to Erin, watching Jack hurry after his team.

"I'm hoping they do," Erin giggled as she wrapped her silk cloth around herself, making herself comfortable.

Ryan took a moment to appreciate how cute she was before he turned his attention back to Blake's team. As the group faced off against Steve, a fight they were sure to make quick work of, he grinned.

He really did look forward to watching their team continue to grow.

Chapter Sixty

Jack had a smile on his face as he looked around the first room. The group had defeated Steve in record time, and made their way easily towards the second floor. Honestly, Ryan wasn't upset that Steve had gone down like a bag of bones, because now the real fun began.

"Are we sure this is the same dungeon?" Jack asked.

"Dungeons grow at an exceptional rate, Jack," Karan said. "This second floor is likely going to be much harder and sophisticated than the first floor."

Karan, ever the air of rationality, was looking around the room with an appreciative eye. One thing Ryan had noticed: adventurers really liked the style of his second floor.

"You sure know a lot about dungeons," Jack said. He picked up the skull of one of the fallen skeletal fighters and turned the face towards Karan, working the jaw as he spoke. "Tell me, little miss, how do you know so much about these here dungeons?"

The rest of the group broke out in laughter, and even Ryan found it funny. Jack's antics were amusing.

"She doesn't seem to be laughing," Erin said, and Ryan focused on Karan. Her smile seemed forced, and her eyes betrayed some other emotion. Sorrow? Anger?

"Maybe another time." Her tone killed the mood in the room,

and everyone's smiles wavered. "For now, how about we get that bounty?"

Her voice was strained, and the smile she put on was less than convincing. Still, Karan's team members all nodded, and they moved forward.

"So, what do you think the boss is going to be like?" Jack, ever the talkative thief, opened the conversation up, clearing the darkness that was filling the air.

"A new and improved Steve?" Blake offered, grinning back at the thief.

"This time with two arms." Jack let out a laugh, and the group was smiling as they walked into the second room.

"Mobs," Blake called.

His words drew the attention of the group, and the knight headed into the room first. Blake easily blocked a strike from the first skeletal fighter, his dark imbued shield easily absorbing the impact. He countered the attack with a swipe of his glowing sword, and the celestial shrouded blade cut easily through Ryan's mob.

"I mean, he's cool and all. But is that really fair?" Ryan grumbled, watching as Blake stepped forward to dispatch the next skeleton.

Blake had definitely grown a lot stronger.

"Hmm, he does seem stronger than the other Silver Nine knights we've seen." Erin's voice had taken on that dreamy tone again. *Ugh.*

"You know, hun, shouldn't you be a little repulsed by him, given his darkness affinity too?"

"What can I say? I've decided I like those bad boys." Erin winked. "Besides, did you forget I'm stuck with a darkness affinity dungeon?"

Oh, good point.

"Well, yeah, but, um." Ryan hated to admit it, but he was starting to feel a bit jealous of Erin's attitude towards Blake.

"Don't worry, silly, you're still my favorite dungeon core." She giggled as she turned her attention back to Blake's group. "They've made it to the locked door." Sure enough, the group was standing in the room with the locked door, inspecting its three locks.

"So, what do we do now?" Matt looked from the door to Karan. "Can we break it down?"

Ha! Good luck. A few groups had tried to break through the door, but because it was enforced with dark mana, the door hadn't even budged.

"Trying to break down locked doors in dungeons is usually a pointless task," Karan said. "The dungeon has likely reinforced it with dark mana, making it nearly indestructible. It would likely take a low Platinum mage to blast through this door."

"Well, let's get going, then." Jack, surprisingly eager, turned and started walking towards the door to the first key room.

"Just a moment, Jack." Karan smiled sweetly at the thief.

"Yes, ma'am?" Jack asked.

"Aren't you a thief?" It was more a statement than a question.

"Well—"

"Doesn't your class specialize in locked things?" Karan walked towards Jack, her smile growing more sinister. "Shouldn't you be able to unlock a simple door?"

Jack seemed to be growing uncomfortable. He looked past Karan to the others, his eyes pleading for help.

"Well, I wouldn't want to deny our group the chance at the experience the other rooms will likely give us."

Karan's hand landed gently on Jack's shoulder, and she looked up into his eyes.

"You never bought a lockpick set," she said. "Did you?"

Her grip tightened, and Jack winced.

"Well, you see—" he tried again.

"You misplaced it, perhaps?"

"Remember that gambling problem?" Jack said, looking like he had just failed the entire team. "It's to do with that. "

He looked away, and Ryan was certain the thief looked ashamed. He felt bad for him.

With a few groans, the group prepared to head into the next room.

"I'm sorry," Jack said.

"Don't sweat it, Jack." Blake placed a hand on the thief's shoulder as he passed him. "I'm all for extra experience."

He offered the thief a smile, and Jack returned it.

"But, I mean, what type of thief doesn't have, you know, thief tools?" Blake added.

"You know I'm still two ranks higher than you, Blake." Jack grinned as he pulled out his dagger, twirling it easily between his fingers. "That means I've got more points put into my physical attributes than you. I can still hurt you."

"About that." Blake shrugged as he glanced back at the group, which was waiting next to the door for Blake and Jack. "Apparently, dual affinities means dual points as well. So I've currently got three hundred and twenty points in my physical attributes, and eighty points left over for skills."

He offered the thief a smile and started walking away.

"That is *so* unfair," Jack grumbled as he followed Blake.

Ryan was even more intrigued by the dual affinities now. He could only imagine what it would be like to have twice as many mob points as he did right now. Why couldn't he be dual affinity?

"Oh, so now Blake is the second strongest in the group," Ryan said.

"That makes him even more interesting." Erin traced small shapes on Ryan's core with her finger. Was she making hearts?

"I really want to see how strong he becomes," Ryan said, distracted. He was pretty sure she was tracing hearts on his core.

He did his best to ignore Erin's heart shaped tracings as Blake's group entered the first pillar room.

This room introduced his skeletal archers. With them, Ryan finally saw Matt take action. Blake blocked the two projectiles fired his way, and the marksman stepped forward, nocking a pair of arrows to his bow.

"Watch and learn," Matt called out cockily, and he lifted his bow.

With a grin, he drew back, and let fly. A second later, both skeletal archers fell, their skulls destroyed by arrows.

"All right, that was pretty cool." Jack clapped Matt on the back as Emily applauded for her brother.

"Multi-shot. It costs me a point of mana per extra arrow, up to five." Matt walked over towards the skeletons, looking down at his broken arrows. "Unfortunately, bone has a tendency to break my arrows."

He glanced at his quiver and sighed.

"Refilling my quiver after every dungeon run is getting annoying."

"Well, refilling my dungeon after every dive is annoying," Ryan mocked Matt, drawing a laugh from Erin.

"You enjoy it," she chuckled.

"Shhh. They don't know that."

"Well, they can't hear you, silly."

"Maybe I should make the archers have a chance to drop bone arrows?" Ryan was already mentally assigning them as possible loot.

"That could work. I know some dungeons modify their loot so that different types and classes of mobs drop loot specific to those classes." Erin landed back atop him. "For instance, ranged mobs like your archers dropping arrows, and melee mobs dropping melee weapons or related armor."

Ryan could see where Erin was going with this and made a mental note to adjust his loot drops. Previously, he had only been focusing on the rarity of the items he was dropping, but now he realized he could customize it even more.

"I'll keep that in mind. Now," he turned their attention back to the room as Blake reached for the skeletal key, "I bet we get to hear Blake scream."

Just as Blake's hand brushed the skeleton key, the sneks leapt forward, sinking their fangs into his leather-clad arm. He let out a high-pitched cry, leaping backwards, pulling the five bone sneks with him.

"Get 'em off! Get 'em off!" Blake waved his arm around, and Ryan found himself laughing as the sneks clung tightly to him.

"Snakes hidden in a pile of bones, how sneaky." Jack chuckled as he hurried towards Blake, his daggers drawn. "Wonder what they are."

Jack paused, eyes going wide as he checked the names of the mobs.

"Sneks. Sneaky snakes. I love this dungeon." Jack let out a roar of laughter as he slashed at the sneks hanging from Blake's arm.

After a moment, the knight was freed, and Jack was scooping up the loot.

"Gotta say, buddy, that wasn't very manly of you." Jack grinned even as Blake held his bleeding arm towards Karan. As the cleric placed her glowing hands over his wound, the knight seemed to shudder, and he shook his head.

"Why did it have to be snakes? I hate snakes," Blake complained. He continued to mutter under his breath as Jack broke into even more laughter.

Ryan was glad he'd listened in on that one.

"I'm going to remember that, Blake," Ryan said to himself, his mind already working. If the knight hated snakes, Ryan was sure he could find some new uses for his sneks further down the road.

I love this group.

Chapter Sixty-One

Blake stared at the pillar in the third room – the trapped room – which held the final key. Ryan loved this room.

"All right, so this is the last key," Blake said.

"A room with a single pillar, and no mobs," Jack mused aloud. "Totally not a trap."

He walked into the room, his thumbs looped into his belt.

"Good thing I'm here." He offered the group a grin, and took a step forward.

"Bad move," Ryan whispered.

Jack's step activated the first part of the trap room. The mana-infused stone slammed shut behind them, locking them in.

"Oh, yeah, so glad you're here," Blake said dully, looking at the now blocked path. "You are the worst thief I've ever heard of."

Jack offered a sheepish grin and bowed.

"But you have heard of me."

With a flourish, he did a backflip, landing next to the pillar that held the key. Ryan was impressed.

"He is so cool," Ryan whispered to Erin.

Jack really seemed to be showing off his acrobatic skills in the dungeon today, and Ryan loved it. He hadn't seen any adventurers move like Jack did.

"Well, thieves' main physical trait is their dexterity," Erin said. "So I'm sure his mana increases his speed and agility, and not his strength and endurance like Blake."

Ryan nodded, remembering what she had told him of adventurers. It seemed that, depending on the class, their mana amplified certain traits over others. So, while Blake, Matt, and Jack were all physical classes, Blake would be stronger and sturdier, while Matt and Jack were more agile and speedy. It made sense to Ryan and explained how each class brought different aspects to a team. As far as Ryan could tell, Blake's team was the most balanced.

"Hey, Blake," Jack called out as he reached for the key. "Watch out for that snek behind you."

Jack started laughing as Blake spun, his eyes filled with terror. Even as he did, Jack snatched the key with a grin.

"Jack, you—" Blake's words turned into a cry as the floor underneath him opened up, dropping him into a bone maiden.

Oops. Ryan's jealousy of Erin's love for Blake may have been more serious than he thought.

The keyhole opened near the cage, along with the cryptic message.

"A key for a life," Emily read. She looked from Blake, who was staring at the encroaching bone spikes, to Jack.

"Well, crap," Jack snapped. The thief rushed towards Blake and slammed the key into the slot, disabling the bone maiden and opening the door behind the group. Ryan was used to groups struggling over the dilemma of saving their teammate or taking the key and leaving the room. Never had he seen a group react so fast.

"That was unexpected," Ryan whispered, his admiration of the group growing.

"Did you really expect them to leave him?" The smile on Erin's face was a smug one.

She was right. Of all the groups, Blake's would be the last one to leave someone behind. But still, they hadn't even been fazed.

"Thanks," Blake gasped as he dusted himself off. He looked

down at the bone maiden they had freed him from. The bone spikes had receded.

"Hey, man, we're family." Jack offered him a grin, and his words earned him an approving nod from Karan. The thief noticed the nod and winked back at the cleric.

"Besides, Karan would strip me of my gear if I let you die. And while I don't mind the thought of her taking off my clothes —" Karan's smile faltered, and Jack let the comment hang in the air.

"But now we don't have the third key," Blake said, dejected.

He looked around the room for a hint. This was the point where the other teams who had sacrificed the key had turned away. Karan pointed towards the open door, leading back the way they had come.

"I doubt the dungeon would create a trap that required you to sacrifice a teammate to continue," Karan said. "Only an evil dungeon would create such a brutal trap. And I don't think this dungeon is evil. Besides, if that was the case, the guild would likely seal it off or destroy it the moment word of such a trap got out."

"Ahh, she gets me," Ryan said. He felt a flush of happiness run over him. Finally, someone who understood he wasn't evil. Her words also reminded him of how important dungeon etiquette was, as much as he hated it at times.

"Focus." Erin slapped his core, and he could tell she was jealous. Served her right.

"So, you think if we head back, we can find the third key?" Blake asked. He lifted his shield and picked up his sword, which he had dropped when the trap had activated.

"I'm pretty sure we will." Karan nodded at the others. "At the very least, I'd say we should return to the locked door, just to double check."

The group agreed, and they headed down the hallway, making their way back towards the second pillar room.

"Finally," Ryan sighed.

He was filled with excitement. This was the second group to not give up after saving their friend. Ryan had started to believe that no one would figure out that his trap didn't mean they wouldn't be able to keep progressing.

He quickly summoned the mobs he needed to in the second pillar room, knowing Blake and his team would reach it soon. As an added bonus reward, he summoned the skull of his wolf-deer hybrid and placed the skeleton key in its mouth. He figured it would serve as a slight hint of what was to come.

He admired his work for a moment, having plenty of time to prepare as Blake and his team fought back through the mobs. Originally, he had planned on just summoning four skeletal fighters, for a total of twenty mob points. However, since Blake hated snakes, Ryan couldn't resist switching it up just to mess with his favorite knight.

The room was now full of twenty sneks. Blake's screams as they entered the room made the decision worth it, and Ryan found himself chuckling as the team pressed forward. He knew they would find the last key, and it was only a matter of time before they faced Buttercup. Ryan could hardly wait.

Chapter Sixty-Two

Blake's group stood before the door that led into Buttercup's room, preparing to take on the boss.

"I'm so excited," Ryan whispered, his full attention focused on the scene he and Erin were watching.

"Me too." Erin snuggled atop Ryan's core, her silk cloth wrapped tightly around her form.

They were both shaking with anticipation. This was the first time a group had prepared to face off against his boss.

"Is everyone rested?" Karan asked. "This is the most the guild allows us to wait between rooms."

The group stood in a circle, with Karan inspecting each of the members. Everyone had their level triangles glowing on their palms, showing their skill points. Karan was making sure everyone was prepared for the boss.

"All ready to get that bounty," Jack said. He flashed a grin, and the rest of the group broke into smiles. Ryan could practically feel their excitement as well.

"All right. Let's go over the game plan one more time." Karan's words drew a sigh from Jack, but the others nodded. She was being a lot more thorough in planning for this boss fight than ever before. Ryan was curious as to why.

"Before we enter, I'm going to cast divine protection on all of you," she announced. "This spell will constantly drain mana from me, but will heal wounds as you receive them without me needing to be near you."

That seemed like a helpful spell, but Ryan was curious how much mana that would drain.

How much mana does a Gold Four cleric have?

"When we go in, Blake, you will need to draw aggro from the boss," she went on.

"Aggro?" Ryan asked Erin. It was a term he hadn't heard the adventurers use before.

"It's adventurer slang for aggression," Erin explained. "Meaning he is going to get the attention of Buttercup and have our boss focus on him."

"Oh, seems smart."

Having the tank draw the attention of the boss definitely made sense.

"I believe knights have a taunt?" Karan asked. Blake nodded, and Karan turned to the others.

"You three, wait until Blake has drawn its aggro, and do your best to damage the boss while avoiding any surprise attacks it may have." She glared at Jack, who had started to whistle. "That means don't do anything stupid."

The thief cracked a smile and shrugged. "I usually don't try to do stupid things," he said.

"That's what scares me," Karan replied dryly.

The group laughed, and even Ryan and Erin started to chuckle. The tension in the group was lifted, and the air around them was practically buzzing with anticipation. Ryan could barely contain his excitement.

"Here we go, then." Karan raised her hands towards the group and silently began chanting under her breath.

As she spoke, golden mana flowed from her hands, enveloping all four adventurers in a golden light. When she finished, their bodies had a faint shimmer.

"Let's do this," Jack called out, but before he could open the door and rush in, Karan grabbed his collar.

"This is the stupidity I'm talking about." She let him go as she motioned to Blake. "The tank goes first."

"Here goes nothing," Blake said.

Blake raised his shield, shrouded in dark mana, then opened the door, stepping into Buttercup's room. He paused as the others followed closely behind him, his eyes fixed on Ryan's second-floor boss.

"What in the name of the Goddess is that?" he whispered.

Buttercup stood with its empty eye sockets fixed on Blake and his party. The dark mana that covered its body almost seemed to expand and retract, as if the beast was breathing. It raised its antlered head, opening its fanged maw, and let out a bone-chilling howl.

Oh, yes.

Jack stepped beside Blake, his eyes scanning over the boss.

"Wait for Blake's taunt," Karan hissed at Jack.

"What's a taunt?" Ryan asked Erin. He had forgotten to ask in his earlier anticipation, but he was really curious what type of a skill it was.

"Throw me a freaking bone, Karan. Did you see this thing's name?" Jack said before Erin could respond.

As he spoke, the rest of the group finished entering. They all paused and took in Buttercup's name.

"Are you really scared of Buttercup? That's a name you would give a deerling or some other forest creature." Jack started to laugh, but it was short-lived.

His laughter drew Buttercup's attention, and without warning the mob lashed its tail towards the thief, sending a bone spike into his shoulder.

"That was as good as a taunt," Erin giggled, watching as Jack leapt back behind Blake, cursing as he tugged the bone spike from his flesh. As the bone was removed, golden light filled the wound, healing him.

"It's an ability that draws a mob's attention to a certain adventurer."

"Oh, well, that'll teach him," Ryan said, smug. Buttercup's name was still a sore spot for him.

"Are you done being stupid?" Karan hissed, and the thief nodded solemnly back at her.

"But come on," Jack said. "Buttercup? Really?"

The others broke into an uneasy laughter.

"Buttercup, Adventurer's Doom," Blake chuckled, stepping forward.

With a sigh, he steadied himself, before letting out a yell of his own. It seemed as if a dark wave flowed from his body as he yelled, and a moment later, Buttercup was launching bone spikes at him.

"Now *that's* a taunt," Erin said.

"Let's do this," Jack called out as Buttercup and Blake squared off.

Matt branched out to the left, his bow raised as he eyed Buttercup's form. Emily stayed back with Karan, but her little dragon had taken flight and was eyeing Buttercup's antlers hungrily. Meanwhile, Jack's form seemed to slowly begin disappearing into the shadows. Ryan knew that skill.

A moment later, Jack lunged from the darkness, daggers drawn, heading towards Buttercup's side. He sliced at Buttercup, sending blades of air flying towards the beast's side.

"Take that," Jack growled.

Buttercup snorted, and even as it shot another spike towards Blake, Buttercup turned its head towards Jack and his attack. Faster than even Jack's attacks, the antlers atop Buttercup's head detached and began to spin. The dark mana moved the spinning bone mass in front of Jack's attack, easily absorbing the attack.

"Oh, that's new," Jack said.

He skittered to a stop and dove out of the way as Buttercup's tail sent three bone shards flying in his direction. He dodged two and blocked the third with his dagger.

"Your taunt sucks," he called out at Blake.

"He just really doesn't like you," Blake called back, and he sent another wave of dark energy towards Buttercup. The mob shook its head angrily and turned back towards the knight.

"Maybe you should apolo—" Blake's words were cut off as Buttercup let out a howl and charged towards him.

The boss's long legs gave it increased speed, and Blake was barely able to raise his shield and plant his feet as Buttercup crashed into him.

"Blake!" Emily yelled as Buttercup's skull smashed into his dark-shrouded shield.

The blow should have sent Blake flying, but instead, he held his ground.

"I'm good," he grunted as he fought against Buttercup's massive form. His foot began to slip, and Buttercup reared up, hooved legs crashing down on the knight. A hoof smashed against his skull, sending him flying backwards, blood dripping from the wound.

"That looks painful," Ryan whispered. He was glad to see Blake slowly getting to his feet as his skull healed.

"Buttercup is doing quite well," Erin whispered, eyes fixed on the battle.

The boss mob turned towards Blake as the knight got to his feet. Without warning, Buttercup whipped his tail in Blake's direction, sending three more spikes flying at the knight.

"Oh no," Ryan whispered.

There was no way Blake was going to get his shield up in time. That attack was going to hurt.

"Over here," Matt bellowed, and three arrows crashed into the bone spikes, creating an explosion of wood and bone before the spikes could reach Blake.

Buttercup turned towards the marksman, and Ryan could tell his boss was irritated. Even as Matt offered Blake a smile, his face turned to horror as Buttercup rushed towards him.

"Cynder, now!" Emily shouted.

Her body glowed red and at the same time Cynder's form took on a scarlet hue. The dragon opened its mouth and let out a wave of crimson flames at Buttercup. Fire met bone as Buttercup's spinning antlers intercepted the attack.

Buttercup was forced to halt its charge on Matt to turn his attention to Cynder, allowing the marksman to move further away from the boss.

"We've got this," Blake called out, and he rushed towards Buttercup, having been completely healed by Karan's spell. Darkness rolled off of him as he taunted Buttercup, just as Cynder's flames dissipated.

"All together," Jack instructed from the darkness, though the thief was nowhere to be seen.

"I don't have the mana to buff Cynder for another minute,"

Emily said as the dragon zipped around in the air. The red glow had faded from both the dragon and Emily.

"That's fine, we can hold him for a minute," Blake replied, smashing his shield against Buttercup. The attack was blocked by the spinning bones, and the knight barely managed to jump back as the boss mob reared up again.

"My divine protection will only hold for maybe a minute." Karan's voice was strained, and Ryan could tell she was worried. He guessed holding that spell on the entire team was tiring, and the group had been taking some damage from Buttercup. Especially Blake.

"Let's finish this, then," Matt snarled.

He launched three more arrows at Buttercup's side, and as the spinning bones moved to intercept, Jack appeared, launching slashes of wind towards Buttercup's other side.

The wind cut into Buttercup's dark mana. The mob let out a howl of rage and spun its body quickly, shooting spikes back into Jack.

The swift move caught the thief off guard, and the three spikes landed in his stomach, sending him flying backwards. At the same time, Buttercup kicked backwards, sending a startled Blake flying.

"Oh no." Erin's cry of concern echoed Ryan's thoughts.

Was Buttercup about to finish off his favorite team? He may have named his boss Adventurer's Doom, but he didn't mean for it to be the bane of Blake's team.

"Goddess, that hurts." Jack coughed up blood as he pulled the bones from his stomach, golden light healing his wounds. He leaned against a wall, struggling to stand. Blake got shakily to his feet as well, and Matt launched the last of his regular arrows to stop Buttercup's bone spikes.

It really wasn't looking good for the group. Ryan was certain he saw the shimmering golden light surrounding the adventurers waver.

"Run away," Ryan whispered, begging his favorite group to just escape.

There was no reason for them to fall here. Any other team, he wouldn't care, but not Blake's team.

"I can't watch." Erin put her hands over her eyes, peeking through her fingers.

"We need to retreat." Karan's breath was coming in gasps, and the golden shimmer had all but disappeared from around the adventures.

"No. I want that bounty," Jack countered. He struggled to his feet and looked around at his group.

"A bounty isn't worth our lives," Karan snapped. Her face was white, and she had blood dripping from her nose. If Ryan had to guess, she was nearly out of mana.

"We can't stop this boss," Blake said. He taunted Buttercup once again, giving Matt a reprieve. The archer only had three bone arrows, which he had received as drops from skeletal archers, remaining.

Jack wasn't convinced.

"Psh, come on. You guys aren't the only special ones here." Jack sheathed his daggers, his eyes beginning to glow green. "This isn't even my final form."

The thief cocked his head back and let out a long, powerful howl. Ryan watched as the thief's face seemed to elongate, his mouth filling with fangs. Grey fur sprouted from his flesh, and his hands grew long, deadly claws.

What's more, Ryan could see the thief's already defined muscles begin to grow and bulge. The final change to appear, as Jack's howl died down, was the appearance of a wolf-like tail from underneath his shirt.

"Let's do this," Jack growled as he drew his daggers, his voice deeper, more bestial, than before.

He lunged towards Buttercup, faster than even Ryan could track. To the boss's credit, Buttercup's spinning antlers moved to intercept the attack, but Jack was just too fast. Two long cuts opened up in Buttercup's dark mana, and the beast cried out in pain.

"Don't just stand there," Jack snarled at the others. "Help me."

He was still moving, never slowing, as more slash marks opened up across Buttercup's dark fur-like mana.

The others seemed to come out of their daze, and with a cry,

Blake rushed forward. He slammed his shield into Buttercup, landing a solid hit as Ryan's boss was still trying to unsuccessfully stop Jack's sudden flurry of attacks.

"I'll immobilize him." Matt drew the last three bone arrows and closed his eyes.

Blue mana flowed around the bones, and Matt once again turned his bow parallel to the ground, aiming directly towards Buttercup. As he launched his three arrows, Jack leapt over Buttercup and sent two wind blasts into Buttercup's back, drawing the spinning antlers above the boss.

It seemed to Ryan that the bones tried to block the most dangerous attacks, meaning multiple attacks at once could overwhelm his boss's defenses.

Interesting.

Matt's three arrows impacted three of Buttercup's four hooves, and as the arrows connected, the blue mana around the arrows turned to ice, pinning Buttercup in place.

"Let's end this," Blake cried out, and Emily once again began to glow red.

As she did, Cynder let out an excited cry, and a wave of flames washed over Buttercup. The boss cried out, its swirling bones trying to block the flames even as Jack rolled under the boss, cutting into its stomach. Buttercup was covered in countless cuts, its dark mana torn and tattered, and Ryan knew Blake's team was about to win.

As if on cue, Blake's sword began to glow even brighter, and with a cry, he swung the blade at Buttercup's head. Unable to block against the attack, Blake's celestial-clad sword cut deep into Ryan's boss.

Buttercup's form collapsed, bones scattering as the dark mana animating them faded away, and Ryan let out a sigh.

They had done it. They had defeated Buttercup.

He smiled as he watched the group look around, the room suddenly quiet, their threat gone. Jack quickly resumed his human form. Cynder flew down to Buttercup's scattered bones, and the little dragon let out an excited roar as it latched onto one of Buttercup's antlers, trying, unsuccessfully, to drag the large bone away. The dragon's antics caused the tension from the battle to lift, and the group began to laugh.

"They did it." Ryan felt the tension flee from his core room as he watched the group celebrate.

Once again, Blake's team had demonstrated what it meant to be a group of adventurers. Once again, they had filled Ryan with excitement and passion to be a dungeon core. He could feel the last remaining fear of the necromancer fading away.

Ryan wasn't going to get stronger *just* to make sure the necromancer couldn't kill him. Ryan also wanted to get stronger so he could continue to watch Blake's team grow.

He grinned to himself as he noted the loot Buttercup had dropped and decided to add one more piece. He had planned on introducing his newest item in the next week, but now he changed his mind.

They'd earned it

Chapter Sixty-Three

Blake sighed with relief as the group sat around their normal table. After claiming the bounty for defeating the second floor's boss, as well as counting out the coin they had received and the items they sold off, they had each earned over thirty gold pieces. Added in with what Blake had been saving, he had enough for his class gear, and he knew Matt did too.

"Oh, man, that bounty was so nice," Jack said.

"I'm surprised you didn't sell off that card," Blake said as he eyed the large steaming steak before him. Karan had treated them all not only to drink, but also steak for their job well done. Blake couldn't remember the last time he had such a fine cut of meat.

"Eh, I'm keeping this as a souvenir." Jack shrugged.

He pulled out a leather-bound journal from his cloak and opened it up, revealing the final item that dropped in the dungeon. It was the size of a playing card, but that was where the similarity ended.

Atop the card, in golden letters, was the name "Buttercup: Adventurer's Doom – 2nd Floor Boss Mob." Beneath that was an image of the mob in all its horror. The way the card shone in the light, Blake was certain it was inlaid with silver. Underneath the image of the card, there was information regarding the boss itself. Then on the bottom, in silver again, the number '50.'

"I wonder if there will be more," Matt said, reaching out to look at the card.

Jack closed the journal and shot him a wink. "If there are, I'm going to collect them all."

Karan shot the thief a knowing smile. "Am I going to need to confiscate your purse, so you don't run around spending all your gold on cards?"

"Hey now, I'm over those problems." Jack tucked the journal away and took a long drink from his hot chocolate.

"So, lockpicks?" Karan raised an eyebrow as she spoke.

Jack's response was to choke on his drink, sending chocolate flying all over the table.

"I'll get 'em tonight, don't worry," he said, clearing his throat. "But first, I'm going to enjoy this delicious meal."

He licked his lips and cut into his steak, taking a bite. His face erupted in pure pleasure. Before he was even finished chewing the first, he was preparing a second bite.

"Man, you're tearing into that like some sort of beast." Blake grinned at his own joke, but his comment caused Jack to pause.

The thief lowered his food-laden fork back to his table and slowly finished chewing, his eyes sad.

"Look, please." He glanced at the others, his eyes pleading. "Don't mention that to anyone, all right?"

"So, you're a..." Blake lowered his voice. "Wolfkin."

Jack shook his head.

"No, I'm not," he sighed.

"But—"

"I'm a mutt." Jack said the word as if it pained him.

"What does that mean?" Blake asked.

Karan interrupted. "It means he's a half-breed. One of his parents was a wolfkin, the other was a human." She turned towards Jack, her eyes filled with sympathy. "You must have had such a hard upbringing."

Blake shared a look with Emily and Matt, and he could tell they weren't following what was going on either. What they could tell, though, was that it was a painful topic for Jack. Even Cynder had paused chewing on a piece of Buttercup's antler.

The little dragon glanced from Karan to Jack, before jumping off Emily's shoulder and carrying her antler piece towards Jack. With a slight nudge, the baby dragon pushed the antler against Jack's hand.

"Thanks, little one." Jack smiled as he picked up the antler and held it back out to Cynder. "But you earned this. I'll be all right."

Cynder let out a small cry, then grabbed the antler and rushed back onto Emily's shoulder.

Blake looked at the group, wondering how to break the awkwardness around them. Uncertain, he blurted the first thing that came to mind.

"By the way, Karan, the Guildmaster said she misses you."

Karan looked as if Blake had slapped her, and suddenly all attention was off Jack, and on Blake and Karan.

"She said that?" Karan's voice was barely audible as she stared down at her plate. She poked at her steak before setting down her silverware.

"Yeah," Blake said, taken aback by her reaction. "It was the last thing she said to me before I came back to town."

He looked at the cleric thoughtfully. What was her relation to the Guildmaster?

"I suppose it has been over ten years since I last saw her." Karan let out a long sigh. "I guess, since we've all been sharing tough secrets today…"

She turned from Blake to Jack.

"I can share mine with all of you."

Suddenly, everyone at the table was leaning in, their attention fixated on Karan. She was the most secretive of all of them.

"I'm sure you've all had suspicions about how I know so much about dungeons."

They nodded.

"Well, when I was Bronze, I had the opportunity to form a party, much like this one, and train in a new dungeon."

Oh, no.

The last dungeon to form, before the Bone Dungeon, was a notorious fire dungeon. Blake had heard horror stories of that dungeon. It had claimed so many lives that the Adventurers' Guild had banned adventurers lower than Platinum from diving in it. Blake had known Karan had experience with dungeons, but not *that* dungeon.

"The Dungeon of Ashes?" Jack asked, interrupting Blake's thoughts. His voice was gentle. Blake guessed Jack had come to the same conclusion as he had.

"Yes."

Karan's eyes seemed to become lost in the memory as she began her tale.

"I was a young adept, having only been in the Adventurers' Guild for about a year when the dungeon first emerged. I was so excited when it formed, and even more excited when I was allowed to join the expeditionary party."

She allowed herself a bittersweet smile.

"At first, it was much like this. I was picked up into a group filled with other Bronze adventurers. Our leader was a Gold Five sentinel named James."

Where have I heard that name before?

"James was amazing. He made sure none of us took any damage as we began our dungeon dives, instantly taunting every mob in every room, even letting the mobs hack away at his mana so that we could have practice fighting."

"You fell for him," Emily whispered, and Karan nodded.

"He's the reason I became a healer. I didn't want him to get hurt, and I wanted to be able to heal him if anything ever happened to him." Her voice cracked for a moment, before she regained her composure.

"James had special connections, and we were able to dive into the dungeon every day. As such, we climbed the ranks faster than any other group had, and we broke into Silver before the dungeon had even transitioned." She shook her head. "Sometimes I wish we hadn't grown so fast."

"Then what happened?" Blake's question sprang unbidden from his mouth, so enthralled was he by her story.

"By the time the dungeon hit Silver, we were already in the mid-Silver ranks, having farmed the first floor so many times. We easily cleared the second floor once it was created and continued our rapid growth." She took a drink, her hand shaking. "We didn't notice the dungeon was becoming more violent.

Many adventurers were starting to fall to it, but we couldn't understand why. Everything it threw at us, James simply taunted, and we easily dispatched them."

Her knuckles turned white as she gripped her mug, sudden emotion taking hold.

"The next time the dungeon closed to undergo a change, it was down for two months. During that time, we completed our ascensions to Gold, and James and I began seeing each other." Her eyes were distant. "He even introduced me to his mother."

"Alice." Blake suddenly remembered where he had heard James's name before.

That was the name of the Guildmaster's only son. The son that was killed in the Dungeon of Ashes.

"Yes, James was her only child," Karan said, her voice barely more than a whisper. "She adored him, and was so protective of him. Just like the Guildmaster, James was strong-willed, and he rarely allowed his mother protect him."

Blake knew firsthand just how strong-willed Alice was.

"Just like his mother, he threw himself into dungeons, pushing himself to grow stronger, and working to protect those around him. Because of this, we were the first group back into the dungeon once it reawakened."

Tears started to fall from Karan's eyes, and it was Jack who acted next. The thief placed his hand gently on Karan's, offering her a small smile.

"It's all right, Karan," Jack said.

She placed her hand on his and gave him a small, sad smile, before she cleared her throat to continue.

"We cleared the first two floors with ease, just as we always had. The moment we got to the third floor, though, everything changed. The third floor was simply a massive cavern, filled with streams of lava. James led our group cautiously into the floor, scanning the room for enemies. We were so fixated on looking for enemies, we didn't notice the door behind us lock closed."

Blake brought his hand to his mouth, even though he knew where the story was going.

"Once we reached the center of the room, sinister laughter filled the chamber. James turned to us, and his smile, the smile he had always worn, was gone. Fear had taken it from him. He screamed a warning to us, but it was too late. Horned humanoids burst from the lava around us, their eyes burning with hunger."

"What were they?" Blake had never heard of a creature that fit Karan's description.

"I'm not sure." She shook her head. "Sometimes I wonder if I simply imagined them, given the panic and chaos that ensued. We rushed back towards the door, only to find it was locked. We tried to teleport out, but the dungeon's magic kept us from fleeing. So we turned to fight."

Blake could hear the pain in her voice. It cracked as she went on.

"No matter how many we killed, more kept appearing. One by one, our members fell, until only James and I remained. I remember that moment so well." She broke down into tears, sobbing. "He was so hurt, and I just...I didn't have any more mana to heal him."

"He saved you somehow, didn't he?" Emily's voice was barely audible, and Blake glanced at her, noting her eyes were filled with tears as well. In fact, they all were on the verge of tears.

"Somehow, we survived the final wave. He killed the last mob before us and turned to me. That was when the room began to shake, and the laughter returned. James took my hand, and before I could speak, he placed a single crystal into my palm."

Tears ran down Karan's face, but she lifted her chin, determined to finish her tale.

"He closed my fist around it, breaking it. Suddenly I was back in Alice's office, covered in blood and wounds, grasping at nothing, crying out James's name."

Karan wiped at her tears, looking around at the group.

"The crystal was a legendary item that Alice had given James. It had the ability to instantly teleport a single person back to a set point. Alice had given it to James, had made him promise to use it if he were ever near death. Instead, he used it to save me."

She turned back towards Blake and offered him a small smile.

"I haven't seen Alice since that day. The moment I explained everything to her, she teleported to the dungeon town and I ran away from her. I wandered aimlessly for a while, broken, beyond repair I thought, until I met Sean."

"My father?" Blake asked.

"Yes. He helped me find a purpose, told me I was saved so that I could save others. He helped me to cope with James's death, and find a new purpose in serving the Goddess of Justice." She pulled out an emblem, the two scales of the Goddess. "He gave me this, and I promised that I would repay his kindness if he ever found a way for me to."

She let out a sigh and offered the group a large smile.

"Go figure his way for me to repay him would see me once again in a dungeon with a party of adventurers."

The group rubbed their eyes, and all offered Karan rueful smiles of their own. Blake couldn't imagine the strength it took for Karan to lead a group of adventurers into a dungeon after what had happened to her. He was suddenly much more appreciative of everything she had done for him and the group. He also understood now why she had been so strict with them.

"I've made a promise to myself that I'll never let another adventurer fall while I'm in their party," Karan said.

"Well, maybe I'll try not to be so reckless next time." Jack offered Karan a sheepish grin, though his eyes held sincerity.

"You just keep me on my toes." Karan returned his smile, and even seemed to blush slightly.

"Ay, well, you know—"

Jack stopped mid-quip, his entire body going stiff. A moment later, a figure appeared behind him. Sasha.

"Sorry to interrupt the chat here, cuties, but Marcus wants to speak with the knight." Sasha pointed a finger towards Blake, beckoning him.

As she did, she leaned down to Jack's ear, and whispered something to him. A moment later, Blake, Jack, and Sasha were heading out of the inn, towards Marcus's headquarters.

Viktor

He took a sip from his ale, watching the group as they shared their stories. He was too far away to hear what was being said, but he could tell it was an emotional story. Truly, they were pathetic creatures.

His eye caught the flash of silver on the young man's hand, and sure enough, he could make out the shape of a wolf's head on the ring. This was the lowly being that would be his target.

Now he just needed to get the man alone. He planned to follow the man to his tent and forcibly drag him back into the dungeon, but a moment later his plan was ruined.

Viktor's side flared with remembered pain as Sasha appeared at the group's table, and he fought down his rage. The earring the Exalted One had given him allowed him to completely hide his presence, even from the assassins. In addition, it applied a sort of glamour over him, which allowed him to pass unnoticed through the town and blend in.

But if he made a move now, the glamour would break, and he would likely have to deal with not just Sasha, but an entire town of adventurers, her twin, and Marcus. Viktor was confident in his own strength, but that battle was outside of his ability for now.

With the Crown of Sorrows, though... Viktor licked his lips in anticipation. All he needed to do was complete this task for the Exalted One, and then revenge would be his.

Sighing, he moved away from his table, and out of the inn. He would need to keep an eye on the young man, so that he could complete his task and claim his reward.

Chapter Sixty-Four

The walk to Marcus's office was a quiet, awkward one. Sasha didn't say a single word, and even more eerily, neither did Jack. The thief spent the entire walk with his head down, not even glancing around. Blake was curious what Sasha had said to him but was afraid to break the silence that hung over the trio.

Once they reached Marcus's office – one of the nicer buildings in the dungeon town, given it was the Adventurers' Guild headquarters for the town – Sasha simply motioned for Blake to enter. Then she turned and walked away with Jack on her heels.

"I hope he'll be okay," Blake whispered as he headed inside. He had no idea what she could possibly want with Jack, but Blake had a feeling it had to do with Jack's newly revealed wolfkin bloodline.

"Don't worry about your friend." Marcus's voice pulled Blake's attention to the center of the room, where a large desk was sitting. Behind it, legs propped up on the table, sat Marcus the Platinum rogue.

"Sir?" Blake bowed towards Marcus, uncertain why he had even been summoned to speak with him.

"Sasha and Rasha just need to chat with your young thief friend. I believe Sasha wants him to join her pack." Marcus offered Blake a grin. "Though, if I know Jack, which I do, I doubt he will leave you guys." Marcus motioned towards a chair besides his desk. "Now, come. We have something else we must discuss."

Blake walked slowly towards the chair and hesitantly sat down. Blake only ever saw the rogue out in public, where he often came off as a gruff, serious leader. But now he seemed completely relaxed and carefree, which was concerning Blake.

"First, let me congratulate you on defeating the second-floor boss." Marcus pulled his feet off the desk and leaned forward, staring at Blake. "It's rare for an unknown boss to be taken down for the first time without a single casualty. Your team is very—" Marcus paused before he said the next word. "—interesting."

Blake opened his mouth to speak but closed it quickly. He had no idea what to say to the rogue.

Marcus held up his fingers and started counting off. "A Gold Four cleric, the sole survivor of the Dungeon of Ashes dive that killed Alice's son. A half-breed thief. A summoner with a baby dragon." He paused with three of his fingers down, smiling knowingly at Blake. "A dual affinity knight." The fourth finger went down. "Four out of five interesting members in your party. I wouldn't be surprised if your archer does something crazy when he hits Gold, just to make your party even more unique." Marcus started chuckling.

"How do you know—"

"So much about your team? Or about your dual affinities?" Marcus waved a hand at Blake, stopping him from responding. "I'm in charge of this dungeon town, Blake. I am the eyes and ears of the Adventurers' Guild in this area. I know everything that goes on." His eyes twinkled and he offered Blake a grin. "I even know who fancies who in this here camp. And I must say, Blake, you have a few admirers." He shot Blake a wink, causing Blake to blush. The rogue was keeping him completely off balance in this conversation.

"But just because I know everything doesn't mean others should." Marcus suddenly took up his bored, serious tone that he often used to address the group. "So far, only a handful of people know about your dual affinities, and I have been asked by Alice to ensure it stays that way."

"How?" Blake finally managed to speak, and that was all he got out.

"Well, for one thing, you are banned from training in public."

"Wha—" Blake's outburst stopped as Marcus narrowed his eyes. A warning, which Blake obeyed. His mind, however, was racing. How was he supposed to get stronger if he couldn't train?

"I have spoken in detail with Alice on this fact. While you are not allowed to train in public, I have agreed to allow you to train in secret in the dungeon at night. This will not only give you a safe place away from prying eyes, but easy mobs to practice skills on."

Blake stared at Marcus in disbelief. Only groups of five were allowed in, and only during the day.

"Before I give you such access, I need you to promise me two things." He tossed a dark stone towards Blake. "First, you can only train in the first room of the dungeon. If you dive in further and die, Alice won't forgive me." Blake nodded as he took the stone, eyeing it. "That stone will allow you to pass through the barrier we have enacted at the dungeon entrance without setting off the alarm. No one knows of it, but I had a barrier there to keep unwelcome visitors from entering the dungeon without my knowing."

"And the second thing, sir?" Blake asked as he pocketed the stone.

"Well, speaking of unwelcome visitors." Marcus rubbed his eyes and offered Blake a small grin. "You're going to do me a huge favor before you start your training."

"I... How can I help, sir?"

"You remember the team that dove into the dungeon before it was opened?" Blake remembered that team. The sole survivor, Todd, was a likeable enough guy, though no one had taken him into their parties since the event. They considered him cursed.

"Yes, sir, I remember them."

"Well, Todd has been begging me to allow him to go back into the dungeon to pay his respects to his team. I'm certainly no babysitter, but I also haven't had any poor saps to task with this." He flashed a mischievous grin at Blake. "Until now." Blake didn't like where this was going.

"I've already sent word to Todd that you are going to take him into the dungeon, but only to the first room. There, he will pay his respects to his fallen team. Afterwards, he has promised to leave this town and stop pestering me."

Blake sighed and nodded. He hadn't planned on going to train tonight, given how tired he was from his boss fight with Buttercup. But he supposed he could at least lead Todd into the first room and let him pay his respects. None of the mobs in that room posed a threat to Blake, especially not now. By clearing the first and second floor, Blake, Matt, and Emily had all reached Silver Seven, while Jack had reached Silver Six. That meant Blake now had 600 mana points, with 480 points increasing his physical attributes. Even though he was Silver Seven, he was as strong now as a Silver One adventurer. He was a lot stronger than he had been that morning.

A knock on the door pulled Blake's mind from his growth, and Marcus motioned for him to go. "That must be our friend Todd. Keep him safe and prove to me you are capable of going into the dungeon on your own."

"I won't let you down, Marcus." Blake stood and turned, preparing to leave.

"One last thing, Blake." Marcus's words caused Blake to pause, and he turned back to the rogue.

"Sir?"

Marcus looked down at a piece of parchment and back at Blake. He opened his mouth and then closed it, shaking his head. "Never mind. Just…" His voice softened. "Be careful out there."

"Will do, sir." Blake offered him a confident smile and opened the door. How hard could it be, keeping Todd safe?

Chapter Sixty-Five

"Little skrat, doo doo doo doo doo doo," Ryan hummed to himself as he scanned over his mobs. It had been an exciting day, especially with Buttercup's defeat at the hands of Blake's team.

"Bigger skrat, doo doo doo doo doo doo."

Ryan flipped through his mobs and compared them to the cards he had made. The first card to drop was Buttercup's, given to Blake's team. Now, Ryan was planning to add them to all his mob's loot tables so that adventurers would be able to get little information cards on each of his mobs.

"Infested skrat, doo doo doo doo doo doo."

He paused as he looked it over. Currently, the paralysis on that particular mob was rather weak. What if he tried to evolve it more? He generally didn't like zombies, but a stronger paralysis or poison-type mob could be useful in the future.

"Well, you are in a good mood," Erin laughed, a wide smile on her face as she flew lazily around the room. She was in just as good a mood as Ryan was; he could feel it through their bond.

"Blake's team has that effect on me." Ryan flipped back through his mobs, grinning as he looked at the next two on his list: the final forms of his skrats and skuirrels. Well, for now, anyway. He silently assigned cards to each, careful to not give their existence away. Rule number one of skeletal fight club, after all.

"Mm-hmm. You seemed really excited to drop that card, too. You didn't tell me you were going to do those." Erin crossed her arms as she floated lazily on top of his core. "That was brilliant."

"Thank you." Ryan beamed at her praise. He was sure his core brightened just a little. "I wanted a way to help adventurers learn about the mobs in my dungeon," he said. "I got the idea of cards after absorbing countless sets of playing cards from the adventurers. It seems they really like these little cards with drawings on them."

Erin gave him a smile, but at the same time, Ryan could feel her emotions start to drop.

"I wish I could help you come up with new ideas like that."

Oh, no.

Ryan knew where this was going. He was not about to be guilt-tripped again. Not this time.

"You help me so much, hun," he said quickly. "I just wanted to surprise you, show you just how much I've been learning from you."

Ha, that'll stop her in her tracks.

"Oh, stop it, you." She started giggling and Ryan could feel her mood lifting.

Crisis averted.

"So, do you have anything else you are secretly working on?" Erin asked.

Oh, crap.

"Nothing right now, hun."

He instinctively glanced at level two of his skeletal fight club as he spoke. So far, the new skeletal mobs seemed to need a lot more experience battling each other before reaching a new form.

Ah well, we have time.

"Oh. Maybe we can think of something together?" Erin closed her eyes and rested her chin on a tiny fist. She really was cute when she did that.

"I'm always happy to try and figure out new ways to improve *our* dungeon." Ryan stressed the word 'our', knowing how happy it would make her. Sure enough, her eyes flew open and a giant grin erupted on her face. She gave him a hug.

"I love it when you say it's our dungeon," she giggled.

"I know, hun."

Ryan was just about to go back to his card assigning task when something at the front of his dungeon caught his eye. Two figures were walking casually towards his entrance from the town. It was definitely too late for more adventurers.

For a moment, fear rushed over Ryan. What if it was the necromancer? What if he had brought someone with him?

"Erin." Ryan's voice was a whisper, filled with fear. "We may have company."

She looked into his core as he focused on the duo. Erin's face grew pale, and Ryan knew she was thinking the same thing he was. Just a few more moments and they would be able to confirm their fears.

Ryan listened closely.

"Thanks again for doing this, Blake."

One of the figures' voices carried over, and Ryan had to pause. Did he just say Blake?

"No problem, Todd. But remember, we can only go into the first room."

That is definitely Blake's voice.

"It's Blake!" Erin's shriek of excitement made Ryan wince.

The two figures drew closer and Ryan tried to make sense of the man that was with Blake. He was sure he'd seen him before.

"Do we know that second guy?" he asked. As he spoke, he watched Blake hold out a dark stone.

A moment later, the air in front of Ryan's entrance seemed to shimmer and part, as if a barrier had been erected. Weird.

"He looks familiar," Erin mumbled.

She was so helpful at times.

The two stepped in, and Ryan quickly pulled up the second figure's information. Todd, Bronze Ten fighter.

Oh, I remember.

"It's Squeaker," Ryan chuckled. He had always wondered what happened to that poor adventurer. And now here he was with Blake. Wait, why was he here with Blake?

The two descended from his entrance towards his first room. Blake was leading the way, walking easily, oozing confidence. A cursory glance showed the knight had leveled up to Silver Seven after his dive earlier today. That meant he was more than a match for the first room.

"I think it is noble of you to want to pay your respects to your team," Blake began, and Ryan turned his attention to the conversation.

Why does Squeaker want to pay his respects to the team? They were jerks.

"Yeah, I know nobody really liked Josh and the others." Squeaker paused as they neared the entrance to the first room. "But," the fighter went on, tearing up. "They were my team, you know? They were the first people to actually let me be a part of a team."

"They were like your family." Blake turned and offered the fighter a smile. "I can understand that."

He walked into the first room, motioning for Squeaker to stay where he was.

"Let me clear out the mobs in here," Blake said. "Then you can come in and pay your respects."

"Thanks, Blake." Squeaker stood by and Ryan watched as Blake closed his eyes.

The skuirrels in the room hadn't seemed to notice him yet. That was, until Blake opened his eyes and sent a wave of celestial energy throughout the room. It was the same taunt as earlier, but this time with celestial energy.

"Oh, so you got celestial energy?" Squeaker exclaimed. "That's so cool!"

He watched in awe as Blake offered the man a smile, his sword and shield erupting in golden light.

Strange. Why isn't he using his darkness affinity?

A moment later, all the mobs in the room came rushing from their holes, leaping crazily towards Blake. The knight grinned, slashing at them with his glowing sword. His movement was noticeably faster and smoother than it had been earlier in the day.

Ryan found himself transfixed as he watched Blake cut down each mob. The knight had no reason to infuse his shield with mana, as no skuirrel, not even the victorious skuirrels, got past his sword.

As the last mob fell, Blake turned towards Squeaker and sheathed his sword. The knight had a huge smile on his face, and Ryan knew he had enjoyed that.

"Alright, Todd, that should be—"

Blake's voice stopped as a bone spike suddenly shot through Squeaker.

The attack seemed to come from the darkness behind him, and caught even Ryan by surprise. He hadn't sensed anything. No one else had entered his dungeon, he was sure of it.

Squeaker fell to the ground, a look of confusion on his face. A moment later, dark laughter filled the dungeon, and a figure clad in shadows stepped forward.

"Oh no," Erin whispered, and Ryan felt a chill fill him. He knew that laughter. He knew that form.

Viktor the necromancer had returned.

Chapter Sixty-Six

"Todd," Blake cried, drawing his sword. Ryan had to give it to the knight; Blake definitely responded a lot quicker than he used to.

"Ah, was that the poor soul's name?" The necromancer, Viktor, spoke as if bored. He motioned towards the body and a moment later it rose up. The zombie Squeaker turned towards Blake and drew its own sword.

"Pity he was so weak," Viktor went on. "But this should at least offer me a moment of amusement."

Darkness flowed from the necromancer, swirling around the zombie. The gloom seemed to infuse him, and Ryan watched as Squeaker's muscles bulged. Then the blackness started to solidify over his body, covering him in a shadowy armor.

"What... what have you done?" Blake breathed, his face suffused with horror. Ryan noticed Blake's sword shaking. Squeaker's death had definitely scared him. The fighter's sudden undeath had likely shaken him up even more.

"What's he doing?" Ryan whispered to Erin, watching as the darkness finished its enhancements of Squeaker's form.

At the same time, Ryan began going through his list of contingency plans for Viktor. Because Blake was in the dungeon, Ryan couldn't use most of his plans, one of which included dropping the entire room on the necromancer. That meant he would need to get a little more creative.

Erin's voice cut into his thoughts.

"I think he is using his mana to upgrade Squeaker from a basic zombie to an armored zombie."

A what?

Ryan scanned his mob list as fast as he could. It really was hard to prepare a modified contingency plan, scan a mob list, watch a zombie getting enhanced, and talk at the same time. His mob list showed zombie and hardened zombie as possibilities. If he had to guess, armored was the Gold version of a zombie.

"I think Blake's in trouble," Ryan whispered as the Armored Squeaker Zombie, or ASZ, advanced.

"Me too," Erin whimpered, wrapping herself in her silk cloth. The poor fairy was shaking. Then again, Ryan was certain he was shaking a little too. He needed to do something, and fast. He was already formulating a plan, but he needed time.

Stupid. If Viktor was going to use a mob against Blake, what was stopping Ryan from using mobs against the necromancer? He literally had an army of mobs at his disposal. Yeah, the necromancer was strong, but Ryan had gotten a lot stronger since last time. He sent mental commands to all of his mobs, ordering them to assemble in the second room of his first floor.

"I've improved your friend," Viktor said. "He is now a Gold-level zombie. Fastest advancement from Bronze to Gold ever."

Viktor let out a dark laugh.

"If you can defeat him, perhaps I'll let you live long enough to tell you who I am."

ASZ lunged at Blake. The knight parried the attack with his sword, stepping back.

Blake surrounded his sword and shield in celestial light as he eyed ASZ warily. Ryan could tell he didn't like the idea of cutting down his former friend.

"Oh, a celestial knight? Were you hoping to become a paladin?" Viktor laughed and his mob lunged once again at Blake.

ASZ's sword smashed against Blake's shield, and to Ryan's surprise, the light around it wavered as Blake was forced back.

"Tell me, O noble knight, do you know about affinity bonuses?" Viktor chuckled as ASZ swung again. Blake blocked with his shield, and Ryan saw the knight wince. That zombie was tough.

"Most affinities have strengths and weaknesses against other affinities." Viktor's voice carried a hint of glee. The necromancer was enjoying this, which was both creepy and perfectly fine for Ryan right now. His mobs had been making their way to his second room on the first floor at an impressive pace for undead creatures.

Obviously, Steve and the skeletal rodents had already arrived there, and as Ryan checked on his mobs from his second floor, he saw they were already in the tunnel leading to Steve's room. Just a few more minutes and they would be ready. His other task was taking longer than he would like, but it was also much more complex.

"For instance, wind affinity is strong against earth affinity. And fire affinity is strong against wind affinity."

Another strike from ASZ; another grunt from Blake. The knight swung at ASZ, and his golden sword smashed into the mob's side. For a second, the zombie was knocked sideways, and appeared surprised. That blow seemed to have done some damage.

"One set of affinities are both strong and weak against each other." Viktor's voice was reaching a higher level of amusement. "Can you guess which?"

"Celestial and dark?" Blake's voice was strained, and Ryan could tell it was taking all his willpower to fight the zombie.

"Correct." Viktor cackled. He was like a child playing with a toy. "So, while your holy light is great for cutting down the darkness, it is actually making you take more damage when you try to defend with it. How unfortunate for you."

At this, Blake's grimace turned to a dark smile. A moment later the light from his shield faded and dark mana enveloped it.

"What in the name of the God of Death?" Viktor staggered back in surprise, and for a second, even the zombie faltered in its advance on Blake.

"Fortunately for me, celestial isn't my only affinity." Blake

324

had a grin on his face, but it did not extend to his eyes. The knight was not enjoying this.

ASZ swung at him, and this time when Blake absorbed the blow with his shield, he didn't grunt. Instead, he was able to push against the zombie's sword, and land another blow against the creature. The light from his sword cut easily into the mob's side, leaving a large wound.

"Well, aren't you an interesting specimen." The way Viktor said those words would have made Ryan's skin crawl, if he had any. "It seems this job comes with an unexpected bonus."

ASZ swung at Blake for a last time, but the knight stepped in, easily blocking the attack and severing the head from the body. The corpse fell to the ground as the dark mana animating it dissipated.

Yes!

Ryan's forces had finally assembled. Now he just needed to send them from his second room to his first, across his narrow walkway.

Darn it. In his panic to work on the main part of his contingency plan, which was still taking him a frustrating amount of time, he had forgotten to enlarge the pathway from his second room to his first. That narrow walkway wouldn't do to send his forces across. At the same time, Ryan realized he could have easily just unsummoned his mobs from his second floor and re-summoned them here, saving even more time.

No use crying over lost time. He could only hope his error wouldn't cost Blake his life. With a silent growl he rapidly began enlarging the bridge.

Surely Blake can hold out for a few more minutes.

"You're going to pay for what you did to Todd," Blake growled, turning his full attention to Viktor. The necromancer simply laughed, and a moment later a bone spear flew out of Squeaker's corpse, impaling Blake through his sternum.

Or not.

"Blake!" Erin screamed out in panic, watching as the knight struggled against the bone spike.

Blake managed to pull it out of his stomach, and the moment he did, golden light began healing the wound, but too slowly.

Ryan winced at Blake's state, but hoped the knight could hold out a little longer. He was almost ready to stop the necromancer.

"Funny, no one expects a bone attack from a zombie corpse." Viktor floated lazily towards Blake, now lying on the ground clutching his stomach.

"You would think," the necromancer went on, "people would expect necromancers to use bones whenever they were available."

More bones shot from the corpse towards Blake, but this time, the knight summoned a shield-shaped wall of dark mana.

"Ah, it seems you have a bit of fight left in you, eh?" Viktor raised a dark-clad hand, and bones began swirling around it, forming into tiny points. A second later, the bone pieces flew into Blake's shield of darkness. With each strike, Ryan could see Blake's shield waver and the knight's face grow strained. Still, the boy struggled to his feet.

"Why?" Blake managed as he started to push forward, trying to draw closer to the necromancer. His wound was healed, and his sword was wrapped in golden light.

How much mana does Blake have?

"Personally, I have nothing against you," Viktor said. "But that ring of yours – I need it." Blake glanced at his left hand, and Ryan noticed a wolf-shaped ring sitting on his finger.

"I'd rather die."

With that, Blake dissipated his shield, charging at the necromancer. His sword cut deep into Viktor's dark aura.

I won't let you die, Blake.

Even as the knight cut at Viktor, Ryan's skeletal army was approaching the first room. In just a few more seconds, the reinforcements would arrive.

In the light of the celestial blade, Ryan could see Viktor's form, and waves of disgust filled him – an impressive feat, given Ryan's constant interaction with zombies and skeletons. The necromancer's body was a strange collection of various mismatched body parts. Many appeared to be in a state of decay, and all were seemingly connected with flowing dark mana. He was a monster made from corpses. The only part of him that didn't appear to be rotting was his head.

Viktor's true form seemed to catch Blake off guard as well. The knight was frozen, staring at Viktor even as the darkness began to reform around the necromancer. That moment of pause proved costly, as Viktor's dark tendrils sent more bone spikes flying.

The shards cut deep, lodging deep into Blake's torso. He fell to a knee, gasping as his golden light began trying to heal his wounds.

But Ryan could see Viktor's dark mana pouring into the wounds, keeping the celestial energy from dislodging the bones.

"Now, I could kill you quickly, and just take the ring." A bone scythe emerged from Squeaker's body, the corpse now limp from its deboning. "But that wouldn't be fun."

The scythe lashed forward, severing Blake's left hand. The knight cried out, and Erin's scream of anguish accompanied it.

"Make it stop," the fairy whispered.

"Gladly," Ryan said.

A split second later, Steve and his skeletal gang burst into the room. The cavalry had arrived.

"Really, dungeon?" Viktor's tone suggested he was more annoyed than startled as he turned away from Blake to face the new threat. Blake's severed hand disappeared into Viktor's robe.

"This completes my task," Viktor said, bowing with a flourish, as a bard might at the end of a performance. "Now for the encore."

Black spikes shot from the cocoon of darkness that surrounded him, skewering any mob that came within five feet of him. Bones scattered all across the room, and every time one of Ryan's mobs fell, Viktor's bone armor grew stronger.

It was a losing battle, fighting the necromancer with skeletons, but Ryan wasn't planning on winning. He was stalling, trying to buy time to finish his plans.

Ryan glanced at the battle for a split second, just in time to watch Steve burst into a thousand pieces. That was the last of the reinforcements. Blake was on his own once more.

Ryan really hadn't expected Steve to put up much of a fight, but how had his army been defeated so quickly? Where was Buttercup?

I need more time.

Ryan's consciousness raced around his dungeon, and he made two swift realizations.

First, Buttercup was too large to leave through the door to his room, so Ryan quickly absorbed the boss mob. Second, he realized his skeletal fight club mobs were still trapped below. That was eighty-eight points of mobs that had not joined the fray.

He couldn't send fight club level two; it would take too long, as the human skeleton mobs were slower than his beast mobs. Plus, level two existed under his second floor; he didn't have the time. However, he could definitely make use of skeletal fight club level one.

How had Ryan forgotten about fight club? Maybe he followed rule number one too literally.

Well, rules are meant to be broken.

"And now I'm going to cut you apart, piece by piece," Viktor said, his eyes glowing with malevolence. "Perhaps I might make you my manservant. Normally, trying to bring back someone with a celestial affinity doesn't end well, but with your darkness affinity..."

The scythe rose again, preparing to swing.

"I can't watch," Erin shrieked, covering her eyes. Ryan, however, had every intention of watching.

Even as the scythe fell, the floor in front of Blake opened up, and a heavily armored mob blocked the massive scythe. Whereas Viktor's scythe had blasted his earlier mobs apart, this new mob withstood the blow.

The fruits of fight club had joined the battle. Ryan had unleashed the final evolutions of his skrats and skuirrels.

"What is that?" both Viktor and Erin exclaimed, though in greatly different tones. Ryan couldn't help but beam with pride, and snicker at their reactions.

"That, Rin, is a plated skrat, the final evolution of a skrat. It costs five points and is covered completely in thick bone plates earned from countless battles."

Even as the scythe smashed into the creature again, destroying it, another took its place. At the same time, white blurs leapt from more holes, launching themselves at the necromancer. They moved so swiftly his dark mana spikes actually missed.

"And those are bladed skuirrels. They also take five points, and have increased speed and agility, as well as lethal bone blades all along their body."

These were the results of his months of skeletal fight club. These mobs were the secret weapon he had forgotten to unleash on Viktor. Where his other mobs had failed, these mobs were able to do exactly what he needed them to. These mobs bought him time.

"You will pay for this, dungeon," Viktor spat as the ebony energy surrounding him pulsated. His bone scythe instantly became clad in darkness, and it ripped through three plated skrats at once. His black spikes grew thinner and more numerous, piercing through the fast-moving bladed skuirrels.

Psh, I can keep this up all day.

That technically wasn't true, but thanks to the absorption of Buttercup and skeletal fight club level two, Ryan was able to keep summoning these mobs even as they were getting destroyed, not to mention the mob points refunded to him from Steve and the bone army's destruction.

"This cannot kill me." Viktor let out a defiant laugh, and all of Ryan's mobs in the room shattered apart. It appeared the necromancer had turned the broken pieces of bones from the plated skrats and bladed skuirrels into a mass of projectiles, and now used these fragments like sling stones, shattering mobs as fast as they spawned.

No duh.

Ryan wasn't stupid. He knew his plan wouldn't kill the necromancer, though he had been slightly wishing it could. No, this was a diversion.

For while Viktor was distracted, Ryan opened up the floor below Blake, dropping the mortally wounded knight into a bone maiden, minus the bone spikes, sealing him in. Ryan was not going to let Viktor have the boy.

"You know what, dungeon?" Viktor turned towards where Blake had been and paused.

At the same time, Ryan dropped a ceiling layer on top of him. With Blake safe, contingency plan one was back on the table. Viktor's form became encased in a spinning wall of bones just as a ton of rock fell on his head. As the dust settled, Viktor's form remained.

"Your silly games are tiresome," the necromancer's voice said.

In response, Ryan opened the floor below Viktor, hoping to drop him into a massive bone maiden. However, the necromancer simply glanced down, floating easily above it.

How is that even fair?

Viktor let out a dark laugh, and raised both hands, summoning all of the bones around him. They began taking shape, forming a lance even larger than before.

"You are not going to survive this—" Viktor paused, letting his hands drop, as he turned his head back towards the entrance.

Ryan glanced outside, and could see lights in the distance, moving towards the dungeon.

"Tsk, it seems my time here is at an end." Viktor turned towards where Blake had been. "I'll let you keep him for now. Perhaps you can make him into a mob that will amuse me when I return."

Viktor's darkness surrounded him once again, completely hiding him.

"For the next time I return, I will destroy you."

And with that, he disappeared.

∾

Viktor

Viktor's hand moved away from the pendant around his neck as he let his darkness fade away. He was mad he had let the boy's body, as well as the dungeon, escape his grasp.

But the mana he had left at the outside of the village, to alert him of possible movement towards the dungeon, had been triggered. He wasn't going to wait around to be ambushed in a hostile dungeon. Next time, though, he would destroy everything.

"Do you have the ring?" A female voice caused Viktor to flinch, and he turned to watch as a robed woman approached.

"Of course I do." He held out the boy's hand towards the female, smirking as her eyes widened at the sight of him. She had never seen his true form before.

"You are so vile." Her voice seethed with distaste as she took the hand from Viktor.

Viktor took great pleasure in his form. It was his greatest achievement. By slowly transforming his body, he had become nearly indestructible.

"Always a pleasure." He turned his rotting palm towards her. "And my reward?"

"The Exalted One will have the crown to you within the month. Obviously, obtaining such a powerful object, which has been sealed by the church, will take a little time."

She turned and began walking away. For a split second, Viktor imagined what she would be like as a zombie. The thought flew from his mind, though. The Exalted One had purposefully sent her this time, and Viktor knew she could kill him instantly if he tried to attack her.

He may have bolstered his powers through taboo means, but hers were bolstered by something even more sinister: chaos.

Instead, he watched her teleport from his castle, likely to return the ring to the Exalted One. Perhaps after he used the Crown of Sorrows on the town, and killed the dungeon, he would pay her and her cult a visit.

Killing the dungeon would add another dungeon core to his collection, amplifying his power even further.

Slaughtering that cult would give him an army of chaotic affinity minions. With both, he would be unstoppable.

Chapter Sixty-Seven

"Where did those come from?" Erin sobbed. She was nearly hysterical as Ryan absorbed all of his bladed skuirrels and plated skrats.

"Skeletal fight club." His nerves were so frayed from the encounter with the necromancer, he spoke without thinking.

"Skeletal what?" Erin's voice was filled with questions, but Ryan didn't have time to explain right now.

"Not now."

He reabsorbed all the fallen debris and brought Blake's body back to the surface of the room. The poor knight was losing blood fast, and Ryan could tell his aura was fading.

"We need to save him." The lights were drawing closer, but Ryan could tell Blake would be dead by the time help arrived.

"I, we, uh…" Erin's face was filled with pain as she tried to speak.

"A celestial feather can heal him, right?" Ryan asked, frantic.

Blake was unconscious. There was no way he could use the item. But if Erin flew out there and used one on him, that could save him.

Erin broke down in tears, shaking her head.

"We can't," she sobbed, continuing to shake her head.

"Yes, we can." Ryan's tone was harsh. "It's easy. You fly out there, I summon a celestial feather. What's the problem here?"

Why is she fighting me? Blake is dying, and we can save him.

"It's against the rules." Her voice was shrill as she broke down in more tears.

"What rules?"

"The Dungeon Master's rules. The Goddess's rules. Celestial feathers are legendary. Only the Goddess's dungeon is supposed to drop them, and even then, she has to choose who to give each feather to."

"I don't care," Ryan growled, and he turned back to Blake. The adventurer had so little time left. They needed to do something.

"Ryan, you know I want to save him too. But I can't. It will upset the balance of the world."

Ryan really didn't care about the balance of the world. His favorite adventurer was about to die because of that necromancer. Ryan wouldn't forgive himself if Blake died. It wasn't fair. It wasn't right. It wasn't—

Ryan's thoughts froze as a brilliant light erupted from Erin's body. Her eyes filled with golden light and a strange, serene look appeared on her face.

"It isn't just, for him to die here." The voice coming from Erin wasn't her voice. Ryan was certain he had heard it before, though.

"Greetings, dungeon." The not-Erin turned its glowing eyes towards his core. "I am the Goddess of Justice."

Well, this is unexpected.

Ryan tried to speak, but his mind couldn't process what was going on right now.

"This is highly unorthodox, and if the balance were not in peril, this would not be happening." Erin's form disappeared and reappeared besides Blake. "However, forces are at work to disrupt the entire balance of the world, a world I have worked so hard to preserve."

The Goddess pulled one of Erin's feathers from her wing and held it over Blake's forehead.

"This young man, just like you, shall be given another chance by me. A chance to help me keep the balance in the world." The feather glowed brightly, and golden light engulfed Blake's form. "I believe in you, dungeon. Do not let me down."

Even as the light surrounding Blake faded, so too did the golden light that had been enveloping Erin. The fairy fell onto Blake's lap, even as the knight began to regain consciousness.

Blake opened his eyes and saw Erin, whose eyes were also open and staring directly into his. Before the knight could open his mouth, Erin let out a scream and quickly flew off, zipping far away from him.

"What have you done?" Erin demanded of Ryan. Apparently, when the Goddess took over her body, Erin had not been aware of what was going on.

"Um, well, the Goddess possessed you, and saved Blake."

"She what?" Erin's voice was shrill through their bond. All the while, Blake was staring at Erin's fluttering form, confusion on his face.

"What happened?" he asked groggily. He slowly raised his left arm to his head and stared blankly at the spot where his hand should have been.

"My hand…"

The way he spoke left no doubt in Ryan's mind that he was still in shock.

"Why didn't the celestial feather heal his hand?" Ryan asked through the bond.

He could feel Erin slowly calming down as the fairy came to terms with the fact the Goddess had intervened.

"Celestial feathers can bring adventurers back from the brink of death and heal their wounds. It does not regenerate limbs, though."

Well, that made the item just a little less powerful, but it was still easy to see why they were legendary.

"What's going on?" Blake cried out.

They needed to explain the situation to Blake. But what should they tell him?

"You were almost slain by a necromancer," Erin explained, cutting to the chase. "The Goddess of Justice saved you."

Blake looked around, noting the scatterings of bones, and then his eyes rested on Squeaker's decimated form.

"Can we save Todd?" Blake's eyes were filling with tears, and Ryan couldn't help but feel even more impressed with the knight. He had almost been killed, and now he was asking if he could still save his friend.

Erin shook her head, flying closer to Blake's face. "We can't."

"But you saved *me*." Blake looked at her, his eyes pleading.

"You were only mostly dead," Erin started, and she landed lightly on Blake's lap. "We cannot bring the dead back."

"Well, technically," Ryan started, then stopped. He really did have a bad habit of saying stupid things when he was so mentally distraught.

I could absorb Squeaker and bring him back as a zombie. But that's not what Blake wants.

"So... were you sent by the Goddess to save me?" Blake looked down at Erin, and the fairy turned away, looking, Ryan knew, towards him – as if he knew what they should do in this situation. *Sheesh.*

"What do you want me to do?" he asked through their bond. It was apparent Erin wanted him to talk to Blake, but it wasn't like he could just communicate with the adventurer. The only reason he could talk with Erin was because of their link.

"Talk to him," she sent through their bond.

Like I didn't think of that.

"And how exactly would I do that?" Ryan asked, wishing he had eyes to roll.

Erin huffed and looked from Blake to Ryan, and back to Blake. As she glanced at him, her eyes moved towards his neck, where his pendant sat. Her eyes filled with excitement as she turned back to Ryan.

"Can you make one of those pendants, and communicate with him through it?"

Ryan stared for a moment at Erin. If he had a face, it would have been full of surprise. That actually seemed like a good idea. He knew the adventurers used those to communicate with each other.

Having absorbed more than a few, Ryan was sure he could mimic that ability. He created a crystal pendant in the room before Blake and sent a pulse of his mana into the pendant, linking it to himself, before Blake grabbed it.

The knight picked up the pendant and held it up, examining it.

"Can you hear me?" Ryan sent his thoughts into the pendant and was delighted to hear his voice resonate from it.

Blake nearly dropped the crystal in surprise.

"Ye...yes."

"Good." Ryan was ecstatic. Now he could speak to someone other than Erin.

"Is this the dungeon?" Blake asked hesitantly.

"No, this is Ryan." He broke out laughing, glad he had a new person to torment with his jokes.

"Focus, Ryan!" Erin yelled at him out loud, drawing a smile from Blake.

"Sorry," he apologized through the crystal. "Yes, this is the dungeon."

"And you are named Ryan?" Blake put the pendant around his neck, his face full of confusion.

"Yes, I'm Ryan the Darkness Dungeon, and that is my celestial fairy, Erin."

Erin did a small curtsey, spreading her wings as she smiled up at Blake. Ryan figured if the Goddess trusted Blake, that gave him the okay to tell Blake about what Erin was.

"A dark dungeon, and a celestial fairy." Blake whispered the words, but Ryan could hear them. "So that's what she meant."

She who?

Ryan made a mental note to ask Blake about that later.

"Do you have any idea why that necromancer wanted your ring?" Ryan asked, conscious of the approaching lights. Viktor scared him, and he had no idea why the necromancer would focus on Blake.

Blake shook his head, looking down at his stump.

"My father gave it to me. It was passed to him from his father. But it was just a silver ring."

"Well, whatever he wanted it for, Viktor got it."

"Viktor?" Blake asked.

"The necromancer." Ryan sighed. He had hoped Blake would

be able to help shed some light on what the necromancer was up to. Oh, well.

"So, what happens now?" Blake looked from the pendant down to Erin.

"The Goddess said you and I are supposed to help keep the balance," Ryan said. *Whatever that means.*

"So, I guess we should just both get stronger?" Blake asked. "Until she tells us more?"

That seemed to be the correct path in Ryan's mind. The stronger he got, the more unlikely it was that people like Viktor could threaten him.

"My hand," Blake groaned as he looked down at his stump again. That was his shield arm. Without his hand, Ryan guessed he would have trouble using his shield. If only that feather had given him his hand back. It wasn't like Blake could just grow a new—

Duh.

"I can make you a new one." Ryan quickly began shifting through his bone collection.

Too small. Too big. Oh, just right.

He found a skeletal hand that matched Blake's proportions, and quickly summoned it next to Blake. The knight screamed.

"What is that?" Blake grimaced with disgust at the hand.

"Seriously. You've been in my dungeon how many times? It's a bone. More precisely, it's a skeletal hand."

"Well. Yeah." Blake looked at Erin questioningly. The fairy simply shrugged.

"Do I have to hold your hand as I walk you through this?" Ryan laughed even as Erin groaned.

That was a good one.

"You have darkness mana, right, Blake?" Ryan asked.

The knight nodded.

"Well, if you use it, you should be able to manipulate that hand as if it were your own."

Blake glanced once more from Erin to the hand.

"How?" he asked.

"Well, uh..."

That was a good question. Ryan just willed the mana into the bones, and then they did as he wished. He had no idea how mana worked for humans.

"Um, try pushing your dark mana into it," Ryan suggested.

Blake stared at the bone hand, and a dark tendril of mana flowed from his stump to it. The darkness flowed over the bones, covering them with a small layer of darkness.

"Now," Ryan went on, "try to attach it to your stump and will it to stay there."

Blake did as Ryan instructed, and when he let go of the skeletal hand, it stayed in place. It had worked.

"There you go. Good as new." Ryan was proud of his work, and he watched as Blake looked at his hand.

It was staying in place, but it wasn't moving. The knight's brow furrowed, and after a moment, one of the fingers twitched.

"This may take some getting used to," Blake muttered.

"I believe in you, Blake."

"Thanks." Blake rose to his feet, grabbing his sword and sheathing it with his right hand. He picked up his shield and placed the straps on his arm, unable to move his hand to grab it.

"Always happy to help, Blake." Ryan's voice started out as cheerful but took on a serious tone. "But now that I've helped you, mind if you help me?"

Blake stopped moving and looked down at Erin. Once again, the fairy simply shrugged.

"I rarely know what he's up to." Erin flapped her wings, and gently flew up to the air. "Oh, and Ryan? We still have things to discuss after Blake leaves."

Judging by her tone, Ryan knew exactly what she hadn't forgot about. *Skeletal fight club.*

To Blake, Ryan said, "I need you to tell whoever is in charge that that necromancer is planning to come back. I don't know when, but he said he was going to come back and destroy me."

"Why would he come back?" Blake asked, glancing from the exit to Erin.

"Not really sure," Ryan said. "I may have turned down his offer to join him, and I don't think he appreciated that. He also mentioned something about using my core to help him become even more powerful. Quite honestly, I'd rather not die. Especially not to him. So, if you could help me stay alive, that would be great."

Blake nodded, and looked once more at Squeaker's body.

"I will tell Marcus what happened. He has a group of necromancer hunters with him. I'm certain they can keep you safe."

Unlikely, since Sasha failed to kill Viktor last time.

Ryan kept his thoughts to himself. Blake's warning to Marcus would have to do.

"In return," Blake started, "can you help me get Todd's body out of here? I'd like to give him a proper burial."

Blake's voice cracked, and tears filled his eyes as the knight glanced at Squeaker's mangled form. Ryan was certain that wouldn't be the prettiest sight, but he figured he could help Blake out.

"Sure, but I'll need you to leave the room." Blake's face took on a questioning look as he glanced at Todd's form, but the knight walked to the path that lead out of the dungeon. Blake's aura was interfering with Ryan's ability to absorb objects in the room, and he also didn't want Blake to watch what he was going to do.

Once Blake was out of the first room, Ryan absorbed Squeaker's form. Then, using his powers, he summoned a new version of Squeaker. He tried to make the body as pristine as he could, though his powers demanded he make the body have at least a little bit of decay, since in essence, he was preparing to create a zombie. Once the new Todd was created, he left the form lying on the ground, unanimated.

"All right, you can come back," Ryan said through the pendant, and Blake stepped back into the room, looking with surprise at the body on the ground.

"How did you do that?" Blake blinked with disbelief as he neared the body, leaning down to pick up Squeaker.

"I'm a darkness dungeon," Ryan said. "I kind of have power over these types of things."

Ryan could see Blake's eyes filling with tears.

"And I figured if you were going to give him a proper burial, his body should at least be all there."

"Thank you," Blake whispered, his voice cracking.

"No problem, buddy. One last thing," Ryan said as Blake turned to begin his exit.

"Yes?"

"Don't tell anyone about me, Erin, or the Goddess."

Ryan figured secrecy was going to be important on those facts. Remembering how crazy the mage had gotten over just a celestial feather, he could only imagine the chaos if people found out just how sentient the dungeon was, not to mention the fact it had a celestial fairy and that a Goddess had appeared.

"Deal," Blake said, and he began walking out.

"I really do hope we can stop Viktor," Ryan whispered as Erin made her way back to the core room.

He watched Blake exit the dungeon with Todd's body, heading towards the group that was rushing towards the dungeon entrance. Ryan had no idea when the necromancer would attack again, but he knew he would need to get even stronger to stop him.

Chapter Sixty-Eight

"Dungeon's closing tonight, Blake," Ryan sent a mental message through his crystal, giving the knight a heads-up.

He had found the pendant allowed him to communicate with Blake all the way to the town. He wasn't quite sure how far the pendant would allow them to communicate, but he enjoyed being able to chat with Blake when he wanted to. It had been a little over a month since Viktor's second attack, and since then, Ryan had been steadily moving towards Gold.

Now, thanks to the carelessness of a few stray nobles – unfortunately not A-a-ron – which resulted in a good amount of fallen high Silver and Gold guards, Ryan had the experience he needed to ascend.

"Giving him and his group one last chance?" Erin shot him a knowing smile.

Blake's group was one dive away from reaching Gold themselves. Blake told him so the other day. Ryan really wanted to give his favorite knight the chance to gain the experience he needed. He also just wanted Blake and his team to do one last dive before Ryan closed the dungeon down. Last time, he had been closed for a month. He had no idea how long his Gold renovations would take.

"Well, I'd rather his group ascend to Gold while we are building," Ryan said. "That way, they can jump right in and see our new surprises."

Ryan had already been toying with ideas for his new boss mob. One thought was to see how much he could evolve his sneks, and then ascend them into boss-hood – a special present for Blake. It was just a matter of whether the mob would work. His other idea was more realistic and involved his skeletal mages.

"You know that puts his team in more danger," Erin warned.

She was right. Letting Blake's team be the first on his new floor when he turned Gold would likely present more danger to the group. However, if there was any group Ryan believed capable of thoroughly exploring his new floor, and making it out alive, it was Blake's team.

"I believe in him," Ryan whispered.

"What was that?" Erin turned her head towards Ryan's crystal, a grin on her face. They had both come to really like Blake ever since the necromancer's attack. Being able to speak with him, even if only when he was away from his team, made it even better.

"I said I believe in him."

He hated admitting that fact, and she knew it. She was just as team Blake as he was – heck, even more. She often went out and watched him train during his nightly sessions, which was where they developed a relationship that led to late-night chats.

"Did anyone die?" Blake's voice resonated in the core room. Ryan had linked the crystal to his core, so when Blake spoke through his pendant, Ryan and Erin could both hear it.

"Some noble. His guards triggered the trap and abandoned him."

It wasn't the most noble way to go, but Ryan had found many of these nobles deserved such a fate. They treated their guards terribly, and many simply saw their guards as replaceable fodder. Ryan wasn't surprised the guards had left this one to his fate.

The worst of the nobles had been A-a-ron, but Ryan hadn't seen him yet. He had a special trap for A-a-ron.

"Well, I guess I'm glad it wasn't an adventurer." Blake's voice held a tinge of sorrow. Ryan knew Blake didn't like how Ryan needed to kill in order to gain experience.

He'll get over it in time, just like I did.

"Hurry up and get your team," Ryan sent to Blake, and turned his attention back to his dungeon.

He had made a lot of changes since he was a low-ranked Silver dungeon.

The first change Ryan made was introducing a shortcut to his second floor. Because the first room of his first floor was directly over his second floor's first room, Ryan had created a staircase that connected the two. The door to this staircase, on the first floor of the dungeon, needed a special two-part key in order to open it.

Steve dropped the first part of the key for any group that didn't already have it. Buttercup dropped the second part. Once adventurers had both pieces of the key, they were deemed worthy by Ryan and could skip his first floor.

The next big change Ryan had put into his dungeon, other than improving his mobs, was the introduction of roaming mobs. After Viktor's attack, Ryan had created massive tunnels all throughout his dungeon, connecting every single room in some way with secret passages.

Using these tunnels, Ryan had a set number of mobs that would roam around the dungeon. That meant they could attack adventurers from anywhere in the dungeon, at any time. It proved a great source of amusement for Ryan and Erin.

Ryan's third addition to his dungeon was the introduction of new mobs. Now that he was Silver One, Ryan had a total of 600 mob points to spend. He left his first floor the same, sitting at its sixty-five points, with the same mobs he had left it with since becoming Silver. His second floor, though, saw many mob improvements.

First, Ryan upgraded all of his basic human skeletons to hardened skeletons. These skeletons had much harder bones reinforced with darkness mana and cost him fifteen points each. He placed two hardened skeletal fighters each in his first and second mob rooms. His third mob room on his second floor had two hardened skeletal archers, seven sneks, and an infested snakie.

His earlier experiments with having zombie snakes become infested with the mushrooms had worked, much to his delight. The infested snakies had mushrooms where their poison glands would have been. Ryan had found combining them with different mushrooms gave them different effects. On top of that, the snakies took on the color of the mushroom that infested them.

Red infested snakies were the deadliest, as they held an actual poison in them that would knock an adventurer out within ten minutes of being bitten. Yellow infested snakies held the same paralysis poison that infested ratbies had. Purple infested snakies, Ryan's favorite, had the hallucinogenic property of the mushroom. Those bites led to the most interesting, and sometimes chaotic, reactions from adventurers.

Of course, Ryan had ensured that the mobs had the chance to drop the mushrooms that could heal the bites, and many adventuring groups, at least the smart ones, had begun carrying antidote potions in case of an infested snakie bite.

Ryan's fourth and fifth rooms were now outfitted with even more mobs. He had been tempted to add in his skeletal mages but decided to save them for his third floor. They just seemed too strong to justify adding into his second floor.

In his fourth room, Ryan placed three hardened skeletal fighters, and two hardened skeletal archers, for a total of seventy-five points. He then added in five sneks that could drop down from the ceiling onto adventurers, for added distractions and fear factors. And just because the thought of Blake having a snek fall onto him made him smile.

His fifth room, still meant to be the hardest room before his boss, held four hardened skeletal fighters and four hardened skeletal archers, for a total of 120 points.

On top of all these improved mobs, Ryan pumped 110 mob points into his roaming mobs. These mobs included six plated skrats, six bladed skuirrels, five of his two-headed sneks, and five infested snakies. The one advantage adventurers had of not skipping the first floor was there was a chance they would be attacked by the roaming mobs in a less dangerous room, rather than being ambushed on the second floor.

The final changes to his second floor were his improvements

to Buttercup's room. First, he made the room much larger. Buttercup had incredible speed, and a good ranged attack. He wanted his boss to really be able to stretch its legs and make use of that fact.

Ryan also needed the room to be bigger so that he could add three more mobs into the room. He had found that after groups figured out how Buttercup fought, they could easily swarm his boss mob and take Buttercup down. As such, he had decided Buttercup needed friends.

He had first planned to add a multitude of different mobs into the room, but Erin had suggested he use the hybrid mob that he had created Buttercup from. He agreed, under the stipulation that he was naming this mob. The last thing he needed was for Erin to call them "Buttercup's woodland friends" or something else ridiculous. As such, he named the ten-point wolf-deer hybrid skeletons horned howlers. The three of them cost a combined thirty points, and Buttercup cost fifty, making his boss room cost eighty points.

Altogether, through all the upgrades, Ryan's first floor cost him sixty-five points, his second-floor cost him 385 points, and his roaming mobs cost 110 points, totaling at 560 points. That left Ryan with forty points for—

"How's skeletal fight club going?" Erin had her cheek pressed against his crystal, a grin on her face. After her initial anger, which led to a week and a half of Erin not talking to Ryan, she had come to really enjoy skeletal fight club. Especially after Ryan convinced her it was just a strict training environment to help his mobs evolve, and definitely not a mob fight group built for Ryan's enjoyment.

"Eh, for some reason they still haven't evolved." Ryan currently had eight basic skeletons fighting each other. Four were skeletal fighters, and four were skeletal archers. No matter how many fights they undertook, and how many they won, they still hadn't undergone changes like his skuirrels and skrats had. He was almost beginning to wonder if human skeletons could evolve this way.

"Laaaame." Erin rolled off his core and spread her wings. "I wanted to see another evolution before we ascended."

"Well, we could go back to the evolution chamber." Ryan started to turn his attention to it, but Erin simply shivered and shook her head.

Last time, Ryan's curiosity had gotten the better of him, and he decided to see what would happen if he tried to combine skeletal mages of different types. Just because he wasn't using them on his second floor didn't mean he couldn't see what might happen with them, after all.

The resulting explosion had created an earthquake that reached the town outside his dungeon and had led to a panicked message from Blake. He had quickly assured Blake he was all right and promised not to try and create such a combination again. Apparently, the earthquake had done a good amount of damage to the tavern.

Oops.

"We're here." Blake's voice echoed across the room, and a relieved look crossed Erin's face. It seemed they didn't have time for mob evolutions.

"Blake! My hero." Erin fake-swooned as she settled atop Ryan's core, and Ryan turned his attention to Blake and his team as they entered the dungeon.

Chapter Sixty-Nine

Blake unleashed a taunt, sending a wave of dark energy into the horned howlers. Ryan had to admit the knight was cool.

The week prior, Blake had found a way to merge his two affinities as they imbued his sword and shield, and the resulting visual effects were, for lack of a better word, awesome. His sword and shield, instead of being covered in golden or black light, were surrounded with an ever-shifting gray, mist-like mana. Blake called it ethereal mana.

The three horned howlers turned their heads away from Matt, who had three arrows nocked in his bow, and rushed towards Blake. The knight planted himself firmly on the ground and closed his eyes.

An instant before the three mobs smashed into him, he opened his eyes, and the ethereal mana surrounding his shield erupted in all directions, creating a massive, eight-foot shield of ethereal mana in front of Blake. The taunted mobs had no chance to slow down, and they smashed into the mana shield.

"Nice one, Blake." Matt turned his bow towards the stunned howlers and launched three arrows, all covered in blue mana, into the mobs.

The moment they hit, ice encased the mobs.

"My turn." Emily's body flashed red, and Cynder let out a cheerful chirp before she opened her mouth, sending a solid wave of flames into the three frozen howlers. The combined heat and cold caused the mobs to literally shatter.

"She's sooooo cuuute," Erin cooed at Cynder, who had flown to the ground and begun picking at the bones, looking for a suitable antler to chew on.

"Blake is getting way too strong," Ryan grumbled as he watched the fight.

Blake was Silver One, but because of his dual affinity, he had twice as much mana as any of the other Silver Ones, and every knight ability he used was stronger and more impressive than any other knights Ryan had seen. Ryan was both excited and scared to see what Blake would be like when he became Gold.

"Well, the Goddess did choose him," Erin said.

She was right. Just like Ryan, the Goddess had saved Blake. That meant for some reason she needed them both to get much stronger. Ryan was just jealous of how strong Blake had gotten so quickly.

"Ya'll going to help me any time soon?" Jack's voice, though filled with amusement, sounded strained. The thief, in his wolfkin form, was dashing around Buttercup, launching slashes of wind into the boss whenever he got the chance.

"What? I thought you could handle Buttercup all by yourself," Matt laughed as he called back to Jack, and Ryan noticed the archer was grinning as he looked down at his quiver.

"I don't like that grin," Ryan groaned.

So far, Ryan had seen new skills from Blake and Jack. The way Matt was grinning, he was certain Buttercup was about to be on the receiving end of a new skill from Matt.

"Well..." Jack paused as he dodged away from three bone spikes Buttercup had launched at him. The thief lobbed a dagger back at Buttercup, only to have the blade blocked by the boss's shield.

"I have a date tonight," he shot a wink towards Karan, even as he dodged another set of spikes, "and I don't want to wear myself out."

"Oh, are they dating?" Erin's face filled with excitement, and Jack's comment had piqued Ryan's interest. He made a mental note to ask Blake later. How could the knight have failed to mention their blossoming relationship?

Sheesh.

"The sooner the fight is over, the sooner our date can start." Karan shot a wink back at Jack, making the thief pause mid dodge. The distraction caused him to take a bone spike to the knee.

"Nooooo, my adventuring days," he cried out as he grasped at his knee.

A moment later, he was grinning again, thanks to the golden healing light from Karan's divine protection. That spell was way too strong.

As the Silver members of Blake's team grew stronger, they had begun to kill Buttercup before Karan even got close to running out of mana. Ryan had wondered why Karan wasn't leveling up and had been informed by Blake that until they were all Gold, her share of the experience went to the team.

The fact she had been adventuring with them for so long without any experience gain had increased Ryan's opinion of the cleric. He still hated the class, but he held a good amount of respect for her.

"You weren't much of an adventurer," Matt called back, and Jack flashed him a fake hurt look. "Now get out of my way and watch this."

The thief dropped to all fours and was quickly away from Buttercup. The boss turned towards the group and let out a roar.

"Ice storm!" Matt bellowed, and he launched over a dozen arrows in a high arc towards Buttercup.

The arrows, all glowing brightly with blue mana, shattered as they reached their peak. Hundreds, perhaps thousands of ice shards rained down on Buttercup, completely decimating the boss mob, and ending the fight.

"How much mana did that cost you?" Jack called out as the thief returned to his human form.

"Five mana per arrow. Plus another twenty to make them shatter." He offered Jack a grin, then stumbled.

"Yup, that's what I thought." Jack walked towards him, hand

outstretched, grinning. "You nearly ran out of mana with that trick."

"Hey, I wanted to finish off the boss for once." Matt smiled as he took Jack's hand, steadying himself with his bow as he stood.

"Well, be careful about mana expenditure," Jack said. "There's no need for us to be overly reckless."

He shot a small smile to Karan, who returned it with a warm smile of her own. Something was definitely going on between those two.

"Says the guy who was just having a one-on-one with Buttercup," Matt shot back.

Jack's grin faltered, and he let out an awkward laugh.

"Well, you know. Do as I say, not as I do."

"Hypocrite." Matt walked towards Buttercup's form. His eyes widened at the loot it had dropped.

"Hey, Jack, I think I see another Buttercup card."

"Dibs." The thief's body nearly blurred as he rushed towards Buttercup's remains, his eyes darting over the loot drops. After a moment, he reached down and picked up another of Ryan's mob cards.

"I thought you were done with those," Karan said.

Jack paused, having already pulled out a leather journal and slid the card into it.

"Well, I, uh—"

"He lost his first Buttercup card in a game of Dungeon Mobs the other night," Blake chuckled, pulling a Buttercup card from his own leather journal. "So his collection was no longer complete."

"I still want to know how you got a full set of infested snakies," Jack complained. "There is no way we've killed that many."

Ryan laughed. He had given Blake a set of all the infested snakie cards in exchange for a few items from the dungeon town. He found Blake was willing to trade him quite a lot for those cards.

Of course, Erin had informed him before he even started such trades that he couldn't simply give Blake blatant valuables like gold and gear. That would, as she always nagged, breach etiquette.

"I can't believe how big of a game everyone has made of those cards," Karan said, pulling out her pendant. "Everyone ready?"

They all nodded, and a moment later, they were gone.

"All right," Ryan said. "Now we just wait till dark, and we can begin our ascension."

He scanned his dungeon. Since Blake's team was the last one of the day, Ryan simply absorbed the remainder of his mobs, and didn't summon any new ones.

"Want to watch some special skeletal fight club matches while we wait?" Ryan asked. He had also absorbed the eight basic human skeletons that had inhabited the massive fighting arena.

"Oh, what are we going to do?" Erin had taken a liking to skeletal fight club.

"A super special fight. I plan on using the skeletal mages when I ascend to Gold, so I'm curious to see just what they can do. With 600 points, I was thinking we could have four teams of skeletal mages fight. Each team would have one dark skeletal mage, and then one of the four affinities."

Ryan knew from Erin that dark skeletal mages could heal other skeletal mobs, so he was curious which affinity would reign supreme in a free-for-all match. It was all going to be part of his experimentation for his next floor.

"Let's do it," Erin cheered.

Ryan flipped through his collection, deciding the easiest way to summon his skeletal mages was to mass-summon the dark ones first, then summon each individual element next. This was in part due to the requirement that the bones for the mage had to come from someone with the appropriate affinity.

After a moment of searching, Ryan found a complete skeleton with a dark affinity, and summoned four sets of those in his fighting arena. As he animated them, dark mana swirled along their bones, and around their hands, globs of black energy glowed eerily. Where their eyes should have been, two void-like pits seemed to swirl. If these effects carried over to the other elements, Ryan was instantly going to fall in love with these mobs. They were just too cool.

Excitedly, he rushed through his bone collections, finding the appropriate skeletal remains for the four affinities he was looking for. Instead of animating one at a time, he first summoned all four sets of bones into the arena, one in each corner, next to his dark mages. From there, he animated them.

Sure enough, as his dark mana filled these mobs with unlife, a myriad of colors began to fill the arena. The fire affinity mage had a crimson glow around his hands, with wisps of fire mana tracing along its body. Its eyes were two floating flames.

The water affinity mage had blue energy clinging to its form, with watery orbs encapsulating its bony hands. Its eyes were a pure, icy blue, which Ryan was sure would send shivers down any adventurer's spine.

His earth affinity skeletal mage had green energy, appearing almost as moss along its body, while its eyes shone with an emerald light. The mass of earth mana covering its hands seemed thicker, almost like dirt with grass atop it.

Wind affinity, to Ryan's surprise, was the coolest of the four. He had always been curious about wind affinity's color, and now, as his skeletal mage came to life, wondered no more. The color appeared to be almost silvery, with tinges of blue and purple swirling around it in small gusts, and the energy around its hands was creating spiral-like patterns.

Ryan mentally prepared himself for the fight, ensuring the mobs all had their commands and were in the correct position. He had secretly been looking forward to this fight for a while now, and he was glad he finally had the time to do it before ascending to Gold.

With one last long breath to steady himself, he sent the order for his mobs to begin. It was time for the most epic skeletal fight club match to date.

∽

Viktor
He teleported into the dungeon town unnoticed, thanks to the earring

from the Exalted One. Quietly, he hurried past the adventurers that milled about the streets and alleyways. They were of little importance to him.

In his excitement, he didn't even take in the features of the adventurers he passed. Besides, soon they would all be dead. He had been waiting for this moment for almost a week but needed the right time to launch his attack. The Crown of Sorrows could only be activated during a new moon, a night of absolute darkness.

His earring kept the guards from noticing him as he headed away from the town and dungeon. He needed the town's attention to be as far from the dungeon as possible if he was to truly enjoy this.

It was nearly night time, and all the adventurers had gone back to town for the night. Viktor used the shadows as dusk fell to search for any threats. The last thing he needed was for the twins to interrupt his use of the Crown of Sorrows. He wanted this moment to be perfect.

After a moment, he confirmed there was no one with any mana around him. With hands shaking with excitement, he pulled a bone crown from his cloak. It was a beautiful sight: a crown formed from intertwined finger and toe bones, lashed together with tendons and dark mana. Laced throughout it were countless flawless opals.

The Crown of Sorrows was a legendary artifact, last used by the greatest necromancer to walk the land. He was eventually defeated by the cursed Goddess of Justice's forces, the church, and the crown was thought to have been destroyed. Viktor had no idea how the Exalted One had gotten his hands on the crown, but it didn't matter.

Viktor lowered the crown to the ground and stepped back. Then he pushed his dark mana into it, sending tendrils of mana flowing all around the crown.

At first, nothing happened. Then the ground beneath the crown began to crack, and slowly a massive skeleton rose from the ground. Before Viktor stood a lich: A Diamond-tier skeleton mob.

"What is your command?" the lich's voice rasped into Viktor's mind.

"Destroy the town," he said as he began to make his way, cloaked in shadows, towards the dungeon.

The lich could destroy the town and its residents. The dungeon was Viktor's. He had a bone to pick with it.

Chapter Seventy

Blake stood in his tent, looking at his gear. Slowly, he reached down, grasping the gauntlet that hid his left hand. With practiced ease, he slipped the piece of armor off, followed by the leather glove underneath it, revealing his skeletal hand.

Dark energy wrapped around it, and with a thought, he flexed it. This hand was a reminder of his weakness. A reminder of his failure to save Todd. It was also a dark secret, as only Marcus knew the full extent of what went on in the dungeon. Blake hadn't been able to bring himself to tell the others of his skeletal hand, and as Ryan had asked, he kept their link a secret.

"Tomorrow, I will take the step to greater strength." Ryan flexed the hand and slid his leather glove back over it, setting the gauntlet on the ground.

The most recent run in the Bone Dungeon, Ryan's dungeon, had given Blake and the others enough experience to ascend to Gold. According to Karan, they would be apart for roughly three months while they underwent their class training.

He didn't want to be away from his group that long, but he was brimming with excitement over the thought of becoming a paladin. Especially since he knew a certain dungeon that was going to become Gold, and which also had a dark and celestial connection, that he could pledge to. If he had been a paladin when that necromancer had attacked, he may have been able to save Todd.

"We're under attack!" A panicked cry pulled Blake from his thoughts, and he quickly grabbed his gauntlet, sliding it back over his hand as he grabbed his sword and shield.

As he rushed out of his tent, all he saw was chaos.

Dark fires burned all along the perimeter of the town, and as Blake turned his attention towards where the cry had come from, his blood froze. All along the street, cracks were forming in the ground, and from them, rising up, were countless undead forms.

And then he heard it.

"Despair as you face your death. Allow me to fill your hearts with sorrow as you fall to my army."

The voice filled Blake's mind. All around him, adventurers froze, glancing around, and he could tell they had heard the same voice.

"What's going on?" he called out as he saw the familiar face of a Gold Six centurion he sparred with from time to time.

But before the centurion could reply, the wall near their tent exploded, and from it, a horde of skeletons rushed in. The skeletal army filled Blake with dread. Such an attack could only mean one thing: the necromancer had returned.

"Get the others to safety, Blake. I'll hold the line." The centurion turned to face the skeletons, his body instantly encased in solid stone armor.

He sheathed his sword, knowing he couldn't help the centurion. While Blake, as a Silver One, had the same amount of mana as a Gold Seven, he didn't have access to the skills that would give him an edge in the battle.

"Embrace sorrow as it washes over you."

The voice caused Blake to pause, and he felt a wave of despair rush over him. At the same time, he heard a cry of pain. He turned to see the centurion's body lifted from the ground,

impaled upon a massive sword made of bones. And holding it…
was a monstrosity.

"No!" The cry ripped out of Blake's mouth, and his hand
grasped his sword.

In front of him was a massive skeleton, clad in robes of dark
mana and wearing a strange crown made of bones. It was far
more powerful than him. But he couldn't – no, he *wouldn't* – flee
from the monster.

"Let us handle this, Blake." A gruff voice accompanied a
strong hand that pushed down on Blake's, sheathing his half-
drawn sword. Marcus's form materialized before him.

"The Crown of Sorrows," the rogue whispered, a touch of
dread in his voice.

"Viktor," came another voice, and as Blake turned, he saw
two massive wolfkin approach.

While Jack only seemed to grow a few inches when he transformed into his wolfkin form, these two beasts had to stand
nearly nine feet in height. One was covered from head to foot in
brilliant silver fur, while the other was all black.

"So, a Diamond-level boss mob," the silver-furred wolfkin
said. "A lich. That means his army is Gold and Platinum-level
skeletons."

From the tone of the voice, Blake could tell it was Sasha, the
female twin.

"This shall be fun," the black-furred wolfkin, Rasha, growled,
as two wickedly curved daggers made of black mana appeared in
his hands.

"If we beat the lich, his army falls," Marcus said, and his
entire form became enveloped in wind.

An instant later, his form flew forward, blades moving in a
blur. The twins let out howls and joined in the fight, leaving
Blake watching in awe.

"Blake!" Jack's cry pulled his attention away from the fight,
and he jerked his head in its direction.

"Jack," Blake called back, watching as the thief, and the rest
of his party, rushed towards him. The relief on their faces was
palpable.

"We need to get out of here, man." Jack's voice was panicked, and as he spoke, the ground around them began to split, with zombies and skeletons preparing to claw their way out of the earth.

"Marcus ordered the evacuation of the town," Karan said. "Everyone else is already fleeing. Let's go, now."

She winced as she looked past Blake, and he turned to see the lich send a bone spike into Sasha's side.

"We have to help them." Blake drew his sword.

"There's nothing we can do," Jack said. "Marcus is Platinum Two, and the twins are freaking wolfkin royalty. If they can't handle that mob, we would die in a second."

Blake's mind raced. He had no idea what being wolfkin royalty meant, but the way Jack said it, it must have meant they were extremely powerful. And he had a good point: Marcus was one of the strongest rogues in existence. If he was struggling, what more could Blake's group do? Besides, Sasha had mentioned the mobs that lich had summoned were Gold and Platinum level. The town was desperately outmatched.

As his mind raced for a solution, a single name came to him. "Viktor"

An idea formed. Maybe if they defeated Viktor, they would be able to stop the lich. And if they stopped the lich, the army would fall as well, saving the town.

"The necromancer that showed up, killed Todd, and nearly killed *you*?" Jack stared at him in disbelief. "You think he's here?"

"He has to be. Who else would send a skeletal army after the town?" Blake scanned the area. There was no way he would miss the necromancer if he saw him. He had to be somewhere.

"Yeah, but how are we supposed to find—" Jack began.

"Hey, uhh, Blake?" Ryan's voice silenced the thief, coming from one of the two pendants Blake wore around his neck.

Every member of Blake's party stared at him as he pulled the pendant from his neck.

"Please tell me you're contacting me about Viktor." Blake's voice was frantic, even as the wolfkin let out anguished howls. Marcus and the twins were barely holding their own.

"Never thought I would hear you say those words," Ryan said. "But yeah. He's here, right now. He's coming for me."

"We're on our way," Blake said, and looked to his team. "Viktor's attacking the dungeon. We need to go help."

He put the pendant away and sprinted in the direction of the dungeon. He wasn't sure his party could stop the necromancer, but he wasn't going to let fear stop him, not now.

"I'm sorry – help who?" Jack asked, running alongside Blake.

"Ryan. He's the dungeon," Blake replied.

This was not the time for secrets.

Chapter Seventy-One

"This is all your fault." Erin sat atop Ryan's core, covered completely by the silk cloth. "If you hadn't insisted on that last fight club match—"

"Whoa, now. You wanted to see it just as much as I did."

Ryan was only half listening; his main focus was on the necromancer currently making his way through Ryan's first floor. The necromancer was taking his time, leisurely strolling through. His dark laughter echoed off Ryan's walls. Viktor was enjoying this.

"I didn't know it would take so long."

The fight had just finished, the water skeletal mage team claiming victory, when Ryan had noticed a figure covered in swirling darkness approaching the dungeon.

Viktor.

As the necromancer drew closer to his entrance, Ryan watched as a small army of undead woodland creatures began to surround Viktor. Had Ryan not been so scared of Viktor, he was sure he would have had a joke or two about the necromancer's forces. Instead, he had done the first thing he could think of. He called Blake for help.

"We both know how this is going to end, dungeon," Viktor's voice taunted as the necromancer stepped into the boss room of his first floor.

Ryan had been creating walls of mana-enforced stone at the entrance to each room, to try and slow Viktor. It was supposed to take a Platinum-level mage to break those walls, but Viktor had been utilizing one of his trusty mana-infused bone lances to drill through each wall.

It didn't make sense to Ryan. Why was the necromancer so strong? On top of summoning walls to slow the necromancer, Ryan dropped stalactite after stalactite on top of him. His efforts weren't making a large impact, but he was really just trying to slow him down. Blake and his team had to be getting near.

"Yeah, with your death" Ryan whispered. Quite late on the comeback, but he knew the necromancer couldn't hear him.

As Viktor drew ever closer, Ryan created a massive stone slab to seal the necromancer into Steve's room, reinforcing the way out with dark mana. Constantly creating walls was draining more mana than Ryan could regain, but he had no choice.

"We're almost here." Blake's voice pulled Ryan away from the necromancer, who was about halfway through the wall blocking the path down to the second floor.

Ryan was so glad his core room was no longer directly behind Steve's room. Ascending to Silver had made his core safer. If only he had ascended to Gold by now, he could have had an entire new floor, and even more distance, away from this deranged necromancer.

"All right, take the shortcut and make your way to the room before Buttercup's." Ryan had a plan, but he needed Blake's team to help him.

"I do hope you put up a little more resistance on your second floor, dungeon. Or have you simply given up?" Viktor let out a dark laugh, sending chills through Ryan's core.

"Just you wait," Ryan whispered, watching as Blake's team entered the dungeon. They were definitely ready for a fight, and Jack had already assumed his wolfkin form. That was good.

"Blake," Ryan said quickly. "Once you've all reached the room, I'm going to need you guys to buy me as much time as possible."

"Buy you time?" Blake's voice was filled with uncertainty, but Ryan didn't have time to explain.

"Just… trust me. I have a plan. Buy me time, and when I tell you to, run into Buttercup's room."

Ryan watched as Viktor broke through the barrier and started floating casually down to the second floor. In retrospect, the fact that he had put his second floor's entrance under the first room of his first floor was a blessing in disguise. It meant the necromancer had to make an even longer trek to get to him, and allowed Blake's team to take the shortcut from the entrance of his dungeon to get ahead of Viktor.

If not for that, Blake's team wouldn't be able to get set up like Ryan was planning. Thankfully, the necromancer appeared to be taking his time to torment Ryan, and didn't seem to notice Blake and his team's presence. That was also good.

"All right, Ryan. But you owe me."

"Yeah, yeah, as many cards as you want," Ryan grumbled back.

"I knew it." Jack's voice broke the tension for a moment, and Ryan chuckled weakly, exhaustion from mana expenditure wearing on him.

As the group of adventurers rushed through his second floor, he closed each path behind them, reinforcing it with mana.

He was definitely nearing the end of his mana reserves, but he wanted Blake and his team to have as much time as they could to prepare. A few extra mana-enforced walls had to slow the necromancer down a little, right? Ryan was also hoping his efforts could tire the necromancer out, at least a little. After all, Ryan had spent an entire Silver One dungeon's worth of mana on sealing the way.

He really hoped his plan worked. He didn't want Blake's team, or himself, to die.

"You're just making me angry," Viktor called as he smashed into another wall. "You're not going to like me when I'm angry."

The bone lance floating beside the necromancer grew, and the darkness around Viktor seemed to condense. *Uh-oh.*

"All right, Ryan, we're here."

The adventurers stood, panting, in the room before Buttercup's, looking grim-faced towards the door that Viktor would eventually come through.

"Right, so, I'm going to slow him as much as possible." Ryan did a quick check of his dungeon, making sure he could enact the next part of his plan.

"Why don't you just send waves of mobs at him again?" Blake asked, and Ryan mentally shook his head.

"No good. He's too strong, and my mobs just get destroyed too easily right now. What's more, he can then use their bones against me."

He did not need Viktor's bone arsenal getting any larger. In fact, that was part of why he needed Blake and his team here: to help whittle away at Viktor's defenses. The necromancer had to be less intimidating without his arsenal of bones, right?

"We need to beat him, Ryan," Blake said. "He's got an army destroying the town as we speak. I'm not sure how, but I'm certain if we beat him, the army will fall." His voice was panicked, and irritated. Ryan could guess the young knight did not like being powerless. Neither did Ryan.

"Trust me, we will," Ryan promised.

The dungeon shook, and Ryan noticed Viktor had transformed his bone lance into a massive bone hammer, which he used to break into the second floor. *Uh-oh*.

"So yeah," Ryan said. "Hold him off. I'll be back."

With that, Ryan closed off his communication with Blake and his team and summoned his level and experience triangles. If he planned to beat Viktor, he needed something new, something powerful.

The most powerful thing he could think of was a Gold-level boss mob.

Chapter Seventy-Two

"Are you sure about this?"

Erin pulled herself off Ryan's core, her eyes filled with fear. He could tell her emotions were in turmoil. Truth be told, he wasn't certain of anything right now.

"It is dangerous to ascend when you're so low on mana," she wailed. "Normally you would wait until you were completely full of mana to try this."

"This is our best chance of beating him. We don't have the luxury of time, Rin."

Just as he had before, Ryan pushed the two triangles together. The shapes flashed and combined, once again creating a six-sided star. The star began to spin, and the room was suddenly filled with crackling dark energy. The energy condensed around the swirling star, and Ryan stared into the darkness of the void.

Where before a single light had appeared in the darkness, this time, two spots of light appeared, and it almost seemed to Ryan like the void was staring back at him. A moment later, he felt his consciousness ripped into the void, and the world around him was consumed by darkness.

≈

---- Blake---

"Ryan, are you there?" he yelled into the pendant, but the glow in the crystal was gone. For some reason, he could no longer contact the dungeon.

"So, Blake, what's going on?" Jack asked. He stared at the door they had entered as the entire dungeon shook once more. The tremors had been growing in frequency, and Blake knew Viktor was drawing nearer.

What if he had led them all to their deaths?

He shook his head, fighting that feeling, and tried his best to steady his nerves.

"We're going to work with the dungeon to bring Viktor down."

"So, so many questions about you and the dungeon's relationship," Jack began, but Karan raised her hand.

"Just how strong is Viktor?" she asked. Her eyes were shifting across each member, and Blake knew she was worried.

"According to Marcus, Viktor is a Gold One necromancer," Blake said. "But Marcus mentioned Viktor is much stronger than a Gold One should be. Perhaps even Platinum level."

Karan's sharp inhale was easily heard.

"We're doomed," she whispered, and her eyes filled with tears. "Once again, my party is going to fall."

Their cleric, who had always been the stable one, who had always supported them, dropped to her knees.

"Snap out of it, Karan." Jack lifted her up. His wolf-like face had a strange, tender expression on it as he stared into her eyes. "We aren't going to fall to some guy that has a hard-on for bones." He offered her a toothy grin and winked. "Besides, I'm not about to die before I get a first kiss."

Karan wiped away her tears as she smiled back at Jack. "You're going to have to live for quite a while, then."

"So, what's the game plan, Blake?" Matt had his bow drawn and was glancing between Blake and the door. They could tell Viktor was near.

"Ryan has a plan," Blake said. "We just need to keep Viktor occupied until Ryan tells us to head into Buttercup's room."

It really wasn't much of a plan, but it was all Blake had to go off. He pulled at his mana, enshrouding his sword and shield with ethereal mana. Using both affinities at the same time doubled the cost of his skills but amplified the strength of the abilities even more.

"Right," Jack said. "Keep the scary necromancer that nearly killed you occupied so that the magical dungeon, which has also nearly killed us, can help us defeat him."

Jack had drawn all of his daggers and had them floating behind him in an arc. He called it a blade fan, and Blake knew he could easily sling those daggers at foes and then retrieve them magically with his wind mana.

"Seems like one of our simpler plans," Blake said. He offered the thief a smile as Karan placed divine protection on the group and began making her way to Buttercup's door. Being the healer, she needed to stay as far away from danger as possible.

"Cynder is excited to get new bones," Emily called out, taking her place next to Karan. Her form glowed red, and Cynder began to glow red as well, while the dragon let out a happy chirp. At Silver One, Emily had enough mana to constantly enhance Cynder, making the dragon faster and stronger, on top of increasing the power of the baby dragon's flame attack.

"Right, guess I'll just provide cover fire," Matt muttered.

He walked to one of the corners of the room and nocked an arrow. Blake knew the archer hated not having any special skills to show off, especially since his ice storm nearly drained him of all his mana. That was not an attack to use at the opening of a fight.

"All right. I'll make sure he doesn't get past my shield." Blake steadied himself, shield raised as he stared at the door. Cracks were starting to appear, and dark tendrils were seeping into the room.

Viktor had arrived.

~

---- Ryan ----

"Ryan!"

A voice cried out his name, but it was muffled by darkness.

"Ryan!"

The voice came again, but it was quieter this time.

Who is Ryan?

His consciousness floated along in darkness, countless images passing him by. The colors, the visions – everything he saw moved so quickly it simply faded to black.

"Ryan." The cry came again, fainter this time. He wasn't even sure he heard it. Perhaps it was simply a figment of his imagination. He turned his attention back to the two golden lights, the only source of hope in the dark void. The 'eyes' stared into him.

"You're an odd one, dungeon." A gravelly voice echoed out from the 'eyes', and a skull, ever changing in shape, slowly began to appear. "Why do you seek more power?"

Why *did* he seek more power? What was he doing?

"Ryan." There was that voice again.

It tickled at his memory, and slowly, the darkness in his mind lifted. He had something to do. He had to… he had something to protect. An image filled his mind: a small female figure with magnificent feathered wings.

Erin.

"I need power to protect the one I love." His voice sounded strange in the void, and for a moment, there was silence.

Then the skull before him seemed to smile, and a dark laughter echoed around him.

"Never would I have thought a darkness dungeon could understand love." The skull looked down at Ryan, and the light in its eyes seemed to burn with even more brilliance. "You have amused the God of Death this time. I shall allow you to ascend to Gold."

Ryan felt the grip on his consciousness slipping as the darkness began to release its hold on him.

"Know that I will expect more from you when you decide you are ready to ascend to Platinum. That Goddess is not the only one with plans for you."

With those parting words, the darkness freed him, and Ryan was suddenly back in his core. Power flooded his very being, even as he tried to make sense of what had just occurred.

"Ryan." Erin gazed into his core, her eyes filled with tears.

"I'm here," he whispered back.

He summoned his level triangle, confirming he had reached Gold Seven, and he grinned at his mob points. Ryan now had 1200 mob points.

"I thought I lost you." The fairy broke down in tears as she hugged his core.

"I'll never leave you." Ryan wanted to say more, but he couldn't stay in that moment. A quick check showed Blake and his team had begun their fight with Viktor, and he didn't have time to waste.

Viktor launched another attack on Blake. So far, Blake's ethereal shield had been able to block the attacks, but every strike of the bone lance drained more of his mana.

"You are a resilient one, aren't you?" Viktor cackled.

"You're one to talk." Blake gritted his teeth, pushing back against the spinning lance. As he did, Jack darted past the necromancer, his knives launching themselves at Viktor's shrouded form. Blades met bone, and the necromancer once again blocked every attack. Three glowing blue arrows flew over Blake's shoulder, smashing against even more bones.

So far, they hadn't managed to land a single blow on the necromancer, but slowly, the number of floating bones he had at his disposal were decreasing.

"Now!" Blake called out, and Cynder let another wave of fire blast down onto the necromancer, coating his entire form in brilliant flames as Blake and Jack leapt away from him. Bones turned to ash in the heat of those flames, and even more of Viktor's bone armor faded away.

"Ye—" Blake's cheer was cut short as a bone spike shot from the flames, catching him by surprise and piercing his side.

Even though Karan's divine protection healed the wound, it was more wasted mana, and reminded Blake that Viktor was not someone they could let their guard down around

"I grow tired of this," Viktor said.

Dark tendrils erupted from the flames, extinguishing them. Cynder cried out in alarm and the baby dragon darted away, just in time to avoid a spear of darkness. The gloom around Viktor sank back into his body, and the shroud solidified around him, revealing his true form to Blake and his team.

Blake had seen a glimpse of the necromancer's body once before, and the sight had revulsed him. Now, as he got a good look at the necromancer's entire form, it scared him to his core. Viktor's body was a mismatch of rotting body parts, all connected with twining bits of dark mana. Some of the body parts didn't even have flesh on them anymore and appeared just like Blake's hand. The only part of the necromancer not in a state of decay was his head, and Blake was certain that was the vital part they needed to target.

"Go for his head," Blake cried out, trying to shake the paralyzing fear that washed over him. He wasn't sure if that was the result of an ability, or just his own panic. Even as he spoke, dark mana created a set of black armor around the necromancer, protecting both body and head.

"Allow me to finish this quickly," he said from behind the helmet of darkness, as his form drew closer to the ground.

The moment his feet touched stone, tentacles of darkness shot out around him, each one clutching the last of his bone fragments.

"Watch out!" Blake warned.

He poured his mana into his skills, summoning a massive, ten-foot ethereal shield. The bone spikes launched towards all the members of Blake's team, and while his barrier blocked most of them, Jack and Matt, who hadn't managed to get behind Blake in time, were cut dozens of times by the bones.

The shards were expelled from their bodies by the golden light of divine protection as it started to heal their countless wounds, but Blake knew that amount of healing had cost Karan a lot of mana. The cleric wouldn't be able to keep it up much longer.

"Everyone, move closer to Buttercup's door," Blake ordered, backing away as he pumped more mana into his shield.

Jack and Matt scrambled behind him. They had gone in an instant from being on the attack to barely being able to defend themselves.

"Matt, how much mana do you have?" Blake whispered

through gritted teeth as his already depleted mana pool emptied even further.

"Enough," the marksman whispered, and he pulled all the arrows from his quiver.

A second later, his bow was raised, and in a swift moment, he let fly all the arrows.

"Ice storm!" he shouted.

Thousands of tiny shards rained down upon Viktor's form, cutting into his dark armor, finally piercing his skin. The necromancer let out a slight cry of surprise, and a grunt of pain.

"That... actually hurt a little." The necromancer's eyes flared from behind his dark mask. "Just for that, I shall kill you slowly."

He laughed as his arms and legs stretched, making a sick cracking sound as they did so. They detached from his body with a tearing of flesh, and they floated like waiting arrows above.

Blake was certain he wouldn't be able to block all of those limbs when the necromancer attacked. He may have Gold Seven levels of mana, but he was still limited to a knight's abilities, and his shield was just a wall, not an encompassing protective aura like that of a paladin. Viktor could simply attack from around it.

"Head for Buttercup's room," Blake whispered, reabsorbing his shield.

Karan threw open the door behind him, and they turned and ran, Viktor's laughter following them.

"Blake." Emily's cry came just as he caught a glimpse of a bone blade flashing past his shoulder.

The world around Blake seemed to slow. He didn't have the mana for another shield. He didn't have the energy to sprint to Emily's protection.

Chapter Seventy-Three

Ryan knew none of his Silver-ranked mobs would be strong enough to stop Viktor, not even Buttercup. But a Gold-tier boss mob might just be strong enough. Especially if Blake and his team did their part.

"Well, I guess this situation is going to dictate what boss I summon." Ryan had been hoping to experiment between his two choices, but given the current situation, he knew what he had to do.

He had one mob planned for boss transformation, and he knew it would do the task.

"Let's make a boss."

"Ryan, I'm glad you seem confident and all, but Blake's team is struggling." Erin shook with fear, and her eyes were filled with concern as she watched Blake's team fighting against the necromancer. Even the five of them didn't seem to stand a chance against Viktor, but they were doing what Ryan had asked, and he was certain he could finish in time.

Ryan found the mob he was looking for, and quickly summoned it. It was the water affinity skeletal mage that had won his skeletal mage fight club battle.

Without another thought, Ryan summoned his level triangle, and slammed his mana into the skeleton. He watched as the numbers quickly dropped from 1150, until it froze at 950. By that time, the skeletal mage was completely encased in darkness. Now, he just needed to wait for it to hatch.

But even as he waited, he saw Viktor's darkness become armor, and tendrils of darkness launch countless bone fragments into Jack and Matt.

"Hurry up, egg." Ryan's sense of calm wavered for a moment, but as he checked on his boss mob, he saw the egg was cracking.

"Yes!" He let out a cheer, and for a second Erin seemed to forget her fear as she looked eagerly into his crystal.

More cracks, and then the new boss mob was born. Normally, his skeletal mages simply had glowing hands, depicting what type of mana they could use. This new boss mob had so much more.

Despite the danger, Ryan spared a half-second to admire his new creation. Its entire form was covered in what appeared to be a robe of blue mana, with a second layer of ice armor beneath it. As it took a step forward, ice spread from its feet, covering the ground in a light frost.

"Now for the final step." Ryan absorbed the boss mob, gaining the pattern from it, and grinned. The pattern for it appeared clearly in his mind, but whereas before he had to choose bones with specific affinities, this new boss let him choose the affinity he wanted it to have before he summoned it. And he had enough points to summon *four* of them.

Oh, yes.

He glanced at the room where Blake and his team were fighting Viktor, and his sense of urgency returned.

Oh, no.

Karan was reaching for the door, and if they entered the boss room before he was finished, he wouldn't be able to summon his mobs.

Even as she turned the knob, Ryan quickly summoned four of his new skeletal mage bosses, one of each affinity. He placed them in the back of the room, hiding them in the shadows. They animated just in time.

Ryan watched as the adventurers fled into the room, and panic filled him. The moment Blake dropped his mana shield and turned to follow the group, Viktor launched an attack towards Emily. There was nothing Ryan could do for them.

Then, to his surprise, Blake threw his left arm out. His hand and shield detached, perfectly intercepting Viktor's attack. The save was impressive, but judging by the look on everyone's faces, Ryan figured Blake hadn't shared his skeletal hand with the group.

"Can I lend you and your team a hand?" Ryan asked. Somehow, joking calmed him.

"I hate your jokes," Blake whispered as he and the others moved further into the boss room.

"Ah, but I had this great joke about a necromancer that walked into a boss room..."

Even as he spoke, he fully expected to see the necromancer burst into the final chamber. But it appeared Viktor was hesitant to enter knowing that Ryan's full roster would be held within.

Ever since his ascension to Gold, and his meeting with who he assumed was the God of Death, a new calm had filled Ryan. This was his dungeon, and he had been granted the power to protect it, and the one he loved.

Viktor was in for a world of hurt.

"You should run to the back of the room. Now," Ryan ordered Blake and his team, and the knight and the other adventurers quickly did as he instructed.

Jack let out an unmanly screech as four forms stepped away from the wall, moving towards the center of the room.

Ryan's bosses were ready to fight.

Only then did Viktor enter the chamber, his torso and bone-bladed limbs floating at odd angles.

"Come, now, are you afraid of the dark?" Viktor's chuckle filled the room, his eyes searching for Blake and his team. Buttercup's room was the largest in the dungeon, and the darkest, meaning Viktor couldn't see halfway across, much less to the back of it, where Blake's team lay in wait.

"Come out, come out, wherever you—" Viktor faltered as four glowing forms came into his view, the mages' lights pooling on the stone around them in an ethereal glow.

"Wha—" was all the necromancer got out before the four mages launched their elemental attacks.

"Yes!" Ryan and Erin exclaimed in unison as the attacks landed. Dust billowed as the dark form flared with light, followed by a deafening roar.

"Not so tough now, are you?" Ryan shouted, triumphant.

Then Viktor spoke.

"Always so full of surprises." Viktor's voice echoed in the room, and as the dust cleared from the skeletal mages' attack, Ryan and Erin both gasped.

The necromancer was missing his right arm, and if Ryan had to guess from the fragments still floating there, he had used its flesh and bones to create a shield to absorb the elemental attack.

"I'm going to make you pay for this, dungeon," he roared, and the fragments whistled forward.

"I don't think so," Ryan growled.

With practiced ease, gained from countless skuirrel targets, Ryan dropped stalactites in a plummeting barrage. Rock met bone in a series of earthy explosions, leaving Ryan's mages unharmed.

"Very well, dungeon," the necromancer hissed.

Viktor's legs swirled and twisted, morphing into twin bone lances poised above him.

"I'll replace these limbs with those of the adventurers you are protecting," Viktor cackled.

And with that, the lances shot forward.

Ryan ordered the mages to scatter, even as he summoned a wall to block the lances. He didn't have the time or mana to strengthen it, so although he slowed the lances a little, one still found its mark. Ryan's earth skeletal mage took a glancing blow, and its arm was ripped away and pinned to the wall behind.

"Return fire," Erin screamed.

As if they had heard her, the skeletal mages launched attacks of their own in retaliation. The boss room was suddenly filled with flashes of light and explosions, spell after spell streaking towards Viktor.

But the necromancer only laughed, his levitating body darting back and forth with impossible speed. Those spells he couldn't avoid were absorbed by his bone shields.

How is he so strong?

"We need him to stay still," Ryan groaned, his confidence sinking.

The mage bosses had the power to blast apart the necromancer, he was certain of it. But if they couldn't land their attacks, it was pointless.

Ryan had an idea. He just needed Blake's help.

"Blake?"

The adventurer was standing in the corner with his dark shield barrier up, protecting his group from stray spells and debris.

"Tell me," Blake instantly replied.

"Think you could use that hand of yours to hold Viktor in place for a few seconds?"

"I... I can try." The knight's voice was not filled with confidence.

That was not encouraging, but to his credit, Blake switched his shield to his right hand.

"Happy to lend a hand," the knight growled.

Ryan nearly cheered. If the situation wasn't so dire, he probably would have rained loot down on the knight for that pun. However, they had a final boss to fight first before anyone could relax.

"You cannot defeat me, dungeon." Viktor continued his taunts, and Ryan could tell the necromancer knew it was only a matter of time before the four skeletal mages were defeated. The bosses were already worse for wear, injuries and mana depletion taking their toll. The four only had enough mana for one last big attack. Apparently, the downside of these powerful bosses was that the moment they ran out of mana, they were essentially no better than regular skeletal mobs.

"I'm ready," Blake said.

"Here goes nothing," Ryan whispered.

Now!

The mages each lifted a skeletal hand, the bones glowing with mana. Viktor shook his head with a dark smile.

"That's not going to—"

A skeletal hand whipped across his mouth, the fingers grasping his head.

"No!"

That single muffled word was all Viktor managed before the mages unleashed the last of their mana in a single combined attack, beams of multicolored light roaring across the room.

Held in place, the necromancer screamed as the maelstrom of elemental energy crackled through his dark armor.

Then:

BOOM.

~

Viktor

Even as the explosion tore his body asunder, he could feel his mana leaving him, life slowly fading. His detached head cracked against the wall, and he watched as the remains of a dozen dungeon cores scattered across the floor.

Life still clung to his blinking, shattered skull, enough to mourn the loss of the cores. The loss of his power. Acquired over a century, defeating dungeon after dungeon. By harnessing dungeon cores and channeling his energies into them, he had gained powers greater than even a Platinum adventurer could have.

In doing so, the gods had stopped him from ever levelling again, a curse for perverting the cores that held the souls of dungeons. Now, the consequences had finally caught up to him.

Viktor closed his eyes, and for the first time, he felt dread. Was this what everyone who had stood before him felt? Was this how it felt to stare death in the eyes?

He silently cursed the Exalted One as the knight approached his head, the boy's sword glowing with the strange gray mana. Viktor smiled up at him even as the sword descended, even as the cold dark of the void called to him.

A single, final thought gave him solace in his loss. An excuse. A reason for his failure. This dungeon and adventurer had been chosen.

Chosen by the God of Death.

Epilogue

It was a week after their battle with Viktor. Following the fight, Ryan had absorbed the necromancer, and with him, many new and wonderful items – not to mention the shattered diamonds. He had questioned Erin about these stones, and the sight of them had been met with revulsion from the fairy.

According to her, they had once been dungeon cores. They could be used, like other gems, to improve an adventurer's mana capabilities. The difference was, anyone using one was able to store vast amounts of power in the gems as well, just as the dungeon cores once had. Erin told him it was taboo to ever do that, and doing so would cut an individual off from the gods who created the dungeons. That explained why Viktor was so strong at Gold One, and why he had not grown in level since they had first encountered him.

Blake and his team had teleported out of Ryan's dungeon to check on the town, where Viktor had somehow summoned a Diamond-level lich boss mob. Blake informed Ryan that the skeletal army and lich were gone. It seemed defeating Viktor had stopped the attack on the town.

After Blake passed on the message that everything had calmed down, Ryan absorbed his four new boss mobs, making a mental note to name them at a later time. He was exhausted from the fight. Now that it was over, the physical, emotional, and mental drain hit him. Ryan decided he was going to take a break before he started his Gold expansion, and slowly closed the mouth of his dungeon.

Only now, one week later, Blake had arrived outside his dungeon mouth, and seemed to be looking for a way in.

"Blake?" Ryan asked aloud. Erin, slumbering on top of Ryan's warm core, stirred.

"My ethereal prince," she whispered, still half asleep. Because she looked so cute in that moment, Ryan decided he would let that comment slide... this time.

"What's going on, Blake?" Ryan sent through the crystal, and the knight paused just before his entrance.

"Mind letting me in?" Blake held up a cloth bag, offering Ryan a grin. "I've got a present for you."

A present!

Ryan lifted the wolf's jaw just enough that Blake could crawl through.

"Seriously?" Blake grumbled as he dropped down on his hands and knees. The moment he entered, Ryan closed the dungeon back up.

"So, what did you bring me, buddy?" Ryan eyed the bag greedily. Swiftly, he began making cards for his new skeletal mages. Generosity begot generosity, after all.

"Well, I've got two things, and a favor to ask, actually." Blake sat against a stalagmite, placing the bag in front of him.

"Don't worry, you'll get the new boss mob cards," Ryan chuckled.

"That's not what—" Blake stopped and licked his lips. "I mean, yeah, that sounds like a fair trade."

"Deal."

Ryan summoned the four new cards for Blake, dropping them into the knight's lap. He loved watching Blake's reaction to them. But he suspected he would love what Blake had in the bag even more.

"So, what'd you bring me?"

Blake pulled out a leather journal and placed the four new cards inside. A wicked grin crossed his face.

"Jack's going to be *so* jealous," he said.

"You're like a drug addict," Ryan said, not unkindly. "Now, about those presents…"

"Ah, right. So, first." He pulled a strange crown from the bag. The crown appeared to be made of human bones and was lined with opals. Ryan could already sense its power.

"Marcus wants you to dispose of this – it seems only a powerful dark being is capable of doing so. It's the item Viktor used to attack the town. The lich it summoned nearly killed Marcus, Rasha, and Sasha before the necromancer fell."

So that's where the twins went.

Ryan had wondered why he hadn't seen either of the twins over the past week. Just how powerful was this item?

"Sure, I'll take it."

Blake set the crown on the ground. A moment later, the knight drew in his aura, allowing Ryan to absorb the crown. Before Viktor had arrived, the pair had learned that if Blake condensed his aura internally, Ryan had the ability to apply his influence in the area near the knight – allowing him to absorb items and summon mobs in particular. Normally, adventurers' auras prevented these two actions, though curiously, Ryan could still summon loot when auras were present. Ryan figured it was just part of the magical rules of being a dungeon.

"Oh, wow," Ryan whispered through his bond with Erin. "This is a legendary item."

He quickly scanned over the crown, taking note of its magical properties. No wonder it had caused the town so much trouble. How had Viktor got hold of an item like the Crown of Sorrows?

Ryan now had two legendary items in his possession, but even without Erin's warning, he knew he should never replicate them. Or at least, not until he was much, much stronger.

"So, what's the other item?" Ryan turned his attention back to Blake.

The knight pulled his shield off his back and set it down on the ground. Ryan hadn't noticed before, but this was a brand-new shield. It glowed with its own light, and on the front, emblazoned across it in gold, was an engraved set of scales, equally balanced. One side of the scales had an opal inset above it, while the other had an onyx.

"This is a paladin's shield," Blake said, tracing a finger over its surface. "But I can't use it yet. According to the Guildmaster, I need the help of a dungeon if I'm ever to ascend."

Blake paused, as if hesitant to go further.

"I'm listening," Ryan said.

Blake cleared his throat and continued.

"You see, paladins are a form of elemental knight. They present a shield emblazoned with the Goddess of Justice's insignia to her God-tier celestial dungeon. The dungeon then absorbs the shield and resummons it, imparting its own mana into the item."

Ryan was beginning to understand.

"At that time, the knight must push their experience and mana into the shield within the dungeon, which allows them to ascend to Gold. In doing so, the knight and the dungeon become linked and the knight ascends to become an elemental knight, unlocking the skills associated with that affinity."

"So, you want me to absorb the shield, and then remake it for you?"

Seems simple enough.

"Yes," Blake said, a hint of pleading in his voice. "Since you are a darkness dungeon, but *also* have a connection to the Goddess of Justice, I should be able to ascend and unlock the skills of a paladin, even with both affinities…"

Blake trailed off, and he ran a hand across his face.

"What is it, Blake?" Erin asked, talking into the pendant.

"Well, there is the chance this doesn't work, and I become a death knight instead."

Oh, that sounds cool.

"Won't know till you try, right?" Ryan said, excited by the prospect. "Are you ready?"

Blake did not reply, but Ryan sensed Blake's aura pull away from the shield. The boy had his eyes closed tight, and his hands were balled into fists.

That was answer enough. Ryan absorbed the shield, noting it was classified as a rare item. He checked it over and decided to make a few minor improvements. He removed imperfections and improved the grain structure of the metal it was made of, and replaced the gems, which had minor flaws, with the perfect versions he had acquired over his time as a dungeon.

Then he replaced the gold in the insignia, which was just gold leaf, with actual gold. His final change was to the back of the shield. On a whim, he traced the symbol that was imprinted on his crystal core, the skull representing his darkness affinity, into the metal.

Happy with his work, he summoned the shield, allowing himself a twinge of pride as he saw the rarity had increased to ultra-rare.

Oops.

"Are you ready?" Ryan asked.

"Yes."

Blake placed both of his hands on the shield, forcing his mana into the object.

Instantly, the room burst into light. Ryan watched in awe as darkness mana and celestial mana twisted and danced around the sitting figure. Blake's body was engulfed within the two contrasting manas, and it almost appeared as if they were trying to overcome each other.

Minutes ticked by, the battle between the two elements raging. Then, with a pop, the two seemed to equalize, darkness on Blake's left half, light on his right.

Even as the light began to fade, the twin elements began to twist and swirl, the maelstrom flinging dust in a tornado of power and crackling energy.

Blake cried out in pain, and Ryan almost tried to pull the shield away. But the boy's yell was followed by a deep sigh as the two manas suddenly converged, creating the strange, beautiful mana that Ryan knew to be ethereal.

It settled into Blake, permeating his body, then slowly faded until he was just a boy again, clutching a glittering shield with shaking hands.

Slowly, Blake rose to his feet.

"How'd it go?" Ryan asked, his interest piqued. He checked Blake's information, and let out a wry chuckle.

Oh, this was going to be *interesting*.

~

???

"*Exalted One, I bring grave tidings.*"

It was a woman who spoke, prostrated before his throne.

"*Viktor has failed,*" *she bemoaned,* "*and the Crown of Sorrows is lost.*"

She was clad in robes of red, and to the bare eye, she was achingly beautiful. But beneath that beauty, he knew she was the vilest creature imaginable. Well, close to the vilest.

He let out a chuckle, and the woman flinched.

"*Worry not, my daughter.*" *he said, smiling at her fear.* "*The necromancer accomplished all I needed of him when he brought me that ring.*"

He grinned and turned to his right, where the fruit of Viktor's labors stood, silent and obedient.

The ring had acquired him a being of immense power. That small, tawdry piece of jewelry was worth more than the crown had ever been.

The woman looked up, confused.

"*But, the Crown of Sorrows—*"

"*Was a useless legendary artifact that only a necromancer such as he could use. Viktor was the last of his kind, so you see, it had no value to me.*"

The woman bowed her head once more.

"*Now, I expect you to carry out the next stage of our endeavor.*"

"*But of course, Exalted One,*" *the woman said, pressing her forehead closer to the ground.* "*My brethren and I will begin at once.*"

Slowly, she backed away, and he turned his eyes back to his prize. He allowed himself a rare, cruel smile. Everything was going as he had planned.

Soon, after countless ages, he would finally have what he wanted. He would finally have his revenge.

Afterword

On behalf of myself and the Portal Books team, I would like to first thank each and every one of you for reading my story, Bone Dungeon.

I had a blast writing this story, and there were many Skype calls with my editors during its development that may or may not have gotten sidetracked covering the crazy shenanigans I wanted to put into the story...and eventually did — looking at you, skeletal fight club...and Steve...and Buttercup...and yeah, I think you guys get the point.

Anyways, this story means a lot to me, and the fact you have picked it up, given it a chance (and made it through to the end) also means a lot to me.

It has always been a dream of mine to one day write a story worth getting published, and thanks to Portal Books, that dream has now become a reality. If you enjoyed this book, I would love it if you could leave a review, share it with friends and family, even give it a shout out on social media.

If you hated it, why not share it with your worst enemy? (I'm a new author. I'll take the views where I can get them, bwahaha...kidding!) But really, while Bone Dungeon is my first book, you can bet it won't be my last.

I am hard at work on Bone Dungeon's, and also writing

another fun novel on Royal Road. If you wish to follow my work, feel free to check that one out at:

https://www.royalroad.com/fiction/21501/dco--dungeon-core-online

or join my Discord, where I post writing updates and chat with my readers:

https://discord.gg/DkJ9mMc

Also, you can follow the Portal Books Facebook group for updates about my books and those of their other amazing writers at:

www.facebook.com/groups/LitRPGPortal/

Finally, if you'd like to sample FREE content from other incredible authors at Portal Books, you can do so by signing up to the Portal Books mailing list.

You'll get access to 40,000 words of LitRPG novelettes, including *Rising Tide* by Oliver Mayes and *Survivors* by Alex Knight. Click through below and subscribe, and we'll get the eBooks straight to you:

https://portal-books.com/sign-up

By signing up you'll also be the first to hear about all our titles such as:

Occultist (Saga Online #1) by Oliver Mayes
God of Gnomes (Godcore #1) by L. M. Hughes
Mastermind (Titan Online #1) by Steven Kelliher
Warden (Nova Online #1) by Alex Knight
Aether Frontier by Scott McCoskey
Dungeons of Strata by Graeme Penman
Cryoknight by Tim Johnson
Battle Spire (Hundred Kingdoms #1) by Michael R. Miller

For more general discussions about the genre, these groups may be useful to you.

www.facebook.com/groups/LitRPGsociety/

www.facebook.com/groups/LitRPG.books/

www.facebook.com/groups/LitRPGGroup/

Best wishes,

Jonathan Smidt

More LitRPG from Portal Books

Portal Books will release 8 new titles this year - it's going to be a big one. But out right now is the sci-fi themed LitRPG, **Warden: Nova Online**.

"Imprisoned for a murder he didn't commit, Kaiden's only hope of early release is in serving as a Warden in the game-world of Nova Online.

It's available on Kindle Unlimited and on Audio.

Also out now is **Occultist (Saga Online #1)**.

Welcome to the world of Saga Online, the newest fantasy VRMMORPG. Join Damien as he discovers the rare Occultist class and summons an army of demons to save his mother's life.

It's available on Kindle Unlimited and on Audio.

Last, but not least, is **Battle Spire: A Crafting LitRPG Book**.

Battle Spire is a meeting of *World of Warcraft* and *Die Hard*, using crunchy LitRPG mechanics with a heavy focus on crafting. Readers can expect to find in depth item and spell descriptions, along with stat tables and profession recipes.

It's available on Kindle Unlimited.

Join the Group

To learn more about LitRPG, talk to authors including myself, and just have an awesome time, please join the LitRPG Group.